Dedications

To my writing partner and dear friend Jess E. Owen. You really helped me level up with this book!

"A lot of people will say, like, 'I'm an aspiring artist,' or, 'I'm an aspiring writer.' No. You're a writer. You're an artist. If you're doing that shit every day, that's what you are." **– Dan Avidan**

Brothers at Arms

Book Two

From the Guardian Archives

By R. A. Meenan

Starcrest Fox Press

Tick. Tock. Tick. Tock.

The massive grandfather clock along the back wall of Assistant Mayor Sheldon's sitting room ticked so loudly, it stung Trecheon Omnir's ears, even hidden in the rafters of the vaulted ceiling. But he had to stay silent. Time was running out if he wanted to get this job done. Just needed the right opportunity.

He had to hope that'd be soon. She was supposed to be alone, but got some random calling from a mob crony. A Fawn Family mob crony to boot. Trecheon had just been about ready to do the job too. The scramble to the rafters was completely unplanned.

Thank Draso for the quilar-sized balaclava holding in his fur and quills, keeping them from making sound and masking his scent. The weight of the fist sized gem in his pocket helped with counterbalance too, weirdly. One more use for the good luck charm Granddad had given him. He adjusted his grip on the wooden beam, a difficult task with biomechanical arms, and flicked his red, catlike ears forward, hanging on every word, waiting to strike.

"I wish you'd reconsider," Sheldon said, arms crossed. "I'm so close to getting this law passed. If you just--"

"It's out of my hands, I'm afraid," said her guest, a gray feline in a fine three-piece suit, holding up her paw. The pair sat in opposing armchairs, lit only by the dim light of a fireplace and a handful of candles. Two muscle-bound bodyguards, a bison and a reindeer, stood behind her, silent, hands behind their backs and eyes hidden behind sunglasses, despite the time of night. The scene had been practically ripped from a mafia movie. The feline continued. "I'm only bringing a message on behalf of Triple Fawn."

Trecheon shuddered. Shit. Triple Fawn.

"Damn those doe," Neil Black muttered in Trecheon's earpiece radio, a "gift" from Triple Fawn – long lasting, extremely comfortable, and perfect for monitoring Neil and Trecheon's hits, whether they wanted it or not. The puma decorated his words with hisses. *"I thought it was fishy when someone showed up unannounced. Are the Fawns trying to get us killed?"*

Not likely, Trecheon thought. Not when he and Neil owed them a hefty one million dollars as ransom for Neil's younger brother Philip. Not when they were still six hundred thousand short. Their goal seemed impossible at times.

Sheldon frowned, running a hand through her shock of red hair. "Surely--"

"Look, lady," the feline said. "There's nothing I can do. This partnership ends now. Boss's orders."

"The sisters have always been friendly with me," Sheldon continued. "They're the reason I have this position in the first place. Why are they ending this?"

The feline raised an eyebrow. "It has come to our attention that you are heavily involved in the Starshine trafficking ring with Brown Fox." The feline shook her head with a *tsk tsk* sound. "Records show, and I quote, that your job is to 'procure product, break it in, and dispose of it when no longer useful.'

'Product' being children, Ms. Sheldon. Middle school and lower. Guess Brown Fox likes 'em young, huh?"

Sheldon's gaze hardened.

"We've seen evidence of the gravesites, too, for 'expired product,'" the feline continued. "Filthy. You must have gotten quite the bonus for doing this yourself. Or maybe you just like getting your hands *dirty*."

Sheldon snarled, almost animal-like. "Why should my hobbies matter to you?"

Neil gagged over the headphones. Trecheon felt ill himself.

"You know how Triple Fawn feels about children." The feline twitched her tail violently, her expression growing cold. "You signed your career's death warrant there."

Neil snorted in Trecheon's headphones. *"If they really cared about children, they wouldn't be holding Philip hostage."* Trecheon silently agreed.

Sheldon rolled her eyes and crossed her arms. "So you're breaking ties with me. Fine. Brown Fox pays more anyway."

"For now." The feline smiled, her sly persona returning.

Sheldon narrowed her gaze. "What does that mean?"

"Your actions have marked you, Ms. Sheldon," the feline said. "Rumor has it the White Assassin is none too happy."

Trecheon's blood ran cold. That damn cat! That'd put Sheldon on high alert.

Sheldon sat straight up and glanced around the room, frantic, all smugness vanishing. "The White Assassin? Are you kidding me?"

The feline stood, adjusted the collar of her suit and fiddled with her tie. "Good luck, Ms. Sheldon." She left with her bodyguards chuckling behind her.

Trecheon furrowed his brow. Shit, shit, *shit*. Curse Triple Fawn!

Sheldon leapt to her feet, panicked. She glanced around, hair whipping about, before running for her bedroom.

"Better hurry!" Neil said. *"She's got a pistol in her bedside table."*

Damnit. Trecheon dropped from the rafters, careful not to make any sound, and pulled out the wire garrote. He dashed after her, silent as could be.

Sure enough, the mayor ran for her bedside table.

Trecheon tackled her to the ground before she reached it. She yelped, reached into her belt, and stabbed at his arm with a short knife. The blade glided right off the metal prosthetic. She stared a moment, shocked, then threw the knife instead.

Trecheon twisted to avoid it, letting her go, but it caught in his leg. He yelped, bending his leg about to avoid getting blood on the carpet.

She dashed for the table again.

Trecheon leapt forward, careful of his leg, and got the garrote around her neck, dragging her to the floor. She fought, kicked, gasped, ripped at the fiber wire, but couldn't get a word out.

Trecheon pulled at the garrote, tugging it tight, cursing his metal prosthetic arms for the thousandth time. They could only strain so far, and since he couldn't feel through them anymore, there was no way to know when he neared their limit.

Sheldon gagged, a wet, throaty sound, as her face turned blue. She got one word out. *"Stop."*

"Funny that," Trecheon whispered. "All those girls you kidnapped shouted the same thing as your people violated, abused, and killed them. And you did *nothing*." He glared. "Think I'll follow your example."

Slowly she stopped moving. Trecheon held the garrote a moment more, just to be sure, then let her go and lowered her to the carpet. Target or not, corrupt or not, he respected the dead. Not that she deserved it.

"Did she hurt you?"

"Knife in the leg. I've got it." Trecheon pulled out a piece of cloth, wrapped it around the knife handle, holding the knife in place, hissing. It'd just have to stay there until he got off the grounds. Couldn't risk bleeding out. Or worse, contaminating the crime scene. Damn that feline. Made him sloppy. Last thing he needed was to be hobbling around on a bum leg while he escaped.

Granddad's gem beat against his leg. He frowned. Maybe there was another way. He pulled out the fist-sized jewel. It shined dull red, but it hummed quietly. Maybe that meant it would work this time. He hadn't been able to get it to do anything since Neil nearly killed him by accident several years back. But he had to try. He held the jewel to his leg.

The humming grew louder and buzzed against his fur as the gem glowed slightly. A feeling of quiet, soothing calm washed over him. He lolled his head back. Peace. Good Draso, when did he ever truly know peace?

The moment was gone all too quickly. But it worked. The knife carefully slipped out of the wound, leaving behind fresh skin and fur. The gem healed him. He stuffed the jewel, knife, and cloth back in his pockets, but then frowned. Three incriminating drops of blood decorated the white carpet. "Leg's good, but I've got a hazard here. Hope she's got some peroxide."

"Master bathroom, under the sink," Neil said over the earpiece. *"Feeling a bit righteous there, Trech? It's not like you to talk to your hits about why you're killing them."*

"Don't call me Trech," Trecheon said, but didn't offer anything else. "I'm going to find the safe. You got the number?"

"09-10-28," Neil said. *"Don't mess up or you'll set off the house alarms."*

Trecheon found the safe under a loose floorboard under her bed, just as his employer had said. A small, but heavy safe, anchored to the foundation, meant for documents. Trecheon fiddled with the knob. 9. 10. 28. The safe opened.

He lifted the heavy door, listening to his mechanical arms groan and creak, then ripped the contents out and dumped them on the bed. One good thing about mechanical arms. No fingerprints. "Done."

"Good," Neil said. *"One more level ten hit in the bag."*

And one step closer to getting Philip back, Trecheon thought. Neil's younger brother was turning nine this year. Three years in foster care, held hostage against adoption by Triple Fawn, one of El Dorado's top mobs because of Neil's reckless decision to take out their leader. Draso's horns, why did they let this get so out of control?

"I got a lead on a level four hit next week," Neil said. *"Small, I know, but we've taken out a lot of big targets lately. Gotta lay low a little before the cops catch on. I'll take this one. I can do it alone."*

"Understood," Trecheon said.

"Now get the hell out of there," Neil said. *"I'm sure Triple Fawn's cronies are hanging around, hoping to remove incriminating evidence."*

"I've got to take care of this blood," Trecheon said. "Can't leave that behind."

"We'll take care of it," a cool, feline voice purred over the receiver. *"Gotta gather the tithe first after all."*

Trecheon froze up. That cat from before. He cursed. The "tithe." Evidence that would pin this crime on Trecheon and Neil, should Triple Fawn choose to use it against them. They already had more than enough to keep him and Neil pressed under their thumbs. The worst catch-22. Keep working to make that money for Philip, make more evidence for Triple Fawn. Leave Triple Fawn or go to the authorities… they use that evidence against them, putting them away forever. Endless cycle.

"Thank you for your service, White Assassin." She clicked off.

Neil growled. *"I hate it when they do that."*

"At least they don't do it often," Trecheon said. "I'll see you back at base." He turned off the comm, then looked back at Sheldon.

She stared blankly at him, dead-eyed, fearful, puffy and blue. Not a nice way to go. Draso's mercy. He was such scum. She absolutely deserved what she got coming to her, but she should have been brought to the courts. He even said it himself. He followed her example. Killing her, while she begged him to stop, made him no better than she was. Good Draso, he was disgusting.

You should turn yourself in.

That tiny voice, after every kill. *Turn yourself in. Admit fault. Spend the rest of your life in prison. Hell, beg for the chair. You're no better than the people you've killed.*

But if he did that… what would happen to Philip? He couldn't stand the idea of him living his life in foster, alone, a child of a corrupt system.

He pressed his hand to his face. He flexed his hand, listening to the mechanisms creak. That'd need repairs. Damn this life he was stuck with.

But he was stuck with it.

He said a short prayer over Sheldon's dead body, then slipped out of the mansion, counting the days until he could finally drop the name of White Assassin.

CHAPTER 01

POST-TRAUMA

"Welcome to Fencing 101," Matt Azure said, glancing out over his students, as Ouranos of the Athánatos observed the classroom. The newly-inducted Golden Guardian stood on a short stage at the front of the room, holding a training sword. Ouranos watched Matt fidget quietly, his white, blue tipped quills rustling in the subtle gusts from the mechanical air conditioner.

Matt's ever-present rosy dawn filled Ouranos' mind with light through the social bond between their focus jewels. But there was also a thin line of dark blue hidden behind it. Nervousness. Ever so slight.

Ouranos sat on a stool near the back of the room, trying to keep a neutral face. His time on Zyearth necessitated that he trade his royal Athánatos garb for a practical Defender novice uniform, a pair of plain black pants and a long sleeved black jacket. The black clothing blended with his own black fur and made him nearly invisible in the dark corner of the exercise classroom.

A white, black streaked wolf named Pasadena Terrill took the stage alongside Matt. She eyed Ouranos carefully, running her fingertips over the hilt of her own sword.

Ouranos attempted a smile, but was sure he failed. Pasadena must have noticed his attempt however, and managed a sad smile herself, though with ears flipped back. He could not blame her, really. After all, Ouranos had killed her brother. Cix.

It had been necessary, sad to say, after Ouranos' father, the Basileus, had taken over Cix's mind and broke the bond with the wolf's Lexi Gem. Saving him had not been possible.

But murder is not easily forgotten, Ouranos thought.

It's not murder if it's out of your control, Ouranos, Matt spoke into his mind. He offered Ouranos a gentle smile. *Pasadena is a soldier. She knows that. It's why she's trying to be friendly. It's just hard. Give her time.*

Ouranos twitched an ear and nodded, but kept his face impartial, his emotions under control.

A much easier task now that the Basileus lacked the power to bend Ouranos to his will. It was a priceless gift Matt had passed to him that could never be repaid.

"You'll be learning the basics of swordplay in this class," Matt told the students. "But you'll also learn terminology and tactics, so it's best if you take notes. Paper and pens out, please."

Twenty-four students nodded nervously and a few muttered to themselves. They scattered over the soft blue mat covering the floor of the classroom, digging pens out of their bags. The dull sounds of footsteps, claw scrapes, and feather rustles danced off the sound-dampening walls.

Matt sheathed his sword, crossed his arms, and took a deep breath, bending one white, blue tipped ear back. He looked tired, unsettled. And Ouranos knew why.

Six months. It had only been six months since the incident with the Shadow Cast. Not even half a year by the Zyearth calendar.

But Zyearth had already begun the return to normal, as if the incident had never come to pass. As if the Defender's labs did not house over two hundred of their soldiers, trapped in the stolen, inky form of a Shadow Cast. As if the Basileus' victims had not died.

As if Earth, its inhabitants, and Ouranos' own people, did not face war.

Ouranos still trembled at the thought of the battles with his father on Zyearth, fighting for control of himself while trying to stop the Basileus' destruction. The experience carried with it mixed feelings.

On the one hand, his social bond with Matthew had granted him power over his father that he had not known in decades.

On the other, hundreds of lives lay ruined at his feet, until the Defenders discovered a way to break the bonds of a Cast.

If the Defenders discovered a way to fix the Cast. Decades of research among his own people, the people who had discovered the means for making Cast in the first place, had resulted in nothing.

As luck would have it, clues led the Defenders to believe that Lexi acid, a substance produced by overpowering one of their magic Gems, could possibly neutralize the effect of the Cast Charms that had turned them. But so far, all experiments had ended in failure. The Defenders had vast resources and scores of scientists and Gem magic experts attempting to solve the problem, but the formation of Cast were beyond both fields of study. His skull pounded thinking about it.

The battle may be won, but the war was far from over.

Matt glanced at the corner. Ouranos flicked his ears back. He had asked Matt if he could observe one of his classes, saying that he wanted to get a feel for how a Defender trained. Perhaps he could learn something for his fight against his father, or at the very least, allow himself a temporary distraction from the deeper issues at hand.

But if he had judged correctly, the students were none too happy to have him here. A reasonable thought, though it still stung.

"Alright everyone, pay attention," Matt called. The class fell instantly silent and every eye fixed on their teacher. Ouranos perked his ears as well. "Pasadena and I are going to give a demonstration of swordplay. This is what your final exam will look like."

Pasadena drew her own sword and faced Matt with a wolfish smirk. Matt held his sword out. He stared his partner down.

Pasadena began the engagement, swinging her sword down hard. Matt blocked easily, pushing against her and forcing her to take two steps back. The wolf lifted her weapon and swung back. *Clang, clang, clang!* The swords bit at each other with every swing. Ouranos watched with a deep fascination.

Athánatos were not violent by nature. Ouranos, however, had been acutely exposed to violence for the last several decades. It was something embedded in him. Even now as he watched the pair square off, his brain pressed images into his mind's eye. Every clang flashed a memory of cruelty.

His sister, Melaina, being forcefully transformed into a half-finished Cast by their father.

The stink of blood and death on the Athánatos battlefields while fighting the Basileus.

The war on Sol – screaming children, dirt stained red, the cries for mercy, falling on deaf ears.

The Omnir, ruined and broken before him, dying in fits.

His role in the War of Eons, watching human and zyfaunos alike die in ways no description could do justice.

And then the violence on Zyearth.

Roscoe Gildspine transformed into a Shadow Cast in a scream so powerful his ears still rang with the memory.

The crushed bodies of the Cast's victims.

Cix begging for death after the Basileus stole his mind.

The jewel fusion with Matt, the battle against Theron, the destruction Ouranos' actions caused. Without realizing it, his thoughts drifted beyond the exercise room and into that recent past.

He found himself back in Corinth Woods where he had first crash landed, facing off against Matt, desperately trying and failing to fight off the Basileus' control. Magic strewn everywhere, so thick it stung the throat. He crashed into Matt, hands alight with power. Matt gripped his hands, his own covered in the thick Black Bound elixir.

Their jewels bonded.

The immediate aftermath burned his brain. A thousand thoughts bombarded him. *Izzy, Guardian, Jaden, Master Guardian, Charlotte, Defender.* Emotion after emotion ripped through him. Hate, fear, worry, elation, despair, joy, horror. Pain threatened to tear him apart, so thick and deep that his senses faded beyond reach, until he was only a shell.

The screams of the Cast, the smell of blood, the stinging, acid taste of magic on his tongue, the feel of horror in the air with that final battle.

The Basileus staring at him through Cix's yellow eyes. *You were supposed to die when I left you. Alone, out of sight, out of mind. I had no intention of wasting my time watching.* The Basileus commanded Cix's body as a puppet, lighting his hands ablaze. *But now I will relish every scream as you burn to ash!*

"No!"

Everything stopped. The sword clangs ceased, and the room fell quiet again. Ouranos opened eyes that he did not remember closing.

Every student had wide eyes trained on him.

Ouranos furrowed his brow, slowly pulling his hands off his ears. That final scream. He did that. Out loud. Without even realizing it. He frowned, his ears flushing from fear and embarrassment, and huddled closer on his stool. "I apologize. Forgive me."

Matt frowned, splaying an ear and eyeing Ouranos. *You okay? Should we stop?*

Ouranos simply shook his head and glanced down at the floor. He tried to speak to Matt, to encourage him to continue, but words failed him. Gradually the students turned their faces away. Matt cleared his throat to command attention.

"Class," he spoke clearly, steadily, to his credit. "Who won?"

The students exchanged looks with each other. Several mumbled and one or two people threw out vague answers.

Ouranos stared out at the students, picking up nervous glances and worried frowns. Fearful. Uncertain. Several shot looks in his direction. Matt tried to keep his ears perked up, but he failed.

"We both won," Pasadena said, her voice clear and steady. She shot a glance and a forced smile at Matt. The students focused their attention on her.

Matt nodded. "That's correct. Neither of us are hurt. Our weapons are intact. In this Academy, we teach you to fight, but our overall goal is to protect. If we can come away from a fight intact, that's ideal. But if we can avoid a fight entirely, if we can use our words instead of our actions to avoid a conflict, we win. We're intelligent beings. Critical thinkers. Our ability to rationalize is what separates us from animals. There's beauty in solving a conflict without war, and there's no victory in death."

The Guardian dug into his backpack and pulled out stacks of paper. "For now, let's just go over the syllabus and get out of here for the day. We'll start proper fencing next class." He handed half the stack to Pasadena and they passed out syllabi. "There will be a quiz on this syllabus next class, so don't zone out. Think of it as practice being on the battlefield. Zone out there and you're dead."

Ouranos shuddered.

Matt spent the next hour explaining the syllabus with occasional interjections from Pasadena, then he dismissed the class. The students filed out slowly, still tossing glances at Ouranos. Ouranos sat on his stool, doing his best to ignore the stares.

When the last student filed out, Ouranos padded over to the stage and leaned against the wall. "That was some demonstration, Guardian."

Matt frowned. "You okay?"

Ouranos stared at the floor. "You know the answer. It would be pointless to lie."

"Maybe you'd like to fill me in on some details," Matt said.

Ouranos sighed. "As the two of you fought, my memories brought me to my previous battles." He took a heavy breath and chanced a glance at Pasadena. "I relived our last moments with Cix."

Pasadena frowned. "Ouranos, that isn't your fault. Cix was already lost. What you did was mercy." She pasted her ears back. "You know that."

"Logically I know this," he said. "But convincing my heart proves difficult. I have spent too many nights wondering what I could have done different."

Pasadena's tail drooped, but she walked over and gave Ouranos a short hug. "I should leave you two to talk. I think Matt can handle this better than me. But if you need to talk to me later, I'm here, okay? Don't suffer alone. Cix wouldn't want that." She nodded to Matt. "See you both later." She left the room.

Matt sat on the stage and invited Ouranos to do the same. "Sorry I had to have Pasadena do the demonstration today," he said. "Normally I'd have Jay do it, but their injury flared up and Pasadena is the only other swordsmaster who can really keep up with me."

Ouranos shrugged like it did not matter, but he knew Matt would sense differently. "At least she is forgiving."

"She is, yeah." Matt leaned on his hands. "So you're having PTSR episodes?"

Ouranos sat down, then lifted a brow and perked an ear. "I am not familiar with this term."

"Post-traumatic stress reaction," Matt said. "After a traumatic episode you might relive the moments. It's not uncommon."

Ouranos bent an ear. "The term is fitting."

"This has been going on for a while," Matt said. "I've been feeling it."

Ouranos fiddled with his hands. "I know, and I am sorry."

"Don't be sorry for having emotional responses to trauma, Ouranos," Matt said. "It's perfectly natural and you shouldn't feel like you have to hide it."

"Perhaps. But I should have brought this up with you sooner," Ouranos said. "Honestly, I have been having nightmares ever since Cix's funeral, but this is the first time that I have experienced this while awake."

Matt shifted. "I had a feeling. I was waiting for you to come talk to me about it, but I wanted it to be on your terms."

Ouranos leaned back and stared at the ceiling. "Thank you for giving me the space."

"Of course." Matt sighed. "We need to go after your father. Finish all this. Then you could start to heal."

"There are reasons why your Master Guardian has chosen to stay here for now."

"What reasons?" Matt snarled, startling Ouranos with his sudden anger. "Earth is in danger. The Basileus has perfected the Cast. It's only a matter of time before things start getting out of control." Red hot rage floated through Ouranos' mind.

"We cannot fight the Cast, Matthew," Ouranos said. "You know that. Until we know how to fix them, going would only plant a Black Bound Gem user on Earth for the Basileus to use."

Matt scoffed, bending an ear. "So what, we just sit here and hope the Basileus doesn't figure out how to create the Cast without the Black Bound elixir? He knows a lot now, it won't take him long to figure it out."

"It is not a pretty truth," Ouranos said. "But until we really understand how to cure the Cast, how can we expect to win? And more than that, you are still healing. Your military has faced a terrible event. Admittedly, by my hand."

A cool blue wafted through his mind. Worry. "Your father's hand," Matt said.

Ouranos narrowed his eyes. "I could have fought him off if I had only tried harder."

"Ouranos, we've been over this. The Basileus--"

"Could have been fought off had I not acted selfishly. There is no room for discussion," Ouranos said. Matt tried to protest in his mind, but Ouranos squelched it. "What is done is done."

Matt sighed, leaning his elbows on his knees. "We need a cure for the Cast. Darvin's been complaining about it for ages, being stuck in that lucid Cast state. He's going mad. We're just so *close.*"

Ouranos eyed him.

Matt shifted. "Okay, maybe not that close. We know Lexi acid does something, but every time they try some new technique on Darvin, he just ends up screaming and nothing changes. And Roscoe won't even let them near him with the acid." He shook his head. "It clearly neutralizes the Black Bound elixir. We've seen that in a hundred experiments. Hell, it even neutralized the

Cast Charms you made. But since Cast don't have normal bodies, no one has a clue where to apply it to neutralize the charm in *them.*" Matt ran a hand through his quills. "I don't know the damn answer."

"And it would be folly to attempt fighting the Basileus without this knowledge. I cannot, in good conscience, ask for your aid."

"Ouranos," Matt said. "You can't do this alone."

Ouranos disagreed, holding on to his thoughts so Matt could not feel them. The only choice was to do this alone. If only to prevent anymore death at his hand. But he kept silent on the matter.

Matt stood. "We should get you to a therapist. It'll help with the PTSR episodes."

Ouranos perked an ear. "What will they do?"

"A therapist will talk to you, help you identify the issues bothering you, and work with you to find coping mechanisms," Matt said. He gripped Ouranos' shoulder. "Let me arrange it, okay? Then when you're feeling better, we'll continue this discussion about letting us help."

"If the Master Guardian will allow it."

"He will, in time," Matt said. His fur bristled. "I hope we *have* the time. Gem users in general are extremely rare on Earth, if there are any at all, and Black Binding is even rarer. His plans will have to be put on hold for now. Though I don't doubt he's trying to find other ways to create them."

Ouranos raised an ear. "I thought I had heard your Master Guardian mention that, though I struggled to believe it. There are really no Gem users on Earth?"

Matt shook his head. "The practice of Gem binding ended during the escape from Zyearth. The same event where your ship came from. Most Gems disappeared or broke over the millennia, since no one used or maintained them. There are planets who use Lexi Gems, but Zyearth is really the only planet with zyfaunos where the majority of the population uses them."

Ouranos flicked his tail. "I was unaware, being so isolated."

Matt shrugged. "There are probably a few unbound Gems floating around different worlds. Sol had some, but no one knows how to bind them, and an unbound Gem is just as useless to Theron as a rock."

"I suppose that is true," Ouranos said. Matthew was right. And it was impossible to force a Black Bind. Or at least improbable. Perhaps he could relax a little. "I will take you up on that therapist, if you believe it will help."

"It usually does," Matt said. "And if it doesn't, we'll look into other options. There's a lot we can try." He sighed. "Come on, let's get some lunch. I need a distraction."

A distraction would be nice. "Then let us go." As they walked toward The Grill, Ouranos thanked Draso that he had managed to avoid the sticky issue of the war. But he knew that would not last.

No victory in death, Matthew had said. Perhaps there was some truth to this. But the Basileus did not believe this. His victory was in destruction. Genocide. And he would murder everyone who got in his way. Even these new friends that Ouranos had made. *Especially* these new friends.

Ouranos had an obligation to stop his father. He did not have an obligation to put Matthew and Isabelle, his friends, in danger. He must move forward with this philosophy. He could have no more incidents like the fight with Cix.

He would protect his friends, and all those the Basileus set his eyes on, even if that meant his own death.

CHAPTER 02

EAVESDROPPING

Matt did indeed arrange for Ouranos to see a Defender therapist, a golden-brown doe with a kind voice and a sympathetic ear named Dr. Angelwing. After two months in Dr. Angelwing's care, Ouranos' nightmares became less frequent, though his resolve to protect the helpless, even at his own expense, did not waver.

"You're holding awfully tight onto this sudden extreme selflessness, Ouranos," the therapist said, bending a long ear. The pair sat in Dr. Angelwing's office, a comfortable room with a tidy desk, floor-to-ceiling bookshelves, and cozy furniture, all darkened with reds and browns. The smell of coffee permeated the air. "Why do you think that is?"

Ouranos leaned back in the plush maroon chair, frowning, cautiously sipping his coffee. "I cannot say, if I am honest with myself. Perhaps after decades of feeling my father's wrath and letting it bleed into my conscious mind, I feel that doing so will repay those I have hurt."

"At your own expense?"

Ouranos shook his head. "For that, perhaps, I blame Matthew. It was his selfless sacrifice that allowed me to think myself capable of protecting others, despite my bonds to my father and my personal shortcomings."

The doctor bit her lip, bending both long ears down. "So do you believe it's acceptable to put yourself in danger?"

Ouranos shifted. "If it is necessary to protect my friends, yes." His tail drooped. "They have already risked so much for me, when I have done nothing to deserve it. I cannot ask them to risk more. That is for me to do."

"Do you think Matt would want you to put yourself at risk for him?"

Ouranos frowned. "Well… no. But that does not change my feelings on it. He has done too much for me."

"Hmm," the doctor said. "I think you need to bring this up with Matt. He cares deeply for you, and I'm sure you for him."

"More than words can say," Ouranos said.

She smiled. "I'm glad you have a solid support in him. But we need to call on that support. Matt would want that for you. Don't be afraid to turn to him. That's what he'd want. Okay?"

Ouranos nodded. Perhaps she was right. But… that changed nothing. He could not ask for more from his friends. Matt specifically.

This was his fight.

He gave her a quiet thanks and left.

"Sir, I'm sorry if I caught you at a bad time, but you asked us to update you as soon as we had new information on the White Assassin on Terra," a quiet female voice said, wafting down the silent halls in the mental health wing of the hospital.

Ouranos paused, turning his head toward the voice, straining. It sounded like a Defender he knew, a white arctic fox named Sami Girsougon. The halls were empty, so she must be around the corner toward the exit into the lobby.

A soft sigh. "Can it wait half an hour? I'm late for a therapy appointment."

Ouranos perked an ear. That voice he knew unquestioningly. The white wolf with astounding ice powers. The Master Guardian of the Defenders. Lance Tox.

Hmm. Matt had said that he would try to get the Master Guardian to approve their intervention on Earth, and implied that he might do so even before they were ready. It was perhaps a long shot, but Ouranos may be able to convince the Master Guardian otherwise. He walked toward the voices.

"I know, but it should only take a minute," Sami continued.

"I've already told Galactic InterPol to dismiss him," the Master Guardian said. "We've given them all the info we can get remotely. We've pinpointed his residence to El Dorado City. He might be using a car repair shop as his cover job. He's connected to a Terranian mafia running casinos, something apparently rather common in organized crime there. He's not a focus jewel smuggling powerhouse like the FJS spooks thought he was." He sighed. "Unless this is some life-altering information, I'm going to recommend we close this case."

"I don't know if I'd call it life-altering, but it is potentially important," Sami said. "Though if you've already informed FJS, we can always dismiss it instead, sir."

The Master Guardian snorted. "I'm already late. Might as well tell me so we can shut the door on this."

Sami rustled her papers. "We think the White Assassin might be related to the Omnir tribe."

The shocked yip from the Master Guardian was so uncharacteristic that Ouranos stopped in his tracks, nearly falling over.

But the name. He did not miss its significance. His body grew numb.

The Omnir tribe. They had survivors. After everything he had done… Ouranos snuck closer, coming to the end of the hall where it branched into another corridor, hoping to hear more.

"In here," the Master Guardian said. "Shut the damn door." A door around the corridor slammed.

Ouranos chewed his lip. He could not miss this information. He rounded the corner and pressed his ear against the nearest door. Their voices were muffled, but he could make out enough.

"Are you sure? The Omnirs?"

"We aren't, sir, not yet," Sami said. "But the assassin uses the name Omnir as his last name and he is that characteristic red. We just need a DNA test to know for certain." A pause. "The team was hoping you'd authorize sending the Golden Guardians to check, but if you'd rather close the case--"

"The Guardians are not to know." Lance's voice sharpened into a snarl, causing Sami to yip in surprise. "And in fact, I want this whole case Vaulted right now. Consider it top secret, top level only. And it would be beneficial for you and your team to forget it yourselves. FJS got their info. They don't need more."

A pause. "Sir?"

"You know what the Omnirs did to the last pair of Golden Guardians," Lance said. "This White Assassin might be an Omnir, but I can't expect Izzy and Matt to go after him with capture and questioning in mind. Their first thoughts will be to shoot first, ask questions later." A pause. "Wait, you said he was red? Why call himself the White Assassin?"

"We're still looking into that, sir," Sami said. "Perhaps as a way to throw people off his trail." Another pause. "Sir, do you really believe that the Guardians couldn't handle this neutrally?"

Lance sighed. "I don't know at this point. I'd have to evaluate them and see for myself before I decide." He let out a tiny growl. "Frankly, I don't want any excuse to send them to Terra. Earth." He whined quietly, pausing a moment. "Draso knows they'd use that to try and go after the Basileus." He huffed. "They are not to know. Understand?"

"Yes, sir," Sami said, though she seemed hesitant. "I'll have this Vaulted immediately."

"See that you do."

Ouranos rounded the corner, away from the door. His brain struggled to comprehend all he had heard, starting numb and slowly giving way to urgent shock.

An Omnir. A real Omnir. He had thought them all dead after the genocide on Earth. Dead because of his father's dreadful experiments and Ouranos' poor decisions. But if they were alive... If even one Omnir had survived, could he consider himself redeemed? Perhaps there were even more than one, considering the genocide had taken place nearly six decades prior. Any living zyfaunos taking the Omnir name would have to be quite old or the offspring of an earlier generation. The Omnir tribe did not use focus jewels and had no means of obtaining long life.

But they could. Sisters alive, they could use focus jewels. They had the biology, just like the Sol tribe, the tribe Matthew had sprung from. Matt said they would have some time before the Basileus was able to create Shadow Cast on Earth because of a lack of Gem users and the rarity of Black Bound Gem users.

But there were Gems. There were potential Gem users. Fear immediately crushed the elation of discovering a wayward offspring of the tribe Ouranos felt responsible for.

If the Basileus knew that there were some surviving Omnirs, he would bear down on them and attempt to force them into a Black Bind, like Matthew. And with the Black Bound elixir, he could create Cast.

He could *create Cast.*

Ouranos pushed the panic back down his throat. Matt had said it was unlikely that Theron could force a Black Bind, but that would not stop him from trying. He needed to do some research.

"Ouranos?"

Ouranos jumped and turned to his left to see Sami staring at him with her head tilted. He let out a sigh. "Sami. You gave me a start."

"Sorry," Sami said. She bent one ear back and her body tensed. "What are you doing here?"

Ouranos tried to calm his fast-beating heart. "I am seeking therapy sessions here, at Matthew's request, to help me calm my post- ah… post-… Forgive me, I do not remember the term."

"Post-traumatic stress reaction?"

"Yes, that," Ouranos said. "I just finished one such session with Dr. Angelwing."

Sami seemed to relax at that news. "Ah, good. Is it helping?"

"It seems to be working," Ouranos said. But an urgency clawed at his chest. This was not the time for idle chit-chat. And the last thing he wanted was to accidentally let it slip that he had been eavesdropping on Sami's conversation with the Master Guardian. "If you will excuse me, I am supposed to be ah, meeting with my sister."

"Of course," Sami said, and walked down the hall.

Ouranos turned and jogged out of the building, into the sunlight. Consulting a campus map, he found the library and trotted in that direction hoping to find answers.

CHAPTER 03

RESEARCH

Ouranos pushed away from his desk and the open book on it, sitting back in the large wing-backed chair with a broken sigh.

His research had carried him long into the night, far past the library's open student research hours. It had been a trick to avoid the librarians asking students to leave and continue after they were gone. He had hidden among the towering shelves, the sliding ladders, oak desks, and private study rooms, trying to escape their notice. He finally ended up hiding in one of the washrooms, hoping it did not have a lock.

But he had managed it, which allowed him several hours alone among the smell of old books, wood polish, and library dust. He exited into near darkness, with only floor lights and desk lights remaining lit.

Here held a wealth of knowledge far beyond anything Ouranos could hope to comprehend, and more besides. The tomes he had found on Gem binding were fascinating. Gems were bound to a user's lifeforce by a zyfaunos already in possession of a Gem, who used their own power to force the binding. A mesmerizing process.

His research also granted him more knowledge about Matt and Izzy's Black Binding. He knew that binding oneself to a Gem was rare, but to learn that only twelve cases of survivors had ever been reported in Zyearth's long history really struck him.

Matt and Izzy's case was even rarer, one-of-a-kind in fact, since after they had each bound themselves, some speculated Matt had bound the two Gems together. Much like how he and Matthew had bound their focus jewels together.

Matt had mentioned he had done research on it, but not that he and Izzy shared a social bond. Though based on his experience with their social bond, he could not blame him. Their bond was comforting and precious, but also difficult and invasive. Not one shared with others outside that bond.

However, it was also among these essays of Gems and binding that Ouranos confirmed his fears.

A leading Gem specialist speculated in one essay that anyone with focus jewels powerful enough could bind a zyfaunos to a Gem. Ouranos absently ran a hand over his own Ei-Ei jewels, nuzzled around his eyes. They were definitely powerful enough. Even he had enough power, despite missing one of the sets of jewels. And his father certainly had enough power.

And his father had gleaned much information about binding from his time in Matthew's head.

The only question remaining is whether he could force a Black Bind. Black Binding apparently arose out of a period of extreme stress and emotional mayhem, and it needed a vast amount of power to achieve. Most who had started the process of Black Binding died before the bind was successful. The fact that Matt and Izzy had survived their own Black Binding was no small miracle.

But certainly his father could attempt a forced Black Bind. He was quite knowledgeable about creating periods of extreme stress and emotions.

Ouranos sighed and pulled his chair close to the desk again. Regardless of his father's knowledge, the Omnir on Earth was in danger. And that left Ouranos with a choice. He could go to the Master Guardian, admit he had eavesdropped, explain his fears about the Omnir and his father, and hope to Draso that he would be willing to send his Defenders to Earth to prevent disaster… or he could attempt the journey to Earth on his own and stop his father himself.

Given the Master Guardian's concerns about the army and Ouranos' reluctance to bring his friends into danger, the latter seemed more inviting. He closed the book on his desk, the thump of the cover slapping the first page reverberating in the cavernous silence of the library.

Then a flood of lights turned on. Ouranos froze.

"Ouranos?"

The voice made Ouranos sit straight up. He turned his head cautiously and faced Isabelle Gildspine, the other half of the Golden Guardians, and Matthew's close friend and partner. The golden brown quilar held three heavy books in her hands and wore only her battle dress pants and a white camisole. She blinked at Ouranos with her big blue eyes, frowning.

"Ah, um," Ouranos stuttered. "Good evening, Isabelle."

"It's morning, technically," Izzy said. "And I've asked you many times to call me Izzy. Isabelle is too formal."

"I suspect you will have to tell me many more times, as I am not used to shortening names," Ouranos said. "May I ask why you are visiting the library so late?"

"I could ask you the same thing. It's almost one in the morning." Izzy eyed the book on Ouranos' desk. "What are you reading? A book on Gem binding?"

"Ah, yes," Ouranos said. This was quite a dilemma he found himself in. "I was curious about the process of Gem binding and I perhaps lost track of time."

"The librarians come around and let people know when student research hours are over," Izzy said. "They wouldn't have missed you."

Ouranos' face grew hot, flushing his inner ears. "I… ah, perhaps I was out of hearing range."

"They're very careful to clear students out of the library before they lock up," Izzy said. "Only those with the right clearance level can enter or leave after hours without setting off alarms. No one is allowed to stay behind." She eyed him. "Unless you were trying to avoid them."

Ouranos splayed both ears now, but said nothing.

"You were, weren't you?"

Ouranos took a deep breath. "Admittedly, yes."

"Why?"

Ouranos weighed his options again. His only real choice was to attempt an escape to Earth by himself. He could no longer ask his friends to endanger themselves.

And yet, he saw no way for him to get to Earth on his own.

Izzy, however, could get them to Earth. But to ask her to do so would be to put her in danger. And Lance had expressed worry about Izzy and Matt staying neutral and professional in concerns with the Omnirs.

But Izzy was a soldier. A healer. And not so hot-headed as Matt – Matt had told Ouranos so himself. Stoic. Strong. Practical. Maybe… maybe if he had to involve one of them, she would be the best. He could protect one friend easily enough, and keep her apart from the Omnir if need be. Though, he would have to keep secret the Omnir's suspected occupation as an assassin, if he were to expect Izzy to approach him neutrally.

Ouranos would also have to keep his own involvement in the Sol Genocide a secret. Draso only knew how she would react if she knew Ouranos was responsible for her father's death, even indirectly. But he could make it work.

Perhaps, by bringing Izzy here, Draso had granted him the means to accomplish his goals.

"Ouranos?"

Ouranos pointed to a spare chair. "Have a seat. I am afraid this will take quite some time to explain."

REVELATION

Izzy carefully placed her hands in her lap after Ouranos explained everything, hoping to calm the shaking.

An Omnir had been found on Terra. On Earth. An actual, living, breathing Omnir. She'd have to check the databases again, but she was near certain that they'd been wiped out not long after the Sol genocide on Terra. She didn't know enough history to remember exactly what had destroyed the Omnir tribe, but the unpleasant feeling growing in her gut from the memory of learning about it suggested it hadn't been pretty.

A catastrophic destruction of an entire group of people. No one had survived. At least, that's what the Defenders had thought.

"And you think there may be more than one?" Izzy asked Ouranos.

"Possibly," Ouranos said. "The genocide happened nearly sixty years ago, yes?"

Izzy pressed her lips together. Sixty years. Good Draso. She had been only four years old when the genocide had happened. She was fifty-eight now, still barely a young adult in the eyes of the long-lived Zyearthlings. "That's pretty close, yeah."

"Omnir are not long-lived naturally," Ouranos continued. "Any surviving Omnir from the genocide would likely be in their eighties or older, possibly nearing the end of their life. From what I gathered from the Master Guardian's discussion, the Omnir they found works in vehicle repair." He frowned. "Admittedly I knew very little of what that entailed, but my research suggests that it is a job for the young. He is likely an offspring, meaning there could be more."

Multiple Omnirs. Living among the mainland inhabitants, with normal jobs.

She chewed her lip. Living peacefully, likely. She had to keep telling herself that. Peacefully. They weren't hiding, or using fake names, or planning genocide, or murdering left and right.

He wasn't something to be feared then. He was just a random car repairman who happened to be possibly related to a dark place in her past. She looked up at Ouranos.

"And you think your father would go after him if he knew he was alive?"

"Yes," Ouranos said. "He needs a Black Bound Gem user to create the Shadow Cast. He knows Omnirs can be bound to Gems. If he catches even a breath that there may be a living Omnir, he may attempt to force a Black Bind on them."

"Ouranos, you know that *any* zyfaunos can be bound to a Gem, right?" Izzy said. "Hell, if you weren't already bound to your Ei-Ei jewels, you could probably be bound yourself. For all I know, you might be able to be bound even *with* the Ei-Ei jewels, though I don't know if anyone has ever tried to bind to more than one type of focus jewel. But still, he doesn't need an Omnir to do that."

Ouranos splayed his ears. He shook his head. "Regardless, the Basileus does not know this. His knowledge will be limited to Omnirs. And to be frank, I am not even certain he would know how to bind a Gem to an Omnir even if he found one, let alone force a Black Bind. But he spent much time listening to me and Matthew speaking, and discussions about Black Binding came up. I cannot think him entirely ignorant."

"No, you can't," Izzy said, chewing her lip. "And actually, if he gets whiff that any zyfaunos can be bound to a Gem, he may just go after any random one. Even if he fails trying to force a Black Bind in one zyfaunos, he has literally any of them on Earth to keep trying it on. Either way, it might be better to be there before he realizes this. We thought we had more time." She took a deep breath. "Though you know, Ouranos, even if he doesn't know about the Omnirs, if we go after him, we're essentially dropping a Black Bound Gem user in his lap."

Ouranos' ear twitched. "I am aware. But you are trained. You have fought him and won."

"Not alone. I had help."

"And you will have help," Ouranos said. "You cannot expect me to send you alone."

Izzy shook her head. "Not alone, no. But until we know how to fix the Cast, anyone who goes is going to face a lot of danger. Going with a small strike team might be better."

"A well-made point."

"I think," Izzy continued. "To keep things as simple as possible, maybe just the two of us should go."

"I agree."

Izzy perked an ear. "You agreed to that awfully fast."

"I was contemplating trying to find my own way to Earth, alone, before I found an ally in you," Ouranos said. "I do not wish to put anyone else I care about in danger. In all honesty, I am not entirely comfortable asking for your aid either, but I do not see how I can accomplish this without help, and you are a kindred spirit in this."

And Matt would not be, Izzy knew. Just hearing the name Omnir would make that difficult for him. Matt had too many awful memories of that past, and was old enough at the time of the event for many of them to still haunt him today.

Izzy had her own bad memories too. An aching belly while waiting to be rescued and vague images, smells, and fears that sometimes entered her nightmares.

But she could put distance between those and reality. Matt could not. And more than that, he shouldn't have to. She and Ouranos could do this without him. Drop to Terra. Find the Omnir. Get him some place safe.

Matt would never have to get involved. And he wouldn't have to face all those horrible memories again.

She stood. "Right then. I guess it's just the two of us." She placed Ouranos' Gem book on top of her stack, walked to a shelf and dumped the pile on it. "We're leaving tonight."

Ouranos stood, ears perked. "Tonight?"

"If we leave tomorrow, we'll have all kinds of questions to answer," Izzy said. "I can Spook the X-Zero and cut the communications to buy us some time. We'll take Pilot. We haven't fully retrofitted him yet, so while he's pretty well equipped to help navigate, he doesn't have tracking software yet." She crossed her arms and gave him a lopsided smile. "These are the Defenders, Ouranos. We won't be able to hide from them forever. But we might at least get a head start and that's better than nothing."

Ouranos twitched his tail. "Indeed."

"We have a name, an occupation, and a general location to find this quilar. That should be enough, especially since the name Omnir will be really rare in the phone directories. If we're lucky we can get to Earth and get the Omnir safe before they can stop us."

Ouranos frowned. "I ah, see your point."

"Good," Izzy said. They exited the library and into the open air.

"Isabelle--"

Izzy rolled her eyes. "Izzy, please, Ouranos."

Ouranos shook his head. "Izzy. This action you are taking. Leaving without permission. Will you face consequences?"

Izzy paused. They'd be going AWOL – absent without leave. That was no small matter. Especially being so young in her Guardianship.

But this was too important to ignore. This was why she became a Guardian in the first place.

"Yes," she told Ouranos. "But I can't let this go. It's my job as a Guardian to stop these things."

"And the Master Guardian will prevent you from completing this job."

"Ouranos, we aren't ready to fight the Cast right now," Izzy said. "Lance knows this. The risk is too great. He'd stop us."

"Because it is dangerous."

Izzy took a deep breath. "Because this is ludicrous. But we have to do it anyway." She pointed toward the dorms. "Get to your room. Pack up and meet me in the hangar. I'll get Pilot for you."

Ouranos pressed his lips together, but nodded. "I will. And thank you."

Izzy watched him walk off before jogging to her own suite. This was probably one of the most reckless things she had ever done in her life, but Ouranos had a point.

This was too big to ignore.

PARTY OF FOUR

Izzy entered her suite, huffing. Snatching a duffle from her closet, she stuffed T-shirts, camisoles, and pants into it. She found her military grade Gem holster as well as the cloth holster and tossed those both in as well. She paused, thinking.

Draso's breath, if only she could get Matt involved in this. They needed a small strike team yes, but what Ouranos really needed was a battle partner. Her healing was great, but also useless against the Cast, and her hammer only did so much. She shook her head and searched for the rest of the equipment she needed. As she zipped up her duffle, she caught sight of her dresser.

Roscoe's wedding coil sat next to her jewelry box. Roscoe had always done a good job keeping it polished and clean and Izzy had continued the practice while… while he was stuck as a Cast. Draso's breath, some days were really hard without her husband.

She picked up the coil and dropped it in her bag as a memorial. Then she glanced over her jewelry box.

Ouranos would need a means of contacting her if they got away from each other. She dug into the box and pulled out a plain black Defender pendant.

It was the first one Izzy had ever gotten. An unofficial pendant made for her by her adoptive father, Jaymes, as a way to contact him if she ever needed him. She had been given strict orders not to wear it, as Matt had with his, but now it might come in handy. She pocketed the pendant, then ran outside the suite.

A small black puddle waited outside for her.

She jumped back. The Cast lifted an inky, dripping stag head out of the flat puddle, glaring at her with three swimming blue "eyes" and damaged antlers. Izzy grabbed her chest with a sigh. "Roscoe, you *ass*. What are you doing?"

"We could ask you that too," a blubbering voice said, and a second puddle appeared beside Cast-Roscoe.

Izzy frowned, staring at the second Cast. The black blob grew up from the ground, forming a stag head and torso, complete with antlers and the three blue eyes of a Cast. A strong smell of deer musk filled the air. The Cast crossed his half-formed arms in an affected look of defiance.

Izzy smirked. "You're getting better at that, Darvin."

"Yeah, well, it's not like it's something I want to get better at," the strange half Cast said, opening his too-wide mouth in a jagged black grin. His voice bubbled and spat like sound forcing its way through water. "But it's at least a little closer to normal. Now," he lowered his eyes down his snout and tilted his head. "Stop changing the subject and tell me what's going on."

Izzy splayed an ear. "How did you even find out something was going on?"

"Because Roscoe follows you around like a sick puppy," Darvin said, pointing at the other black blob. "And he's gotten really good at escaping the labs, so when he leaves, I follow." He pointed a dripping black finger. "Stop changing the subject."

"We are leaving," Ouranos said, coming up the grassy hill behind Darvin. He held a duffle bag on his shoulder. "For Earth."

Darvin shot a glance at Ouranos. The force of his head turning broke one of his inky antlers off and dropped it into the puddle of his body with a splash. He shook himself, then carefully grew another antler in its place.

"In the middle of the night?" Darvin asked, incredulous. "By yourselves?"

"We're going to investigate something. The Basileus might have found a way to create more Cast on Earth," Izzy said.

Darvin raised an inky brow over one of his three blue eyes. "Might have."

Izzy shifted. "Yes. Might have."

Darvin snorted, shooting black ink to the grass. "By yourselves. With no way to fight the Cast, no backup at all, no certainty that your enemy really has found a way to increase his army, and a definite certainty that you could face a court martial or dismissal from this. Also, dropping a Black Bound in the Basileus' lap."

Izzy frowned. That sounded really bad when he put it that way. This really was the most senseless, foolhardy thing she had ever done. "That about sums it up, yeah."

"Awesome," Darvin said. "Count us in."

Ouranos frowned. "We do not want to endanger anyone else."

"Who are you going to endanger?" Darvin said. "We're Cast, remember? We're invincible. Hell, for that matter, you might benefit from having us there. We can spy for you. Besides." He nodded to Roscoe. "He won't let you go anywhere without him, Izzy."

Izzy glanced down. Roscoe had affectionately wrapped himself in a half circle around her ankles. She caught a wink of a smile.

She never could resist that smile.

But she frowned. "They're going to know you're missing."

Darvin tilted his head. "You think they won't know you're missing too?"

"The labs are guarded," Izzy said. "They'll figure it out way sooner than if Ouranos and I just left by ourselves."

Darvin scoffed. "I'll drop a couple of the other Cast in our lab," he said. "They think we sleep at night. No one will question it."

Izzy wrinkled her snout. "Darvin…"

Darvin lowered his gaze. "You're not going to get out of this, Izzy. You need us. You shouldn't be doing this just the two of you."

Izzy threw up her hands. "Okay, fine, you make a good point. But hurry up with your plan. We don't have time."

"Yes, ma'am," Darvin flipped a hand up and smashed it into his chest, affecting a Defender salute. He and Roscoe slithered back toward the labs.

Izzy took a deep breath.

"Isabelle," Ouranos said.

"Izzy, Ouranos."

Ouranos chewed his lip. "Izzy. You know. If… when Matthew discovers us missing, he will know where we went. And he will follow. I struggle to believe even the Master Guardian could stop him."

Izzy pinned her ears back. "I know." And there was nothing she could do about it. There wasn't enough time to try and prevent him from following. But they weren't going to fight the Basileus. They were going to save an Omnir. This was search and rescue, not war. Hopefully anyway. She met his gaze. "Natassa will do the same. She has once before."

Ouranos flicked his tail, frowning. "I know."

She headed toward the hangar. "We just have to hope we have a big enough head start."

CHAPTER 06

WAKE-UP CALL

Matt woke up groggily to pounding on his door and the muffled sounds of someone calling his name. He sat up in bed, shook his head, and checked the time. 3:34 AM.

Adrenaline shot through his system and he sprang out of bed. He threw on a pair of blue pajama bottoms and his Defender pendant.

"Matt, wake up *now!*" the voice demanded.

"Coming!" He zipped out of his room, not bothering with a shirt, and jogged to the front door.

Ouranos' sister Natassa, and Sami Girsougon, an arctic fox, stood at his front door. Both had their ears pasted back and they wore frowns.

Matt tilted an ear. "I'm glad I had the sense to put some pants on. What's going on?"

"Izzy and Ouranos have gone *missing,*" Natassa said. Her black fur made her nearly invisible in the dark hallway, made worse by her deep maroon pajamas. The cream-colored fur on her snout and around her eyes reflected the hall light with a ghostly glow. "Ouranos never came home today. I tried going to ask Izzy for help in finding him, but she is not in her suite."

"Darvin and Roscoe are missing from the labs too," Sami said, swinging her long white fox tail back and forth in agitation. Her teal and black battle dress uniform was rumpled, mirroring her anxiety. "I was on shift to watch the Cast in the labs and they weren't in their own lab. Two other Cast were in their place. I can't find them anywhere."

Matt frowned, fighting the sleep from his eyes. Ouranos he could probably forgive. He had seen him walking the grounds early in the morning several times since the incident with the Cast and The Basileus. Probably one of the few times he could walk around and be fairly confident he wasn't going to run into any glaring Defenders. He was likely out walking around right now.

Just to check, he prodded the edge of his consciousness for Ouranos' presence in his mind. But he found nothing. Still, not that surprising. Six months of practice with the social bind and both of them were getting better at preventing the bleeding effect. He considered calling out to him, but thought better of it. It was 3AM. He didn't want to startle Ouranos.

But Izzy wasn't answering anyone either. That wasn't like her. Unless she was deeply asleep, which wasn't unreasonable to assume. And he still wasn't ready to try and test their social bind. "Are you sure Izzy just didn't hear you? She's a pretty deep sleeper."

"She will not answer my calls either," Natassa said. "Even when I tag them as emergency calls. Please, Matt, we need your help."

Matt ran a hand over his face. That was a problem. "Alright, we'll go check out her suite." He shut his door, walked across the circular hall to Izzy's suite, then pressed his pendant against the wall opener next to her door. The door chimed, then opened and he walked inside with Natassa and Sami at his heels.

Matt flipped a light switch, lighting up the suite. A few dishes sat on the kitchen counter, and an open data slate was propped up on the large wood table in the dining room, playing a waterfall screensaver. Everything smelled like fresh cleaning.

But no Izzy.

She was probably asleep. Rather than shout and scare her, Matt waved Natassa and Sami to the couch in Izzy's sunken living room, then headed for her bedroom, a large spacious room at the end of a long hallway.

The door was shut, so he knocked. "Izzy?" He waited a moment, but didn't hear anything. Cautiously, he opened the door and flipped on the light. The massive bed was made, completely undisturbed. A snatch of adrenaline ran through Matt's veins.

No Izzy.

"Izzy?" No answer. He shot a hopeful glance in the bathroom, but Izzy wasn't there either.

He pressed his lips together. Now he was worried. He pulled up his pendant and pressed his thumb to the back of the dragon shaped communicator. A list of call codes came up and he called Izzy.

"Connection failed," the tiny computer beeped at him. *"Pendant out of range."*

Matt frowned, pressing his ears back. Out of *range?* That didn't make sense. The communicator ranges were international. She could be anywhere on Zyearth and still be in range. The only way she'd be out of range is if she had somehow left the planet--

Electricity lit up his spine and his fur stood on end. "Draso's *breath,* Izzy." He dashed out of the bedroom and toward the front door. Natassa and Sami stood.

"She's not there?" Sami asked.

"No," Matt said. "But I have a hunch as to where she disappeared."

Without bothering with shoes or a shirt, Matt ran out of the Guardian Edifice and dashed across the wet grass toward the Defender's cliff hangar, unsheathed toeclaws digging into the dirt. Natassa and Sami ran behind him. He prayed that he wouldn't find what he expected to find there.

When he arrived, he typed in his code, pressed his pendant to the door for identification, and shoved the door open, turning on the huge overhead lights. They warmed and bathed the entire hangar in a dense white light.

The deep-space travel X-Zeros sat next to the single-fighter S-Wings, atmosphere-ready Delta-Zs, elemental drones called Epsilon-Ones, and their only grounded Delta-H. Dozens of Pendragon troop transports lined one wall. Matt jogged across the cold metal floor toward the X-Zeros, making a mental count of the planes.

One of the X-Zeros was missing. Specifically, Izzy's personal plane.

"Fire and ice, Izzy," Matt muttered. He ran back to the codepad and pulled up the most recent activity. Sure enough, Izzy had logged in an entry, just two and a half hours ago. And, apparently, she had taken her X-Zero.

"Matt?" Sami said. "What's going on?"

Matt shook his head and ran toward the hangar door. "Go pack a bag and meet me here. We're leaving."

AWOL

Matt jogged up the ramp leading into his personal X-Zero, granted to him after he had earned the Guardianship. He wore his battle dress pants and a green T-shirt and carried a large duffle and a field pack. He dropped his duffle and pack in the tight sleeping quarters, then headed toward the cockpit.

It had taken him over half an hour to supply the ship. And every minute, Izzy was getting farther and farther away. Lightning and air.

He'd noticed Izzy's code all over the machine too. He did them the favor of erasing both their tracks, though he knew it wouldn't do a whole lot of good.

Lance would find out eventually.

He poked at the edges of his mind for Ouranos again, louder this time. Nothing. Damn it all.

"I am here," Natassa walked on board, carrying a duffle and wearing a pair of tan pants and a white T-shirt. Like her brother, Natassa had traded her traditional Athánatos garb for some modern Zyearth clothing. She frowned at Matt. "Do you know where we are going yet?"

Matt flicked his ears back. "I can only assume they're headed for your home. Earth, Terra... Can't think of anywhere else they'd rush off to in the middle of the night without permission. That's where we're headed."

"To face my father."

Matt lifted an ear. "Possibly."

Natassa shook her head. "Certainly. Izzy and Ouranos are after him. I can feel it. I cannot believe that you will go all the way to Earth just to berate them and demand they go home."

Matt bent an ear. "Natassa. As much as I want to kick his sorry tail – and trust me, I *really* want to – we can't. We haven't figured out how to fix the Cast yet. Hell, even going there is giving him exactly what he wants. Black Bound users. We're giving him the means to make more."

Natassa twitched her tail. "Then why go at all? We could wake the Master Guardian and have him put a stop to this."

Matt rubbed his arm. She had a point. But… "Izzy is my partner. She'll listen to me. We need each other. I just need her to come home."

Natassa flattened one ear. "You may fool yourself, Matthew," she said slowly. "But you do not fool me. We are leaving to face the Basileus once and for all." She entered the plane silently.

Matt flicked both ears back.

Sami appeared at the door in her still-rumpled uniform, carrying a duffle on her shoulder and one more box of food. She looked harried, holding her ears back and keeping her tail close to her legs.

She glanced at Matt with a stern frown. "So this is it then? We're just leaving?"

"You don't have to come if you don't want to," Matt said.

"I do have to come. Darvin is going to Draso knows where and he doesn't have his Gem," Sami said. She put down her box and held out a colorless Gem, which still sparkled in the dim light. It had been months since Darvin had been able to properly touch the jewel, let alone use it, and it had started losing its color.

Matt nodded to the Gem. "Is Darvin even going to be able to use that?"

Sami shrugged. "You never know. I packed Roscoe's too, since they were in the labs." Sami pressed an ear back. "We're really going to leave without asking or talking to Lance about this at all."

Matt wrinkled his snout. "Do you really think Lance would let us go if we told him what was going on?"

Sami twitched her snout. "No, probably not."

"Then we go without asking."

Sami lowered her gaze and eyed him with one of her large purple eyes.

Matt splayed his ears, but he tilted his chin up. "Defender Manual Section 5, Paragraph Q states 'upon recognizing a packmate is in danger, assist as soon as possible.'"

Sami twitched a whisker. "Paragraph R states that the Defender assisting should consult their superior officer if they believe their actions will also put them in danger, or risk a court martial."

Matt bit his lip, but waved a hand. "Paragraph S waives that requirement if time doesn't allow for consultation."

"That's for the battlefield though, Matt," Sami said. "Ouranos and Izzy have at least a month before they hit Terra. Lance won't take your nonsense from Paragraph S."

Matt flicked his ears back. "…I know. But if I actually follow this to the letter, he won't let us go at all. Izzy and Ouranos will be on their own. I can't do that. Especially after I abandoned her so much when we fought the Basileus the first time. I'm not going to lose my partner."

Sami wrinkled her snout. "Okay, I get it. But you realize this really could mean a court martial, or even a dismissal from service." She pressed her lips together. "You could lose the Guardianship you worked so hard to get. Are we prepared to face that?"

Matt frowned. She made a good point. But Izzy couldn't do this alone, no matter what she thought. He wouldn't let her face that again. He'd bring her home.

"Izzy's in danger," Matt said. "And Ouranos. They're too important to me to leave behind. That's why I became a Guardian in the first place. It's worth it. Don't you think?"

Sami perked both ears in surprise. She smiled. "Yeah, I do."

Matt plugged his Gem into the energy slot, activated the Gem shards that powered the plane, then nodded to Sami. "Sami, why don't you take Natassa to the sleeping quarters and get your bags stowed away? I'll get started with launch procedures." Sami nodded and led Natassa to the back.

Matt started up the plane, closed the door, and pressurized the cabin. He started the thrusters and cautiously led the plane out of the open hangar doors. Hovering over the channel water, he watched the hangar doors as they shut, then took a deep breath. After a moment, he pulled up the intercom and told Natassa and Sami to strap in. He flew the plane far out over the ocean, a good distance away from the Defender campus, then prepped it for escape velocity.

"Get ready for the real take off, everyone," Matt said over the intercom, then blasted the plane with power and sent it into the upper stratosphere. Ten minutes of extreme G's later and they had well escaped Zyearth's pull. Matt pulled up the intercom. "Everyone okay?"

Sami tapped the intercom back. "We're fine. Natassa's a little woozy though. I'll get her through it."

"Good," Matt said. "Get some sleep if you can. I know you've both been awake for a long time, and we're in this for the long haul."

Matt set the plane on autopilot, watching the hours tick by until it read 7AM, local time on the Defender campus. Likely Lance would already be up, but hopefully he wouldn't be aware that his two Golden Guardians were missing. He opened up the communications module.

Lance picked up almost immediately, glaring at the camera with a snarl on his black wolf lips. Defenders ran back and forth behind him in the main communications center, looking harried. Footage of Matt and Izzy's trek through the hangar played on the wall screens.

"Matt, where in Draso's Holy Palace are you and Izzy? I've been trying to get you on the COMs for hours!"

Matt winced. So much for that hope. A lump grew in his throat. Maybe he wasn't really okay with court martialing or dismissal. Better get this over with, straight and to the point.

"Sir, Izzy is missing. We believe that she, Ouranos, and the Polttarit brothers took her plane and are headed for Terra. I'm going after her."

Lance widened his eyes, bending both ears back. "Whoa, whoa, whoa, what? Give this to me a little at a time. Izzy is missing?"

"Izzy took her plane with Ouranos, Darvin, and Roscoe at about one in the morning," Matt said. "I'm taking Sami Girsougon and Natassa and going after her."

Lance curled his black lips in a snarl. He craned his neck, trying to get a good look behind Matt. "And that's why I see you in a plane."

"Yes, sir."

Lance rubbed the fur between his eyes. "Fire and ice, Matt. You gave us all heart attacks. You know where Izzy went for certain?"

"She took Ouranos. I can only assume she's headed for Terra." He swallowed. "For Earth."

"Did you try contacting her?"

"She's got her plane Spooked," Matt said. "I can't track it and she's not answering pings. Trust me, I tried. That's why I'm going after her."

"Did you try your ah…" He frowned. "Your social bond with Ouranos?"

"Yes sir," Matt said. "Either he's out of range or he's blocking me. It's also possible their Spooked plane is messing with it somehow."

Lance eyed him. "Your plane is also Spooked."

Matt shifted in his chair. "Yes, sir."

"And it didn't even occur to you to ask me about going after her before you dragged Sami and Natassa into this 'rescue' mission with you."

Matt pressed his lips together. "No, it definitely occurred to me. But Izzy was already far ahead and time was limited, so I took initiative according to Section 5, Paragraph S, and went anyway. Sir."

Lance took a deep breath, wrinkling his wolfish snout. Matt couldn't tell if he was snarling or smiling. "Paragraph S doesn't cover this situation and you know it."

Matt stayed silent.

"But you went through with it anyway," Lance said. "Because you knew I'd say no."

"I had a hunch."

Lance shook his head. "Are they going after the Basileus?"

Matt gave a slight shrug. "I assume so. I can't imagine what else would send them over there in such a hurry."

"Lightning and air," Lance swore. He glared at Matt with an anger he had never seen in the wolf before. "You're not just going after her to bring her home, are you. You're planning to fight him too. Unequipped, unable to stop or fix the Cast, unable to do anything but give him another Black Bound Gem and the means to create more Cast."

"With all due respect," Matt said, keeping his voice steady. "I'm aware of the gravity of the situation, sir. As much as I'd like to go after the Basileus, it's not possible at this stage. I don't know why Izzy took off, but for now, the plan is to chase her, find her, and bring her home."

Lance eyed him. "For now."

"Yes, sir," Matt said. "Since I don't know what encouraged Izzy to go to Terra, I can't say how the situation will change. But, for now, that's the plan."

Lance's lips curled in a snarl. "This isn't a game, Matt. It's a serious issue. You're AWOL. By all rights, I should dismiss you. You, Izzy, Sami, and the Polttarit brothers. This is reckless and foolish."

Matt pressed his ears back. "I'm aware, sir."

"You just won the Guardianship. You're putting all that at risk."

"It's a risk I was willing to take, sir," Matt said. "Even if it means giving everything up. Izzy left for a reason and I'm not going to abandon my partner."

Lance's face softened, just slightly, but he held the frown. "I don't have to remind you that going into a hot zone unprepared is what killed your father." His voice lost some of its bite at the last few words.

He closed his eyes a moment. Lance was right. This was exactly what had killed his father. And Izzy's. Going into something they couldn't handle. Hell, it was even likely to happen around the same site of his father's death, if he remembered the location of Natassa's home correctly.

But that didn't change the situation.

"Sir, this is exactly why I fought so hard to become a Guardian," Matt said. "Why my father and grandfather became Guardians. To fight impossible odds. It didn't stop them, and it won't stop me. And because he fought, he saved me, Izzy, and Charlotte. I'm willing to do the same to save my pack."

Lance let out a low grow. "This isn't the *same*. This is dropping two Black Bound users in Theron's lap. This is putting the whole *planet* in danger."

"I'm *aware,*" Matt said. "Sir. Which is why it's not my intention to stay. I'm planning to bring Izzy home. But I couldn't wait for permission. Izzy's putting herself and Ouranos in danger. Even the Polttarit brothers, despite them being Cast. But I have to do what I feel is right. That's why I wanted to be a Guardian. Sir."

Lance lowered his gaze. "Your father gave me that same line more times than I want to remember. And your grandfather." He waved a finger at Matt. "Go after them. Bring them home. And for the love of Draso, don't try any heroics, okay? I can't send more soldiers your way. Not to a silent planet. Not when we can't fight back. We've lost enough." He closed his eyes a moment. "I don't want to lose all of you too."

Matt nodded. "Yes, sir."

Lance sighed. "You're… you're just like your father, you know that?"

Matt tilted one corner of his lips up. "Yes, sir."

"Try to come back in one piece, okay?" Lance said. "This isn't over yet. We're going to have a serious discussion about this behavior. This is completely unacceptable." He shook his head, releasing another sigh. "And I want you alive to have that discussion."

"Understood."

Lance ran a hand down his face. "I'm sending you Galactic Accord protocols for dealing with a silent planet. Make sure you follow them to the letter. We don't want to open their ears if we can avoid it. Terra is violent enough without it. Understood?"

"Yes, sir."

"Let me know when you're coming home. Master Guardian out." He closed communications.

Matt sat back in his chair, taking as deep a breath as his lungs would allow. *Good Draso, Izzy, why now?*

True Purpose

Matt spent the trip in a state of constant unease, trying to work through any possible reason that would send Izzy and Ouranos to Terra. To… to Earth. Each one was as unlikely as the last.

His frustration led him time and time again to the digital library, poring over old Earth histories and information, desperate to learn anything that might explain why Izzy ran off for Earth. Three weeks into the month-long journey and he still hadn't found anything.

Sami caught him in the library on the start of the fourth week. She leaned against the door frame, watching Matt flip through digital titles on a holographic rotating bookshelf projecting from the table in the center of the room. He growled, "tossing" aside a digital book in frustration. The hologram projection flew across the room with a simulated flutter of pages before dissipating in a flurry of pixels.

Sami nodded at him. "Something wrong?"

Matt shook his head. "I just don't understand, Sami. Why did Izzy and Ouranos take off for Earth? Why now of all times? Lance was right when he pointed out we have no way of really tackling the Basileus. What do they know that we don't?"

Sami sat in one of the soft red chairs, one of the few on the plane that wasn't hard synthetic. Her ears flattened and she frowned, furrowing her brow.

Matt blinked, staring at her. He pinched the bridge of his nose and narrowed his eyes. "There's something you're not telling me."

Sami pulled her tail in her lap and picked at the fur. "Yeah, actually."

Matt splayed an ear, frowning. That wasn't good. He sat back in his chair. "And it's something that might have to do with Izzy's mysterious flight to Earth."

Sami perked an eyebrow. "To Terra."

"To Earth," Matt said, though his voice cracked a little. He took a deep breath and composed himself. "Use the locals' term. Silent planet rules."

"Okay, good point..."

Matt lowered his gaze. "So this secret sent Izzy and Ouranos to Earth."

Sami looked away, hunched slightly. "I don't know. Possibly."

"Why haven't you told me?"

Sami smoothed her tail. "The Master Guardian asked me not to tell you or Izzy. He wasn't sure you'd handle the news all that well."

Matt crossed his arms.

"I don't honestly agree with him on it," Sami said. "You're made of stronger stuff than that. But he's the Master Guardian. I had to follow orders. But now that we're AWOL and probably headed for dismissal..." She shook her head. "Honestly, I've been fighting with myself about whether or not to tell from the moment we took off. But we're so close now, and I think you need to know."

Matt furrowed his brow. "Okay then, out with it."

Sami lowered her gaze, piercing his with her violet eyes. "You have to promise you'll remain calm and professional."

Matt's bones buzzed. That wasn't a good sign. "Uh. Sure."

She pressed her black lips together, frowning. "We've been tracking an assas-- ah, a mechanic on Terra-- I mean, Earth for a few months. He's a bit unusual, since he's a… a red quilar."

Matt's vision blurred for a split second, as if someone had punched him in the face. No. No, it couldn't be. Not that. But memories flashed in his mind.

A red quilar hovering over his mother's broken body.

A red quilar chasing Matt, Charlotte, and Izzy, screaming at them.

A red quilar stabbing at Izzy's father.

A red quilar killing Matt's father, Jaden, his ghostly screams echoing off the sanctum's walls as the room filled with light from his broken Gem.

Matt winced, revisiting the pain from his Black Binding, which had happened right after his father's death. As a result of that death, really.

That could not be one of those quilar.

"Why have you been tracking him?" Matt asked, his voice wavering. He hid his hands further in the crooks of his arms to stop the shaking.

"Well," Sami said slowly. "You know that the Omnir tribe was wiped out not long after the Sol Genocide. With them, the gene for red fur in quilar on Terra died too. The only red quilar still around are on Zyearth, and even that is rare. When we received word that there was a red quilar running around on Terra… pardon, Earth, we felt the need to investigate."

"Sami, no offense, but that's horse spit," Matt said. "What's the real reason?"

Sami shrugged slowly, splaying her ears. "That's the only reason I was told. I wasn't in charge of the investigation."

Matt pressed his eyes closed and rubbed the fur on his brow. "I assume you think that this is an actual Omnir then."

"Maybe," Sami said. "We only need a DNA test to know for sure. But it seems really likely."

"Draso's breath," Matt said. Emotions swirled, chasing questions in his mind.

"Matt," Sami said. "Your hands."

Matt glanced down. His fists were so tight they were shaking. He forced his hands to relax and sighed. "Sorry." He shook his head. "How did Izzy find out?"

Sami shifted. "Ouranos found me in the medical office building right after I had talked with Lance about this new information, the day that Izzy took off. I didn't think Ouranos had heard anything, but he must have."

Which would explain why he'd go to Izzy about it. Ouranos had mentioned the Trinity Islands briefly during their time fighting the Cast and Theron, and while Matt had never confirmed with him, it was pretty clear Ouranos knew something about the Omnirs. But that still didn't explain why Izzy had gone to... Earth.

"I can't picture Izzy going to Ear... going that far just get petty revenge," Matt said, though the idea that revenge against them was "petty" was completely wrong, if he had anything to say about it. "They must still have new information that we don't, but I think it's safe to assume that that's what prompted them to leave." He pinched his snout, frowning. "Fire and ice..."

"I'm sorry, Matt," Sami said.

Matt forced himself to relax. "It really shouldn't affect me this much. It was what, over fifty years ago? I was just six. And it's not like my whole life was horrible after that. But, damn it, Sami, if you had been there..." He shook his head. This wasn't a productive reaction. He needed distance. He looked Sami in the eye, on purpose, and pressed a smile on his lips, hoping it looked genuine. "Thanks for telling me when you did. We have over a week of travel left and that'll give me time to work through this a bit."

Sami gave him a shy smile. "If you ever need to talk about it, Natassa and I will listen. Okay?"

"I'll be fine," Matt said. "But thanks." He sat back in the chair again, with a sigh. "I think I'll find a nice fiction piece and try to relax a bit. See you for dinner?"

"Sure," Sami said. She stood up and though it was completely unnecessary, she swung her fist in a simple salute, then left.

Matt picked up a digital book and spread it on the book stand on the table, giving Sami a few minutes to leave. He consciously regulated his breathing, trying to convince his heart to slow.

Damn. *Damn* it all. It had to be this. It was bad enough that he was headed for Earth for the first time since he left it at age six. But now he really was facing all the same elements his dad did when he had gotten killed. Same unpredictable hot zone, same location, and now facing the same quilar. His body shuddered involuntarily.

He wrinkled his snout. It couldn't be as bad as that. He wasn't facing a mob of bloodthirsty tribal warriors. He was confronting a car mechanic. Car. Mechanic. You couldn't hardly get a more innocuous job than car mechanic, unless he was some daycare nurturer. And if he was a car mechanic, he'd likely be young. Too young. Probably the offspring of some surviving Omnir, not involved with the genocide at all. Harmless.

Lightning, air, and *fire*, he had better be harmless, or he'd face Matt's blade and he wouldn't feel the least bit sorry.

CHAPTER 09

WHITE ASSASSIN

Trecheon Omnir, proprietor of the "illustrious" Red's Garage in El Dorado's industrial district walked casually down the stairs of his apartment to the garage's office at the ungodly hour of 7AM. He unlocked the front door and poked his head out into the still foggy world of El Dorado City, snatching up the paper in front of the garage's office. Glancing over the headline, he flipped the sign in the window from "closed" to "open."

Serial Killer Strikes Again, Assistant Mayor Slain, the headline read. A much-too-flattering picture of the young red-haired woman grinned under the headline with teeth so white it almost hurt to look at them. Trecheon frowned, entering his office, his red, black-streaked quills bouncing like a thick broom on the back of his head. He poured himself a cup of coffee from a battered old coffee pot and sat at his dented metal desk.

His metal fingers clinked against the ceramic mug, a constant reminder of his war injuries. Two biomechanical arms, going right up to the shoulders. He shoved aside his discomfort and skimmed the article.

It detailed the Assistant Mayor's death and the investigation, but it was the commentary that caught his attention.

A disturbing trend has become apparent among the serial murders over the last several years. Investigators report that nearly every victim by this alleged professional has been involved with some deep criminal activity, Assistant Mayor Sheldon included. Because of the strange MO of this serial murderer, some are claiming police aren't making a significant effort to find the killer. Others have started calling the murderer a vigilante hero and are actively cheering for them. One social media group has started a 'fan club' and have nicknamed the murderer the 'White Assassin' after a popular video game.

Trecheon fought his churning stomach. Fan club. Good Draso. This wasn't something to be celebrated. He was a goddamned murderer, for Draso's sake. Scum. Didn't matter who he took out.

He tossed the paper on the desk along with all the others telling of his assassin exploits. It wasn't like he wanted to be an assassin. His old war buddy Neil Black had dragged him into it during a time they were both struggling for money.

Killing was one of his only good skills. Blame the war for that.

He downed his coffee in one swig, then walked over for another. The War of Eons memorial practically glared at him. He wandered over to the wall, glancing over the various medals, newspaper clippings, his Mameluke saber, and souvenirs he had collected during the war.

Reminders of all the people he had lost to that damn war. Neil was the only one left.

One particular piece caught his eye, as it often did. A single dog tag. The only thing remaining of his friend and fellow soldier. Carter. Trecheon didn't even have a picture of the quilar, and years of suppressing war memories meant he could only put together a vague image of the soldier in his head. Carter had been in Trecheon's black ops team, codenamed Outlander, and had gone MIA right after Trecheon had been honorably discharged for massive injuries. Right after the war had stripped him of all the people important to him.

A single piece of paper was pinned next to the tag. Carter's elongated handwriting on a ripped piece of paper from the journal he'd always carried around with him.

SOMEDAY YOU'LL REMEMBER ME. WHEN YOU DO, COME TO WHERE WE FIRST MET.

A cryptic message straight out of a comic book. Carter always had had a tendency toward dramatics. Trecheon had found it in his pocket but he still didn't have a clue what it meant.

Damn him for being so obtuse.

The door to his office opened and his lead mechanic, a young Latino human named Christian, walked in with a grin. "Morning, *Jefe*. What've we got for today?"

"The Mobiüs is back in with some energy conversion problem," Trecheon said. "And we have a couple of scheduled oil changes from some petrol cars."

"The Mobiüs, eh?" Christian leaned against Trecheon's desk, combing his black hair out of his eyes and curling his thick arms in a mocking gesture. "Your favorite customer! What was she wearing this time?"

"Ugh, she's anything *but,* and you know it," Trecheon groaned. "And the last thing I want to do is think about what she was wearing."

"Gotcha Boss," Christian said with a laugh. "I'll get started ASAP." He nodded to Trecheon's arm. "See you got your arm back from the shop. Did you ever figure out what happened?"

Trecheon winced. Several weeks ago, he had fallen asleep in the office after a long night of paperwork and woke up to find his right arm on the floor with a massive hole in the center of the bicep, like someone had shot it. He couldn't get it to attach properly, let alone function.

How someone had gotten past the cameras and shot his arm without him waking up spooked the hell out of him. It was a message, he was sure of it.

After the incident he'd replaced all the locks and upgraded the security system. He had been on edge ever since, even taking to sleeping with his gun. He'd be paying off that security upgrade for years.

He hadn't seen or heard anything about the intruder since. He was almost disappointed. If they had just finished the job instead of dropping some pointless message, he could end this miserable existence. That was probably why Trecheon hadn't made any significant effort to find the perpetrator himself. The only reason he had even bothered upgrading security was because of Neil. Trecheon couldn't let himself get offed like that. That would leave Neil alone to fight for his brother Philip. Unacceptable.

He schooled his face. "No," he said. "Cameras all bugged out and didn't catch anything, and the repairman couldn't find any trace of a bullet. Just a bunch of dirt and pebbles, like someone dragged it through the beach."

"Damn," Christian said. "Whoever did that went to *lengths.*" His expression darkened. "Maybe it's that White Assassin guy."

Trecheon forced himself to roll his eyes. He reached over and tapped the paper. "Yeah, I'm sure after hits like this, he's totally interested in scaring some piddly ex-Marine mechanic with no assets."

Christian leaned over Trecheon's desk and glanced at the newspaper before walking over to the coffee pot. "I think the Assassin is less concerned about assets and more about corruption. I assume you read about the Assistant Mayor's human trafficking 'hobby'."

Trecheon eyed him. "That's your first response? Nothing about the fact that she was killed?"

"No sympathy for criminals," Christian said, taking a sip of his coffee. "Especially when it involves kids. Though to be fair, I'm not on the side of this White Assassin guy either. She should have been brought to court rather than murdered. But this vigilante must think that's the only way to get rid of corruption, I guess."

Trecheon frowned, running a hand over the paper. "Maybe."

Christian lifted his mug and glanced at the war memorial. "We all lost a lot in this damn war, didn't we?"

Trecheon took a deep breath and nodded. Christian had lost two brothers and his father in the war, though all three were war heroes, considering the battles they were attached to. One had even stormed the Desert Wall, though he'd gone MIA for his troubles.

"Do you ever miss him?"

Trecheon glanced up. Christian nodded not to Carter's dog tag, but to the one image Trecheon had kept of his brother Ryota after the bastard had gone rogue. A picture of their childhood, before the military and war corrupted Ryota's mind.

Trecheon took a determined swig of coffee. "No."

Christian eyed him.

"No," Trecheon said again. "The brother I miss isn't the murderer from the war. Ryota died long before the shell he left behind had vanished in DC."

"So what would you do if he turned up again?" Christian asked. "He's MIA."

Trecheon frowned. He pressed his lips together. Images of his last encounter with his brother entered his mind. A gruesome blood trail. Neil's leg damaged from some strange explosive device. All his own squad missing or dead. Ryota nowhere to be found. "I don't know," he said finally. "But thankfully, I'll never have to worry about that."

Christian turned away from the memorial. He scratched his thick goatee. "Likely so. Sorry about that. Didn't mean to start the day so grim."

Trecheon shrugged. "Better to start the day grim than not start it at all."

Christian chuckled. "True, true." He downed the rest of his coffee. "I'm gonna go start on the Mobiüs. Let me know if you need anything. I wanna get as much done under the hood as I can before it gets too hot."

"Understood," Trecheon said. "Thanks."

Christian nodded to him, then walked into the main garage, snatching up the Mobiüs coupe's keys as he slid through the door.

Trecheon glared at the paper. Who was he to be judging his brother anyway? His dead brother. After all, Trecheon was also a murderer. He had the same blood on his hands. At least Ryota had believed he was doing something good.

Trecheon wasn't worth the air he breathed.

He shook his head. "To be honest, Christian, I'm not on the side of the White Assassin either." He sat back in his chair to look over the day's work orders, trying to ignore the implied glare from Carter's dog tag.

By mid-afternoon, the heat of El Dorado's late summer had roasted Trecheon's garage enough that he was fairly certain he could cook a turkey in the cabin of one of the cars in for an oil change. He made sure his team was well hydrated and cool, then spent the hottest part of the day inside the poorly air-conditioned office doing paperwork.

He had just settled in to tackle the paperwork for one of the hydrogen cars, when the phone rang. He picked it up. "Red's Garage."

"Goooood afternoon Mr. Red!" a fake, overenthusiastic voice blared over the receiver. "Can I interest you in our fantastic insurance policy for all the door hinges in your house?"

Trecheon pulled the phone away from his ear a moment, wincing. He growled into the receiver. "Cut the crap, Neil. I know it's you."

"Yeah, I figured you'd know," Neil said with a purr. "I'm just pulling your leg, Trachea."

Trecheon covered his face with his palm. "One of these days, Neil, I'm going to rip out *your* trachea for calling me that. Real name, please."

"Sure thing, Trech," Neil said.

Trecheon gritted his teeth. "One last chance, Neil."

"Fine, *Trecheon,* sheesh," Neil said. "Bet you're fun at parties."

"So is there a purpose to this delightful exchange, or are you just calling to harass me?" Trecheon asked. "Because if it's number two, I'll happily hang up this phone. I've got paperwork to deal with."

"I, uh, might need your help on this job," Neil said, his voice growing suspiciously quiet.

Trecheon splayed an ear. An assassination. And a hard one. "The level four? I'm detecting reluctance."

"Well, this, uh, isn't a paying gig."

Trecheon splayed both ears now. He shut his eyes and counted to five before speaking. "Neil. The last time you took a free gig, your parents were *killed,* your brother ended up a ward of the state, and Triple Fawn put us on a very short leash. They're likely listening on us right *now*."

"This isn't the same, Trecheon," Neil said. His voice lost all sign of jest and it carried a rare seriousness. "There isn't magic here."

No magic here. Code word for the magic hit. The hit that many assassins felt compelled to believe in. The final murder that might save lives from oppression, corruption, and drug abuse. The hit that was supposed to make it all worth it.

But Neil had stopped believing in the magic hit after his run in with the Fawn Family, the mob behind Triple Fawn Inc. They'd be working the rest of their lives to get the "ransom" money to adopt Philip and get him out of the foster system.

But taking a free gig wouldn't help earn the money. "Why are you taking a free gig, Neil? Especially if it isn't magic."

"I think you'd be better off seeing the details in person," Neil said. "The usual spot?"

Trecheon frowned. This had to be serious if Neil wasn't comfortable sharing the information over the phone. "Sure. See you later." Neil said goodbye and hung up.

Trecheon put the phone back in place and stood, his body buzzing. This was not good.

CHAPTER 10

BROTHERS

Trecheon sat on his wobbly chair at the kitchen table, listening to the radio spit out old rock music, trying to keep his nerves down. He had his Lowry 9mm laid out for cleaning. The sun had long disappeared over the El Dorado Bay and the moon hung high in the sky.

He usually met up with Neil in the dead of night when discussing jobs. It was by far the best way to avoid being overheard. And normally he'd catch some Z's before heading out, but the puma's serious tones still echoed in his head and sleep was impossible.

He finished cleaning the barrel with a brush and fresh cloth, then started reassembling the parts. A difficult job with the biomechanics. He missed the proper articulation of fingers, not to mention the ability to feel through the parts for grit. But, close enough. Not like he had any other choice.

As he worked, he thought back to the Sheldon hit and his strange jewel. He lifted the loose floorboard under the kitchen table, opened the hidden safe, and pulled the jewel out.

Little rainbows floated over his walls in the light. It had once belonged to his grandfather, who gifted it to Trecheon, then disappeared. It had somehow magically healed him after Neil had accidentally shot him in the side a few years ago, and again with that last hit against the Assistant Mayor.

Draso, he missed Granddad at times.

And other times he wanted to strangle him for abandoning their family right before the war. As helpful as the jewel was, it was also a constant reminder of Granddad's desertion.

He took the gem to the table, polished it up, and dropped it in his pocket. Time to go find Neil.

Their usual meeting place was a cave buried deep in the canyons just outside town in an area so rocky, the only way to access it was on foot. Trecheon navigated the craggy path to the cave and got there around 3AM.

Neil was already there, deep in the back of the cave. He had a small electric lantern and a cup of coffee waiting for Trecheon. He wore a mask of severity as he passed Trecheon the coffee, twitching his puma tail with a nervousness and irritation Trecheon hadn't seen in some time. Neil waved him to a rock. "Have a seat."

"This had better be good, Neil," Trecheon said, bending his ears back. Neil's serious look unnerved him.

Neil said nothing. Instead, he handed Trecheon a battered old phone with a video on pause. Trecheon blinked at it, then pressed the play button.

The picture was stationary, with grainy, dull colors, like the footage from an old CCTV camera. The background showed a pyramid shaped building, overgrown with foliage. Trecheon lifted an eyebrow and glanced at Neil.

"The old casino strips?" They had been abandoned years ago, in favor of newer, better building foundations, and had never been torn down. The place was a ghost town.

"Just keep watching," Neil said, nodding to the footage.

Trecheon turned his attention back to the phone. As the video moved along, he noticed a small red figure walking out of the Great Pyramid into the empty, cracked sidewalks toward a long pier overlooking the bay.

Trecheon's adrenaline spiked. "No. No, that's--"

"Shh!" Neil said. "Just watch."

The cameras followed the red figure, each picture becoming slightly clearer. They wore plain black pants and a dark colored jacket. They had catlike ears and blood red quills, just like Trecheon's. Trecheon pulled the phone closer to his eyes, noting the quickening of his breathing and heartbeat.

Then a camera caught the quilar's face. Blue eyes. Familiar snout shape. The figure glanced up at the camera, then turned and disappeared into one of the broken casinos. The video ended.

Trecheon carefully placed the phone on a rock near his knee. He stared at Neil in disbelief.

Neil gave him a sympathetic smile. "I saw this while following that level four. Turned out to be a dummy hit, but I still got this out of it. That is unmistakably--"

"My brother," Trecheon finished. "Ryota."

They sat in silence for a moment. Trecheon's mind spun. Ryota. After he had long gave him up for dead. To see him here, alive, and apparently just a few miles from Trecheon's home, sent his blood boiling.

"Neil, what the hell is he doing out here? How is he even alive?"

Neil just shrugged, bending one ear back, twitching his tan tail. "Hell if I know. I'm just as confused as you."

"And what do you want me to do with this information?"

Neil shifted on his rock, frowning. "I was hoping you'd be willing to help me finish the job we started back in the war."

Trecheon's ears rang with the shock. "You want me to hunt him down and kill him."

"If that's what's necessary, perhaps," Neil said. "Look, we both know he's a deceptive, dangerous little bitch. I don't feel right just letting him roam free." He shrugged. "We could try talking to him. Maybe he's changed. But if he's hiding among the casino ruins, I sure as hell don't think so."

Neil had a point. Shit. It had been six, almost seven years, since Trecheon had last seen his brother. Or had last thought about the fact that he might need killing. Draso's damned *fire*. He couldn't do this. Not again. Not after all the shit Ryota had pulled before.

And it wasn't like they could go to the police or… or the military over this. Not with Trecheon and Neil's dealings as the White Assassin. They couldn't draw attention to themselves. He couldn't imagine trying to explain why Neil had a tap on the old casino cameras.

"Whether we need to take him out or not, I don't know," Neil said. "But we at least have to go see what the hell he's up to, yeah?"

Trecheon shut his eyes and rubbed his temple, trying to wrap his mind around everything. He took a deep breath.

"Trecheon?"

"Yeah," Trecheon said eventually. "Yeah, you're right. We need to see what's going on." He glanced up at Neil. "I don't suppose you tried researching any of his old traitor buddies, see if any of them got out of prison yet."

"Way ahead of you," Neil said. He spread out several pieces of paper. "These are all the people that were eventually attributed to being a part of Ryota's band of traitors. From what I can tell, everyone here is either dead,

MIA, or still behind bars." He coughed. "A few of the MIAs are apparently now a part of Angel."

"You're *kidding.*"

"I wish," Neil said.

Trecheon's blood ran cold. Angel. The rogue team of military-sanctioned assassins. In rumor anyway. There was a saying in the military – Fear the Angel – though who exactly they were and who they reported to was completely unknown. But one thing was certain. When Angel went after you, you were a goner. Full stop. Trecheon splayed his ears.

"Is that worth the risk then?" Trecheon asked. "If he's with Angel…"

"From what I can tell, Ryota isn't involved with Angel," Neil said. "Chadwick reached out to me recently. He's got a list of Angels going, since three of their team's members turned Angel. Ryota isn't one of them."

"Chadwick?" Trecheon said. "He and Jordan went MIA after the Desert Wall Assault."

"I was surprised too," Neil said. "But he and Jordan are alive and well, looking up all of Ackerson's old black ops teams. Partially to warn them about Angel because apparently they're big targets, but partially to make sure they aren't Angels themselves. I cleared you with him, which is probably why he hasn't approached you himself." Neil shifted. "They think Ackerson is running Angel himself and they want to take him down."

"That's *suicide.*"

"Yeah, well, after half their team went Angel, they want answers," Neil said. "But good news is everything points to Ryota being alone."

"At least that." Trecheon glanced over the papers, trying to calm his nerves. His gaze caught one familiar face and he lifted the file. A female gray fox with soft brown eyes stared up at him. A lump caught in his throat. "Rebekka."

Neil pasted both ears back and frowned. "Apparently. I'm honestly not surprised, considering DC."

Trecheon chewed his lip. "Is she in Angel?"

"Unconfirmed at this point," Neil said. "Chadwick can't even confirm her actual status. For all we know, she's dead."

Trecheon tossed the sheet down, unwilling to unpack the complex emotions that came with the news. He'd have a good cry about it when he was done with his brother. "Do we even know Ryota's still here?"

"I've still got my tap on the cameras," Neil said. "It's fuzzy, but I've seen him every night this week hanging out by the Great Pyramid Casino at around midnight. Just him, no one else. I don't know what he's doing there, but he's not exactly hiding. He hangs out in front of the casino, right in the view of the camera." He tapped the screen of the old phone. "Every. Night. There's the invitation."

Trecheon narrowed his eyes. "Almost like he wants to be found."

"I thought so too," Neil said. "Are we going to disappoint him?"

Trecheon furrowed his brow. "I say we accept."

Casino Nights

Trecheon took his helmet off after Neil pulled into an abandoned parking lot about half a mile from the main casino strips. Stars hung overhead, barely dimmed by the neglected streetlights, overshadowed by the half-moon hanging in the sky. A distant echo of ocean waves accompanied the briny smell of sea water, riding on that ever-present El Dorado wind. It had rained the night before, and puddles had gathered everywhere.

Trecheon pulled himself out of the side carriage on Neil's motorbike, splashed in one such puddle, then dropped the helmet on the seat. "You're sure the bike will be okay here?"

"No one's around for miles," Neil said, hanging his own helmet on the handlebars. "We don't even get homeless or drug dealers around here. There's rumors that the place is haunted and no one is willing to test it."

Trecheon raised a skeptical eyebrow. "You're joking."

"Not at all," Neil said with a grin. "The people around here are crazy superstitious. Trust me, I checked into it with that dummy hit. I was surprised myself, but I've never seen anyone else around. We'll be fine."

Trecheon pulled a bag out of the foot well of the side carriage and slung it over his shoulder. He checked his holster, making sure his Lowry handgun was secure, then swung the cloth pocket for Granddad's gem around his waist and tied it. He pulled his jewel out of the carriage and dropped it into the pocket.

Neil watched him with a curious ear perked forward. "You've been bringing that jewel on every hit lately."

"It saved my life once," Trecheon said. "Possibly twice, if Dr. Laskey was correct about the state of my shoulders when Carter brought me into the hospital."

"But it hardly ever works."

"It healed my leg with the Sheldon hit."

Neil twitched his whiskers. "Alright, I'll give you that." He shouldered a long pack. "Come on, let's get going."

They walked in silence down the wooden beach walk toward the casino strip. Trecheon kept a close eye on the tall sea grasses and overgrown landscape bushes on the sides of the walk. His heart pounded more and more with each step, as if he expected Ryota to leap out of the bushes at any moment.

Draso's fire, Ryota. By all rights, he should be dead. Trecheon had treated him as such. He was done mourning. Done telling himself over and over again that he should have done more to keep his brother in check. Done with the what ifs and the silent guilt.

A few minutes later, they got to the casino strip proper. Dozens of buildings lined a wide street right along the beach. Most were shaped after some kind of ancient monument. The Great Pyramid, an Egyptian Sphinx, a Babylonian palace, a Japanese temple, and even a mockup of Stonehenge. A couple of scattered streetlights still worked, though barely. None of the buildings had light in them. All of it was heavily overgrown with vines, grass, and unpruned trees.

The buildings themselves were relatively untouched though. Trecheon had expected graffiti and broken windows, but the only sign that they weren't lived in was the overgrowth and dust. A shiver ran down his spine. It was almost as if the inhabitants had just up and disappeared without warning. Creepy.

Neil handed Trecheon an earpiece. "Normal code names," he said. "I doubt the Fawns are listening in on an unpaid hit, if that's what this turns into." He pointed to the Sphinx. "There's a step up there that I can fit on quite nicely. I'll spot you. If you really want to try talking to him, I won't stop you, but I'll at least cover you."

Trecheon eyed him. "Don't shoot unless I tell you to."

Neil glared. "He's a literal traitor, Trecheon."

"He's my *brother,*" Trecheon said. "And I don't have many people left to care about."

Neil flicked his tail. "Okay, sure, I'll give you that." He gripped Trecheon's metal shoulder and tilted his head down. "Just be careful. I brought you into this because I know you'd hate me if I didn't and because I really don't want Ryota running free when we both know what he's capable of. But I don't want to lose my best bud. I don't have many people left either."

Trecheon splayed both his ears. "You just need me to help you get that million-dollar ransom money."

"Well, admittedly, that's a nice aspect of our friendship," Neil said with a somewhat sarcastic grin. "But I'd rather be able to share the spoils of that million bucks with a friend, you know? Philip would too. You're like another brother to him."

Trecheon forced a smirk. "Yeah, sure."

Neil patted Trecheon's back, careful of the biomech mounts, then nodded to the building. "Keep your eyes and ears open. I'll see you in a bit." He started climbing.

Trecheon watched Neil climb, then glanced back down at the street, frowning, trying to squelch the fear squeezing into his veins. Good Draso. He didn't want to lose Neil either. He had lost too much already.

Though he wasn't deserving of that kind of friendship. Not after the way he treated Neil. Not when he was a Draso-damned murderer.

He shook his head and set himself up outside the pyramid casino where Ryota had appeared in that video, avoiding puddles, keeping his ears open. He tried to focus, but the silence ate at him.

Will Ryota try to kill me?

No more than he deserved.

As it neared midnight, he heard tapping in his headset. One tap. Target spotted.

Adrenaline filled Trecheon's veins and he ducked into an alley and waited, glancing out over the street.

A red quilar emerged in the dim light, lighting a cigarette. He leaned against a lamppost across the street and glanced up at the moon. He was dressed head to toe in black, complete with a long black trench coat.

Trecheon's heart pounded. That was Ryota. It *had* to be Ryota. Smoking his stupid cigs, hanging out in the open as if he owned the world. He was only about twenty feet from Trecheon. If he was careful, he could get close without Ryota ever noticing. He crouched and inched his way out of the alley, slowly pacing after his brother.

He was halfway across the street when he stepped on an old empty bag of chips, crunching it under his feet. Ryota stood up straight, ears perked, and glanced around. He caught Trecheon in his gaze almost immediately.

Trecheon cursed silently. He stood up and held out a hand. "Ryota. It's Trecheon. I just want--"

Ryota's eyes widened. He threw his cigarette at Trecheon and dashed away.

CHAPTER 12

RYOTA

Trecheon side stepped to avoid the hot cigarette, then ran after Ryota, splashing through the puddles lining the street. He tapped the headset. "Where'd he go?"

"He's headed for the pier," Neil said, urgency in his voice. "One block down, make a left. He's getting out of my sight. I'm coming after you."

"Hurry!" Trecheon ran for the pier. He couldn't see Ryota anymore, but he could hear him splashing through puddle after puddle. He clung to that sound. He had to catch him.

He turned down a street on the left and saw Ryota's figure far down the pier. Trecheon pushed himself. *Move, legs, move!* He slammed down hard on the wood of the pier, leaping over puddles, black with the night sky. The rotted wood creaked under him. "Ryota, please! Stop! I just want to talk!"

"Get the hell back, Trecheon!"

"We aren't in war anymore, Ryota!" Trecheon said, despite the strange lump that had grown in his throat at the sound of Ryota's voice. It was him. It was really *him*. "Can't we just talk like adults?"

"No!" Ryota shouted. "Stay back or I swear to Draso I'll kill you myself!" He pulled something from a holster on his hip, then vanished into the dark.

Trecheon's heart raced and he pulled his pistol from his holster. Damn it, he just wanted to *talk. Don't make me do this.* "Come on, Ryota. I just want to--"

Ryota slammed into Trecheon from the left, knocking his gun free. The pistol slid down the wooden pier. Trecheon fought against his brother's strength, but Ryota was surprisingly powerful. Within seconds, he pinned one of Trecheon's biomechanical arms against the wood and had his own arm to Trecheon's throat.

"Think I won't kill you? Huh? After what you did to my squad?" Even in the dark, Ryota's eyes terrified him. He was manic.

"We--!" He gagged. "*We* were your squad, Ryota!"

"You were just *liars!*" Ryota shouted, pressing his arm against Trecheon's throat. "You weren't stopping the war, you were just encouraging it! Killing left and right, not caring who died! You just--"

Blam! A muzzle flash lit up the night sky, and a bullet whizzed by Ryota's ear. He yelped and leapt back, releasing Trecheon. Trecheon scrambled to his feet, coughing, but Ryota had already turned tail and run further down the pier, clutching his ear. Trecheon glanced behind him.

Neil stood on the pier, glaring into the darkness, holding Trecheon's discarded pistol.

Trecheon gaped. "Neil, you just--"

"I saw trouble and I stopped it," Neil said, his face a hardened mask, as he often wore in war. "He was trying to kill you. Not acceptable."

"But now he's getting away!"

"He can't leave the pier unless he wants to try swimming to the Vanishing Island," Neil said. "Come on, let's go--"

One of the puddles leapt up and wrapped a long, inky black tentacle around Neil's arm. Neil yelped and tried to pull away, but another puddle grabbed his other arm. *"What the hell is this?"*

Trecheon stared, his heart racing. "Neil--"

Another puddle lifted off the wood and smashed a thick and wet tentacle into Trecheon's head, sending him sailing toward the edge of the pier. He scraped against the wood, desperate for purchase, but his metal hands slid on the slick lumber. He smashed into the rotten wood railings, broke right through it, then fell into the darkness, clawing the air with a gasp. He caught the very edge of the decaying wood, which snapped and knocked him around, but didn't break completely. Trecheon breathed a thanks to Draso and pulled his body up to grab the pier with his other hand.

Neil screamed.

The scream gave Trecheon a jolt, and he missed catching the pier with his free hand. He had never heard Neil scream before. Not ever. Not even in war, when he had every right to scream. He pulled his free hand up and grabbed the wood.

Neil screamed again.

"Neil, I'm coming!" Trecheon shouted, but he didn't know what he'd even do when he got there. Neil had his weapon.

Gunshots fired over and over, echoing Neil's screaming. Trecheon snarled. He tried pulling himself up with his arms, but the faux muscles and hydraulics screeched and moaned. Cursing, he swung his legs up as high as he could, eventually catching the edge of the pier with one foot. He pulled hard, managed to get his body up on the wood, and rolled away from the decayed railings, forcing himself to his feet.

Neil was nowhere to be found.

Panic mushroomed in Trecheon's chest as he frantically searched the area, running up and down the pier. "Neil! Neil, I'm here!"

No Neil. *Shit.*

He turned back toward the entrance to the pier and ran, hoping to find some clue. Instead, he found a black puddle with a strange round bulge in the center.

Trecheon stopped in his tracks.

It had an inky swell like a large bubble, ready to pop. Three small blue lights arose out of the puddle, and the swell opened up with what could only be called a large, jagged grin.

"Oh, *shit.*" Trecheon turned to run, but two more puddles stood behind him, mimicking the one in front. Long tentacles bulged out of their "bodies" and reached for him. Trecheon stepped back, breathing fast and flattening his ears. He was trapped.

"Trecheon!" Neil's voice. Trecheon turned. A gunshot rang out and the puddle in front exploded like a balloon. He saw Neil at the entrance to the pier, holding Trecheon's gun and waving to him. "Come on!"

Trecheon didn't look back. He ran as fast as his legs could carry him. Occasionally he'd catch a glimpse of one of the strange puddles out of his peripheral vision, but Neil hit all of them dead on before they got close.

Neil cursed. "Damn it, these things won't stay down!" He waved to Trecheon. "Come on, back to the bike!" Trecheon nodded and they pounded down the sidewalk toward the parking lot. He chanced a glance behind him as they ran.

A dozen of the puddle monsters followed closely behind. Trecheon yelped and pushed his legs harder. But as he ran, his foot caught the edge of a broken sidewalk, and he fell hard on the wet pavement. His leg snapped and he shouted out in pain.

Neil stopped and turned back. "Trecheon!" He ran back, firing the pistol into the oncoming wave of black puddles, for what little good it did him.

Trecheon gripped his leg, gritting his teeth and growling fiercely. Draso's *hot blood,* it was like *fire* running up his leg. Every other sense blurred, forcing him to focus all his attention on the injury.

But those damn puddles.

He pushed his mind through the pain and glanced up.

The puddle things were right on his tail and Neil was too far away. Even if Neil could get there in time, he'd never be able to help Trecheon back to the bike fast enough. He was a dead man. He faced the puddles, hoping it wouldn't hurt much.

A wave of heat smacked Trecheon in the face and fire blossomed in the center of the advancing monsters. The fire sent the blobby monsters fleeing in all directions, shrieking something out of a Draso-damned horror movie. Trecheon shielded his eyes against the heat and light of the fire and looked around frantically, trying to figure out where it came from.

Didn't take long to find the source. Two figures ran alongside the sidewalk across the street, chasing after the escaping monsters.

One of them had their hands on fire.

CHAPTER 13

SAVIOR

Neil was at Trecheon's side immediately, going to one knee. "You okay?"

"What the hell do you think?" Trecheon snarled. He pointed to the two figures. "You said no one else was here."

"And I wasn't lying," Neil said. "I don't know where they came from." He squinted. "Did that guy just throw a *fireball?*"

Trecheon stared. The only thing he could really discern is that they were two quilar, one of them feminine and the other masculine. He shook his head and rubbed his leg and wincing. The fire shot through his veins at full force again. He glanced back at the two figures.

The tallest figure, the masculine one, stood black against the night sky. He paused several yards ahead and held his arm out and his hand ignited. Trecheon jolted in surprise, despite the pain. The quilar tossed fire at one of the nearby blobby monsters. The monster wailed and disappeared down an ancient storm drain. Holy shit, he really *was* throwing fireballs.

Trecheon blinked. No way had he just witnessed that. He turned to Neil, but couldn't make the words come out.

Neil stared, ears perked. "Hot *damn.*"

The masculine figure sprinted after several more puddles, throwing fire at all of them, chasing them out of sight. Next to him, the feminine one hunted down stragglers. Her golden-brown fur glinted in the shallow light from the few working streetlights. She brandished a large war hammer, which she smashed into the puddles with a grace and precision that could only come from years of training.

Two other puddles followed behind them, shrieking as well, but unlike the others, their wails sounded more like battle cries and they tackled the other monsters, almost as if they were being directed by the two quilar ahead of them. Trecheon couldn't be sure, but he thought he caught words in their wobbling shrieks more than once.

Within a few minutes the strangers had the monsters cleared off. They regrouped a few yards ahead, apparently oblivious to the fact that Neil and Trecheon were close by. He thanked Draso for the fact that they were hidden in darkness. The smaller figure wiped her brow.

"That's not what I expected to find coming here," she muttered. This close to the beach, the waves nearly drowned out her voice. Trecheon strained to hear it.

"It is worse than we feared," the tall one said. "We are too late."

The small figure glanced at one of the storm drains that the puddles had disappeared down. "After all the trouble he had to go through to create Cast on Zyearth, I'm really struggling to believe he's already found out how to replicate that on Earth. There are way too many factors against him. Something else is going on."

Trecheon eyed Neil. "The hell is a cast?" he whispered.

Neil just shrugged. "The hell is a Zyearth?"

Trecheon furrowed his brow.

"We best find our target soon then, and see what we can salvage of the situation," the tall one said.

"I kind of regret coming alone," the feminine one said. "You need a proper offensive partner."

"You are more than sufficient," the tall quilar said. He glanced around. "Are you sure your plane will be safe among these buildings?"

Plane? Cast, Zyearth, and now a plane? These two were insane.

"I Spooked the plane and it doesn't look like anyone has been down this beach in ages," the feminine one said. "It'll be fine."

"Come on," Neil whispered in Trecheon's ear as the pair continued talking. "Let's get out of here while we can, before those people find us." He tried helping Trecheon to his feet.

Trecheon bit his tongue to stop a scream. *"Stop that,* you asshole, my damn leg's *broken."*

Neil frowned. He poked a little at Trecheon's left leg. Trecheon bit the sleeve of his jacket and yipped before slapping Neil's hand away. *"What in Draso's name are you doing?"*

Neil bent an ear. "Damn. This is serious."

"No *shit,* Sherlock," Trecheon said. There was no way he'd get out of here quietly, not even with Neil's help.

Neil perked his ears. "Wait. Try that jewel thing of yours."

Trecheon wrinkled his snout. He lifted the gem out of the pouch, pursed his lips, then pressed the jewel to his broken leg. The thing glowed slightly, and the pain lessened, just a little, but then the glow faded. He tried moving the leg, but the fire came right back. "Damn. No dice."

Neil snorted. "Then you'll just have to deal. Hold on, and try to keep quiet." He wrapped one of Trecheon's metal arms around his neck and started lifting him. Trecheon drew a sharp breath, growling.

Two black puddles sneaked up on the strange vigilantes. One grew several feet in the air, growing a jagged grin and horns.

Trecheon's eyes widened. "Watch out!"

The pair jolted and glanced around, fire blossoming around their ankles. The puddle collapsed, just as the small quilar met eyes with Trecheon. She frowned and pressed both ears back, glancing at her companion. The tall one glanced at Trecheon, then nodded to the other, waving a hand. Strange that the hand didn't look damaged, despite the fact that it had been doused in flames a few minutes ago. He took a deep breath.

The feminine one walked up to him, brow furrowed. She crouched down until she was level with Trecheon. He stared into her blue eyes. She seemed… uncertain. Curious. The dim light didn't frame her face very well. Her expression softened slightly, as if she was trying to smile, but failed. She took a deep breath and spoke.

"Is your name Omnir?"

CHAPTER 14

OMNIR

Izzy stared at the quilar, waiting for his answer. Her heart pounded against her ribs like it was trying to escape, and even though she had tried to smile at him, had tried to look friendly, she just couldn't make herself do it.

He certainly looked like an Omnir. Standard Earth quilar, with blood red quills and fur, though his also had some streaks of black in the tips and one on his forehead. She did note, with some relief, that he was quite young, probably late twenties at most, meaning he couldn't have been alive during the genocide. He wasn't the enemy. He was just a random quilar trying to make a living. Hell, he might not even be an Omnir.

Unless he also had a Gem. The Gem would slow his aging and would explain his young looks quite nicely. It could also explain the existence of the Cast, if he was somehow Black Bound.

But that wasn't likely. Silent planet. She mentally called up the protocols. Gotta keep their ears plugged… somehow. She thanked Draso's archdragons she had thought to bring Ouranos up to speed on them on the trip over.

The quilar stared at her for a half a minute, then shook his head, raining water down from his quills. "Yeah, um… My name is Omnir. Last name. Um. Who are you?"

Izzy held in a swear. "Izzy." She pointed behind her. "That's Ouranos."

"A pleasure," the prince said, taking a small bow, though he shook slightly. Whether that was from the shock of the news or the battle they'd just finished, she wasn't sure. He had a small cut on his ear, probably from the battle. She made a mental note to take care of it soon.

"Uh, Trecheon," the quilar said. "My first name. Trecheon." He jerked a thumb at his puma companion. "That's Neil."

Neil bent an ear back, eyeballing Izzy and Ouranos. "*Thanks*, Trecheon."

Trecheon glared at him.

"We, ah," Izzy began. Lightning and air. She and Ouranos had spent days talking about how they'd handle the Omnir once they found him. But looking at him now, all those plans flew out the window. She expected to find him working in a shop, not in the dead of night, suspiciously near a bunch of Cast.

"You still there, lady?" Trecheon said.

Izzy wrinkled her snout. "We were, um, looking for you."

Trecheon glanced back, raising an eyebrow. "For me? Why?"

Draso's fire. Describing the situation with Theron and the Cast was hard enough, but throw in the fact that Izzy was a magical, long-lived quilar from a different planet, and the best she could expect from him was for him to laugh her all the way back to Zyearth. Not to mention the fact that it'd break every Galactic Accord rule about silent planets. Should've thought of that one sooner.

"It's kind of a long story," Izzy said. "Maybe we should find a better place to talk, if you're willing. Would you mind?" Not that she was really planning on giving him a choice.

Trecheon bent an ear, frowning. He waved at his left leg. "I can't exactly move right now. Leg's broken. So unless you're willing to help Neil get me to a hospital, I'm not going anywhere."

"Oh, that's easy to…" She paused. Silent planet. No magic. Problem.

Neil pasted both ears back, twitching his whiskers. "Lady, his leg is freakin' *broken*. This isn't an easy fix unless you've got magical healing powers or something."

Ouranos frowned. "Isabelle?"

She glanced up at him, frowning.

Ouranos lifted a brow, then his eyes grew wide and his ears flattened. "Oh. Yes, that is a problem…"

"I'd say it is," Neil said. He pointed to Ouranos. "I know this dude here's a freakin' giant, but you can't go dragging Trecheon all over the beach. You'll make the leg worse."

He had a point. But…

She looked over the beach. Broken leg… and Cast, hiding in the dark. They wouldn't stay hidden for long. She sighed and shook her head. "I don't think I have a choice, Ouranos. We're vulnerable here."

Ouranos twitched his snout, but he shrugged. "You know better than I."

Neil flicked an ear back. "You've got some weird subtext going on here, and I don't like it."

"Sorry," Izzy said. She took a deep breath and met Trecheon's bright blue eyes. "I can fix your leg. But you have to promise not to freak out… and you have to keep what you see here absolutely silent. Okay?"

Trecheon leaned back, eyeing her. "You aren't filling me with trust here, lady."

"I know," she said. "And I normally wouldn't do this, but who knows when…" She paused and shook her head. "Just trust me. For now." She pulled her Gem out of her holster and activated it, listening to the quiet whine and using the light to examine Trecheon's leg.

Neil's eyes widened and his ears shot straight up. "No way. Trecheon, that's just like yours!"

"What?" Darvin's gurgly voice roared so loud that Izzy winced, pressing her ears back. Darvin rose to the full height his Cast form allowed, over a meter and a half, and he glared down at Neil and Trecheon with his blue Cast eyes.

Neil fell back on his tail and skittered away. "Whoa, whoa, whoa! Stay back!" He fumbled for his pistol.

Ouranos held his hand out. "Do not be alarmed. He is our ally. He will not hurt you."

"Like hell I won't!" Darvin bubbled. He furrowed his inky brow, squinting all three eyes and bearing jagged black teeth. "Is *this* the reason you came all the way here? To find an *Omnir?"*

Izzy glared at him. "To find someone Theron could *abuse,* yes."

"But an *Omnir?"* Darvin growled. "You can't *trust* these damn Omnir. He's already got a Gem! And right near the Cast! And you want to *help him*? For all you know, it's his fault they're here!" He turned the scowl on Trecheon. "How do you have a Gem?"

Trecheon narrowed his eyes, half-snarling. "Why do you even care?"

"Because Earthling zyfaunos don't *use* Gems anymore!" Darvin growled. "They don't even know how to bind! Where did you get it?"

"That's none of your business," Trecheon said.

"You--"

"Be quiet, Darvin," Izzy said, scowling at him. "This outburst is exactly why I didn't bring Matt along. Don't make me regret bringing you here."

"Well, I'm glad that *someone* here has some sense," Darvin snarled. "Though that should be *you,* Izzy. You're a *genocide survivor* and you want to help the enemy! What the hell are you *thinking?"*

Trecheon frowned. "What genocide?"

"Look at him, Darvin," Izzy said, growling. "He's too young."

"Not if he's bound to a Gem," Darvin said.

"You don't know that," Izzy said. "He could have been bound later."

Darvin threw his blobby hands in the air, spraying drops everywhere. "So what? Think he can't be influenced by those involved? They destroy *everything.*"

"How can you know that if you don't even *ask* him first? For all you know, he was raised completely away from all of that stuff," Izzy said.

"He has a Gem," Darvin said. "That's proof enough for me. Weren't they after the Sol's Gems? For all you know, he has one of the Sol Gems!"

Izzy paused. She shook her head. "Does that really make any difference?"

"Influence, Izzy!"

"I really don't appreciate being talked about as if I'm not here," Trecheon growled. "What in Draso's Palace are you two going on about?"

Izzy sighed and pressed her lips together, looking over at Trecheon. "I don't suppose you'd let me look at the Gem."

Trecheon leaned back, suspicious, but then hissed, gripping his broken leg.

Izzy splayed her ears. "Maybe after I heal your leg. Would that be a fine trade-off?"

"Just do it," Trecheon said, wincing. "Then we'll talk."

"Or you'll just run off," Darvin snarled.

"Darvin, *shut it,*" Izzy said, glaring at him. "You're not helping." She turned back to Trecheon's leg. "Give me just a moment and I'll have this all taken care of."

"Right," Trecheon said, eyeing Darvin.

Neil leaned close to Trecheon's leg. "So you've got actual magic? That healing thing actually works?"

Izzy eyed him. So much for silent planet protocols. "Yeah, no problem," she said, feeling around Trecheon's leg for breaks. She glanced at Trecheon. "Can I assume you're a healer then?"

Trecheon gritted his teeth, watching her poke around his leg. "I don't even know what that means."

Izzy frowned. Hmm. "It means your Gem's specialty is healing."

"It must be!" Neil said. "Trecheon healed himself three times with the thing since he got it. They were kind of by accident though. Does that mean you know how to do it on purpose?"

Izzy's hands froze on Trecheon's leg. She looked at her patient with wide eyes. "You healed *yourself?*"

Trecheon shrugged. "I guess so. Doesn't always work though. I tried just now and couldn't get much out of it."

"Why, is that a big deal?" Neil asked.

Izzy kneeled back, hands on her knees, frowning. Gem users couldn't be affected by their own magic. Healers couldn't heal themselves. It was one of their biggest failings, at least in her mind.

And here was someone who had supposedly done so *three times.*

She shook herself and went back to Trecheon's leg. "Let's just say I'm extremely interested in seeing your Gem now." She poked around a little longer, then sat back again. "You've got two breaks, but they're pretty clean from what I can tell. Give me just a moment." She replaced her Gem back in the Gem holster and held her hands over his leg.

Trecheon winced slightly. "Will this hurt?"

Izzy raised an eyebrow. "Did it hurt when you healed yourself?"

Trecheon blinked, shook his head, then waved a hand to his leg.

Izzy took a deep breath and pressed her hands over Trecheon's leg, pumping cooling healing energy through her fingers. She worked her hands up and down, feeling for the breaks, and enticing the bones to knit properly. Trecheon lolled his head back. Neil just stared in wonder.

Izzy kept her gaze on Trecheon's leg. She wasn't expecting to find a Gem-bound Omnir. An Omnir, yes, but one that hadn't been bound. Someone unconnected to the Gems, to Sol, to the genocide as a whole. Someone she could protect to help fight these stewing feelings of anger and hate. And if he really was bound, maybe he was older than she realized. Maybe he had been around during the genocide.

She shook her head. No. Innocent until proven guilty. A staple of the Defender creed. Darvin could shove his xenophobic rant right up his blobby ass.

But there were Cast… and right near a Gem. Draso's fire. Maybe she should have brought Matt with her after all. She needed her partner.

Healing wasn't going to cut it anymore.

Trecheon breathed a sharp hiss and reached for his leg. "Hey, *watch it!*"

Izzy refocused and saw her hands. Black staining ran up her fingertips. She cocked an ear.

Her Black Bound powers had activated. And the elixir that had caused so much trouble on Earth coated her fingers. Her whole body buzzed.

"Ow!" Trecheon wrenched his leg away. "What the hell? I thought this wouldn't hurt!"

Izzy pulled her hands back and the black staining slowly faded away. She glanced at Trecheon. "That hurt?"

"Yeah, it did! Damn!" he pulled his pant leg up, hissing in pain as he did.

Izzy helped him, and leaned back at what she saw.

Under the pant leg, looking gray and sickly against the healthy red fur, stood a patch of dead hair.

CHAPTER 15

BROKEN

Izzy gasped into her hands, then ran her fingers over the fur. It disintegrated as she touched it leaving behind pale, bald skin. "Draso's mercy, what have I done?"

"That's what I want to know, lady," Trecheon said. "You said you were going to fix my leg, not strip my fur!"

Izzy picked up a piece of the dead fur and ran it between her fingers. The fur was gray and brittle, like it had aged a hundred years and died off. Fresh panic ran through Izzy's chest.

Ouranos walked up to her. "Isabelle, are you okay?"

She turned quickly and faced him, catching a glimpse of his damaged ear. She pressed her lips together. "Let me heal your ear." A tiny flesh wound was simple. Fast. Not like a broken bone.

Ouranos lifted a hand and ran it along the damaged flesh. He frowned. "If you wish."

Izzy lifted a hand to his ear and pressed healing powers into it. Instantly her fingers grew black stains and Ouranos jerked his head away, gripping his ear. "Sisters alive, Izzy, that hurts!"

She drew her hand away, taking dead fur tufts with her. The ear wasn't healed. Terror gripped her as she watched her hands soak up the black staining.

Her healing powers were broken.

Healing powers weren't like most Gem powers. Healing Gems granted the user command over the cells of another person, giving them extra energy and allowing them to speed up the body's natural ability to heal.

But this was different. This wasn't commanding cells to heal.

It was commanding cells to die.

Izzy fell to her knees, crossing her arms over her chest and hugging her shoulders. Her breath quickened and she flattened her ears, failing to hold in the horror.

If her healing powers broke… if she couldn't use them at all… then she was worthless. Worse than worthless. She couldn't be a Guardian with broken powers. She couldn't even be a Defender. She couldn't be *anyone*.

Cold metal pressed against her bare shoulder. She jumped and turned to see Trecheon looking at her with a furrowed brow of sympathy.

"If it makes you feel better, I do think you fixed my leg."

Izzy stared at him a moment, frowning, then glanced down at her shoulder and gasped. "Your hand! It's--"

"Biomechanics," Trecheon said. "Both arms. Lost them in the War of Eons. You'll pardon me if I squeeze too hard. I'm lucky enough to have enough usable nerves to power the damn things, but I can't feel through them anymore."

"Draso's horns, that must be awful," Izzy barely whispered. "You can't feel *anything?*"

Trecheon shrugged. "It's a tradeoff. I could get technology that could essentially send me messages about temperature and texture and such, but it greatly reduces reaction time and articulation in the arms, and I can't have that as a mechanic. We really don't have anything that truly replaces feeling at all."

Izzy furrowed her brow, splaying her ears. "I'm sorry."

Trecheon chuckled. "Don't be. It's been so long, I can't really remember life before them, so I don't miss it. At least it's easier to clean motor oil off them and I don't have to worry as much if I catch a finger in the moving parts in an engine. I'd rather pay for repairs than deal with the pain."

"Right," Izzy said, trying to draw herself back to reality. Refocus. Get Trecheon somewhere safe. Healing wasn't necessary for that. She stood and held a hand out to Trecheon.

Trecheon smiled, gripped her hand, and she pulled him to his feet. He tapped the previously broken leg on the ground and walked around. He grinned. "Good as new."

"Aside from the bald patch," Izzy said, chewing her bottom lip.

"Better bald than broken," Neil said with a grin. "Tell chicks it's a scar from the war. They love that shit."

Trecheon rolled his eyes.

"Trecheon, I am so sorry," Izzy said. "I don't know what happened." She stole a glance at Ouranos' ear. Maybe she had healed that after all. Maybe she wasn't broken.

But the ear was still damaged. Damn it all.

Trecheon waved a hand. "The fur will grow back. Now," he reached into a cloth pocket tied around his waist and pulled out a Gem. Izzy watched it with a growing hunger. He passed it to her. "I believe we had a deal?"

"What do you know?" Darvin muttered, his inky body bubbling like a pot of water at half boil. "Omnirs do know how to keep a promise."

Izzy glared at him, but then took the Gem gingerly from Trecheon.

It wasn't like any bound Gem she had ever seen. It had only slight color – straight red. Almost orange, in fact, like the color had been leeched from it. And though it looked like it had been recently polished, it didn't shine with the spark of a bound Gem. More like the faded color of a Gem that hadn't been touched or used in a while. Half bound, maybe.

Izzy glanced up at Trecheon. "How old are you?"

Trecheon perked an ear. "Uh, twenty-eight. Why?"

Izzy raised an eyebrow. "And that's your real age?"

"What reason would I have to lie?" Trecheon crossed his arms.

"Give me your hand a moment," Izzy said, holding her hand out. Trecheon raised an eyebrow, but did as he was told. Izzy held his hand and glanced at the Gem, frowning. Even with metal arms, the Gem should react to him if it was bound to him. He must not be bound, at least not fully.

But if it wasn't bound, it shouldn't be able to heal. Or have color. Something wasn't right here.

"Look, I'm glad you're fascinated with the jewel and all," Trecheon said, taking his hand back from Izzy. "But I really don't have all night to let you stand here staring at it." He plucked the jewel from Izzy's palm. "I've got to find my brother."

Panic welled up in Izzy. "You can't just leave--" She paused. "Wait, did you say brother?"

"Oh *great,* there's more than one of them," Darvin said.

Trecheon glared at Darvin. "Look, buddy. I don't know what you are or what you have against me, but keep it to yourself, alright? I haven't done anything to you."

Izzy stepped between them before Darvin could say anything else stupid. "You say you're looking for your brother?"

"Yes, and I've wasted enough time here," he said. "Thanks for fixing my leg." He nodded to Neil and the two of them turned back toward the pier.

Izzy stepped in front of them. "Wait! Let us help you find him."

Trecheon frowned. "Why?"

"Because we understand how to fight the Cast," Ouranos said, moving next to Izzy. "We can keep you safe if they come back."

Neil crossed his arms now, one hand holding his pistol, twitching his tail. "Ryota is a dangerous madman. We're not just here to talk shop with him. We can't just let anyone go after him, whether or not the Blob is after us."

Trecheon elbowed Neil in the ribs. "If we can get him to talk, we *will* talk with him."

Izzy eyed the pistol in Neil's hand and swallowed hard. She pushed the feelings aside. "I'm a soldier. I can fight if need be."

Trecheon crossed his arms. "We are too. Doesn't make you special."

"It can. Besides," she pointed to Trecheon's Gem. "If you let me stick around, I'll show you how to use that thing properly."

Trecheon narrowed his eyes. "You don't even know me, last name or not. Why do you care?"

Izzy chewed her lip. "Does that matter right now?"

"Of *course* it does."

Izzy thought fast. "Let me rephrase. Does that matter right now when there are wild puddle monsters running around that you can't possibly fight?"

Trecheon eyed her. "Is that a threat?"

"It's a *fact,*" Izzy said. "When these things attacked my base, they killed and maimed *hundreds*. Casualties were through the roof. You're two zyfaunos with a pair of ineffectual firearms. These things *will* come back. Do you really think you'll be able to fight them off on your own?"

Trecheon's eyes widened. "They attacked a *military base?* Which one? How come I haven't heard of this?"

"They covered it up," Izzy said, which wasn't entirely lying. Lance had kept the whole incident as removed from the public as possible. "Do you think the military wants the public at large to know about these things? It'd cause widespread panic." She formed a fist. "You need us."

Trecheon furrowed his brow. He sighed. "Okay, fine."

"Trecheon!" Neil said. "Seriously?"

"What choice do we have?" Trecheon said. "If those puddle things come back we won't be able to fight them. Besides," he tapped his Gem. "Maybe it's about time I learned about this damn thing."

Neil rolled his eyes. "Fine, whatever. Let's just go or we'll lose Ryota completely, if we haven't already."

Izzy sighed relief. "Thank you."

"Don't get comfortable," Trecheon said. "This isn't a partnership. Soldier or not, you can't get involved with this fight with Ryota. That's our job. Stay back. Understood?"

She flicked an ear back. They were dead serious. Though if this Ryota was connected to the Cast, she'd have to get involved.

But she didn't have to tell Trecheon that. She nodded. "Understood. Lead the way." She sidestepped to let Trecheon and Neil go past. Ouranos followed behind and she took up the rear with Roscoe and Darvin. Trecheon took the gun from Neil as he walked by.

Darvin followed slowly, half formed from the torso. "I don't trust them."

"I don't remember asking," Izzy said, splaying her ears.

"Izzy, they're out here, by themselves, claiming to be soldiers, but out of uniform chasing some supposed villain," Darvin said. "Doesn't that seem a little suspicious?"

"Of course it does," Izzy said. "But I don't have enough to prove anything. Innocent until proven guilty. Defender honor code. Besides that, we're not exactly being truthful either, are we?"

Darvin growled. "Why are we doing this anyway? What does this have to do with finding the Basileus and kicking his sorry tail?"

"The plan was to protect the Omnir, not fight the Basileus," Izzy said. "Ouranos said that if the Basileus learned that there were Omnirs on the mainland, he'd come looking for them to try and force a Black Bind."

"He's clearly *already* got someone in a Black Bind," Darvin said. "He's made Cast. He'll overrun the whole planet if we let him. We need to take this fight to him before he makes *more.*"

Izzy flattened one ear. "I know. Big change of plans. But we can't go gallivanting into the Basileus' stronghold with just the four of us. So for now, we stick with the Omnir. If Ouranos is right, the Basileus will come looking for him. That's our chance. Besides," she pointed to Trecheon. "I've just met the only healer in the known universe that can somehow heal himself. I'm not just going to let that go. Especially…" she paused. "Especially with my powers not working right."

Darvin sighed, a gurgling sound like a babbling brook. "I didn't quite get it, but… it looked like your powers are hurting people instead of healing them."

Izzy shifted her weight. "That seems to be the problem, yeah."

Darvin shrugged. "Well, you always did want offensive magic." He slunk down into his inky Cast form and hurried after the rest of them.

Izzy stopped in her tracks. She *had* always wanted offensive magic. She had been thinking about it on the whole trip here. Hell, she was even thinking it when her Gem started going haywire. And now, suddenly, her healing powers had become offensive. She stared at the Gem.

She swore it stared back, if only for a moment.

CHAPTER 16

HOMECOMING

Matt hovered his plane over El Dorado Bay near a long strip of what looked like a collection of rotting Earth monuments, bathed in half-moon light. A quick look at the map told him that the beach housed an old casino strip. He cross-referenced some Earth news sites and learned that it had been abandoned years ago. That'd probably be the perfect place to hide his plane. And according to Sami's knowledge, they were close to where the Omnir they were hunting lived.

Not far from Omnir Island, where they originally came from. That didn't escape Matt's notice.

Sami sat in the co-pilot's seat, and Natassa stood behind them in the doorway. The Prinkípissa let out a shuddering sigh. "I am not sure whether to be terrified or relieved to finally be home."

"I know the feeling," Matt said. He glanced out over the bay. Three islands towered over the sea. The one farthest north was massive, though the other two were significantly smaller. Trinity Islands, as the locals called it.

The middle one, the one closest to the big island, was Matt's birthplace. His home. The island of Sol.

He supposed in some distant part of his mind, he could consider this homecoming a triumph. He had overcome the disaster of the genocide, grown up strong and intelligent, and came back to his birth home as a Guardian instead of dying like his neighbors. As far as anyone knew, he, Charlotte, and Izzy were the only zyfaunos that had survived the genocide.

Well, that and the Omnirs, though they had also faced some horrible catastrophe not long after the Sol genocide.

Matt had spent the last week of their trip to Earth researching the Omnirs, and was surprised to find that no one was quite sure what had happened to them. Reports and pictures showed obliterated shadows, bones, and bits of flesh, all spread out from a central point near one of the largest structures on Omnir island.

A few essays had compared the pictures to that of the damage done by the atom bombs during one of Earth's world wars, but the Omnir's island didn't have any of the damage to suggest a bomb had hit them. The trees, buildings, and crops were mostly untouched, sporting only stains and chars that faded quickly. The only things damaged were the inhabitants. A creepy phenomenon no one could explain. It made Matt think of the disaster he and Ouranos left behind when they bonded their jewels.

Though even in the face of that much death, he had a hard time fighting the feeling that they had deserved it.

The destruction of the Omnirs' home had also obliterated the already rare color red from Earth quilar genes, so any living red quilar would have to be related to the Omnirs somehow, if distantly. Their target had to be an Omnir.

From what Matt could gather, the islands had been labeled sites of memorial and wildlife preservation, so the only people allowed on them were the occasional scientist, biologist, or anthropologist. Apparently they were just as untouched as they had been when he had left fifty-four years ago, though it was hard to see how true that was in the dark.

Natassa placed a hand on Matt's shoulder and gave it a friendly squeeze. "We are here to talk if you need to."

Matt reached up and patted her hand. "Thanks," he said, though he didn't intend to talk to them. It was his job to handle this. He was made of stronger stuff. It was a long time ago.

He had this under control.

"Matt," Sami said, pointing to the scanners. "I think that's Izzy's plane."

Matt squinted, glancing out where Sami had pointed. Sure enough, Izzy's plane was there, poking out between some buildings. Spooking made it invisible to the naked eye, but it relied on the supplemental Gem shards. It would need a Gem to hide it from advanced scanners, and Izzy wouldn't have left her Gem behind. Matt nodded.

"Let's go after them then." He guided his hovering plane up the beach.

Several minutes later, Matt had his plane parked and hidden almost as well as Izzy's. He shut down the engines and removed his Gem from the Gem slot up front, then stood up.

"We'll travel light, for now," Matt said. "Though bring your weapons. You never know what you might find in abandoned buildings. Just be cautious when using them. Defense only."

Sami and Natassa nodded and they followed him out of the plane.

Matt jogged along the beach toward Izzy's plane, holding out a handscanner that would detect the plane when they got close. It was nestled behind a building facing the bay, hidden amongst a semi-circle that looked like it was supposed to be mimicking Stonehenge, if Matt remember correctly. He walked up to the plane slowly and ran his hand along the invisible metal.

Sami came up behind him. "Anything?"

Matt nodded. "It's here, and it's cold. They've been here a while." He followed the plane until he got to the door, then opened it and investigated the interior. Empty. He walked back out and locked it up. "They're gone. Not surprising."

"Where do you suppose they are?" Natassa asked.

Matt pulled up his pendant and tried calling Izzy.

No connection. She must have her pendant Spooked. She had to know Matt would have chased her the moment he learned she went missing, so that was expected.

However, if he was lucky, he might get her on a general Defender signal scan. He pressed his lips together, then told the computer to blanket search for Defender signals.

The program tagged him and Sami by name as well as the two planes and Natassa's signal, but to his surprise, he found not just one, but two additional Defender signals. They were horribly weak and they bounced all over as if the computer couldn't properly pinpoint where it was coming from.

He frowned. Even Spooked, his pendant should be able to pinpoint other Defender signals with no issue. Something must be interfering with the pendants, though Matt couldn't begin to guess what, considering they had no understanding of Earth tech.

Time to go a different route. He mentally reached for Ouranos.

But he found nothing. *Nothing.*

Matt choked and stopped walking. What the *hell?* He tried again. *Ouranos? Answer me!*

Nothing.

"Matt?" Sami asked. "You okay?"

"No," Matt said, his voice shaking. "I can't reach Ouranos."

Natassa gasped. "Oh *no.*"

"We need to find them now," Matt said. "Something is wrong and I don't like it." He pointed to the scanners. "The pendants are Spooked, but they're showing up in these two general areas." He chewed his lip. "They're not really static, but close enough."

"What do we do then?" Natassa asked.

"Split up," Matt said, making sure his sword was easily accessible from the sheath on his back. "We'll make better time if we spread out. I'll head to this signal near the pier, you two head for this building here."

Sami frowned. "What if we come across Cast? You should stay with a fire user."

Matt wrinkled his snout, but shook his head. "I'm not worried about Cast. The Basileus doesn't have the tools to create them. Something else is interfering, I just don't know what yet. Keep an eye out." He glanced at Natassa. "Don't let go of that pendant I gave you, okay?"

Natassa nodded, fingering a jet black Defender pendant around her neck. It had been Matt's at one point, an unofficial pendant given to him by Jaymes to communicate with.

"Good," Matt said. "Let's head out. And the moment you find one of them, call me." They nodded and walked off.

Matt sprinted toward the pier, his heart racing. Izzy's Spooked pendant he could forgive. But after half a year with Ouranos in his head, his sudden absence threatened to break him.

RED QUILAR

Matt held up his pendant and projected the map that had Defender signals on it. He watched them bounce around, frowning.

A third Defender signal had appeared.

Where were all these signals coming from? He supposed one of them was Izzy's, and one had a chance of being Darvin's, or even Roscoe's. He didn't remember ever recovering their pendants after they'd been turned.

As he walked, more signals popped up, tagging Darvin and Roscoe by name. They bounced about, like the Spooked signal. Izzy's was likely the Spooked signal and the unnamed signal could possibly be Ouranos. Izzy had an unofficial pendant too, and he wouldn't be surprised if she had given it to Ouranos like Matt had given his to Natassa.

But the third signal… it didn't move. Totally static. Looked like it was near the pier. Actually, it looked like it was *in* the pier. Strange. Matt followed the fading Spooked signal toward the pier on the north end of the strip of beach.

As he walked, he poked at the edges of his mind for his connection with Ouranos again, hoping he could read something, anything. A faint, deep purple colored the edges of his subconscious, the admiration and friendship Ouranos had sparked during the early days of their social bond, mixed with the black and blue of worry. The worry was a quiet, soft worry though, not fear, which he supposed was good. Matt sighed relief. Finally, a connection. Thank Draso. He was beginning to worry that something had happened to Ouranos.

The connection didn't give him any idea of where Ouranos was though. *Ouranos?* Nothing. Hmm. Perhaps Ouranos was blocking him. They had gotten better at those psychic blocks over the months, and since Ouranos had tried coming here in secret, it made sense that he had a block up.

He'd just have to find them the old-fashioned way.

But as he neared the pier, the signal cut out completely. He furrowed his brow and tried finding the source again, but his pendant couldn't pick anything up. He growled. "Fire and ice!"

Something pounded on the sidewalk ahead of him. Footsteps. Matt whipped his head up and caught a glimpse of a quilar ducking into an alleyway across the street.

A red quilar.

Matt thumped after him, his heart racing.

He turned down the alley just in time to see the quilar climb a dumpster and leap over a tall fence.

The image of a red quilar leaping over a stone wall after one of the fleeing Sol quilar during the genocide flashed before Matt's eyes. The memory halted him, and his stomach threatened to bring up his last meal. He shook his head to release the memory, then leapt over the fence and landed hard in the sand. Glancing around, he saw the quilar running toward the posts of the pier.

A memory of a quilar running up the beach after a young Sol kit flickered in his mind, dragging the queasy feeling back. Matt shook his head more violently this time, willing the memories to go away, and followed. "Wait! Slow down, I just want to talk!"

The quilar suddenly slowed and turned. He perked an ear quizzically.

Out in the dim light of the moon, Matt could make out more of his target. A red quilar, definitely, with long thick spines and catlike ears. He wore a simple but modern black outfit with a long black trench coat and a pair of combat boots. Matt thought he caught the faint smell of cigarette smoke.

The quilar inched closer to him, giving him a strange look in the vague glow of the moon. "Carter?"

Carter? Matt shook his head. "No, my name is Matt. Are you... Is your name Omnir?"

The quilar's eyes flashed wide. "Nice try, Carter. I know your voice. What are you doing here?" He paused, a sudden knowing in his eyes. "You're with Angel aren't you. *Both* of you are. You've finally found me and you're here to kill me too, just like you did with Guardian."

Matt held his hand up, bending one ear back. Angel? Guardian? "No, my name is Matt. Matt Azure. I am a Guardian and I'm not here to kill anyone. I just want to know your name."

"You're not a *Guardian*, you're an *Outlander*," the quilar spat. "And now an Angel. Or did he erase your memories somehow? Brainwash you?"

"No…" Matt said. "Please just tell me your name."

"It's *Ryota,* you asshole, as if you didn't know," the quilar snarled.

Matt squinted. "Ryota Omnir?"

"Yes, Ryota Omnir!" the quilar shouted. "Have you lost your marbles?" He paused. "You know what? Don't answer that. Get the hell away from me. Angel can't have me."

"I'm not--"

"Like hell you aren't," the Omnir said. "I don't know how you all found me, but I'm not going anywhere, so just get *back.*" He turned and ran.

Matt growled and ran after him. "If you'd just *talk* to me a moment, I could--"

The Omnir faced Matt and shot a bolt of lightning at him.

"Whoa!" Matt dove left and rolled. The electricity struck the sand several yards away from him and a smell of burning and molten glass permeated the air.

The Omnir continued running.

Matt pulled himself to his feet and followed, adrenaline running through his whole body.

He shot *lightning*. Lightning! He must have a Gem. How the hell he had gotten bound to it was anyone's guess.

And being this close to Sol… he had to have a Sol Gem.

He snarled. It didn't matter how he'd gotten a Gem or how he had bound to it. He didn't have the strength or training that Matt did. He called on his powers and struck the Omnir with a blast of wind, hoping to flip him on his side.

The Omnir tilted sideways at the gust, but rather than crash and burn, he tucked his body and rolled back to his feet. He whirled around and caught the air on fire with twin bolts of electricity.

Matt threw up a shield, but the electricity smashed into it and broke it, sending him flying back several meters. He landed hard, sliding through the sand. He stood, rubbing his back. That Omnir knew more than Matt gave him credit for. This was no amateur.

That only encouraged Matt's theory. He acted like a soldier with years of training. He had to be one of the Omnirs from his youth. Draso's horns! He pulled up his pendant while running after him.

"Sami, Natassa, meet me at the beach," Matt said, throwing a twister of wind into the sand. "I found an Omnir here and he is not friendly!"

Sami and Natassa both acknowledged him. Matt dropped the call and threw the twister of wind and sand at the Omnir.

The Omnir flipped around and blasted the funnel with lightning. The tornado lit up and froze in place, the wind dissipating and the sand sticking up as if it was one solid mass. Matt skidded to a halt in front of it as it leaned precariously. He grimaced and threw a shield up just before the whole thing crashed down on him.

The frozen dust devil smashed into thousands of tiny pieces, raining all over the sand and Matt's shield. Several pieces stuck to his exposed shoe and one cut through it, slicing his foot. Matt yelped and pulled his foot away. Cautiously, he examined his shield, now pierced with dirty fragments, then pushed it away, letting the fragments fall harmlessly to the sand next to him. He stood and stumbled away from the broken pieces, hunting for the Omnir.

He was gone.

Matt cursed. He found a relatively clean spot in the sand, sat down, and gently examined the fragment in his foot. It must be glass. Fulgurite. Dirty glass. Images of fulgurite scattered over the Arena flashed in his mind. That couldn't be sanitary.

Blood welled up around a two-centimeter cut on the top of his foot, staining his shoe. Nothing too serious, though it hurt like hell. He'd have to go back to the plane and get the first aid kit and wrap it, at least until he found Izzy so she could heal it properly.

Footsteps sounded on the beach sand and he looked up to find Sami and Natassa running after him, their toeclaws kicking up loose sand. He held out a hand. "Watch out! There's fulgurite fragments all over the place. You'll injure your feet."

Sami paused, held out a hand and lit the area with fire. She guided Natassa around the fulgurite fragments and they ran for Matt. "Are you okay? Where's the Omnir?"

Matt carefully pulled his sock over his foot and slid his shoe on. "Gone. He got away while I was being rained on by fulgurite." He pointed to the simple glass tubes on the floor. "He made all that. Damn Omnir has lightning powers."

Sami perked both ears. "He has a *Gem?*"

"He must. He has Gem powers. Either that, or he's got some other kind of focus jewel with elemental magic, but I doubt the Athánatos are sharing."

"Certainly not," Natassa said.

Matt gingerly got to his feet. "Damn, that hurts."

"Let's get you back to the X-Zero," Sami said, frowning. "Unless you want me to go after the Omnir?"

Matt thought about that idea for a moment, then shook his head. "I don't know where he went and if he has that kind of power and control, I don't want anyone going after him alone. Come on, let's get back and take care of my foot. Then we can go after him."

"How is he bound to a Gem?" Natassa asked, following behind. "I thought you said the art of binding was lost to the zyfaunos of Earth."

Matt glanced back toward where the Omnir disappeared. "It was."

JEWEL

Trecheon marched along the pier looking for signs of Ryota, already regretting his decision to let these weird strangers tag along.

But it was hard to say no. He had finally met someone who actually knew something about Granddad's jewel. Just his luck, it had to come at the most inconvenient time possible. He shouldn't be dragging along some bizarre vagabonds with powers he couldn't understand. Not when facing a dark part of his past. Not when dealing with Ryota.

He paused near the end of the pier and kneeled down. Cigarette butts. But they didn't smoke when he broke them apart in his fingers, so they were likely cold. Damn his hands for not having feeling in them anymore.

One thing for certain though. Ryota wasn't on the pier anymore. He stood up and headed back toward the beach.

The golden brown one, Izzy, followed him closer than he wanted, trying to catch his eye. He ignored her. The last thing he needed was another conversation. His brother was more important.

But she was like an annoying shadow. He finally turned to her with a growl. *"What?"*

She tilted her ears back, frowning. "I'm trying to decide if you're actually bound to your Gem or not."

Trecheon stopped and faced her, throwing up a hand. "What does that even *mean?"*

"It means the power of the Gem is bound to your lifeforce," Izzy said.

Trecheon frowned. "That didn't clear a damn thing up."

"It means…" Izzy paused pursing her lips. "Draso's horns, I've never had to explain this to a nonuser. Bear with me." She took a deep breath. "It means the Gem's magic is bonded to your life essence and grants you magical powers and other abilities, while also protecting your physical body."

Trecheon stared at her, trying to find the words, but failed.

Izzy continued. "But it doesn't act like a bound Gem."

"Maybe it's not 'bound' then." Trecheon continued down the pier, twitching his ear in annoyance. And maybe he didn't want it to be.

Izzy jogged ahead of him and stopped. "How did you get your Gem?"

Trecheon crossed his arms. "Do we have to do this right now? I'm trying to find my brother and that's a little more immediate."

Izzy let out a slow breath. "Sorry."

Trecheon sighed and continued on to the end of the pier. Izzy fell into step next to him, looking sullen and upset. Trecheon frowned. He really had gotten himself into something ridiculous. He sighed. "It was a gift."

Izzy perked her ears. "Pardon?"

"The jewel," Trecheon said, turning off the pier and heading down the beach. "It was a gift."

"From who?"

Trecheon tilted an ear. "Why do you care? You wouldn't even know him."

Izzy shifted. "I... ah…"

"You know," Trecheon said, turning to face her. "It's really obvious you know something I don't. So why don't you let me ask a few questions before we continue on?"

Izzy pasted an ear back. "Go ahead."

"Your blobby friend over there obviously hates my guts," Trecheon said, nodding to the strange Cast creature that Izzy called Darvin. The black monster glared at him with three blue eyes, rippling his body on the sand. Trecheon turned back to Izzy. "Why? What did I do?"

"If you are truly the age you told us," the tall, black quilar Ouranos told him. "Then you did nothing."

"What does age have to do with it?" Trecheon said. "Are you trying to say I was a part of that genocide you keep mentioning?"

"No, no!" Izzy said, holding up her hands.

More and more suspicious. They were hiding something and he was going to get to the bottom of it. "Then why are you looking for me?"

Izzy slumped her shoulders. "Fire and ice. You want the long version or the short version?" She picked at a quill. "Actually, I doubt you'd even understand the short version."

"Try me."

Izzy exchanged a glance with her tall partner then met Trecheon's eyes. "You're in serious danger."

Trecheon laughed darkly. "Lady, this is El Dorado. I'm a war veteran who was on the wrong side in an unpopular war. I'm a quilar in a primarily human city." *And I'm an assassin under Triple Fawn. Scum of the earth.* "Of course I'm in danger. I'm *always* in danger."

"I promise you, you've never been in danger like you are right now."

Trecheon narrowed his eyes. That was a bold claim. "I doubt there's anything in this world bigger and more dangerous than *war.*"

"I dunno, Trech," Neil said, walking up behind Ouranos. He twitched his tail. "Those Cast things were pretty awful."

"I didn't ask you, Neil," Trecheon said.

"He's right though," Izzy said. "Cast are invincible monsters. They're impossible to kill or destroy. They aren't things you can fight and walk away from."

Trecheon lifted a brow. "You killed them. I saw you."

"We didn't kill them, we just chased them away," Izzy said. "And frankly, I wouldn't want to kill them even if I knew how."

Trecheon frowned. "Why not?"

"Because they're sentient beings," Darvin said, standing up to his full Cast height. "Cast are made from zyfaunos."

Trecheon stared. "You have got to be shitting me."

"Of course not," Darvin said, waving a blobby hand. "You think I was born this way?"

Neil twitched his tail. "How'd they get turned into monsters?"

"It's… it's a complicated process," Izzy said.

Trecheon narrowed his gaze. "And I'm in danger because of those things?"

"You're in danger because of the zyfaunos who created them in the first place," Izzy said.

Trecheon flattened both ears. "Why?"

"Because of who you *are*," Izzy said. "Your last name, your fur color, even your Gem. You're a massive target."

Trecheon snorted. "Bullshit. I'm a former Marine. What can this guy even do to me?"

Ouranos furrowed his brow and threw his hand out. The air around him caught fire, lightning fell from the sky, wind whipped up the sand on the pier, and snow piled up around his feet, all at once.

Trecheon leapt back. "Whoa, whoa! What the hell?"

Ouranos lifted his hand up and it all disappeared at once. "The enemy you face has powers like mine tenfold. He is a madman ready to do anything to achieve his goals." The magic subsided and Ouranos' expression softened. "Your tribe has been… used by our enemy for generations, unfortunately. And if you have truly used the Gem as you have claimed, you have already made yourself known to him."

Trecheon pulled out the jewel, frowning. *Granddad, what on Earth did you give me?* "Why does he want this?"

"He wants you *and* the Gem," Izzy said. "Because he can use you together to create Cast."

CHAPTER 19

BINDING

Trecheon dropped the Gem and backed away.

Izzy dove for it, but their other Cast ally, Roscoe, grabbed it before it hit. He passed it to Izzy. "Be careful with that!"

"That thing can *create* those black monsters?" Trecheon said, staring at it with wide eyes. He waved both hands. "Keep it. You can have it. I don't want anything to do with it anymore. Especially if Cast are really zyfaunos."

"The Gem itself doesn't create Cast," Izzy said. "It's only one component in a much more complicated process."

"And I'm another component," Trecheon snorted.

Izzy chewed her lip. "Kind of? Maybe? It depends on… well, a lot of stuff."

Trecheon narrowed his gaze. "Well, it's got to *wait.*" He held his hands out. "Take the damn thing. I don't want it. Ryota is still out there and--"

"I don't care," Izzy said in a half snarl. Trecheon backed up. "This is a much bigger problem than your rogue brother and it needs taking care of *now.* You can't just drop the Gem and run."

Trecheon growled now. "So what am I supposed to do? Let Ryota run around free? He's just as much a target as I am, even without a Gem."

Izzy flicked her ears back.

"Didn't think about that one, did you?" Trecheon said, arms crossed. "New plan. Ryota is priority number one. After we find him--"

"Trecheon," Izzy said. "As of right now, *you're* priority number one. As much as I don't want Ryota to be the Basileus' victim, he's not the one with the Gem. You are. And being partially bound makes you even more of a target. You literally have all the elements he needs, and you already have an affinity for the Gem. It's only a matter of time before he finds you."

"So what am I supposed to *do?"* Trecheon growled. "Let you guys follow me around for the rest of my life? How am I supposed to protect myself?"

Izzy pressed her lips together. "Let us fully bind you to the Gem."

"Izzy, you can't be *serious!"* Darvin said, sitting up in his black body. "You're going to bind an *Omnir?"* Roscoe gurgled quietly and wrapped himself around Izzy's legs.

Trecheon glared at Darvin. He opened his mouth to protest, but Izzy cut him off.

"Darvin, seriously, *stay out of this,"* Izzy said. "If I bind him fully now, then the Basileus can't force a Black Bind."

"You don't even know if he can force a Black Bind at all!"

"I know he can *try,"* Izzy said.

"That's assuming you could even bind him with your broken magic--"

"Darvin, for the last time, *shut up,"* Izzy snapped. "This isn't your call." She looked Trecheon in the eye. "It's yours."

Trecheon grunted, still keeping half an eye on Darvin. Darvin sneered at him awkwardly with the strange blue eyes of a Cast. Trecheon shook his head. "I need a better reason to bind to this thing than some empty promise that this invisible enemy will stop coming after me."

"There are more powers than just the Gem specialty," Izzy said. "Shielding for example."

Trecheon frowned. "Shielding?"

"Yeah," Izzy said. "Here, I'll show you." She turned to Ouranos and held her hands up. The air around her shimmered with a weird circular rainbow. It turned green, then purple, then it disappeared completely. "Throw a bolt of lightning at me."

Ouranos flicked his ears back. "If you are sure." He held a hand out and casually tossed it forward. A bolt of electricity blasted from his palm at Izzy, smashing into the invisible wall in a bright flash of light. Trecheon winced and shielded his eyes, but when he looked back, Izzy was completely unscathed.

Trecheon stared, then turned to Ouranos. "Do I get powers like that?"

Izzy shook her head. "Gems only specialize in one thing. Since your Gem specializes in healing, you won't get an element. They're kind of rare anyway."

"Damn. Wishful thinking, I suppose." He held a hand out. "May I?"

Izzy nodded to him.

Trecheon walked forward and touched his hand to the invisible shield. It was as solid as stone. He pushed, but it didn't budge. Neil gave a low whistle.

Trecheon's heart pounded in excitement. "And I could do that if I was bound to my Gem."

"If I teach you, yes," Izzy said. "Your healing powers will also get stronger."

Trecheon rubbed his chin. Shielding… if he really was going to face someone with that kind of power, it might be the only thing that could save him. "Could that help fight back against those Cast things?"

"Potentially, yeah," Izzy said.

Neil frowned at him. "Trecheon, are you sure you're okay with this?"

Trecheon crossed his arms. "It would help a lot with… well, everything really," he said, trying to stay vague. "And maybe it'd help protect me against Ryota when we go after him again." He eyed Izzy. "Assuming those shields can deflect bullets."

"Low caliber, but yeah, they can."

Neil flicked his tail. "I suppose."

"I'll do it," Trecheon said. "How do we get started?"

"I admit, I am curious to see how a bind works," Ouranos said.

Izzy stared at her Gem, frowning. She turned. "Ouranos, you have to do this."

Ouranos flicked his ears forward. "Pardon?"

"My powers are going haywire," Izzy said. "I don't know if that actually means anything, but I worry it could damage the Gem bind."

"Hmm," Ouranos said. "You make a good point. And it would confirm that the Athánatos can, in fact, bind Gems."

Trecheon raised an eyebrow. "Hold on. Are you saying he's never bound someone to a Gem before?"

"I have bound Athánatos to their Ei-Ei jewels," Ouranos said. "The ritual is different, but the principle remains the same. I foresee no issues."

Trecheon glanced down at the Gem.

"Trecheon?" Izzy asked.

He glanced at her. "How common is Gem binding?"

Izzy perked her ears. "Why?"

"You said there are lots of people with it, but that's very vague," Trecheon said. "I want to know how safe it really is. So how common is Gem binding?"

"Where I'm from, very," Izzy said. "It's perfectly safe, Trecheon."

Trecheon pressed his lips tight. "Where *are* you from?"

Izzy flicked an ear back, but her face remained as stoic as ever. "Does that matter?"

"Clearly, if you live in a society where they regularly bind magical jewels to their persons," Trecheon said. "Weird I've never heard of them. This have to do with Zyearth? I heard you mention that earlier, though far be it from me to guess what the hell that is."

Izzy exchanged a glance with Ouranos, but then put her hand on her hip and eyed Trecheon. "You think a group of magical Gem-binders are gonna be open and up front about it? You said you're military. Imagine your military with powers like mine or Ouranos'. Then tell me why you haven't heard of us."

Trecheon flicked an ear back. "Alright, point taken." He pointed to her Gem. "Has a Gem binding ever gone wrong?"

Izzy chewed her lip. "Black Bind is kind of a bind gone wrong. But you won't have that problem."

"You've mentioned this Black Binding thing a couple of times," Trecheon said, wary. "Why won't that happen to me?"

"Black Binding means you've bound yourself instead of having someone else do it," Izzy said. "It only happens when you're facing a life-threatening or emotionally traumatizing event at the time of binding. You're fine."

Trecheon raised an eyebrow. "You think what we're going through right now doesn't count?"

"Not even," Izzy said. "I'm talking in the moment life-or-death situations. It's how I was Black Bound."

Trecheon flicked an ear. "What happened to make you bind yourself?"

Izzy's eyes widened, and she rubbed her arm. "I... don't like talking about it."

"But if I don't know--"

"Trech, after everything you've been through in the war, can't you cut her some slack?" Neil said with a growl. Roscoe curled closer around Izzy's feet, gurgling angrily.

"But if I don't *know--* "

"I watched someone get murdered when I was four, okay?" Izzy snapped. "Someone stabbed him and there was a burst of Gem energy and he *literally exploded.* There was *nothing* left." She glanced at the floor. "I still hear him screaming sometimes in my dreams."

Ouranos bent an ear back and looked off.

Trecheon lowered his gaze. "Sorry. I shouldn't have pried."

"You really shouldn't have," Darvin snapped, shaking an inky fist until it collapsed. He turned to Izzy. "Are you okay?"

Izzy stared at the ground, her face scrunched up, her gaze far away as if she wasn't there.

A guilty twinge bit at Trecheon.

Darvin slithered around in front of her. "Izzy?"

Izzy shook her head. "I'm fine. I'm... I'm fine." She looked up at Trecheon. "Sorry."

"...Don't be," Trecheon said. "My fault."

"Still," Izzy said. "But you're fine. You're not in the right position for a Black Binding. It's okay."

Trecheon eyed his Gem.

Izzy put a hand on Trecheon's. "I wouldn't ask you to do this if it was dangerous."

"Said the complete stranger keeping secrets," Trecheon quipped.

Izzy's smile faded to a frown. "No, you're right. I am a stranger, and I am keeping secrets. But you saw what the Gem can do. You know it has powers. Despite all those things, you know it's real." She took a step back with a deep, steady breath. "But I'll let you decide."

Trecheon gripped the Gem. He had seen what Izzy's Gem could do. The good and the bad. Yes, it protected her, yes it healed, but it also apparently turned on her.

Granddad's somber face floated by in his mind's eye - the seriousness of his voice, the urgency in the words. *You'll want it someday.*

Maybe that day was today.

Trecheon took a slow breath. "I might regret this. But let's do it."

Neil bent an ear back with a disapproving grunt, but he didn't say anything.

"Right. Okay. Let's do this." Izzy maneuvered Trecheon until he and Ouranos were facing each other on the sand with barely a foot between them. She pressed her lips together. "Trecheon, hold your Gem out with the point facing up," she instructed. "Ouranos, hold your palms out over the Gem and call power to your hands."

Trecheon held the Gem out, frowning.

"Hold on," Neil said. "What happens if Ryota or the Cast show up while we're doing this?"

"This won't take a minute," Izzy said. "But keep an eye out. If they haven't shown up yet, hopefully they're not around."

Neil eyed her, but he glanced around, squinting. "Seems clear. Go for it."

Ouranos held his hands over Trecheon's Gem. Little tongues of fire danced on his palms among swirls of snow and sand. "Is this enough?"

"It should be," Izzy said. "Ouranos, repeat after me." She took a deep breath. *"Draso, gamen sapura."*

Ouranos wiggled his snout. *"Draso gamen sapura."*

Trecheon's Gem tugged closer to Ouranos' powers. He jerked slightly, but forced himself still again.

Izzy continued. *"Draso, rasta bentome."*

"Draso, rasta bentome."

"Draso, tel rasta separit vasa."

"Draso, tel rasta separit vasa."

"Tel rasta separit Trecheon i Draso."

Ouranos met Trecheon's eyes. Trecheon stared back, trying to hold fast against the tugs of the Gem. *"Tel rasta separit Trecheon i Draso."*

The jewel tugged free completely. Trecheon gasped and tried to reach for it, but Izzy held his wrist. "Let it go. This is supposed to happen." The jewel spun in the space between their hands.

And the power. Oh, it flowed through Trecheon like nothing he had ever felt. A combination of mild pain and powerful elation, it was like the comforting ease of being magically healed combined with the power of raw electricity running through his blood. It felt like he was flying on air and burning in hell all at once.

Izzy glanced between them, then gave Ouranos one more line. *"Draso... bentome i Trecheon."*

Ouranos shut his eyes and repeated Izzy. *"Draso, bentome i Trecheon."*

A blinding light accompanied a jolt of sheer pain through Trecheon's veins. He shouted, but then everything slowed down and the pain stopped. He opened his eyes. The Gem still spun, dancing light over the sand and pier next to him.

The colors had changed. Rather than a solid, faded red, it was now a vibrant red with a blue star in the center. When the light hit the side of the jewel, it glinted darkly. Very strange. He stared at a moment, then reached for it.

Something slammed into Trecheon sending him flying down the beach, out of reach of his Gem. No, some*one*. Trecheon wrestled with his attacker, trying to get a hand to his gun. Flashes of white fur invaded his peripheral – definitely not Ryota. Trecheon managed to get a leg free and kicked at the man. He yelped and leapt back.

Trecheon scrambled to his feet and reached for his gun, but his attacker grabbed his arm and whipped him around. The attacker smashed Trecheon into a pillar of the pier, pinning his back to the rotting wood. Before Trecheon could escape or grab his weapon, he felt cold, sharp steel under his chin.

Standing in front of him, with a face of white fur, a head of blue trimmed quills, and angry green eyes, was a tall, fuming quilar. And he had a long sharp sword at Trecheon's throat.

CHAPTER 20

MATT

Trecheon gripped the sword with one hand and ripped his gun out of his holster with the other, fighting panic. He pushed at the sword, grateful for his metal hands for once, and pressed the gun against the quilar's chest. His fur puffed up and he glared, trying to stop the shaking fear. "Get that damn sword out of my face or I'll shove it up your ass *sideways.*"

The quilar narrowed his eyes and bent his ears back. Trecheon heard a soft whine and a rainbow swirl formed in front of his gun. It faded to purple, then green, creating a shield almost instantly. But unlike Izzy's, it kept a green tint. The quilar snarled.

"Just *try it.*"

Izzy ran toward them. "Matt, *stop!*"

"Stay out of this!" the quilar shouted. A wall of wind and sand darted up between her and Trecheon. The quilar growled. "What the hell was the point of attacking me earlier?"

"I don't know what you're talking about," Trecheon snarled.

The quilar bared his teeth and pressed the sword harder. "You're a terrible liar. Answer me!"

"I didn't do a damn thing!" Trecheon said. "Ask that golden brown quilar over there. She's been with me for the last half-hour."

"Izzy wouldn't stoop so low."

The wall of sand suddenly dropped and Ouranos rushed forward, reaching a hand out to the quilar.

"Ouranos, stay *back,*" the white quilar snarled without turning around. "This bastard attacked me and I'm going to figure out why."

"Matthew, I promise you he did nothing of the sort," Ouranos said. "He has been with us!"

"Please, Matt, don't *hurt him,*" Izzy said. "He's done nothing wrong!"

A white fox rushed up. "Are you kidding, Izzy? He just attacked Matt less than half an hour ago, completely unprovoked!"

Trecheon's eyes widened. No. *Ryota.* "That wasn't me, it was--"

The distinct sound of a rifle bolt chambering a round hit Trecheon's ears and he looked to the side. Neil had his rifle aimed right at the quilar's head. "I know your shields can repel lightning. Wanna try a Lapua Magnum, asshole?"

Matt glared at Neil. "Do you really want to test that?"

Izzy stood between Neil and the quilar, forming a shield. "Neil, *please.*"

"Step aside, lady, or your head's going with it." Neil said, baring fangs.

"Like hell it is!" Darvin shouted, bubbling. He rose to his full height in front of Izzy and Roscoe did the same, shrieking. Neil took a step back, fear flashing across his face, but then he narrowed his gaze and kept rifle trained on Matt.

No one moved.

Matt looked right into Trecheon's eyes. "If *you* didn't attack me," he said slowly. "Then who the hell *did?* There are no other red quilar on Earth. Speak carefully."

Trecheon stared into his eyes, trying to find the words, trying to point the finger at his damn brother. But his brain froze, his mouth paralyzed. Something about Matt's expression, his mannerisms, his voice - all of it felt vaguely familiar. It was on the tip of his tongue like an angry itch.

Then it hit like a brick to the chest. *"Carter?"*

The quilar snorted. "I already told you my name is *Matt*. I'm not an Angel, I'm not an Outlander, and I haven't got a clue who this Carter is."

But Trecheon couldn't drop it - Carter was his savior, the soldier who saved his life after he lost his arms in the War of Eons. He had to know. "You have a brother then, yes? Named Carter?"

"No!" Matt said. "I hardly have *any* relatives, and it's all your *fault."*

Trecheon blinked. "Wait. What?"

"You heard me! Your fault! You and your whole damn family!" Matt snarled at him, but his eyes glistened. "I shouldn't even be talking to you. You should be *dead* after everything you did. Do you hear me?" Trecheon pushed harder against the sword, his heart pounding.

Ouranos stepped forward again. "Matthew, please, see reason! He is not the quilar that attacked your home. He is too young and your enemies are dead." He gripped Matt's shoulder. "Please, my friend, this is not *you."*

Izzy gripped his other shoulder. "Matt, please... Don't do this. Please. Be the Guardian I know you are."

Matt glared a moment longer, his green eyes raging, but slowly his features softened. He closed his eyes, shook his head, then pulled the sword from Trecheon's throat and dropped it. He studied Trecheon. "How old are you?"

Trecheon ran a hand under his throat. It came back clean. He eyed Matt. "Twenty-eight."

"Figures," Matt said. He leaned against a piling and sank down to the sand. "Water below." His voice shook.

Neil lowered the weapon and ran up to Trecheon. "Christ, Trecheon, are you okay?"

"I'm… fine," Trecheon said. He glanced at Matt. "Is he okay?"

Izzy glanced at Matt and squatted near him, frowning. "Matt?"

"This is why you came here, isn't it?" he said, meeting her eyes, his voice still shaking. "To find the offspring of the Omnirs."

Izzy pasted her ears back. "That's one of the reasons, yes."

"And you didn't take me," Matt said. "Because you knew I'd react exactly like that."

Izzy pressed her lips together. "Honestly, yeah."

Matt lifted his gaze back at Trecheon. He narrowed his eyes. "A red quilar attacked me about half an hour ago."

"Well, it sure as hell wasn't me," Trecheon said. "It was my brother. There's a *reason* I'm here chasing him down."

Matt stood and brushed the sand off his pants. He sheathed his sword. "No, you're right, it wasn't. He didn't have black streaks through his quills. Or metal hands, I think. He was wearing gloves." He pointed. "How far do those prosthetics go up?"

"All the way to the shoulders," Trecheon said.

Matt pressed back an ear. He stared at the sand. "Sorry."

Trecheon crossed his arms, glaring one eye at Matt. "For what? My arms or your damn sword at my throat?"

Matt took a deep breath. "Both, I suppose."

Neil flattened his ears. He shot Matt a glare and eyed Trecheon's pistol. "Can someone tell me what in God's name is going on around here?"

"I second that," Trecheon said. "I don't know what the hell your problem is with Omnirs, but I'm sick of being in the dark about it. What's really going on?"

Matt ignored Trecheon and glanced up at Izzy. "What are you really doing here?"

Trecheon flattened his ears. "I asked a question."

"And you can *shove it,*" Matt said, glaring at him before turning to Izzy. "Izzy, talk."

Izzy pressed her lips together, sparing a glance at Trecheon. "Omnirs can be bound to Gems, Matt," she said, turning back to the white and blue quilar. "And Ouranos says Theron would know that. He knows exactly how to create the conditions for a Black Bind. He can even bind someone himself if he wants to."

Matt raised an eyebrow. "You know that for a fact?"

Izzy glanced between Trecheon and Ouranos. She lifted up Trecheon's Gem a moment before passing it to him. "We know that now."

Trecheon gingerly took the jewel and dropped it in the cloth pouch at his side, keeping one eye trained on Matt.

Matt furrowed his brow a moment, then his eyes lit up in understanding. He stood. "Wait, you bound an *Omnir?*"

Izzy took a step back. "With Ouranos' help, yes."

Matt glared. "Do you realize you just gave the Basileus a *weapon?*"

"That's what I said," Darvin said, poking between Matt and Izzy. "I tried to stop her, Matt."

Matt's shoulders slumped. "After all they did, Izzy, why would you *do* that?"

"Matt," Izzy said, holding her ground. "There are Cast here."

Matt's ears perked up. "What?"

"There are Cast here," Izzy said. Trecheon noticed the fox's expression blanked, her jaw loose. Another black quilar with a cream-colored snout and ears like Ouranos, ran up to the group. She wore the same surprised expression. Izzy's frown deepened. "Real Shadow Cast, Matt. I had to do something."

"Having Cast here somehow justifies binding an Omnir?" Matt asked. "I'd think that'd be a good reason *not* to bind anyone and draw attention to yourself. What were you thinking?"

"He was already partially bound," Izzy said. "That made him a potential victim. More inclined to be Black Bound, if Theron pushed it."

Matt glared at Trecheon, sizing him up suddenly, as if this new information meant something. "You really are twenty-eight."

Trecheon splayed an ear and wrinkled his snout. "I said I was. What reason would I have to lie? And what does age have to do with it anyway?"

Matt shook his head. "Wait a second. You said Ouranos could *bind Gems*. And that theoretically, the Basileus could do the same thing."

Izzy nodded.

Matt bared his teeth again. "That red quilar that attacked me earlier. He had Gem magic."

Trecheon whipped his head to Matt. "Ryota?"

Matt nodded. "That is the name he gave me." He frowned at Trecheon, almost sheepishly. "Did I hear that puma call you Trachea?"

Neil snickered, pressing his hands to his snout.

Trecheon gave him a death glare, then turned back to Matt. "Trecheon, actually." He tried to smile, though it came out all wrong. He holstered his pistol and hoped he at least managed a neutral face as he held out a hand to Matt. Better to try to make nice with the strong man with a pointy sword. "Sorry if we got off on the wrong foot."

Matt pressed both ears back, but he took Trecheon's hand. "…My fault."

"I'd argue it's mine in a way, since you all have this intense hatred of Omnirs," Trecheon said. "Honestly, I wish I knew why."

Matt took a deep breath and glanced at Trecheon with a barely contained disgust. "You really don't know."

Trecheon threw up his hands. "If I knew, you think I'd be asking so damn much? Why am I even working with you guys if you can't even answer simple questions?"

Matt crossed his arms. "So you've been completely honest with Izzy then? No secrets at all? Answered everything she's ever asked you?"

Trecheon paused and flicked his ears back.

"Well?" Matt eyed him.

Trecheon snorted. "Secrets don't make for good relationships."

"I don't need to have a good relationship with you to do what needs to be done," Matt countered. "I have my secrets. You have yours. And if there really are Cast here--"

"There are," Trecheon said. "An attacking black puddle is something I'll never forget."

"Then that's more important," Matt said. He turned to Izzy. "I don't think it's a coincidence that the Cast appeared so closely to a Gem bound. Two Gem bounds." He shook his head. "I wish I would have known to look for signs of Black Binding in that other Omnir."

"Hold on a second," Trecheon said. "How do you know Ryota has a Gem?"

"Because he threw lightning at me," Matt said with a growl. "That's why I was in shoot-first-ask-questions-later mode."

Trecheon's quills stood on end. *Lightning?* "How on Draso's green Earth did he get that kind of power?"

"Not important now," Izzy said. "What *is* important is that he has one and he's suspiciously near the Cast."

"Whoa, whoa, *whoa,*" Trecheon said. "Let me get this straight. You came looking for me because I can be bound to this Gem thing and used by this... what, Basileus? Theron? I can't quite make out who the villain is here. But you think you're already too late because he's got my brother in his claws."

"Wait," the white fox said, twitching her ears. "Did anyone else hear that?"

Trecheon stood silent and listened. Just sand and gentle waves bubbling along the shore.

Bubbling? He turned toward the sea, but found the bubbling sound came from the buildings behind him instead. He whipped around.

A rippling wave rose up from the row of buildings on the beachfront - and it headed directly toward them. Black and gurgling and hissing… with little blue eyes catching the streetlights.

CHAPTER 21

CAST ATTACK

Trecheon's fur stood straight up and his skin went cold. "Cast!" And *dozens* of them. He couldn't count how many trios of eyes he saw in the black mess. Neil shrank back too, waving the rifle about, hissing like a feral cat.

But Matt stepped forward and took charge. "Defenders, spread out! Sami, flank right with Natassa and Izzy. Light that hammer up. Ouranos, with me on the left. Stage two firestorm, give them everything we have!"

Without hesitation, everyone followed orders. Natassa, the other black quilar, caught her hands on fire and threw a ball of flame on Izzy's hammer. Izzy rushed forward and slammed the hammer among the wave of Cast.

"Sami, give me more!" Izzy shouted. Sami, the white fox, fueled the blaze with additional fireballs. Izzy spun the hammer about with considerable skill, sending the Cast flying. The three zyfaunos scattered the monsters, each one shrieking as they fled. Darvin and the other Cast, Roscoe, chased them further away. It was wild.

But Ouranos and Matt's coordination was uncanny, almost uncomfortably so. Matt threw his hands forward, whipping up sand in what looked like two thin twisters. Ouranos filled each twister with flames and the pair guided them through the Cast, splitting the wave cleanly in two. There were no words between them, but they worked perfectly, like they were reading each other's minds.

These people were unlike any soldiers Trecheon had ever seen before.

Neil hissed in his ear. "Trecheon, look!" He pointed.

Trecheon turned. A figure in all black with a shock of red quills pounded down the sidewalk away from the Cast. Trecheon gasped. "Ryota!" Neil lifted his rifle, but Trecheon pulled the muzzle down. "Don't shoot him, damn it!"

Neil twitched his tail. "But--"

"No buts, just follow!" He tore off after Ryota. Neil growled, but he followed.

But just as they hit the pavement, a Cast wrapped itself around Neil's legs, dragging him to the sand with a loud thud. "Trecheon!"

Trecheon ripped his pistol out of the holster… but stopped. The Cast had Neil completely tangled up. He'd never get the shot.

The Cast fully engulfed Neil as the puma struggled.

Trecheon cursed, dropped the pistol, and plunged his hands into the Cast. He pulled at the black mass with no effect – it fell apart in ribbons, but held a death grip on Neil. His arm hydraulics strained and groaned.

Then Neil stopped shouting.

Trecheon pulled harder though the Cast shredded in his hands, slipping between his metal fingers. He gritted his teeth, fighting panic, fighting tears. "Damn it, just let him *go!*"

A fierce tornado thrashed up around Neil, knocking Trecheon back. The wind kicked up sand and pulled apart the Cast into little drops. In seconds the tornado moved off, leaving Neil on the ground and the Cast wailing in the funnel. Neil didn't move.

Matt ran up to Neil and fell to one knee. Trecheon scrambled to his feet. "Is he okay?"

Neil groaned.

"He's fine," Matt said. "Cast kill by crushing or suffocating their victims, so if he's moving, he'll survive." Neil responded by turning over and throwing up. Matt furrowed his brow and bit his lip. "Just breathe, okay? I've been there. It'll be better in a second."

Trecheon heaved relief. "Thanks."

Matt ignored him. He turned to Ouranos. Without even a word, Ouranos blasted the Cast with one more bout of fire then rushed over to them. He leaned down by Neil. "You are sure?"

Trecheon stared at them, confused.

Matt just nodded and turned toward the direction Ryota ran off to.

"Hey, wait!" Trecheon snatched up his pistol and ran after him. "Where the hell are you going?"

"After the quilar who attacked me," Matt said. "Stay out of it."

"Hell no, that's my brother!" Trecheon spat. "I'm trying to *talk* to him, damn it!"

"Then you better hope you're faster than me," Matt said. He unsheathed his sword.

Trecheon snarled. No way was this asshole getting to Ryota before him. He pushed his legs and sprinted past Matt. He had to take two strides for every one of Matt's, but he somehow managed to keep ahead.

But Ryota had disappeared. No trace. Both Matt and Trecheon slowed. Matt breathed heavily, but he didn't seem winded. Trecheon leaned on his knees, watching him. He glanced around.

Then he noticed where he was. In front of the Great Pyramid hotel. Exactly where Ryota had come out of in the video Neil had showed him. He turned toward the doors.

Matt turned too and reached for the door's handle.

Trecheon gripped his wrist. Matt flicked an ear and turned, but Trecheon didn't back down. "Look, I haven't seen my brother in nearly a decade. I know he's a bastard, and I know he attacked you, and you have every right to be mad and nothing I say will make it better. Hell, he attacked me when I first saw him, too. The fact that he's so damn dangerous is why I'm here looking for him in the first place. But I thought Ryota was dead. I *have* to talk to him, even if it's just for a moment. I have to know what happened to him. Please."

Matt narrowed his eyes. "He attacked *you?* Your own brother?"

Trecheon flicked an ear back. "We didn't have the best end to our relationship in the war."

"What's to stop him from attacking you again?" Matt said. "He'll kill you. You're newly bound to your Gem. You have no powers and even if you had them, you'd have no idea how to use it."

Trecheon frowned. "I know," he said. "But I have to try." He thought back to Matt's claim about not having any family left. "Haven't you ever lost someone important to you? Wouldn't you want to do the same if you could talk to them again?"

Matt furrowed his brow and his face softened. His gaze grew distant, like some part of him wasn't there anymore. He sighed. "Go ahead. I'll… I'll back you up."

Trecheon raised a brow. "You will?"

Matt shifted and took his hand off the door handle. "Yeah. Because you're right." He looked away. "And it'd be a way to make up for attacking you earlier. For what good it does."

Trecheon flicked an ear. "Okay. I'm putting my trust in you. I don't do that lightly."

"Likewise," Matt said. "On both accounts."

Trecheon took a deep breath. This was quite a gamble. "What kind of magic do you have?"

"I'm a wind manipulator," Matt said. "Don't bother making any jokes about it, I've heard all of them before."

"Not that this is the place to joke," Trecheon said. "If you think there's trouble, you can intervene. But… but don't kill him. I don't want to see my brother die today if I can help it."

Matt's ears pasted to his skull, but he nodded. He sheathed his sword.

Trecheon took a deep breath. That was a start. He closed his eyes, counted to three, then opened the door.

CHAPTER 22

GENOCIDE

Trecheon walked slowly through the hotel reception to the double doors, trying to keep his boots from echoing. The last thing he wanted was to scare Ryota and give his position away. He slowly opened the second set of double doors.

Everything smelled of rotting mildew, dust, and fragrant plants that Trecheon couldn't name. The moon shone through skylights and holes in the ceiling. Its light competed with a handful of flickering artificial lights that still worked, giving the whole place a dying, haunted feel.

His black-clad brother was in the middle of the massive lobby, waving a hand in the air, snarling. "Damn it, it should be here, why isn't it here?"

Trecheon flicked an ear back. He glanced at Matt, who just shrugged. Trecheon shook his head and waved a hand. Matt nodded. He snuck in carefully and hid behind an overgrown palm growing through the cracked marble floor. He gave Trecheon a thumb's up.

Trecheon inched his way forward, as silent as can be, until only a few feet separated him from his brother. "Ryota."

Ryota whipped around and waved his hands. A dozen tennis ball-sized orbs of electricity flickered from his body, hovering in the air around him, casting deep shadows over Ryota's face. Trecheon stepped back, wishing Izzy had had time to teach him how to shield.

Ryota held himself tense, baring his teeth. "Trecheon, I've warned you before, stay the hell *back*. Angel can't have me."

"I'm not with Angel," Trecheon said. "You think I'd want to keep working with Ackerson after all the shit he pulled? Or whoever the hell runs Angel."

Ryota's face softened a bit, but the electricity remained. "Then what do you want? Why are you here?"

"To ask you the same question," Trecheon said. "I thought you *died.* Instead I find you here slinking around these rotting casinos like a damn sewer rat. What in Draso's name are you *doing* here?"

Ryota took a step back. "I'm working for someone."

"What the hell kind of employer has you prowling a ghost town at night?" Trecheon snapped.

Ryota stood straight and lowered his gaze. "Someone who finally has the damn *truth,* Trecheon. I'm so sick of living among *lies. "*

Trecheon raised an eyebrow. "What are you talking about?"

"This!" Ryota said. "This city, this country, this government… all of it a bunch of *lies* and *deception* designed to keep zyfaunos down and humans at the top. But this guy, Trech, he sees through it all. He *knows*. He's going to set things right, and he's asked me to help him."

Trecheon flattened his ears. "The Basileus? Theron?"

Ryota's eyes flashed wide. "How did you know?" He shook his head. "No, wait, you were with Ouranos weren't you. That's why you aren't surprised by the lightning either. Shit." He waved a hand and the electric cages disappeared. "Trech, Ouranos is a *filthy liar*. You can't believe anything he says. Theron warned me about him. He wants to *stop* us, Trech. He's going to stop our only chance at peace."

"What in Draso's name are you even saying?" Trecheon said. "This guy has you afraid of your own brother, your own damn *shadow,* and he's somehow the *good guy?* Open your eyes, Ryota. You know--"

"Don't tell me I don't know who the good guys are," Ryota spat. "We weren't the good guys in the war, Trecheon. We were just tools, and you know it. This country - hell, the whole damn *world* - used us like keys to a treasure, leaving a trail of blood and organs everywhere we went. Humans sit around in their high castles watching us, sipping wine while they train us to exterminate each other in the name of 'good.'" He formed fists. "But Theron will fix that. He's going to get rid of them all, and we'll finally have peace. We..." he paused. "We don't have to die anymore."

Trecheon furrowed his brow. "You're trying to create peace through *genocide.*"

Ryota perked his ears, a little taken aback. But he hardened his features. "It's the only way, Trecheon. It's the only way to stop all this death."

"The only way." Trecheon could hardly believe his ears. "How the hell can you believe that after all we've seen? And you think Theron wants *your* help with this nonsense? Why you, when you could hardly even act in war?"

Ryota snorted, but his mouth curled up in a slight smile. "We've cleansed the world before."

Trecheon blinked. "What?"

"The Omnirs," Ryota said. "Theron's told me all about our history. We were warriors, Trech. Our whole tribe - our whole *mission* - was to cleanse. We--"

"Whoa, whoa, *whoa,*" Trecheon said, holding up his hands. "What tribe? We're just a bunch of nobodies from El Dorado. This guy has you spinning, Ryota."

"Not *us*," Ryota said. *"Granddad.* The Omnir tribe. He led a whole generation in a cleanse, Trech, he--"

"Are you *insane?*" Trecheon said. "Are you accusing *Granddad* of *mass murder?"*

Ryota narrowed his eyes. "Don't come to his defense, like he's some kind of benevolent caretaker. He *left* us, Trecheon. Ayumi--"

"Do *not* bring Ayumi into this," Trecheon snapped. The last thing he wanted was to relive the loss of their sister. He paused. "This other genocide. This... 'cleanse.' Was it also against humans?"

Ryota waved a hand. "No. They took out some lesser tribe of quilar." He reached into a black cloth holster, similar to Trecheon's, and pulled out a Gem. He lifted it, deep, blood red, and tossed it in the air. "To get these. Power should be *used* and they were just letting it sit."

Trecheon's blood ran cold. His mind flooded with the events of the day. Izzy's story about watching someone get murdered, Darvin's accusations of genocide, Matt's anger and hate, everyone's distrust of the name Omnir. That was all of them were talking about. Mass murder and theft... his family's legacy. No wonder they all hated him.

No wonder he took to the assassin profession so easily. It was in his blood. Born to kill and nothing else. Trash. He could practically feel Matt's hate burning the air behind him. And he deserved every atom of it.

But that didn't make any of this okay.

"You seriously think it's justifiable to *murder a whole tribe* just to get some magic jewels." Trecheon said. "Ryota, you've lost your senses!"

The spheres of electricity reappeared around Ryota's head. He stuffed his Gem into the cloth holster wrapped around his waist. "So I take it that means you won't join me then?"

"*Join* you?" Trecheon said. "You're out of your *mind.*"

"A shame," Ryota said. He threw his hand forward and the electric orbs flashed Trecheon's way.

THUNDER AND LIGHTNING

Trecheon hit the deck, wrapping his arms around his head. *Oh god, oh Draso, I'm dead.*

But the magic never hit him. Instead, a series of *pop pop pops* blasted his ears and a bombardment of flashing lights blinded him. Matt had saved him as he promised. He rolled off toward his reluctant partner's position. "Don't kill him!"

Ryota shouted over the din. "What are you--" But he was cut off as a vicious tornado of dust and debris sailed past Trecheon toward Ryota, drowning his words. Trecheon dove out of the way and scrambled to his feet. Matt walked out from behind the palm, hand out, baring his teeth.

Ryota leapt aside in a flash of green and purple – a shield. He got to his feet. "You tell me you aren't a part of Angel, yet you're here with both Neil and Carter? What the hell are you trying to pull, Trecheon?"

"I'm *not* Carter," Matt said, ears flat.

"You think I don't know who you are?" Ryota said. He threw his hands out and a bombardment of lightning crashed down on them. Matt dashed next to Trecheon and shielded. It held, though cracks spiderwebbed through it. Ryota ran for the exit on the other side of the massive lobby.

Matt shoved Trecheon left. "Flank him! We need to get that Gem away from him. He won't be able to use it."

Trecheon frowned. "How do you expect me to do *that?*"

"You any good with that pistol?" Matt ran right. "Just don't hit the Gem if you want him to live."

Trecheon frowned. There goes that plan. Shit. Trecheon pulled out the firearm and ran left. He'd have to hit something else then. Make him drop the jewel.

Matt threw his hands forward and two thin twisters danced across the floor, tearing up broken marble, furniture, and overgrown plants. With incredible precision, he guided the dusty mess ahead of Ryota and plopped the whole disaster in front of the exit, throwing a jumble of dirt and trash into the air and blocking the doors. Ryota skidded to a halt and turned. He gritted his teeth and waved a hand, wrapping himself in magic shields.

Trecheon and Matt stood on Ryota's left and right, blocking his escape. Matt surrounded Ryota with dust-filled twisters, but Trecheon held out a hand, begging Matt with his gaze not to do anything to him. Matt snarled, but held back. Trecheon aimed the pistol at Ryota, staring him in the eye. "We don't want to hurt you, Ryota."

Matt grunted, but he didn't say anything.

Ryota glared at Matt. "Where the hell did you get a Gem, Carter?"

"For the last time, I'm *not Carter,*" Matt snarled. "I'm *Matt.* A survivor of the Sol Genocide."

Ryota's eyes flashed wide. "A survivor? Theron said--"

"Theron says a lot of things." Matt formed a fist, and the tornadoes grew.

This was getting out of Trecheon's control. *"Draso's mercy,* Ryota." He lowered his pistol. "I don't want to do this. Just… come home."

Ryota wrinkled his snout and furrowed his brow. "You are not my home." He threw a hand up, spewing lightning everywhere. But not at Matt or Trecheon – at the ceiling. A big chunk of exposed concrete and metal exploded from the damaged building and tumbled down over Trecheon.

Trecheon gasped and covered his head, sure he was a goner.

But a huge rush of wind drowned everything out and tore around his body, threatening to knock him over and blow him away. A horrific cacophony beat against his ears, but nothing fell on him. He opened his eyes.

All the debris had been scattered to Trecheon's left. Huge concrete boulders, long, bent lengths of metal I-beams, glass, wires, broken light bulbs, and rotting, mildewy insulation littered the ground about ten feet from him, scattered haphazardly about. Trecheon stared, mouth agape. He turned to Matt.

Matt knelt on one knee, teeth gritted, sweat beading on his white fur. He held a hand out. It was covered in some thick black sludge. Trecheon furrowed his brow. All that effort just to save *him?*

"Impossible…" Ryota muttered. Trecheon turned. Ryota stared at Matt, eyes wide. "You're Black Bound."

Trecheon frowned. Ryota knew Black Binding.

Izzy had said she was Black Bound because she watched someone get murdered when she was four.

Matt must have faced something just as bad. Probably during that genocide they kept mentioning. Good Draso, no wonder they hated Trecheon on name alone.

"You're not Carter," Ryota said. "You're the white and blue Zyearthling that Theron went after."

Matt faced Ryota, straightening up. He breathed heavily, but he managed to stand tall. "I'm also the quilar that severed his hold on Ouranos," he said with sudden conviction. "And the one who kicked the Basileus' sorry tail out of my home."

Ryota scoffed. "With Ouranos' help."

"There's no shame in fighting with a partner." Matt stood.

Ryota bared his teeth. "Only the weak need a partner." He held out his hands and blasted Matt with lightning.

Matt crossed his arms in front of him and formed a shimmering shield, but the force of the lightning cracked it and sent Matt sliding backwards on his heels. He growled and strengthened the shield, but it was only a matter of time before it'd break and probably kill him.

So Trecheon had a limited window.

He dashed for his brother and tackled him to the ground. In Ryota's shock, he turned the electric barrage on Trecheon, shearing off one of his artificial arms with one bolt and hitting him square in the chest with another.

Trecheon screamed. Pain ran through his body like needles and knives through his veins, all converging on his remaining arm which twisted around wildly from the extra electrical impulses. Memories of losing his arms in war blasted through his mind, doubling the pain.

He fought for control but the arm had been completely lost to him. He mentally reached for the memory override code. *Right arm, emergency release, passcode IAmTheWhiteAssassin!* A freakin' nice reminder that he deserved this shit coming to him.

The arm fell at his side, spinning out of control, dispersing the electricity, and finally slowing the pain. The world blurred and he listed to one side. Matt called his name, a distant and far cry in his ringing ears, then Trecheon passed out.

HEALER

Izzy curled her lips in a snarl and slammed her fire-bathed hammer in a mess of Cast. "Natassa, herd them this way! Sami, keep an eye on those two stragglers!" Natassa hurled a barrage of tiny fireballs at several Cast and Sami trapped the escaping ones with a fire wall. She turned. "Where are Matt and Ouranos?"

"I am here," Ouranos said. He walked up with Neil, holding the puma up with an arm across his back. Neil gulped air. "Matthew has chased after Ryota with Trecheon."

Izzy flattened her ears. "Neil, what happened?"

"Cast attack," Neil said, breathless. "I thought I was gonna *die.*"

"He should be fine, though he could use a healer…" Ouranos' voice trailed.

Izzy scrunched up her snout.

"No way in hell am I asking you to heal me," Neil said. "Not after what your powers did to Trecheon."

"I still healed him," Izzy said, though she silently thanked Draso that Neil didn't ask for healing. The last thing she wanted to do was hurt anyone with her malfunctioning powers. Even as she thought it, her Gem whined in her ear and her hands grew warm with healing power. She pushed it back, though the tingle of magic stuck to her fingertips.

Neil narrowed his gaze. "Yeah but--"

"Izzy, watch out!" Sami shouted.

Izzy whipped about, swinging her hammer. It connected with a massive Cast amalgamation but rather than break it apart, it stuck fast, like someone gripped the other end. She pulled it hard, trying to get it free, but with a solid tug, the Cast ripped the hammer out of her hands.

Ouranos held out a fire-soaked hand, but another Cast appeared and engulfed it, quickly working its way around both him and Neil. Neil shouted, trying to pull away from Ouranos and the Cast, but without success.

Izzy's ears exploded with her Gem's whine. Her powers activated, instantly drowning her hands in Black Bound elixir. She gritted her teeth as Darvin's words floated through her head. *You always did want offensive powers.* With no other options, she buried her hands in each of the attacking Cast and forced healing magic though her fingers.

All the Cast froze in midair and each sunk in itself like liquid being sucked through a vacuum. They reemerged from wherever they had been pulled into… reforming as zyfaunos. Proper zyfaunos, all Athánatos quilar. One masculine. Three feminine. Each of them had black fur, two with blue streaks, one with red and the final with silver, wearing traditional garments similar to Ouranos' and Natassa's. Staring with shock and surprise, they drew raspy breaths.

Ouranos and Neil stared with slack jaws and wide eyes. Ouranos even named one. "Horras!" he cried, his voice quivering. The masculine quilar turned to him, his face rigid with shock.

For a brief, elated second, Izzy's heart leapt with joy. She had saved a Cast! She brought four back! Draso's mercy, if her malfunctioning healing could bring them back then she could save Roscoe! And Darvin! All the Defenders at home. She reached for one of the Athánatos.

All four exploded, shattering Izzy's elation.

The zyfaunos blasted apart in hideous shrieks, their bodies shredding in a spray of black ink, red, bloody flesh, and fur, raining down on Izzy, Ouranos, and Neil. The shock of the screams locked Izzy's muscles. Lightning ran through her body, heating her face and making her ears ring until she was almost deaf, unable to hear anything beside the four quilar's final shrieks of pain in echoes. Her brain tried to process what had happened, but it… stalled. Broke.

Neil's cry broke her out of it. "What the hell did you *do* to them?"

She turned, panic rushing through her. "I don't know!" Izzy said. She spoke too fast, too high pitched. "I just--my healing powers--I didn't--"

"Your healing powers exploded four people?" Neil shouted. "Christ on a bike, lady!"

"Isabelle…" Ouranos spoke softly, distantly, his body frozen in place. He opened and closed his mouth, but he said nothing more.

Izzy stared at her hands. Fire and ice, what had she done?

"Izzy, duck!" Darvin shouted.

Izzy whipped about and dug her hands into the attacking Cast, still charged with healing energy. The Cast once again sunk in on itself, reemerged as an Athánatos quilar, streaked with brown, then exploded in goopy flesh and ink.

Darvin's words bombarded her. *You always wanted offensive powers.*

But not like this. Not like *this.*

And yet, the Gem whined, personifying pleasure. She fought it back. *Don't do this! Give me my healing back!*

"Isabelle, stop, please!" Ouranos shouted, high-pitched desperation in his quavering voice. "These are my *people!*"

Izzy turned. "Ouranos, I--"

"Izzy!" Darvin shrieked. Izzy whipped about, but a Cast engulfed her before she could react. The black, gooey monster closed around her in that familiar squeezing she wished she didn't have the memory to know.

She could stop this. Stop *all* of this.

But those ruined faces, those shattered bodies, the fear, the *shrieks.*

Ouranos begging her to stop.

Killing the Cast meant looking in the broken expressions of a thousand quilar. Quilar that she should be working to save. She was a *Defender,* damn it. A Guardian. Not a *murderer.*

But she also couldn't fight back. She had no hammer, no element. The monster squeezed harder, stronger. Crushing pain enveloped her, breath escaped her, panic set in.

Her Gem acted without her and her Black Bound powers activated. Mind blank, she pressed magic-engulfed hands against her attacker.

Once again, the Cast sunk into space, emerged as a zyfaunos with green streaked quills, and exploded with a high-pitched scream and a rain of blood and fur.

Izzy frantically brushed the golden fur on her arms, now stained red and black with blood and Cast ink. She shook her head, raining the damning colors on the concrete. Nothing rid her of it. It stained too deep. Damn, damn, damn!

"Sami!" Darvin's panicked voice drained the blood from Izzy's face and she whipped around.

Sami lay on the ground in a pool of some dark fluid, still. Natassa stood in front of her, trying to keep the Cast wall at bay, but with little luck. A Cast dove for Sami's fallen form.

"No!" Izzy rushed for them, hands hot with healing power. It was the Cast or Sami, and she wasn't about to let Sami go.

But before she got to Sami, Darvin slammed into the Cast attacking her and covered her with his body, gurgling loudly like a growl. More Cast attacked, but while they were mindless, Darvin was strategic and he batted them away with thin tentacles, waving them about like whips. Sami groaned and moved under him, gripping her head. She was alive at least.

"Take him!" Ouranos shouted, and hefted Neil onto Izzy. She held him up as Ouranos rushed forward with a wave of fire over the mound of Cast.

But it wasn't enough. The mass of monsters had grown even since they started fighting them, and if Izzy estimated correctly by the many, many trios of eyes, it was more than any single Defender had fought on Zyearth at once. Several Cast wiggled out from under the wall of flame and tackled Ouranos to the ground. Two more grabbed Natassa and pulled her down too.

Neil leapt back and gave Izzy a shove toward Ouranos. "Go save them!" He fell on his tail.

Izzy ran for Ouranos, but just as the Athánatos prince disappeared under the monster's grip, he held a hand out to Izzy. "Do not kill them!" Then he was gone.

Like hell I'm going to let them kill you! She ran up, hands alight with power.

Something smashed into her head, blasting stars in her vision. She fell to the concrete hard, her head bouncing, cutting her vision completely. She had a vague impression that a Cast had her in its grip, but consciousness left her before she could form a complete thought.

CHAPTER 25

BLACK BOUND

Matt stared, his body buzzing. Trecheon had just tackled his magic-flailing brother to the ground. No shields, no protection, no magic of his own, all in an attempt to stop him attacking Matt.

And now he was on the marble, artificial arms destroyed, unmoving, possibly dead. Something dark pooled under his body, though in the dim light, Matt couldn't tell if it was blood or oil from his arms. He had to get Trecheon out of there and get him to Izzy. *Now.*

But that meant getting Ryota out of the way. Which might be difficult with his Black Bound powers running hot. It would have been so much easier to push Trecheon instead, but after what had happened with his high school bully Warren, way back when his powers first broke, he didn't trust himself to use his magic to move zyfaunos ever again. The image of Warren flying through the air and smashing into the cafeteria wall would haunt him forever.

"I… You…" Ryota said. Matt turned.

Ryota stared at Trecheon, frozen, eyes wide, jaw slack. He lifted a hand, twitching. Both of his black gloves and the edges of his sleeves had been shredded in the battle and they hung in loose ribbons over his red fur. He ripped the shredded gloves off and threw them to the ground, shaking. His whole body moved with little jolts, as if he was uncertain what to do. Eventually he closed his mouth and attempted to furrow his brow, though with little success.

"T-that's what you get for fighting me," he muttered in little squeaks.

Now was Matt's chance. He had one goal. Chase Ryota away. He lifted a hand--

Red hot pain ripped through his arm. Matt winced, biting his tongue against a scream. He didn't know what he'd done to it, but damn, that hurt. He lifted the other arm instead and whipped up a tornado, blasting it Ryota's way.

Ryota snarled, and held his hands up, shielding. The tornado smashed into Ryota's shield, shattering it, but the force of the shatter broke apart Matt's magic, shrouding Ryota in a cloud of dust.

Then the dust settled… and Matt saw his hands. Little black blobs had formed on the tips of Ryota's fingers.

Matt stared. "Lighting and air… you're Black Bound."

Ryota blinked, then looked at his hands. He wiped them on his jacket like a kit trying to hide a crime.

"That's how Theron made more Cast!" Matt said. "He's using *you!*"

"He gifted this power to me," Ryota snapped. "I'm not being used. He gave me strength. Long life. Immortality. A treasure--"

"What the hell did the Basileus do to you to get you *Black Bound?*" Matt said. "How did you even *survive?*"

Ryota frowned. "What?"

"Black Binding *kills* most Gem users," Matt said. He shook his head. He didn't have time for this. "Your brother will die if I don't get him to a healer."

Ryota furrowed his brow and glanced at Trecheon.

"Let me take him to Izzy," Matt said.

Ryota whipped about and tried glaring at Matt, though it was clearly forced and lacked conviction. "Give me one good reason why I should."

Matt narrowed his eyes. "Your boss will want to know the Guardians are here."

Ryota twitched an ear and chewed his lip. He glanced back at Trecheon.

"It's as good an excuse as any," Matt said. He carefully inched his way to Trecheon.

Ryota snarled. He pulled himself to his feet and ran for the door without another word.

Matt let him go and rushed to Trecheon. The red quilar lay on his stomach, his face in the pool of black, though up close the pool reflected greasy rainbows. Oil. Not blood.

That didn't mean he wasn't bleeding though. Both of his ruined sleeves carried bloodstains. Matt carefully twisted Trecheon onto his back, careful not to injure him further, or twist his own damaged arm again.

Oil had sunk into Trecheon's red and black quills and fur, though his chest still rose and fell, so that was a good sign. It was shallow though, as was his heart rate. He needed Izzy.

Matt gathered up Trecheon's damaged artificial arms. He glanced them over, frowning, then placed them on Trecheon's stomach and picked his fallen ally up.

Matt's pendant beeped frantically – an emergency call from Sami. Cursing, Matt dropped to the floor and answered it. "Sami, I've got a--"

But it wasn't Sami who appeared in the projected hologram from Matt's pendant. It was a Cast. He nearly dropped the pendant. "What the hell?"

"Matt, they're gone!" Darvin's bubbly voice shook more than normal. His Cast body rippled wildly in his apparent panic. "They're all *gone!*"

Matt's heart nearly stopped. "What? Who?"

"Everyone!" Darvin said. "Izzy, Ouranos, Natassa, Roscoe, Neil... they're all gone! And Sami..." Darvin nearly choked as much as he could as a Cast. "She fell and I can't wake her up and I can't even tell if she's breathing, and--" he fell into panicked, unintelligible mumbles.

Shit. "How the hell did they all go missing?"

"I don't know!" Darvin said. "We were fighting the Cast and Sami fell and I was trying to protect her, but the Cast attacked everyone, and by the time I got them away from Sami, everyone else was gone."

Earth and *stone.* Matt pulled up his pendant and searched for Defender signals.

Nothing. Just his, Sami's, and the phantom one in the pier.

He tried reaching mentally for Ouranos. *Ouranos, answer me, please!* He got a faint wave of colors – yellow worry, a red, which Matt associated with the blood fire of battle... and a deep purple... mourning. Dread roiled in his belly. Ouranos didn't answer, so he dug deeper and connected it to a name. Horras. He didn't know who that was, but it wasn't Izzy or any of his teammates so he had to assume they were okay. Alive, if anything.

But Ouranos wouldn't answer. That terrified him.

But, like it or not, they didn't have time to go looking for them. Not with Trecheon and Sami having issues. "Darvin, do you think you could carry Sami?"

Darvin blinked his three blue Cast eyes. "What?"

"You said Sami was hurt," Matt said.

"I said she might be *dead,"* Darvin snapped.

"She's not dead," Matt said, trying to keep his voice steady. "Her pendant shows normal vitals. You probably forgot to check in your panic."

Darvin's three blue eyes widened, then he sunk in on himself.

"She needs medical attention, though," Matt said. "And if Izzy isn't near you, she clearly can't be the one to do it. We need to take her to my plane and get her under Caesum's care in the med-wing." He chewed his lip. "Trecheon is badly hurt too, and I can't carry them both."

Darvin's Cast body grew a large gap under his eyes, like a mouth dropping open. "You're seriously picking that Omnir over *Sami?*"

Matt narrowed his eyes. "The Guardian Oath demands I protect all creatures--"

"Does that include enemies over friends?" Darvin spat. "That Omnir--"

"Trecheon, Darvin," Matt snarled. "His name is Trecheon and he's not the enemy. He just took a lightning bolt for me, for Draso's sake."

Darvin rippled angrily. "But--"

"Do you really think I should get to decide who lives or dies?" Matt said through gritted teeth. "We can save them both, but only if you act *now.* Can you carry Sami or not?"

Darvin sunk in on himself. "…I can carry Sami."

"Follow my pendant signal and meet me at the plane," Matt said.

Darvin gurgled and cut off the communication.

A twinge of righteous anger ripped through Matt. Darvin was right. He shouldn't be helping this Omnir. His *enemy.*

But he was a Guardian. The oath demanded it, even when he didn't agree with it. And… Trecheon had saved him too.

Damn it all. Matt carefully lifted Trecheon's limp body, pushing through the pain in his arm, and headed out of the casino.

CHAPTER 26

CAESUM

Matt cautiously laid Trecheon on the long metal table in the medical bay on his X-Zero. Carrying him with Matt's damaged shoulder had been hell, but he'd powered through it.

Thoughts warred in his mind. *He saved your damn life, Azure, so treat him with respect!*

The Omnirs destroyed your home, a thousand voices called. The voices of those lost on Sol. *Killed your family, burned your village, made you starve, alone.*

You are a Guardian, the first voice said. *Your job is to defend all creatures.*

But not enemies.

But is he your enemy?

Matt gripped his head, gritting his teeth. *Stop, stop, stop!* All his training, all his time as a Defender, and nothing had prepared him for this.

But it wouldn't do to insist Darvin treat him with respect if he didn't do the same.

The red and black quilar hadn't moved or made a sound during his entire trek from the casino to the plane. He must have gotten a bigger chest full of electricity than Matt realized. Maybe… maybe he'd die from his injuries and Matt wouldn't have to worry about this anymore. Maybe he could just choose not to do anything after all. Defend all creatures. He had done that. He didn't have to carry this guilt.

Why should you get to decide who lives or dies?

Damn it. He mentally beat himself.

As damaged as Trecheon was, the arms would be the bigger problem. The sheered one would need extensive repair of the metal plating and wiring, and possibly some repair on the hydraulic system. The other was worse off. The wires were burnt to cinders and they disintegrated in Matt's hands. He wasn't sure if they were even salvageable.

And his knowledge of the mechanics was limited. But this was far more than basic repairs. And beyond that, Matt knew nothing about Earth tech. Earthling technology in general was grossly inferior to Zyearthling tech and even without that, they were developed differently. For all he knew, there could be nothing similar at all between the two technologies. The archaic hydraulic system was already evidence of this.

He'd have to get Caesum involved. As much as Matt hated to admit it, the dragon AI was much better suited to work through this situation than he was. Caesum had much finer control over the X-Zero's onboard repair station and was well-versed in the mechanical repair know-how. Like it or not, Trecheon's arms and mounts needed a complete overhaul.

He just wasn't looking forward to the inevitable lecture he'd get about being AWOL.

Someone pounded on the door of the plane. Matt made sure Trecheon couldn't roll off the table then rushed to the door to examine Sami. To his surprise, Sami stood by the door on her own power, conscious and alert, though frowning.

"Thank Draso," Matt said, his body flooding with relief. "You okay? Darvin made it seem like were dying."

"I've… had worse I suppose," Sami said with a shrug.

"She woke up while I took her here," Darvin said. His body relaxed into a smooth puddle. "I'd cry if this damn body would let me."

"I'd like Caesum to take a look at you anyway," Matt said. "Think you're up to getting him? He's in his case in the cockpit. Just drop him in the A.I. slot and report to medical."

Sami nodded. "I'll do that."

Darvin shifted. "You're sure you're okay?"

She smiled at him. "I am. Thanks for getting me here." She entered the plane and headed for the cockpit. Darvin moved to follow.

Matt held up a hand. "Darvin, I know you're worried about Sami, but you've got to look for Izzy and the others," Matt said. "I can feel Ouranos is still alive, but I don't know where and he's not answering me. You're the best Defender to go looking for them right now."

Darvin hesitated, but formed a simple stag head with his inky body and nodded. "Yes, sir." He slunk off back toward the pier.

Matt sighed. He didn't like separating like that, but he really didn't have a choice. They needed Izzy. He needed his partner. Pushing the matter to the back of his mind, he headed back to the room holding Trecheon.

He did a quick visual inspection for damage on Trecheon's body. He had a ripped shirt, some singed fur, and several patches of dried blood, but overall, he didn't look too bad, at least on the surface. Incredible for a lightning strike.

He lifted him up to check on his back when he heard something clunking on the metal table.

It was a stained cloth rag. Matt flicked an ear back. He undid the knot around Trecheon's waist, laid the quilar down, and glanced in the pouch.

Sure enough, a Gem occupied it. A real, fully bound Gem, in red, with a blue center, accented in black. A passing memory reminded him that he had seen Izzy handing the Gem to Trecheon right after Matt had attacked him.

Matt's fur stood on end. A real Gem. Just like Trecheon's brother. Anger swirled in Matt's head.

He had to have a Sol Gem. It was too convenient. Right near Sol, where the Gems were easily accessible. He glanced at Trecheon. And Izzy had said he had been partially bound. That could mean he wasn't twenty-eight like he said. He could be one of the Omnir who attacked his home.

Maybe he was working with Ryota and this was just a farce. Maybe he was just as dangerous.

No! Matt gritted his teeth. That didn't make sense. Ryota wouldn't attack an ally. Trecheon clearly didn't know anything about the genocide. He needed to stop looking for problems where there weren't any.

One issue though. Izzy had bound him and he didn't get any answers as to why before the Cast attacked. More than that, he had no idea what Izzy had told him about Gems or the Cast or Theron or hell, even Zyearth. He had to hope she followed Galactic Accord regulations, but there was no way to know for sure. He'd just have to play it by ear.

He pressed a button on the sidewall and a slim glass med reader lowered from the ceiling. The holographic projectors warmed and within seconds the med reader spat out various readings on Trecheon's biosigns. For the most part they looked normal, though there was some tissue damage near the arm mounts. There wasn't much throughout the rest of his body, which surprised him. Perhaps the metal in his arm and mounts sucked the electricity away from the flesh and kept him from too much injury. Matt furrowed his brow.

"Matthew Azure, you *traitor!*" a tinny voice sounded in the room. "Have you gone completely mental?"

Matt glared crossed his arms. Caesum wanted a battle? He'd give him a battle. "You promised me you'd congratulate me when I earned the Guardianship. That I'd earn the title of 'sir.' Well, I earned it. What happened?"

"What *happened* is you decided to go AWOL, you *pathetic excuse for a Defender.*" the blue and purple dragon snorted, flapping about in the hologram lights above Matt's head, spewing motes of blue light. He glared at Trecheon. "And you're helping an Omnir. An. *Omnir.* Your parents' *murderer.*"

"Trecheon did not murder my parents," Matt said, though that righteous anger returned. He pushed it away. "He's too young. I'm more than double his age."

"So he's related to your parents' murderer," Caesum snarled. "It amounts to the same thing."

Matt splayed his ears and glared at Caesum. "It doesn't. That's xenophobic and ethnocentric. Don't say that again."

Caesum snorted. "Your father--"

"Do *not* bring my father into this," Matt said, slamming a fist on the table. "I've got enough to deal with without you bringing him up." He pointed to Trecheon. "You see these readings? This damage? That should be me. He tackled a lightning fabricator. His own *brother.* And with nothing but his own body. No shields, no magic, no ability to do anything to counter the attack, just so he could save me. After I attacked him unprovoked, I might add." He took a deep breath. "So don't go lumping him together with the quilar that killed Dad." Because if he started doing that, he'd give permission for Matt to start hating him. He was having a hard enough fighting that battle.

Though even saying it out loud, he wasn't sure if he believed himself. He breathed out slowly, trying to calm the tightness growing in his throat and chest.

Caesum fluttered into the shadows in the room. "I'm sorry."

"You're not sorry at all, so don't bother lying," Matt said, his voice thick. He leaned on the metal table, forming fists. "I'm having a hard enough time dealing with this situation. Don't give me any more reasons to throw hate on him when to my knowledge, he's done nothing to deserve it. Understood?"

Caesum floated back into view. "Yes, sir."

Finally got his "sir." Good. Maybe he'd get Caesum to do what he needed him to. "Prep the repair module. He has biomech arms. Both of them are broken and I don't have the know-how to fix them. You'll have to do that."

Caesum's long dragon ears flipped back.

"And *don't protest*," Matt said. "Get the module ready. While they're being repaired, you can drop the medi-arm and help me fix and clean the wounds and arm mounts." He glared. "And if he wakes up, let me do the talking."

Caesum narrowed his gaze. "Silent planet protocols--"

"*I know the silent planet protocols,*" Matt snapped. "Doesn't apply anyway. Trecheon already has a Gem."

Caesum's eyes widened. *"What--!"*

"*Say. Nothing,*" Matt snarled. "It's already done. Can't plug up their ears again. I will *handle it.* And you'll keep your maw *shut.* Do I make myself clear?"

Caesum growled, deep and angry. *"Matt--"*

"*Guardian,*" Matt said, baring his teeth. "It's *Guardian Azure,* and don't you forget it. I better not hear another complaint or I will take you straight to Guardian Tox for insubordination. We're already in a desperate situation. The last thing I need is you making it worse. Now, I'll ask again. *Do I make myself clear?"*

Caesum snorted. "Yes, sir."

Matt lifted his chin. "Yes, *Guardian."*

Caesum bared a tooth, but continued. "Yes, Guardian."

"Good," Matt said. "Get the hell out of here and get the medi-arms ready."

Caesum nodded and his ghostly form flicked away in tiny motes of scattered light. Matt took a deep breath.

Fire and ice. Somehow he knew it'd come to blows with Caesum. But at least it was over.

Trecheon let out a shuttering breath, then lay still again.

Matt pressed his eyes shut and flattened his ears.

He couldn't let anyone see how badly this affected him. Right now, he just needed to work on his patient and see if helping his new… ally, would make up for the fact that he had nearly torn his throat out earlier that morning.

Draso's wings, he hoped it would.

SHATTERED

Trecheon woke groggily. He blinked, trying to understand the blurry images in his vision and the odd metallic scents wafting past his nose. His face was wet and somewhat oily. A soft beeping sounded overhead and an echo of tools tinkering mingled with it.

Something was also messing with his shoulder mounts. He jerked left. "Get away," he muttered with less strength than he intended.

"He wakes," a male voice said. Matt, the white and blue quilar. "Welcome back to the world of the living."

"You're a walking cliché, you know that?" Trecheon coughed. He blinked more, turned his head toward the voice, and through watery eyes, his vision focused. His strange attacker snapped into place.

He frowned at Trecheon, ears back. Oil smudges dotted his face, hands and quills, and one shoulder was wrapped in a long support bandage, giving him a grimy, broken look. He looked jittery. Tense. As if ready to spring at any moment. Trecheon held in a shiver.

"I've been told that before," Matt said, reaching for a rag to wipe his oily hands clean. He glanced at Trecheon with a skeptical eye. "How do you feel?"

"Like someone hired me to be a lightning rod and I was broke enough to take the job," Trecheon spat. Something felt wrong, missing. He needed that Gem thing. He could heal himself. Make the pain go away. "Ugh, everything aches."

"That's basically what happened," Matt said. "But the aching is good. It means your nerves are intact. Any sharp pains?"

"Just around the mounts," Trecheon said. "And maybe some phantom pains. I thought I was done with those." He shook his head. "Where's Neil?"

Matt wrinkled his snout. "Missing. Along with most of our pack."

Fresh panic ran through Trecheon. *"What?"*

"I have Darvin out looking for them," Matt said. "We should hear soon, I hope."

Trecheon glared. "I need to go find him *now.*"

Matt flicked an ear back. "Buddy, you aren't even going to be able to sit up on your own, let alone go hunting for your friend. Your arms are still being repaired."

Trecheon moaned and laid his head back on the hard metal table. Right. Damaged arms. Missing. That's what was off. No wonder he was having phantom pains. "Shit."

"I have one of my ah, coworkers working on them," Matt said. "They should be ready soon, at least as well as we can fix them. In the meantime, would it hurt you if I sat you up properly? I'm trying to repair your mounts, but it's really hard to do with you lying down. Once we fix everything, we can join Darvin in looking for everyone, assuming he hasn't found them by then."

Trecheon pressed his eyes closed a moment, trying to calm the panic. Neil would be safe. Someone was looking for him. It wouldn't do any good to panic. Calm. Breathe.

Then in one fluid motion, he hoisted himself up. He spun on the table and faced Matt, legs hanging over the edge. He glanced at the ruined sleeves of his shirt and frowned.

"That was my favorite shirt."

Matt perked both ears. "How did you do that?"

"I've been without arms for a long time," Trecheon said. "You learn to work around it. Gotta work that core to make up for the missing arms."

"Hmm," Matt said. He tilted his gaze up to the ceiling, then turned to Trecheon. "This'll get done faster if my colleague can help, but you gotta promise not to freak out when you see him."

Trecheon raised an eyebrow. "Way to fill a guy with confidence."

"He's not dangerous or anything," Matt said. "Just… unusual. And kind of an asshole."

"Sounds like you two are peas in a pod," Trecheon said with a smirk.

Matt glared, but then sighed. "I suppose I deserve that."

Trecheon forced a chuckle. "If I can take you, I can take him. I'd rather get this done sooner than later. Phantom pains suck ass and Neil needs me."

"Fine then," Matt said. He looked up at the ceiling again. "Caesum, he's awake. If you're willing to help, we can get both mounts done at the same time."

Tiny bulbs over Trecheon's head lit up and he watched as little bubbles of light formed the shape of a dragon straight out of European folklore – leather wings, horned head and tail, thick scales. This one was tiny and an odd mix of purple and blue.

Trecheon blinked at him. "Hi?"

The dragon snorted, blasting the air with petite rainbow streams of smoke, glaring with tiny beady eyes. Matt furrowed his brow and crossed his arms, scowling.

The dragon glared back. "You told me to be quiet."

Matt raised one eyebrow. "You can say hi at least."

The dragon tilted his head toward Matt, then threw up his forelegs and flipped his head back in a miniature display of exasperation. "Fine, whatever!" He turned to Trecheon. "Hello."

"Forgive Caesum," Matt said. "He's never been good at endearing himself to strangers."

"I can tell," Trecheon said, squinting. "What is it?"

"Smart A.I.," Matt said.

Trecheon tilted his head. "Smart A.I. A.I. doesn't even know how many r's are in the word 'strawberry.' How the hell do you have one that's *sentient?*"

Matt paused. "That's ah… complicated."

"My appearance and personality come from a deceased dragon," Caesum said. "Programming fills in the rest and gives me my superior intelligence."

Matt snarled. *"Caesum."*

"What?" Caesum said, throwing his head back. "You said silent planet protocols didn't matter anymore."

"I also told you to keep your mouth *shut,"* Matt said. "Superior intelligence my tail."

"I'll have you know I was a top learner in life," Caesum muttered.

"You're just reading that off your biodragon's profile," Matt said. "Your biodragon came from the dark ages. The most he might have learned is how to use moss to clean a wound or something."

Trecheon watched the exchange with fascination. Something didn't quite fit. "Hold on. Dragons aren't real."

Matt perked his ears, then sighed. He glared up at Caesum. "You woke the dragon."

Caesum gave Matt a sarcastic smile. "You're welcome. Protocols can be fully ignored now."

"I really hate you sometimes," Matt said. He turned back to Trecheon. "You're right. Dragons don't exist here. Not anymore, anyway." He picked up a handful of small tools and dropped them onto the table next to Trecheon. "Caesum, if you could use the medi-arm to get the other shoulder." Caesum grumbled, but a mechanical arm dropped from the ceiling near Trecheon's shoulder with an assortment of tools hanging off the end of it.

Trecheon watched Matt pick at the mount on his right shoulder with a long tool. "What do you mean they don't exist *here.* Where else is there?"

Matt sat up from his work and frowned at Trecheon with a splayed ear. "Guess that answers that question. Izzy didn't tell you?"

"Izzy didn't tell me shit," Trecheon said.

"Hmm." He poked at Trecheon's shoulder. "She followed that protocol at least. But that leaves me holding the Wishing Dust."

Caesum snorted rainbows again. "GA protocols don't just apply to magic, *Guardian.*"

Matt shot Caesum a look, but went back to his work. "Right."

Trecheon pulled away. "Oh hell no. You aren't gonna start this business then leave me hanging talking about protocols like I'm not even here. What the hell is going on here?" He paused. "This have anything to do with that Zyearth thing Izzy mentioned? Never got a straight answer out of her about it."

Matt chewed his lip, standing up straight. "Didn't follow as well as I thought then. What do you think Zyearth is?"

"Some secret society of healers and wizards, apparently," Trecheon said.

Matt smirked slightly. "Well, you're half-right I suppose. Might as well get you the rest of the way there, assuming you'll even believe me."

Trecheon eyed him. "Try me."

"Zyearth is a planet," Matt said. "And we came here from planet Zyearth."

Trecheon's mind froze as he tried to process this information. "Wait. What?"

"We came from Zyearth," Matt repeated, moving back to repairs. "A month's travel with the Gem drives, when we're properly aligned. Once part of the Galactic Accord, now an independent planet. Not that this place would know about it. Even if you managed to pick it up in those pathetic telescopes, you'd probably never be able to figure out that it had life. Silent planet and all."

Trecheon stared. "You're completely insane."

Matt smirked. "I've been told that one too. But we really did come from a different planet."

They came from a different planet. A *different planet.* He listened to the soft tinkering of tools while his mind tried refocusing with this new possible worldview. There were so many things wrong with this imaginary concept that he didn't even know where to start.

"We just barely started a Mars colony," Trecheon said. "How the hell do you have the technology to travel the galaxy like you're on a fishing trip?"

Matt eyed him. "You really think Earth is the gold standard for technology and space travel?"

Trecheon snorted. "Alright, I guess I'll give you that. But we've seen literally thousands of habitable planets in hundreds of solar systems. Where are you even from?"

"Vale System," Matt said. "Like with yours, our planet is the only one in the system that can support life. Well, naturally anyway."

"Never heard of it."

"Of course not," Matt said. "You think we based the names of our solar systems off of Earth's names? Hell, starmaps don't even call this place Earth."

Trecheon lifted a brow. "Then what the hell is it?"

"Terra."

Trecheon rolled his eyes. "Real original." He glanced back at Matt. "How come you speak English then?"

"We invented English," Matt said, laying one tool on the table and picking up another. "We brought it here. Where'd you think it came from?"

"Oh, I don't know, *England?*" Trecheon said, unable to help the sarcasm.

Matt chuckled. "The name actually comes from an old Zyearth word, *englaindia.* Means 'language.' History changed the word's meaning throughout the ages. You'd be surprised how many planets speak some form of English."

Trecheon flattened both ears. "Hold on. You *brought* it here? Does that mean that I came from there too?"

"Technically, though obviously many, many generations removed," Matt said. "All zyfaunos come from Zyearth. Where did you think the term 'zyfaunos' came from?"

"Bullshit."

"Your Gem came from Zyearth too," Matt said, as if Trecheon needed anymore worldview shattering collapses. "All Zyearthlings have one. Well, most. A few choose to opt out."

Trecheon glared. "That doesn't make sense. If zyfaunos came from Zyearth and they all have one, how come we don't all have them on Earth?"

"Refugee ships brought your ancestors here and they used dangerous and hastily developed cryotechnology," Matt said. He poked a corner of Trecheon's arm mount with a tool. Trecheon tried not to wince. "Desperate to escape a catastrophic world war. Lasted for nearly half a century and killed off something like eighty percent of the planet's population. A common problem when a silent planet opens its ears, though our silence breaking happened because of summons, not magic."

Trecheon flicked an ear back. Sounded like something straight out of a space drama.

"It's also why they left in a hurry," Matt continued. "No one had used cryotechnology long-term before, and they found out too late that it caused severe memory loss and actually severed Gem bonds. Zyfaunos came here with damaged, broken Gems, and really, no knowledge of what they were or how to fix it. It's honestly amazing that any of those old Gems still exist. Yours probably originally came from a refugee ship. Or…" He glanced off. "…Never mind."

"My Gem came from my grandfather," Trecheon said, needing to say something to counter Matt's claims.

Matt paused at the tools. "The grandfather that left you and your brother? The one Ryota ranted about?"

Trecheon winced. That stung. "Yeah. That one."

"And did he? Just leave you like that?"

Trecheon's ears bent back. "I'd rather not talk about it."

"Fair enough," Matt said, furrowing his brow. "I'd kind of rather not talk about it either if I'm honest."

"Wait a minute," Trecheon said. "Everything I heard Ryota and Izzy spouting suggests that you and Izzy were somehow involved in that genocide he kept talking about. How are you from a different planet?"

Matt paused again. "I was born here," he said, resuming work. "My father is from Zyearth, but he married an Earthling quilar and was living here for an extended period when we were kids. After the genocide, my sister managed to get a boat and escape the island with Izzy and me. Some zyfaunos from Zyearth picked me, Izzy, and my sister Charlotte up from a beach on the mainland." He shuddered. "I can't really picture it clearly since I was six when it happened, but for all I know, I was picked up on this beach."

Trecheon lowered his head and stared at his feet. He couldn't even imagine that kind of trauma at six.

Wait. Six? Didn't Ryota say *Granddad* was probably involved with the genocide? He glanced over at Matt, frowning. That would make Matt at least twenty years older than him. Forty or forty-five or something. He looked way too young.

"How old are you?"

Matt sat back and scratched his chin, as if thinking. "Sixty? I think I technically had my birthday while in transit here, but space travel always makes that tricky."

"Sixty!" Trecheon gasped. "You don't look a day over twenty-five!"

"And I never will," Matt said, flashing a quick grin. "Not the same way you do here on Earth. A benefit of the Gem. Didn't Izzy explain that to you?"

"She said I'd get shielding and my healing would get stronger," Trecheon said. He glanced around the room and found his Gem sitting on a wire mount on the counter. "She didn't mention any other powers."

Matt frowned. "She didn't tell you how long you'll live on a Gem?"

Uh oh. "No."

Matt shook his head. "Damn it, Izzy. That was irresponsible."

"Why?" Trecheon asked, his chest filling with dread. "How long will I live?"

Matt pressed his lips together. "About four hundred years."

CHAPTER 28

KNOW YOUR ENEMIES

Trecheon nearly fell off the table. *"What?"*

Matt put a hand on his shoulder to steady him. He frowned. "Izzy *really* should have told you. But I guess I'm not surprised she didn't know to. I don't think anyone ever talked to her about the informed consent of Gem binding, with her being Black Bound. We didn't exactly get informed consent. Even my own conversation about that was kind of by accident."

"I can't live that long!" Trecheon shouted, near panic. "I don't want to live that long! What's going to happen to me? Is my body going to break down after a hundred years? Am I going to be cursed with broken knees and bad eyesight for a majority of my life? Oh Draso, I don't want to live on this disgusting planet that long…"

"Calm yourself," Matt said, holding his hands out. "Your body won't be falling apart after a hundred years. If it did that, no one would keep a Gem."

Trecheon wrinkled his snout. "How do I stop it? I don't want to live four hundred years."

Matt furrowed his brow. "You uh, can't. Gem binding can't really be broken."

Trecheon narrowed his gaze. "'Can't really' isn't the same as 'absolutely cannot.' Is there something you're not telling me? Can it be broken?"

Matt rubbed his arm. "I've only known two ways it can break. The first being with the cryotech, which no longer exists, and the second… well, it was really unusual circumstances and resulted in the immediate death of the user…" His voice trailed.

Trecheon frowned. "You speak as if you witnessed it yourself."

"I did," Matt said. "I... held his hands while he died. And trust me, you really don't want to go that way." He closed his eyes and turned his face away for a moment before turning back to Trecheon. "And before you ask, you can't just break the Gem either. Gems are notoriously difficult to break anyway, but if you manage it, the break will cause you to go into power withdrawals and die instantly and painfully. Or the broken Gem's power will vaporize you. So unless you want to die *now*."

Trecheon shifted. Maybe he did. It'd be no more than what he'd deserve. He shook his head. Definitely not time for those thoughts. He eyed the Gem on the counter with a mix of fear and contempt. "What did you people saddle me with?"

"There are benefits too. It's not all bad. Though," Matt tilted an ear. "I wonder why Izzy wanted to bind you in the first place. That doesn't make sense to me, what with you living on a planet without Gems."

Trecheon shifted. "Well. One reason is I can heal myself. I doubt she'd admit that though."

Matt's ears shot up and he dropped a tool. "You can *what?*"

"I'm a healer that can heal myself," Trecheon said. "I've done it three times."

"Before the Gem was bound?"

"Yeah," Trecheon said. He cursed. "I should have asked more questions before diving into it."

Matt frowned. "Typically speaking, Gem users can't use their powers on themselves." He returned to the arm mount and after a few turns of the screwdriver, he pulled back. "If that's the case, maybe you can heal your shoulders then. There's only so much I can do myself. I'm not a healer."

"Need my arms back first," Trecheon said, trying to calm the frustration he felt in his chest. If Matt was right and he could just break the Gem to die, maybe he wouldn't have to live four hundred years. He didn't deserve that kind of life, let alone want it. Though… He glanced at Matt. "Do broken Gems really… vaporize their users?"

Matt frowned. "It depends on how long you've had the Gem and how powerful it is. For you, a new user, it'd likely just fade. It'd probably be pretty quick and relatively painless, though you'd still die. For me, it'd be hours of agonizing power withdrawals and hallucinations while my organs attempted to work without the Gem's energy, if the Gem didn't vaporize me. For someone who had the Gem past our biological lifespan, it would be torture beyond measure. Again, assuming you didn't immediately disintegrate."

Trecheon's eyes widened. "Holy *shit*. Why the hell would anyone use one of these?"

"It's not as bad as it sounds," Matt said. "Like I said, Gems are extremely tough – more so than diamonds. It takes a lot to break one. I can't think of the last time on Zyearth that one broke." He paused, and his eyes unfocused as if he was a million miles away. Trecheon was about to ask what was wrong, when Matt shook his head and went back to repairs. Maybe it was best not to ask.

"What happens when you die naturally with the Gem?" Trecheon asked, his stomach swirling. "Not that, right?"

"No, no, it's nothing like that," Matt said. "It's more of a gradual release of the bond. You lose a lot of energy and your senses will fade just like they would naturally, but it's not painful. I'm told it's quite peaceful, honestly. Way more so than biological death, since there's not usually a disease involved."

Trecheon took a deep breath. At least that.

"Well, I'm finished on my end," Matt said. "It's not a great job, but I'm kind of limited here. It should work decently though. Caesum?"

"…Finished," the dragon said, slightly dejected. "I'll check on the modules." The dragon's ghostly form dissipated.

"What is his problem?" Trecheon asked.

Matt dropped his tools into a drawer then went to a sink and washed his hands. "Honestly, the same problem I have with you."

Trecheon turned his head. "Ah. Sorry I asked."

"Sorry I mentioned it," Matt said. "It's not fair to lump you with the Omnirs that attacked my home. I know that logically."

"Emotionally though…"

Matt hoisted himself on the counter with his good arm and folded his hands into his lap. "Thanks for trying to understand. I appreciate that." He flicked both ears back. "It's a hard pill to swallow, knowing that your ancestors likely killed my parents. My whole family even. My aunt lived with us. I think she was going to get married soon, though I don't remember much." He shook his head. "Ancestors isn't the right word. That's too far removed. Granduncles and… grandfather perhaps. Just two generations removed." He flattened his ears and turned his head.

Trecheon twitched his snout. "What exactly happened?"

Matt lifted an ear. "Pardon?"

"The genocide," Trecheon said. "What happened exactly? Ryota wasn't really clear." He shifted. "I mean, I get it if you don't want to talk about it, but it might give me a better understanding of your feelings on this."

Matt's quills and fur stood on end a moment, then settled back down. "I don't remember everything, admittedly. It's kind of a blur." He took a deep breath. "But I remember smells, emotions, brief images. Everything smelling like blood and fire. I remember seeing my mom's body sprawled out in the backyard. I remember my aunt herding us out of the house, running for the beach. She hid us, then ran off to find my dad, and she never came back. My sister Charlotte, who was nine at the time, decided she should go find Dad herself and we followed."

"Is Izzy your sister too?"

Matt shook his head. "Not by blood. We were adopted by the same person on Zyearth though, so she's good as." He stared off into the distance, like he was transporting back to another time. "Izzy's involvement in the genocide was just coincidental. Our dads were partners in the Defender military and they were just over for a visit. Izzy's dad had brought along my grandfather's Gem because Dad wanted me and Charlotte to get used to carrying one before we were actually bound." He paused a moment, as if collecting his thoughts. "We found Izzy's dad while we wandered the burning village. I… don't know exactly what happened to him, but he was wrestling with one of the red quilar and then just… exploded."

Trecheon winced. "A Gem break maybe?"

"Izzy has her dad's Gem now, so that's unlikely, unless he had one of Sol's unbound Gems."

Trecheon shifted. "Do you pass Gems down through families? Like an heirloom?"

"We do, if the Gem matches," Matt said. "A poor consolation prize, but there's some comfort in it. Not one that I share." Matt shook his head and continued. "We ran all the way to the Sanctum at the top of the village. My dad was there, fighting a red quilar. Dad was doing pretty good until he saw us. Then he faltered and the red quilar got the upper hand. He stabbed at my dad's Gem with a knife and shattered it. The power overload… disintegrated him." He shook his head. "There was literally nothing left but a few strands of hair and a tiny splatter of blood."

Trecheon's fur stood on end. "A *knife* did that to his Gem? I thought these things were resilient."

Matt shrugged. "It's what I remember, but who knows how well I can trust the memory." His voice grew thick. "I sometimes wonder if it's my fault that he's dead. If I hadn't distracted him, maybe he'd be okay."

"Don't fall into that," Trecheon said. Matt looked up. Trecheon twitched an ear. "Trust me, it's really easy to fall into that trap. I've done that with my brother for Draso knows how long. It just eats you up. But what ifs don't fix things. You gotta let it go."

Matt took a slow breath. "You're right." He tightened his lips together. "Somehow the quilar Dad was fighting was completely unscathed in the explosion. He turned and saw me and all I saw was this hateful red quilar who had just killed my dad. My emotions went haywire. I was holding Grandpa's Gem and it reacted to my emotions, bound to me… and I think it killed the quilar that killed Dad. It's hard to remember – all I can recall is pain."

"Is that when you and Izzy were Black Bound?"

Matt raised an eyebrow.

"Izzy mentioned that she saw someone die and that's what made her Black Bound."

Matt shook his head. "Guess you figured out I'm Black Bound too."

"Wasn't hard."

Matt smiled slightly for a moment, then his face fell again. "Yeah, we were both Black Bound then. Me to my grandpa's Gem, Izzy to her father's

Gem." He closed his eyes and turned away. "Sorry. It's still really hard to sit here and stare at you while talking calmly, like we're just discussing some ancient history instead of a dark spot on my past."

Trecheon shrugged, a gesture that probably looked funny without arms. "Hopefully it'll get better with time." Assuming there'd be time to get over it.

"The arms are complete," Caesum said, reforming himself over Matt's head. "I have asked Grandis Chief Girsougon to get them and bring them here."

Matt flicked an ear back. "How is she?"

Caesum waved a clawed hand. "She's got a nasty bump on her head and some pretty bad bruising, but nothing internal. She'll be fine, though she needs rest and a healer."

"Thanks, Caesum," Matt said. "I appreciate you looking over her. You're dismissed."

"You're in no position to dismiss me, Matt," the dragon hissed, then disappeared.

Trecheon lifted a brow. "What was that?"

Matt scrunched up his face, glaring after the dragon. He shook his head. "You're military, right? I've heard you mention involvement in a war a few times."

"Marines. But yeah."

Matt leaned against the overhead cupboards. "We're AWOL right now."

Trecheon's ears perked. "*All* of you?"

"Most of us," Matt said. "Izzy, Sami, Darvin, Roscoe and myself. Ouranos and Natassa aren't military. They're allies."

"You went AWOL all the way from a *different planet* just to go hunting me down?"

Matt winced. "I didn't. Though, I guess in a way, Izzy did. But not for revenge. I guess because she found out that Theron could use Omnirs to create

Cast. Maybe, anyway, if he could somehow get you Black Bound. I just followed her." He shook his head. "I was intending to just pick her up and go home, but that plan's out the window now, considering the Cast and the fact that your brother is Black Bound."

"What?" Trecheon said. "How do you know?"

"He showed signs when I fought him after you passed out tackling him to the ground." Matt twitched his snout and lowered his gaze, looking a bit sheepish. "Thanks for that, by the way."

Trecheon shifted. "In fairness, you had saved me from a huge pile of falling debris." His ear twitched. "Why did you blow the mess away instead of me anyway? I weigh a lot less."

"That's kind of the reason why," Matt said. "It'd be way easy to hurt you." He glanced off. "I know from experience, unfortunately."

Trecheon furrowed his brow, but didn't question it. "And Ryota got away."

"I kind of encouraged him to," Matt said. "If he's really working for Theron, we'll see him again, and you needed help."

Trecheon shook his head. "You're going to have to tell me who this Theron person is."

"Basileus Theron. He's… complicated," Matt said. "The only thing that's really important is that he's the one who created the Cast." He shook his head. "He's also Ouranos' father."

Trecheon perked both ears in shock, then flattened them. "Ouch."

"Tell me about it," Matt said. "I don't know how good a look you got of Ouranos in the dark, but you'll notice he doesn't have pupils. That's not natural." Matt tapped the fur near his eyes. "Ouranos and Natassa have different focus jewels than we do, called Ei-Ei jewels. They're attached to their heads and they grant immortality."

Trecheon snorted. "I guess I should be glad I didn't get saddled with *that.*"

Matt smirked. "True. Either way, Theron did something to Ouranos' focus jewels, which allowed the Basileus to physically control him. He forced Ouranos to come to Zyearth and he used his powers there to create Cast."

"Hold on," Trecheon said. "You said he could *control* Ouranos? What, like a puppet?"

"That's an accurate description, yeah."

"He wasn't acting like a puppet when I saw him."

"No," Matt said. "He broke free of Theron's puppetry while on Zyearth."

Trecheon tilted his head. "How'd he do that?"

Matt pressed his lips together and splayed his ears. "That's… complicated too."

"You don't have to explain, Matt," the female fox said. Trecheon turned his head and saw her come in with his arms, good as… well, not new, but close enough, hopefully.

Matt slid carefully off the counter. "Trecheon, this is Sami."

She eyed him, dropping his right arm on the table near Matt. "Hi."

Trecheon frowned, furrowing his brow. "So does everyone in this Zyearth hate me because I'm Omnir? Does the red fur just boil you guys over or what?"

Sami leaned in near Trecheon's face and spoke in a whisper. "I think it's the *white* part of you that bothers me more."

HEALING

Trecheon's face flushed and his chest tightened.

White. She said *white*. Holy shit, she *knew*.

"What'd you say, Sami?" Matt asked, picking Trecheon's arm off the table.

"Nothing," Sami said. She shifted the left arm with surprising dexterity and faced Trecheon. "Ready?"

He shoved down panic and forced his breathing to slow. He gave Matt a glance, then met eyes with Sami. She gave him a subtle nod.

So. She was keeping his secret from Matt. Probably good, considering Matt already hated him for his murderous family. He didn't need Matt knowing he was an *actual* murderer. Matt would kill him on the spot. As much as he deserved it, that could not happen. Not today. Not when Neil was at stake. He shrugged casually, forcing his heart to slow. "Sure, ready."

Matt pressed the left arm near the slot and Sami did the same on his right. "On my count," Matt said. "One. Two. Three."

They pushed and both arms slid in nicely. Sami anchored his right arm and Trecheon flexed the fingers. Perfect. He reached over and anchored the left arm and tested it. Despite the damage they had taken, they actually looked and worked better than they had in months. Clean, smooth movements, perfect neural connection. "Gotta test one thing. Can you guys release the anchors again and hold the arms? Wanna check out the mental release command."

Matt and Sami both gripped the arms and Trecheon reached for them mentally. *Left arm, right arm, emergency release, passcode IAmTheWhiteAssassin.* Both arms detached cleanly. Trecheon sighed. Some part of him insisted he get that changed. But another said he deserved the mental anguish that came with the reminder. He flicked an ear back. "Thanks. You can push them back in now." They did so.

"I'm going to keep an eye out for Darvin," Sami said. "Call me if you need anything."

"Rest," Matt told her. She nodded and walked out.

"Wait a minute," Trecheon said. "We need to go find Neil."

"That's the plan," Matt said. "But let's heal up first or we'll be useless." Matt walked back to Trecheon's Gem on the counter, still twisting his wrapped shoulder in pain. He lifted the jewel from the wire holder, and took a deep breath before turning back to Trecheon.

Trecheon tried to keep himself from trembling.

Matt pressed his lips together a moment, then lightly shook his head and passed the Gem to Trecheon, plopping it in his open palm.

The Gem felt… different. It was like power and fear and chaos and order. It was almost like being alive. Or like he had the power to control life somehow. Maybe that's what healing did. He wasn't sure.

But more than anything, it felt comfortable. Like home. Like he was destined to have it. He quietly scoffed. The idea was ludicrous. He didn't deserve anything like that. He glanced over at Matt. The blue and white quilar still held himself stiff and tight, slightly trembling, ears not quite perky.

Time to try the diplomatic approach. "So," Trecheon said. "Damage your shoulder, did you?"

"My shoulder and my foot. Fighting Ryota," Matt said, his voice dripping with acid. Acid Trecheon knew could easily be turned on him. "Neither is broken, but it hurts like hell."

"Let me heal it then," Trecheon said. "Like you said, let's heal up. It'd be payback for you fixing my arms. I'll get your foot too."

"Fixing your arms was already paying you back for you tackling Ryota and saving me," Matt said. He rotated the damaged shoulder. "But I would be a lot more useful if I had the proper use of my shoulder and foot."

"And it'd be a good way to break this thing in," Trecheon said with a nod.

Matt pressed his lips together, eyeing Trecheon, but then shrugged. "Sure. Why not."

Trecheon put on a pleasant smile then slid off the table. He held a hand out, frowning. "So, uh, I guess I just touch your shoulder and think about healing or something?"

Matt shrugged. "I don't know, honestly. As I said, I'm not a healer. But I guess that's similar to how I control my magic, so give it a whirl."

Trecheon gingerly pressed his metal hand against Matt's damaged shoulder. "Here goes nothing." He closed his eyes and concentrated on the Gem at his side.

A tiny whine emitted from the Gem, and power surged through him. Under his fingers, he got impressions of the damage in Matt's shoulder, and he could "see" the injury being repaired in his mind's eye. The power continued rolling through him for several minutes until Trecheon couldn't feel any more damage. But as the power rolled through, so did his energy, and by the time he pulled his hand away, fatigue bit at him.

Matt rotated his shoulder and smiled. "Good as new! Not bad for a first timer."

"That takes a lot out of you," he said. "I feel slightly winded."

"I'm told that's normal," Matt said. "Most new Gem users overuse their magic."

"You say that like it's second-hand knowledge," Trecheon said, eyeing him a bit. "Does that mean you didn't?"

"Oh, I definitely did, but being Black Bound makes my Gem relationship way different," Matt said. "But that's a whole different dragon pit and I'd rather not get into it right now."

"Fair enough," Trecheon said. "Foot next, while I still feel confident."

Matt lifted his foot up on the table and Trecheon took care of that too. Matt sighed relief, then removed the bandages. "Thanks. That helps a lot."

"Anytime."

"So," Matt said, reaching down and putting his sock and shoe back on. "I suppose you want to try healing yourself?"

"That was one of the motivations for getting bound, yeah," Trecheon said. He reached a hand up to his damaged flesh near the shoulder mount, cupping the bandage there. He closed his eyes and tried pumping healing energy into it.

Nothing happened.

Trecheon furrowed his brow and tried again. Still nothing. The Gem refused to activate. What the hell?

Images of Izzy's bewildered and shocked face blew through his mind. The look of a zyfaunos who's Gem had just betrayed her.

Panic ripped at him. He tried again, desperate to get the thing to work. But again, nothing.

"It's not working." Trecheon's voice rose two octaves and he spoke too fast. "It's not working! Why isn't it working?"

Matt held his hands up. "Calm down!"

"Calm down?" Trecheon said. "What if my Gem is breaking? What if it's damaged like Izzy's Gem was? What if--"

"Wait, what?" Matt said. "Izzy's Gem is damaged?"

"Her healing powers weren't working," Trecheon said. "They were hurting people instead of healing. What if my Gem starts doing that? What if I lose control--"

"Trecheon, *calm down,*" Matt said. "Your Gem isn't damaged. In fact, it's doing exactly what it's supposed to do. Gems don't normally work on their users, remember? You're fine."

Trecheon shook, staring at Matt. "But--"

"It's fine," Matt said. He splayed an ear. "But Izzy isn't. We have to find her right now."

Someone pounded on the door of the plane.

Trecheon exchanged a glance with Matt. "Darvin."

"Matt?" Sami poked her head back in the small room. She had both ears flattened. "You might want to see this."

Matt frowned and left the room. Trecheon followed behind. As they stepped out of the plane, Trecheon saw Darvin splayed over the sand with his strange stag torso half out of the puddle, gleaming in the early morning light.

There was another puddle next to him too. A smaller one that couldn't quite hold together the same way Darvin did. Two strange white spheres floated to the surface of the puddle. Trecheon squinted, trying to figure out what they were.

A wave of disgust ground through his stomach. They were eyeballs.

"Ugh," Trecheon said, his stomach churning at the sight. "I think I'm going to be sick."

"I found her on the beach," Darvin said, waving an inky hand at the new puddle.

Matt frowned. "Her?"

"Yes," Darvin said. "This is Melaina. She's Ouranos' sister. And she knows where Izzy is."

CHAPTER 30

MELAINA

Darvin's words hit Matt's ears like a physical blow. Images of this same creature floated through his memory. Ouranos had unwittingly shared it with him on Zyearth when they had first bound their jewels.

Ouranos had said Melaina had a lot of the characteristics of a Cast, but wasn't fully formed. He hadn't known what that meant really… but now he did. "Draso's mercy."

"Ouranos' sister," Sami repeated. "Are you sure?"

The new puddle, Melaina, made a strange, high pitched, whistling gurgle. Very different than the normal Cast sounds.

Darvin glanced at her, then nodded. "I'm pretty confident, yeah."

"How?" Matt asked.

"I can understand her," Darvin said. "And when a Cast talks instead of attacks, you listen."

"Ouranos did say something about his sister as a Cast," Matt said. He leaned down to Melaina's height, since she didn't seem capable of rising out of her puddle like Darvin. "You can understand me?"

The puddle gurgled and whistled again.

"She says yes," Darvin said.

"And," Matt paused, taking in a deep breath. "You know where Izzy is?"

The puddle grew a slight bulge and affected a nod before collapsing in on itself.

Matt frowned. "She's having a hard time keeping herself together."

"She has a hard time speaking too," Darvin said. "I can only get broken speech."

A twinge of sympathy ran through Matt.

Trecheon moved on Matt's right. "…Sorry. I shouldn't have made that comment earlier."

Melaina gurgled politely.

Matt furrowed his brow. "Can you take us to Izzy and the others?"

Darvin affected a shrug. "She keeps talking about something called the Veil. I don't know what that is."

Melaina erupted into waves, gurgling loudly against the sand. Her eyeballs rolled over the top like rubber balls on the surface of a pool.

Matt suddenly understood Trecheon's desire to be sick.

"I heard you the first time," Darvin said with strained patience. His inky body went stiff. "But I don't know what the Veil is."

More gurgling from Melaina.

Darvin perked a curious inky ear. "What?"

"What'd she say?" Sami asked.

Darvin shook his head. "I'm still not sure I understand. It's.. it's like the Veil is something that prevents people getting to Athánatos. What?" he turned back to Melaina, whose rippling became even more urgent. Darvin frowned, his lips dripping. "Uh, so I guess that big island is Athánatos Island. And the Veil prevents people from just sailing up to it and getting on."

"We call it the Vanishing Island," Trecheon said. "And she's right, no one can sail up to it. Supposedly it's some big illusion. There's all kinds of idiotic cults and conspiracy theories surrounding it."

"Natassa called it that too," Sami said. "Crown of Trinity Islands. Apparently the science community can't explain it." She shrugged. "Guess I know why now. Makes sense."

Trecheon snorted. "Is it really real then? That doesn't make sense. How can you prevent people from getting on it?"

Matt eyed him with a frown, then nodded to his Gem.

Trecheon lifted a brow, following Matt's gaze. "Oh. Right. Magic. I forgot. Is Neil on the Vanishing Island?"

Melaina rippled at Darvin again.

"Rips?" Darvin cocked his head. "Um, okay, so I guess there are rips in the Veil? And somehow rips act like... uh, she keeps saying 'windows'... but I guess rips let people through the Veil and they can get to the island that way. And that's where the others are, I guess."

Trecheon growled. "Shit." He turned. "Melaina, what do rips look like?"

Melaina gurgled at Darvin. He rippled back at her. "She says they're like... waves in the air, or windows to parts of Athánatos Island. But... subtle, I guess? Almost invisible. You just have to know where they are."

Trecheon turned to Matt. "Do you think that's what Ryota was looking for in the Casino? A rip to get to the island?"

Matt flattened his ears. "I bet it was."

Darvin lowered his body into the black puddle. "Damnit."

"No one could have expected that to go smoothly with that many Cast," Matt said. He shook his head and turned to Melaina. "Can we get through the rip too?"

Melaina fell silent, then a slow ripple gurgled through her body.

Darvin frowned. "She says the rip collapsed. It's gone."

Matt cursed. "How do we get on the island?"

Melaina erupted in movement and gurgled excitedly. Darvin listened with interest, but then collapsed in on himself with a yelp.

Matt perked his ears forward as Darvin rebuilt himself. "What? What is it?"

Darvin only rose about two feet out of his puddle. "Melaina says there's another rip, one that's not likely to collapse."

Matt splayed one ear, dread building up in his chest. "Okay, where is it?"

"You're not going to like it," Darvin said.

"Just come out with it, Darvin," Matt said.

Darvin sighed, shaky and wet. "The rip is on Sol."

CHAPTER 31

RYOTA

Ryota stood in a corner of the underground room, a place he had dubbed "the lair" after all the weird stuff he had seen here. It was built like a super villain's secret base. High walled, ancient brick, thick pillars, dark, save for a few filtered sunbeams through slits in the ground-level roof and a handful of primitive torches in each corner. It smelled of dust and bronze and just… age. Like the smell he could expect if he took a tour of an ancient pyramid somewhere. Stale. Old. Dying.

He hated it. He hated every inch and nook and cranny. He hated being reminded of death.

Cast slithered along the walls and over the floors like the mindless, dirty souls they were, not really living, not really dead, oblivious of everything around them, including Ryota. That suited him just fine. He didn't like the reminder of what they were.

This is your soul when your body is stripped away. Theron told him this when Ryota had gotten his first glimpse of an imperfect Cast years ago during the War of Eons. He had only gotten to look for about two minutes before the half-formed creature exploded in a shower of black rain and screeching, ruined beyond repair.

He still shivered at the memory.

But that wouldn't be him. Because he wouldn't die. Theron had promised him that much. And once he gained immortality, he'd dedicate his everlasting life to ending Earth's orchestrates of wars. He and Theron would finally rid the planet of humans.

No one would ever have to die again.

Though getting the Athánatos king to keep his promise of everlasting life proved to be challenging.

"So the Guardians have come to Earth then," Theron said, pacing back and forth in the room between his slithering Cast.

"That's what he told me, yeah."

Ryota tried not to look too hard at Theron. The quilar's jet black fur, streaked with a rotten orange color, clashed with his angry, hateful silver eyes, and awkwardly shaped ears and long, tufted tail. Theron's not-quite-normal appearance only reminded Ryota of the graceless, unnatural shape of the Cast. The Athánatos king wore long, purple-blue pants with a white-lined *osaa,* a gold band across the collarbone, and little else.

The Basileus' arms were also covered wrist-to-shoulder in woven bracelets, each containing a set of Athánatos Ei-Ei jewels – soul jewels stolen from Athánatos warriors to create the Drifters. One of those, Ryota knew, belonged to Ouranos, though he'd never tried to guess which one.

Ryota scrunched his face. *We are borrowing a few lives for the sake of many,* Theron had said. Sacrificial lambs.

But still.

"Interesting," the Basileus said. "To come after me without a way to fight the Cast. They are foolhardy it seems." He launched into a detailed plan, but Ryota's mind wandered to Trecheon.

Ryota flattened his ears. Why did he have to get dragged into this? He was done thinking about his brother. His betrayal, his desire to run full force into the war. Ryota had promised himself that if he ever saw Trecheon again, he would kill him. It was his brother's fault that Ryota had lost his comrades in war.

But even now, he couldn't convince himself to do it. Trecheon was his little brother. He couldn't... he couldn't kill him. Hell, he couldn't even convince himself to throw a decently charged lightning bolt at him earlier, and even now he cringed thinking about his brother lying motionless in the casino. Death loomed over him.

Ryota gritted his teeth, squeezing his eyes shut.

Hopefully Trecheon was dead. Then Ryota wouldn't have to deal with him anymore.

Ryota formed a fist. In fairness, Ryota should never have been on the mainland. He had been taking infrequent nightly trips to gather up more zyfaunos for Cast, though that became less and less of a thing after Theron had turned the entire population of Athánatos.

Though there was always the chance he'd get a human. That was the prize Theron really wanted. A shame humans never explored the old strip.

But then Ryota had let it slip that there was a serial killer in the city. The White Assassin. Theron wanted all the information he could get on him, meaning Ryota's visits were far more frequent. *He will be a fabulous ally,* Theron had said.

Ryota had never gathered much though. The newspapers and the police were stumped. Or, like the papers suggested, they were happy to let the White Assassin take out the city's corruption. He only got snippets of this guy – he was good at tracking, frequently jumped between bloodless kills and high-powered firearms, probably to avoid a distinctive pattern, and only went after corrupt targets. Matron Fawn's death had eventually been attributed to the White Assassin. That had been a blow. Ryota had all but convinced her to join the cause. She and her money and power would have been invaluable. Her sisters cut off all ties with him after her death.

"Ryota, are you listening?" Theron said.

Ryota shook himself. "Sorry. What was that?"

Theron ran a hand over one of the inky Cast near his feet. "The Cast managed to drag my children through the Veil?"

"And the golden quilar and Neil too," Ryota said. "They're not far from here."

Theron glanced at Ryota, brow furrowed. "You did not capture them."

"How could I?" Ryota protested. "The rip in the Great Pyramid collapsed and they were already long gone by the time I found another one." Ryota snorted. "The other rip dropped me in the Gardens. I couldn't fight all of them anyway. Too many magic users."

Theron scoffed. "This is why I have yet to give you immortality," he said. "You cannot hold your own against other mages. You are too weak to hold the Ei-Ei Jewels' power."

Ryota frowned. That was always the excuse. But time was running short. He needed more practice, damn it, and mages were hard to find on Earth. "Theron--"

"I need the golden brown quilar," Theron said. "She is also Black Bound and far stronger than you. She is a necessary piece in this puzzle."

Ryota flattened his ears. "Let me go get her," he said. "I'm strong enough for that. She's just a healer." And he could prove he was worthy of the Ei-Ei jewels.

"No," Theron said. He opened a thick book on a pedestal, something he often did while thinking. Ryota never had figured out how to read the runes in it. "I will send the Drifters after Ouranos and his allies."

Ryota shivered. If there was even one thing creepier than the bodiless souls of the Cast, it was the soulless bodies of the Drifters. Empty shells. Worse than that. Mindless zombie puppets that didn't react to pain and did whatever Theron told them. Ryota didn't quite understand how he puppeted them with the Soul Jewels on his bracelets, but whenever Theron called them, the colored jewels lit up. Creepy as shit.

"You know, I'm sick of waiting for what you promised me," Ryota said. He kept a cool head, but his body shook with worry.

Theron narrowed his eyes. "After all I have done for you, you still question me."

Ryota flicked his ears back. "If you would just--"

"I have bought you time with your Lexi Gem," Theron said. "A priceless gift that I specifically chose you for. You will get what you asked, but you must be patient."

Ryota flicked his ears back. "But--"

"It is not up for discussion," Theron said. "I have done what I can for you. You need more strength."

"But how do I get it?" Ryota said. "You keep saying that, but you haven't told me *how.*"

Theron stomped a foot and the area lit up with lightning, fire, and ice. Ryota stepped back. Holy *shit.*

Theron eyed him. "Soon. If you prove yourself to me. Until then, enjoy the power and long life from that gift."

Ryota held his hands up, flattening his ears. Some gift.

Theron had first approached Ryota with the Gem not long after he had entered Canada with Outlander during the War of Eons, promising eternal life in exchange for help taking down the human regime that had kept zyfaunos down for so long. Ryota had been giddy with glee. Magic and long life? A way to cheat death? He'd taken him up on it immediately.

Theron had promised the Gem binding would be painless.

It wasn't.

He had given Ryota a colorless Gem, then immediately bombarded him with every element known to Earth. Ryota panicked and the Gem reacted, binding to him. The pain was unimaginable, and his whole world turned red and black while he fought it. When it finally subsided, he was actually perfectly fine. No more pain, no magic scars. And he had a Gem.

Theron had apologized. Apparently it was the strongest way to bind. Black Binding, he'd called it after Ouranos' trip to Zyearth. Theron told Ryota after the bind that most didn't survive the process. Theron claimed his survival made him the chosen one, one that would take down the human regime. He didn't buy into that "chosen one" bullshit, but surviving Black Binding meant Ryota could survive anything.

Then they'd gotten to work. Training, practicing, fighting, forcing the Gem to reveal its magic. Just two months after the bind, Ryota's Gem granted him powerful electric magic.

Then the black elixir started forming on his hands.

"This is proof that you have potential," Theron had said. *"That your power could be limitless. But only if you produce more."*

It was just droplets at first. Tiny black beads barely bigger than a grain of rice. But that was apparently what Theron wanted. He pushed Ryota to make more. Which he did... eventually.

But it wasn't enough. It was *never* enough.

He had managed to use what he could get to turn a couple of captives in war. For a few minutes. Black ink oozing out of every orifice, drowned in gurgling screams. The stuff of nightmares. Most exploded and died within minutes. None survived longer than an hour or so.

Then Theron sent Ouranos to Zyearth. A month and a half later and suddenly he was harvesting every tiny ounce of the black liquid from Ryota. Draso's horns, it had been so exhausting.

Then… Theron started to turn the island's inhabitants. He had insisted it was necessary to go after the humans on the mainland. Ryota's quills stood on end.

Think of something else.

"Then what do you want me to do?" he asked.

"You will go to Sol," Theron said. "There is a rip in the Veil there. Few know about it, but at least one of our enemies has knowledge about its location."

Ryota raised an eyebrow. "Who? The mainlanders don't even know about the Veil, let alone about the rips. They think Athánatos is an optical illusion."

"My daughter, Melaina," Theron said. "She knows and she is somewhere on the mainland. I do not know if she can communicate its location to the Guardian Matthew, or if he will even listen, but I cannot take the chance. If either Guardian learns the location, that is likely where they will head next. Protect the Veil." He gave Ryota a stern look. "And finish what your ancestors started."

Ryota refrained from rolling his eyes. This guy sure had an ear for dramatics. "You're sending me on a babysitter's chore."

Theron shrugged. "If you think it will be too much for you…"

"I'll go, I'll go," Ryota said.

"Good." Theron turned to a wall of shelves, each full of bottles containing the refined form of the Black Bound elixir – Cast charms. There had to be thousands of them at this point.

Ryota pressed his lips together. *Yup. Glorified babysitting.* He bounced a salute off his temple. "I'm out then."

"Ryota."

Ryota turned back.

Every Soul jewel glowed at once, bathing Theron in an eerie multi-colored light, giving him a demonic, haunted look. "Do not fail me."

Ryota hunched down, splaying his ears. "Right…"

Theron nodded and turned back to the wall of charms.

Ryota narrowed his eyes. Screw this shit. He wasn't going to go unprepared. When Theron turned his head, he snatched up a bottle of the Cast charms. He needed backup. And he knew just where to get it. Time to head for the dungeons. Make a few Cast for himself.

Sacrifice a few for the good of the many.

Hardening his resolve, he tested his ability to call lightning to his fingertips and walked off.

This… this was temporary.

This was war.

CHAPTER 32

CHRISTIAN

"I still don't understand why we're here," Darvin said, rippling his anger across his inky Cast body. "This is a waste of time."

Trecheon glanced at Matt in the side car of Neil's bike, watching his strained expression. He seemed like he was trying very hard not to be sick as Darvin slithered his awkward Cast body out of his lap. Trecheon held in a smirk.

After learning about the Veil from Melaina, Trecheon had insisted that he was going with the group to Sol. He had to find Neil. But first he insisted they visit his garage. He had led Matt and the others to Neil's beat up chopper, hoping Neil had left the keys. Which he had. Typical.

The vehicle only had two seats, but Matt refused to let Trecheon go off on his own, especially because Theron would be looking for him.

And Darvin refused to let Matt go off with Trecheon alone. He spent the whole ride over laying across Matt's legs like the spawn of some blobby monster from an 80s horror flick. It took all Trecheon's will power not to burst out laughing at Matt's obvious discomfort.

"It's not a waste of time," Trecheon said, dismounting the bike. "For one, it's Tuesday and I need to close up shop and put up a sign--"

"--As if your business means anything with what we're facing--" Darvin snorted.

"--*And,* I have something that will help us get across the bay," Trecheon continued, glaring at the black puddle. "Because you sure as hell aren't getting that massive plane on that tiny island with no clear space to land. And somehow you space aliens didn't have the foresight to bring boats."

"It's a *space-faring plane,*" Darvin said. "Of course it doesn't have boats."

"Like I said." Trecheon grinned. "Lack of foresight." He waved his hand. "Come on."

He led them to the front of the garage and pulled out his key. But when he slipped the key into the lock, the door slid open. He frowned.

"*Jefe?* Is that you?" Christian's voice sounded from inside the office. The young Latino sounded worried. Not surprising, since the shop should have been open over an hour ago.

Draso's horns. Christian had a key. And he opened today.

"Stay back," Trecheon hissed at Darvin and he gave a warning glare to Matt. "It's me, Christian. Sorry."

"*Dios mio,* Boss," Christian said, worry painted over his tanned face. "Where the hell have you been? You live upstairs, for God's sake!" He eyed Matt with a raised eyebrow. "And who's this?"

Matt had crossed the room and was looking at Trecheon's makeshift war memorial on the wall. Trecheon kept a glare suppressed.

"It's been an… interesting night," Trecheon said. "I'm going to be out of the shop for today. Maybe for a couple of days, I don't know. You're in charge for the time being, okay?"

"And…?" Christian nodded his head toward Matt.

"Don't worry about him," Trecheon said. He rolled his shoulders, trying to make the discomfort go away. "You know the drill. Just keep tabs on the customers and I'll be back soon as."

"Heavens, *Jefe,* what happened to your shoulders?" Christian stared wide eyed at the damage on Trecheon's still-exposed shoulders. Trecheon silently cursed, wishing he would have thought to demand a new shirt from Matt.

"It's nothing," Trecheon said.

"It's not *nothing,* " Christian said. "You're practically smoking!"

Trecheon growled under his breath. "I've got it under control, okay? I don't have time to explain right now."

"Boss," Christian said, lowering his voice and gazing at him with a worried frown. "This has been happening a lot. This going off for a couple of days. What's going on?"

Trecheon frowned. "It's complicated." He chanced a glance at Matt to see if he'd heard, but the white, blue-tipped quilar seemed engrossed in the war memorial. Good. The last thing he needed was Matt getting wise to his other profession. Or Christian for that matter. Had he mentioned anything about his suspicions the other morning when they'd discussed the newspaper article about the White Assassin? He couldn't recall.

But for now, he had to get Christian thinking about something else, and hopefully Matt, if he had heard anything. "Do me a favor." He reached over the desk and pulled out a work order. "I've got a part for one of the hydrogen cars that should be ready for pick up now. I'd normally get it myself, but this issue out-of-town needs taking care of now. Call it a family emergency." Because going after Ryota and finding Neil counted, he thought.

Christian crossed his arms. "You don't have any living family."

Matt perked an ear. He pressed his lips together and wrinkled his snout. Trecheon cursed internally.

"I have Neil," Trecheon said. "He's as good as, and he needs me for something. That good enough?"

Christian frowned and glanced back at Matt, still absorbed in the war memorial, before reaching over Trecheon's ancient desk for the work order. "Sure, Boss."

"And here." Trecheon pulled out a twenty and passed it to Christian. "I know you tend to skip breakfast on days that you open. Lemmie buy this time. I vote for Tam's Donuts, but get whatever you're in the mood for."

Christian eyed him, almost sad. "Yeah. Tams. Sure." He headed out into the garage, shutting the door behind him. Trecheon managed a sigh of relief.

"Protective of you, isn't he?" Darvin said, slipping his inky body under the door.

"He's one of mine, so yes," Trecheon said. "Good mechanics are as good as family."

"So this is Carter," Matt mumbled, and Trecheon heard the familiar sound of the unprotected dog tag clinking. Trecheon turned and saw Matt running his hand over the tag and chain.

Trecheon wrinkled his snout and frowned. "In the most literal sense, since that's all that's left of him. He's MIA."

Matt flattened his ears. "Sorry."

"Don't be," Trecheon replied. "It's not like it's your fault."

"Still," Matt said. "You must have been close if you got his tag instead of his family."

Trecheon sat hard in the beaten old chair behind his desk, rummaging through the drawers for a set of keys. This was not the time to be exploring his friendship with Carter. "You might say that."

"What's this note mean?" Matt pointed to Carter's note, squinting, as if studying the handwriting.

Trecheon shrugged. "Hell if I know. Carter left it with me."

"He didn't tell you?"

"Found it in my pocket with the dog tag after Carter went MIA," Trecheon said. "So no."

Matt eyed him with a frown, but didn't say anything.

Good, because Trecheon couldn't muster the effort to discuss it. At least it seemed that he had successfully gotten Matt's mind off Christian's question about his mysterious disappearances. Hopefully, anyway.

He found the keys he was looking for, then stood. "Wait here. I'm going to change and pick up a few supplies. Be back soon." He turned without waiting for a reply and trekked upstairs.

Damn it all. Matt had to bring up Carter. Especially when some deeply suppressed memory still insisted that Matt looked like him. If only he had a picture, a memento, *something*, that reminded him of what Carter looked like. But their records had been wiped clean when the war was over, or they had at least been put at so high a security level that Trecheon no longer had access to it.

Trecheon stripped off his ruined shirt and threw it in a bin.

His black ops team hadn't exactly been one hundred percent legitimate. Most of his team had been wiped completely – names, pictures, occupations, birthdates, war exploits. Only Neil and Trecheon had escaped the worst of it. Trecheon, for his "miracle" arms, Neil for his prowess as a sniper.

And his notorious PTSD case.

But Carter wasn't there at all. He couldn't even find his likeness in newspapers, or in the program for the MIA Mass. His name was all over the place, since he was the one who had pulled Trecheon to safety after his double amputation, but there wasn't a single picture anywhere.

Despite everything Carter had done for him, Trecheon had somehow mentally blocked him out. He could only recall vague images. White. Blue. Green. Melded together in some dirty, blurred blob.

Guess that could be expected when war stripped you of huge chunks of yourself. He threw on a new shirt, snatched up his spare bike jacket, and stuffed supplies in a shoulder bag. Hell, Trecheon never even got the chance to talk to Neil about it.

Draso's mercy, Neil had better be okay after all this mess.

CHAPTER 33

THE BASILEUS

Ouranos stood in front of Izzy and Natassa with Roscoe the Cast and Neil the puma at his sides, still fighting off a few remaining Cast in a dense, familiar forest of pines and scrub oak. Roscoe beat back the Cast borrowing Darvin's whip technique and Neil had Izzy's hammer. He had no technique as she did, but he did have strength, and he easily broke the puddles apart, if just for a little while. Roscoe and Neil seemed to keep their focus well, but Ouranos was fighting panic.

"Hey, magician, watch yourself!" Neil shouted.

Ouranos turned and shot a wild blast of fire at a flying Cast. He growled. "Natassa, how is Isabelle?"

"She is coming to," Natassa said, though her voice betrayed worry.

Ouranos turned back to the Cast as the last few retreated against his fire. Though he knew his fire was not actually affecting the Cast. They acted as if it did, but somehow being on the island increased their strength.

Ouranos took a deep breath. As if these were not problem enough, he could not summon. A cold emptiness enveloped him.

He had tried communicating with Matt, but could only find dull colors – violet worry, blue unease, gray distrust. Also a violent, but suppressed red anger. But nothing specific, and no words, leaving him with a hopeless, empty feeling.

A gurgling, piercing whistle sounded faintly through the trees.

"They're running," Neil said. He frowned, watching them go off, his tail twitching. "What the hell happened?"

Ouranos watched them run. What indeed?

"Ugh," Izzy muttered. "My head. What happened?"

Ouranos turned. Izzy sat up with Natassa at her side. He frowned at them both and kneeled. "Isabelle. How do you feel?"

A voice in his mind. *Bring her to me.*

Ouranos held his eyes shut a moment. His father. Calling to him again. Strings severed or not, Theron still had Ouranos' Soul Jewels and would attempt to use them.

Ouranos would not obey. He refused.

Izzy blinked at him, then rolled her eyes. "*Izzy,* Ouranos. We've been over this."

Ouranos allowed himself a smile. "Yes, ma'am."

Izzy glanced around. "Anyone seen my hammer?"

"Here." Neil handed it to her. "That thing is heavy as shit. I could barely lift it. I don't know how you handle it like you do."

"Decades of practice," Izzy said. She took the hammer and stood. "Thanks. What happened to your rifle?"

"Hell if I know," Neil said. "I lost it when that Cast attacked me." He glanced around. "Where in God's name are we?"

Natassa looked around at the pine trees and pasted her ears back. "Oh, no."

Ouranos shook his head. "Unfortunately, yes, Natassa." He turned to Neil. "We are on Athánatos Island. Our home."

Your prison.

Ouranos snarled at the voice. *No.*

Neil raised a skeptical brow. "What?"

"I believe you mainlanders call it the Vanishing Island," Natassa said.

Neil lashed his tail, holding his hands up. "Whoa, whoa, *whoa.* That's not possible. The Vanishing Island is just an optical illusion. It's not real."

Izzy looked around, just as Roscoe curled up in his inky form around her feet. "Looks pretty real to me."

"But how did we even *get* here?" Neil said. "They call it the Vanishing Island because if you sail too close, it literally *disappears.* "

"It is the Veil." Ouranos stood, trying to mentally push his father aside without drawing attention to himself. "It protects the island from unwanted visitors. The only way to the island is to enter through a rip in the Veil."

A rip in your mind.

Ouranos clenched his jaw. *My mind is my own!*

"Ouranos," Natassa said, frowning up at him. "If there are rips in public places…"

Ouranos took a deep breath and counted to five before responding. "I know, Natassa."

Neil frowned. "What?"

"Rips are carefully monitored and repaired, if possible," Ouranos said. "But that is usually the job of the royal family. We regularly patrol to check for and repair them to keep them under control. But with all of us absent…"

You abandoned them.

A wave of shame set his fur on end, but Ouranos tried to keep his expression steady.

Neil blinked at him. "You said 'we.'"

Ouranos nodded, mentally gripping for control over his own thoughts. "I did. Natassa and I are members of the royal family."

Neil held a hand to his forehead. "Okay, we're gonna need to cool it with the shattering worldviews for a while."

"Understandable," Ouranos said. He glanced at Natassa. "We need to get back to Matthew and the others."

Izzy glanced behind her. "Can we get back the way we came in?"

Ouranos frowned. He walked behind her, waving a hand in front of him, looking for signs of the rip. A blur of trees, a shimmer of magic, a feeling of brokenness, a scene of the beach. Nothing. The rip was gone. "It appears to have collapsed."

"Can we contact the others and let them know where we are?" Neil asked. "Trecheon will lose his shit if we don't."

Izzy pulled up her pendant and pressed her thumb to the back of the dragon. She played with the holographic controls for a moment, then pasted her ears back. "No can do. There's something interfering with the signal. The Veil, perhaps. I can't even see his biosigns nearby. Or the planes."

"I have tried contacting him myself, but with no luck," Ouranos said. "Something is blocking our connection."

Natassa pasted her ears back. "I... I tried calling on Excelsis and Deo but... they are not answering me."

Ouranos flicked his tail. "Nor are Jústi and Pax." Natassa's expression darkened.

The phoenixes were exclusive summons to the Athánatos royalty, bound by a willful oath many, many generations ago. Only one thing could break that oath and separate the Phonar from the royal family – if one royal willfully killed another royal. By their oath, the Phonar's pact would break and the phoenixes would be free to leave their charges.

It was one of the things that had stayed Ouranos' hand when fighting the Basileus during his war with him – killing Theron meant losing the Phonar. Losing the Phonar meant losing necessary allies against those who created Cast.

The fear was so deep that it had enveloped Ouranos' mind since the war started, especially when the Basileus showed every intent to kill his children. Theron had no qualms about losing the Phonar.

Their sudden absence sent chills down his spine.

Bring the golden quilar to ME.

Ouranos staggered, gripping his head. *No! She is my friend. My charge.*

You destroyed her life. You killed her father.

Ouranos faltered, feeling the truth of it. Ouranos had coerced the Omnir into attacking Sol. He initiated the genocide that took Izzy's father from her.

He shook his head. *No. That was you. You forced my hand.*

You failed to protect them.

Ouranos growled. *Then I will die protecting her!*

You will die alone.

Natassa stood slowly. "Ouranos. Father."

Come to me. Bring them to me! This is your prison!

Ouranos shut his eyes tight and gritted his teeth. "I… I hear him, Natassa."

Izzy stood now. "Ouranos?"

"The Basileus," he said, meeting Izzy's eyes. He could not lie to her. Not now. "I hear him in my head."

Everyone stared at him, including Roscoe. He flattened his ears.

Izzy shifted, but she would not avert her eyes. She gripped his shoulder in a firm, but friendly gesture. "Are you going to be okay?"

She does not care for you. Should she discover your hand in her father's death, she would kill you herself.

Ouranos shut his father out. Izzy would never do that. Not after all they had been through. She cared too much.

No one cares for you.

But that was not true. And that he could cling to.

"I think I will be," he said finally. "For the time being." He eyed Izzy and Natassa. "But if things get out of hand..."

Roscoe suddenly stood as tall as his Cast form allowed him, forming a semi-solid stag body. His three blue eyes and furrowed brow affected a look of determination. He pushed himself between Ouranos and Natassa and gurgled something unintelligible. But the message got through anyway.

He is not strong enough, the Basileus insisted.

But he was. Ouranos smiled. "Roscoe, it would honor me to call on your protection should the need arise."

The Cast-stag nodded once before collapsing into the dirt once more. Though Ouranos thought he caught a glimpse of a smile. He turned to Izzy. "Roscoe will hold me should the Basileus take control. Does that satisfy you?"

Izzy glanced at Roscoe, but smiled. She nodded.

Neil blinked at them both. "Take control? What the hell does that mean?"

Ouranos exchanged glances with Natassa and Izzy.

Izzy wrinkled her snout. "You wanted to avoid more worldshatterings, Neil."

Neil twitched an ear. "Never mind then. What with the magic and the attacking puddles and visiting an island that isn't real, my life is complicated enough right now. Tell me some other time." He crossed his arms. "What are we going to do next?"

-bring them to me-embrace your prison-come to me-you cannot fight-

Ouranos flexed his claws. "We are leaving. Now."

CHAPTER 34

TRUST

By the time Trecheon collected his gear, changed his dirty clothing, and headed downstairs, Christian had returned with the part and donuts and was sitting in his chair in the office, tossing suspicious glances at Matt. Matt apparently chose to ignore him by sitting on the grimy customer couch, flipping through one of the car mechanic magazines Trecheon had lined on the corner table. The donuts sat on the counter near the coffee pot.

Trecheon frowned, staring at Matt. "Do you even know what anything means in that magazine?"

Matt glanced at him over the magazine with a flattened ear and a lifted brow. "I repaired your arm mounts and you have to ask if I know anything about mechanics?" He reached for a donut.

"*Jefe,*" Christian said, never taking his eyes off Matt. "Who is this guy?"

"An asshole," Trecheon said, forcing every ounce of sarcasm into his voice as possible. "Don't worry about it. You got my part?"

Christian shrugged. "They weren't happy passing it off to me, but yeah, I did."

"Great, thanks."

Christian furrowed his brow. "Boss…"

"It's fine, Christian," Trecheon said. Matt gave him a look over the magazine. Trecheon rolled his eyes. "Okay, it's not really fine. Not yet. Neil needs help. But it's under control. Try not to worry too much."

"Kind of hard not to, Trecheon," Christian said.

Trecheon schooled his face at Christian's use of his name. He shook his head. "Just trust me. You can trust me, right?"

Christian smirked. "Like you've ever given me a reason to."

Trecheon crossed his arms. "Funny."

"I trust you, Boss." Christian stood, rigid and uncomfortable. "Just take care of yourself. Okay?"

Trecheon blinked. "Um. Yeah, sure. I'll do that."

"Good." He gave Matt one more suspicious look, which Matt studiously ignored, then snatched up the work orders for the day. "I'm going to make some phone calls. Let me know if you need anything."

"Sure."

Christian let out a sigh, snatched a donut out of the box, then settled into the office chair.

Trecheon flipped an ear back, then motioned Matt into the garage. Darvin stealthily snuck past Christian and followed them both. The door slammed louder than Trecheon intended.

"So," Matt said, turning to Trecheon. "What's this miracle way of getting us across the channel to Sol?"

Trecheon eyed him. Matt had a determinedly blank face, devoid of emotional content.

"It's not a miracle," Trecheon said, a worm of worry crawling through his belly. "I just happen to have a couple of jet skis and a trailer in the garage that a customer left behind about a year ago. They're top quality, so they should get us across with no problem." He pointed. "See? There."

Matt lifted an eyebrow and glanced over the skis. "You really think these things are gonna get all of us to the island? There's five of us."

"Two of us are puddles," Trecheon said. Darvin flipped him an inky black finger.

"Sure," Matt said. He poked at the gas cap. "These things use… what's the word… petrol?"

Trecheon raised one eyebrow. "Yeah, so?"

"How far will one tank get us?"

"Not far enough," Trecheon said. "But I'll bring a spare gas can for each."

"To refuel in the middle of choppy channel waters."

"You got any other bright ideas, space alien?" Trecheon said. "I don't have a boat and ferries are forbidden. Unless your magic can fly us across, I don't see any alternative."

Matt leaned against one. "And how are you going to tow them to shore? That old bike of yours won't cut it."

"It's not my bike, it's Neil's," Trecheon said automatically.

"Still can't haul anything."

"I've got a truck," Trecheon said, trying to keep his irritation under control. "We'll use that."

Matt sighed. "Fine. Guess we're stuck then. Hope you can swim if things go south." He stretched. "Let's hook them up."

Trecheon frowned. Refusing to let Matt unnerve him, he went into the vehicle yard and hauled out the truck.

"So." Matt crossed his arms. "Can I ask a question?"

"You just did, asshat," Trecheon snapped. He hopped out of the cab and leaned down near the tow hook on the back of the bed. "Why stop now?"

"Where *have* you been going off for days at a time?"

Shit. Matt had been listening to Christian's questions. Trecheon forced himself to keep working on the tow hook and spoke as casually as possible. "Nowhere important."

"If it was nowhere important, you would have told Christian," Matt countered. "He's as good as family, right?"

Trecheon narrowed his eyes. "You tell your family everything, space alien?"

"Of course not," Matt said. "But the stuff I keep from them are usually secrets I don't want anyone knowing." He leaned forward with raised eyebrows.

"Is there a point to this conversation or are you just looking for more reasons to hate me?" Trecheon snarled. "Neil is in trouble. Your friends are in trouble. We left them fighting literal invincible monsters somehow being controlled by my idiotic and dangerous brother and supposedly some evil mage with powers beyond my wildest imagination. We don't have time for you to fish for incriminating evidence with pointless questions." And Trecheon couldn't afford to give Matt any reason to keep him from finding his brother or Neil.

The insides of Matt's ears colored, but he wrinkled his snout and bent an ear back. "I'm not trying to look for reasons to hate you. But the Defenders had been investigating you for some reason. Sami was part of it, but she won't say why. Either she really doesn't know or she doesn't want to tell me. But if there's some shady thing you're involved in that's going to cause problems for us, I'd like to know now."

"Well, there's not," Trecheon shot back, though his skin crawled. They had been investigating him? Good Draso. Corrupt El Dorado police and inept

FBI agents he could handle, but he'd never escape if an intergalactic military with wild space magic decided they wanted him dead.

Well. Maybe that served him right. Assassin and grandchild to genocidal maniacs.

He shook his head and pointed. "Just grab that side of the trailer and help me get these skis attached, okay? Like it or not, you need to trust me."

"For now," Matt agreed, and lifted his side of the trailer.

Trecheon hooked the trailer to the truck and let out a sigh Matt couldn't see. He had dodged that bullet. He grabbed a couple of gas cans, filled both skis, then attached additional cans to them.

He tossed one more glance toward the office. Christian still sat at the desk, but he kept his gaze on Trecheon as they left the garage, an anxious frown on his face.

HOME

Izzy followed Ouranos and Natassa as they trekked through an extremely thick forest of pine and oak. The smell of sap from both trees hung in the air like perfume. They had been walking for nearly two hours, trying to stay silent to avoid attracting any Cast. The heavy scent and dark shadows from the trees reminded Izzy strongly of the forest in the Corinth Dead Zone back home on Zyearth. The same place where she had lost Matt for the first time.

Also the same place where she had met Cast for the first time. She didn't appreciate the association or reminder. She gripped her hammer tighter.

"Ouranos," Izzy said quietly. "How much farther to the palace?"

"Not far," Ouranos said.

Neil pushed a pine branch aside. "So, someone wanna fill me in on why we're going *toward* the evil mage king's lair instead of away from it?"

"There is a permanent rip in the Veil that we keep for the purposes of leaving the island, should the need arise," Ouranos said. He paused a minute and grabbed his head, groaning. The moment passed and he shook his head.

"It is the only rip that we can know for sure exists, and it is our surest way of escaping and seeking help before confronting the Basileus."

Natassa twitched her tail, and gripped her brother's shoulder. "Ouranos."

"I am fine, Natassa," Ouranos said. "He does not have control over me."

Natassa splayed an ear, but said nothing more.

Izzy frowned and flicked her ears back. Despite everything, a sudden longing for her own, loving, happy father rose in her chest.

He had died on one of these very islands. The longing vanished in favor of deep, primal aching.

She had never thought she'd come back to Earth. Zyearth didn't have any more ties here, and being a silent planet meant there was no reason for anyone to visit again. It was only after they met the Athánatos that suddenly there was a need to come back. She had always known Matt still had grieving to do here. He had been older. He remembered more. But as she thought about her father's death, the Sol genocide, the destruction of so many lives…

Maybe she had some ghosts that needed laying to rest too.

Some more recent. "Ouranos?"

Ouranos paused and turned. "Yes?"

"I… I want to apologize," she said. "For… for what I did to the Cast."

Ouranos' eyes widened a moment, then he frowned, furrowing his brow. His ears flattened. "You did what was necessary."

"It doesn't mean I shouldn't apologize," Izzy said. "I… I killed innocent Athánatos. It doesn't matter if it was necessary. It's still a problem. They're still your subjects." She took a deep breath. "I know an apology doesn't fix it, but…" her voice trailed. She should say more, but she couldn't find the words.

Ouranos' face softened. He took a deep breath and pulled Izzy into a side hug. She leaned into him, taking in the warmth. "Your apology is accepted," he said. "But for now, let us continue. We can discuss this later, should we deem it necessary." He broke the hug and continued on.

Izzy nodded. "Sure."

"So," Neil said, breaking the uncomfortable conversation. "You said you were royalty, yes?"

"That is correct," Ouranos corrected. "And by law, our father is king."

Neil pasted both ears back. "You mean the voice you hear in your head?"

"The very same."

Neil gritted his teeth in a frown and scrunched his snout, baring a fang in disgust. "Ouch."

"You have no idea," Izzy said.

Neil waved a hand. "Anyway." He gestured around the woods. "If you have a king, then there must be a kingdom, yeah?"

"You are standing in it, yes," Ouranos said.

"So where are your subjects?"

Ouranos paused. Natassa flattened her ears. They exchanged worried glances.

Suddenly the silence felt much more sinister. Izzy stepped forward. "Ouranos?"

Ouranos turned to Neil. "Your question is not unfounded." He chewed his lip. "The Cast we saw briefly returned were all Athánatos quilar. I... do not like the implications that sets."

"...I don't either," Izzy said. "Are we close to the palace?"

"We are," Ouranos said. "And we should have met a sentry by this point."

"Or at least other Athánatos," Natassa said. "We are not sparsely populated, and you will often find children exploring the woods." She chewed her bottom lip. "With my father on the warpath and what we saw with the Cast, I suppose we could forgive the lack of Athánatos in the woods, but the sentries..."

Izzy pressed her lips together. "Obviously something's wrong."

"Something is," Ouranos said. "Stay close as we approach the palace."

Izzy nodded. Thinking back to the Cast she had killed, she reached for her Gem. The moment she touched it, inky black ran up her fingers, staining her fur. She let it go, glaring at the jewel as if it was sentient and working against her. *You always did want offensive powers.* The Gem gleamed at her, almost smugly.

"What's this?" Neil asked. Izzy lifted her head.

Three statues covered in moss and dirt sat scattered in a strange half-circle among the pines. Standing about three meters tall, they looked like Athánatos quilar, only… stylized. One wore a thick cloak covering their eyes and body. Another wore a veil over their face that fell all the way to their feet. The final had huge chunks of their body missing… though this was clearly by design, as the holes left behind were cleanly cut and thoughtfully placed. Once again, the face was missing. The statue also had massive cracks in it, not part of the design, like it was falling apart.

All of them were feminine looking. Each had a plate with runes on their base, though Izzy couldn't begin to understand them. A fourth base stood between two of them, but it had no statue – just a haphazard pile of marble and stone fragments. The top of a shield covered a broken face, leaning against the base.

Natassa drew her hand to her mouth. "Sister's alive… The Seal."

Izzy turned. "The what?"

"The broken statue," Natassa said.

"Did it break during the war, Natassa?" Ouranos asked.

"I cannot recall," Natassa said. She picked up a piece and ran it between her fingers. She turned to the statue with holes in it. "The Purge seems to be nearing the edge of her life too."

"What are they?" Neil asked.

"The Four Sisters," Ouranos said. "They have been here since the dawn of our civilization. Evidence of the first battle with… well, an ancient enemy that we do not have time to discuss. However, it does mean we are close to our destination."

Natassa dropped her marble pebble. "There." Her calm voice soothed away Izzy's worry. Izzy looked up where the princess pointed.

The sight took her breath away.

Across a small field of clovers and tiny white and yellow flowers, spread between monster trees like ghosts in the mist, stood the Athánatos palace. Long, open air rooms and halls stretched through the forest, making way for tree clumps and scattered fountains. Tall pillars with silver gilding held up ceilings and cool shadows invited visitors deeper into the palace. Large, elaborate statuary depicting images of Draso, his Son, Kai, and various ArchDragons from Draso's scripture towered as tall as the pillars, dwarfing the palace. Somewhere in the center, a thin trail of smoke rose, bathing the area in a pleasant bonfire smell.

Draso himself, a large, feather-winged dragon with a long snout, short claws, thick scales, and a patient smile stood gilded in the traditional gold, while other statues bore thoughtfully placed jewels on scales, wings, and around the eyes. Miniature gardens encompassed colorful statues of dragon battles, Athánatos, and even one statue of Mona, the mortal mother of Kai. The bighorn sheep laid at the foot of Kai's cross, a double horizontal beamed piece with feathery dragon wings pinned to the top beam. Her body was draped in actual white and gold fabrics, which blew dramatically in the breeze.

Neil grunted and pasted his ears back. Izzy glanced at him and saw him staring at Mona's statue. She raised an eyebrow, but he waved a hand and turned away from the depiction.

Scattered to the left and right of the palace were small but sturdy looking dwellings, all independent of each other, and much more modestly decorated. The further the dwellings got from the palace, the simpler they were.

But… empty. Silent. Izzy's quills stood on end.

One small field under a canopy of trees held tiny, decorated gold boxes scattered all around the floor in haphazard patterns. Natassa glanced at them with ears pasted back, and muttered the word *féretro*. Her somber expression kept Izzy from asking what they were.

Leading up to what Izzy expected was the main palace, was a long, vine and tree covered path. Athánatos statuary lined the path. Tall masculine Athánatos with smaller feminine Athánatos and what looked to be children at their feet, each group set in bases of gold. One child in each group had a tiny, tasteful crown on their heads, set in silver. Each of the statues had what looked to be real Athánatos Ei-Ei jewels set around their eyes.

All except the last set of statues. Izzy frowned. The final set had the tall masculine quilar and the shorter feminine one, but only the feminine one had jewels set around her eyes. Four children sat at their feet. One masculine. Three feminine.

Izzy's ears perked and she stared. Former kings and their families. And the last statue set was Ouranos' family.

Ouranos had mentioned before that his mother had died. Her death, in fact, was apparently what had made his father go mad. Natassa had mentioned this to her during their many conversations on Zyearth. Their mother's Ei-Ei jewels were already set in her statue.

Izzy glanced over at Ouranos.

The Athánatos prince took a deep breath. "Home."

Izzy bit her lip. It was utterly majestic. Inviting, friendly, open.

But also completely abandoned.

CHAPTER 36

DRIFTERS

Ouranos stared out at the palace.

The silence ate at him. No one. Absolutely no one. Not even a sentry. Even the Basileus was sane enough to post sentries. He was not all-seeing.

And yet the palace gardens and fountains were still in pristine condition. The topiaries, green. The plant-life trimmed and clean. The fountains spilling gorgeous, silver water. But who cared for them?

"Get behind me," Ouranos said. He spread his arm protectively, adrenaline pumping. "We shall enter through the South Wing. Stay behind me several paces. If we encounter a sentry, I may be able to convince them I am here to meet the Basileus, but the rest of you will not."

Rather than enter the flower field, Ouranos turned to the right and led the group through the thick pines, keeping an eye out. The complete absence of citizens filled him with dread.

Had his father turned the whole island into Cast?

They are mine.

Ouranos snarled internally at his father. *They will be yours no longer.*

"There." Ouranos ignored his father and pointed to a small outdoor hall lined with tiny fairy-winged dragon statues that appeared to fly through marble trees. "The South Wing."

"And we still haven't seen anyone," Izzy said, her nervousness apparent in her voice. Natassa gripped Ouranos' arm and Neil twitched his tail in agitation. Even Roscoe, who could not be harmed, rippled his Cast body with anxiety.

You will not leave.

Ouranos led the group down the South Wing Hall.

"Ouranos," Natassa said, shaking slightly. "When we passed Mother's statue… I did not hear her jewels sing."

Ouranos stopped, his body buzzing. "What?"

"The jewels on her statue did not sing."

His eyes widened. "Are you sure?"

"Very."

Ouranos chewed his lip. "We shall have to examine them when this is over. We must have been too far away. I do not imagine them broken."

"Not broken," Natassa said. "Replaced. With false jewels." She shivered. "Stolen."

Ouranos' eyes grew wide. *Stolen?* By who? Surely not his father. The jewels were powerless unless bound. As useless as pebbles.

Ouranos' ears flattened. Though his father's mind had twisted so completely… it was possible he had found some use for them. One more worry to add to their ever-growing list.

"Keep your magic ready," Ouranos said. "If the jewels have been stolen…"

"Father might have found some way to harness their power without a user," Natassa finished. "Or he forced them on someone as a way to control them." She held out her hands. Tongues of fire danced her on fingertips.

They entered the airy South Wing, amid sculpted fairy dragons, silver gilded walls, and marble flooring. Pines grew along the edges and a soft wind through the grasses cooled the building, bathing it in the sappy scent of the trees. The ceiling sported glassed holes to let in the sun, shaped to fit in with the various histories painted and gilded around them. The South Wing was meant mainly for civilian gatherings, and would be quiet with the absence of citizens.

Ouranos shook himself. Hopefully he could save them once his allies reached full strength once more. He walked in carefully.

His home.

Your prison.

"We must be silent, lest we attract the attention of sentries," Ouranos said. "Brandish your magic and weapons." He lowered his gaze. "The Basileus still haunts my thoughts. I am unsure if he can sense my location any longer, but we must act as if he can."

"You're stronger than him, Ouranos," Izzy said. "Block him out. He can't have you."

Ouranos smiled, though said nothing.

Neil tensed, curling his tail between his legs. "My kingdom for my rifle..."

"Stay by me," Natassa said. "We will not allow harm to come to you." He flattened his ears and moved close to Natassa, fur bristled, gaze darting about.

Ouranos led the group around the outside edge, hoping to keep the sound of their footsteps low and keep out of the pockets of light.

They are mine.

Neil followed Natassa quietly, but then tripped, crashed to the marble floor, and let out a yowl of pain. The sound bounced off the ceiling and floor of the room, magnifying.

Ouranos flinched, turning on Neil, but the damage was already done.

I SEE YOU.

Footsteps sounded down the Deep Hall leading to the center courtyard.

Neil gripped his snout and flattened his ears. "Damnit!"

Ouranos swore. "To the Royal Wing. Hurry!" He broke into a sprint, running for the outside hall with the others at his heels.

"Ouranos!" Natassa's cry turned his attention to the Deep Hall. Four Athánatos sentries had emerged, holding long weapons that Ouranos had rarely seen in Athánatos hands before.

Swords. They had *swords.* Long, slender, well-forged swords. Weapons long-thought missing from Athánatos, as their peaceful culture had no use for them. Yet, here they were, prepared and ready.

And more than that, the sentry's eyes were blank. Pupilless.

They are MINE.

Ouranos' gut roiled at the sight of them. Drifters. His own state reflected back at him. And like Ouranos had once been, they seemed completely unaware. Worst still, he knew them by name. Friends, fellow sentries, soldiers that had trained alongside him when he had undergone the ceremonial training that all princes went through.

"Ouranos, go!" Izzy said, shoving him down the side hall. "Run!"

Ouranos nodded and ran.

Natassa shouted, and a thump echoed in the hall. Ouranos turned. One of the Drifters had tackled her to the ground. *Xenos,* Ouranos thought. They had trained together when Ouranos was young.

Xenos lifted his sword above his head.

Ouranos faltered. *He is my friend, my subject!*

But Natassa is my sister!

He begged his legs to move, but he remained frozen, helpless.

Neil leapt forward and body-slammed the sentry, knocking him to the ground as his sword fell to the ground with a loud clang. The tan puma snatched the sword off the ground and stood, ears back and tail twitching in anger. He glared at the remaining sentries with a low growl.

"Come after me, you spineless bastard," Neil challenged.

Ouranos watched as a second sentry charged Neil, sword swinging. Neil blocked easily and swung back, slicing open a wound. The sentry had no form, no talent with the sword, no choice but to swing as hard as he was able. But Neil wielded the weapon as if it were an extension of his own body, blocking each attack and elegantly pushing the sentry back. His form almost perfectly mimicked Matt's…

Another sentry slammed into Ouranos and they flew down the hall. The sentry pinned him. Ouranos scrambled under the body, clawing to escape, but the sentry that had him was too strong. Ouranos tried calling the Phonar again, but still no response. His enemy lifted his sword.

Ouranos caught a glimpse of the quilar's face. "Galen!" He called out the sentry's name. "Stop this! This is not your battle, nor your heart! See your prince and *yield!"*

But Galen paid no mind and swung the sword down.

Ouranos pressed his hands up and formed a thick block of ice to stop the oncoming weapon.

Too late.

The blade ripped through his shirt and chest, spilling hot blood, before catching in the forming ice block, preventing further damage.

Searing pain ripped through Ouranos, screaming through his chest, as he gripped the wound. Blood washed over his hand, and panic filled him.

You are MINE. YIELD.

Galen wiggled the sword free of the ice block and chopped down again, methodic, as if in a trance, slowly breaking through the ice.

The world blurred. Images of war, on Athánatos and on the mainland, thoughts of the battles on Zyearth, reminders of the death at his hands, all his sins assailed him, and he froze in place, unable to move, unable to flee the world his actions had created, unable to escape--

A Cast screech blasted through the hall and Galen's weight lifted from him. Roscoe pulled Galen away. The sentry fought physically, though wore no expression. Ouranos waved the ice blocks away, his memories with it. The pain attacked him full force.

Izzy dropped to her knees by him, her face awash with worry. "Ouranos! You're hurt--" She reached for him, but froze, staring at her hands. Ouranos followed her gaze Her hands were dotted with Black Bound elixir.

She will die. Your actions will complete the genocide. She will die unaware of your hand in her father's death.

Ouranos shoved his father's words away. He tried to say he was fine, but blood in his mouth drowned his words. He coughed, spitting red on the floor.

Izzy shook her head and removed her jacket instead, pressing it to the wound. Her face blanked. "I'm sorry. I don't think I can heal it."

He coughed and spat again, though this time less blood spilled out. Izzy's expression was intended to be reassuring, or at the very least an attempt to hide her fear and therefore keep Ouranos' down. The healer's face he had come to know. But the fact that he realized what she was doing only succeeded in having the opposite effect. Panic gripped him and he spoke too fast and too high pitched. "Am I going to die?"

Izzy shook her head. "It's shallow. Just stay still a moment."

"The blood in my mouth--"

"You bit your tongue," Izzy said, her voice steady and emotionless. The voice of a healer to match the blank face. "You'll be fine. Just stay with me, okay? We're okay."

But they were not. Galen. The other sentries.

A blast of weak fire flew by them. Natassa stood in front of Ouranos, hands out, keeping the sentries at bay. But like Ouranos, it seemed she could not convince herself to use full power and kill them.

"Is he going to be okay?" Natassa asked, breathless, turning her head toward them.

Izzy hesitated. "He's--"

"Why are you not *healing him?*" Natassa exclaimed.

Izzy pressed her ears back, her emotionless mask breaking. She threw her hands out, eyes glistening. "I *can't!* My healing powers *broke--*"

"Guys!" Neil called out. "A little help!"

Ouranos strained to lift his head. Four more sentries converged on Neil, swords in hand.

Roscoe screeched a war cry and left Galen to assist, rippling along the marble like a tidal wave. Natassa turned her fire on them.

But they kept coming. The hall soon filled with them.

Neil shouted and thrust the sword at a sentry, running it through his chest. The Drifter paused a moment, then fell, still without expression.

Ouranos choked.

They will all die. Unless you submit to me.

Galen, now free, snatched Izzy and pulled her away from Ouranos. She shouted, surprised and angry. She snarled at him and, with black hands, she gripped his chest. Ouranos watched in horror as her powers ripped through the sentry. In mere seconds, his body convulsed, he gasped for air, and then fell dead at her feet. She stared at him, breathing hard, confusion, fear, and panic in her face, all at once. Shaking her head, she turned back to put pressure on Ouranos' wound, unshed tears catching the sparse light.

They will all die, by my hand... or yours. Save them all. Submit to me!

But he could not. He could not give in to his father. Not again. Not after everything that had been done for him.

Not if it meant more killing.

I will spare your friends if you submit to me.

Ouranos gritted his teeth, trying desperately to push his father out. *But you intend to use me to KILL!*

You have already killed. Sol... The Omnirs...

His vision blurred and he grew light-headed. *It was your hand--*

IT WAS YOU. His father's words exploded in his mind, a cacophony of hatred. *Submit and your friends will live.*

"Izzy," Natassa said.

Izzy looked up at Natassa. "What?"

"Keep him safe," Natassa said. "Get him out of here. Get to Matt and defeat the Basileus." She looked Izzy in the eye. "Please."

Izzy flattened her ears. "What are you--"

"This way!" Natassa rushed forward, toward the wall of sentries and Neil. "Follow me, this way! You want the Prinkípissa of the Athánatos!"

The sentries turned their heads and, as one, headed for Natassa.

Neil grinned at her. "That's the way!" He ran after Natassa. "Come on, you soulless monkeys, come and get it!"

"Neil!" Izzy called. "What are you doing?"

"Saving your asses," he called. "You tell Trecheon he'd better figure out a way to fix Cast or I swear to Christ, I'm going to kill him myself. Understand?"

"But--"

"Coooome and get it!" Neil called, like he was enticing a sounder of swine to dinner. "Let's go, let's go!" He and Natassa broke through the sentries and ran down the opposite hall.

They did not get far. The wave of sentries flooded over them. Neil swung and several fell, but he and Natassa were not strong enough alone to stop the onslaught.

Ouranos stared, panic shooting through his veins. He would kill them! Did they not understand? He opened his mouth.

Izzy clapped her hand over it. "Don't. Don't waste that sacrifice."

They will die they will die they will die

Ouranos coughed, filling his mouth once again with blood. The world blurred. Izzy kept her jacket pressed tightly to his wound, but she kept her watery gaze trained on Natassa and Neil as they disappeared into the fray.

A fierce fatigue fell over Ouranos. He glanced once more at his sister, sacrificing herself for him once again.

Then the world vanished.

DISCOVERED

By the time they had hooked up the trailer, fought the city traffic, and gotten the truck and trailer to the casino beach, it was already nearing noon. The heat settled under Trecheon's red fur, which didn't help his mood. The damn truck's AC compressor had died last month and Trecheon couldn't bring himself to steal from Philip's random fund to replace the part. Rolling down the windows did next to nothing with the beach-side humidity, and to top it all off, it turned out Cast bodies radiated heat like a freakin' uranium core, making Darvin the world's worst space heater. The whole cabin sweltered, fogging up the windows like a rolling sauna.

It also didn't help that the only sleep he had gotten since yesterday's afternoon nap was from a knock to the head. Matt managed to catch a little sleep in the hot truck on the drive back, but he couldn't be much better off than Trecheon.

About ten minutes before they hit the old parking lot, Matt woke up with a shout and gripped his chest.

Darvin poked out of the footwell. "Matt?"

"It's Ouranos…" Matt said. He squeezed his eyes shut and grimaced. "He's hurt. Bad."

Trecheon lifted a brow. "How do you know?"

"We have a jewel bond," Matt said. "We can sense each other's thoughts and feelings. I haven't been able to speak with him, but--" He groaned. "I can still feel things…" He held his head. "Draso's mercy, my whole head is exploding with red…"

Darvin gurgled quietly. "You've never felt his pain before though."

"No, I haven't," Matt said. "Which tells me something is seriously wrong." He gripped his chest, but turned his gaze to the window. "We need to hurry."

They neared the plane Matt had called an X-Zero (who came up with *that* name?), and Trecheon turned the truck toward the water. Sami sat near the plane with the Cast called Melaina at her side. She stood when they brought the truck nearby, blinking at the trailer with a frown. Trecheon pulled alongside and everyone piled out.

Sami bent an ear back and arched an eyebrow at Matt. "You okay?"

Matt shook his head. "It's Ouranos. He's badly injured and I can feel it."

"That is not good…" Sami said. She glanced over the trailer again and turned to Trecheon. *"This* is your plan for getting across the water?"

"You got a better one?" Trecheon asked. He looked over the skis… then frowned. The spare gas cans were both missing. "Shit."

Matt flattened an ear. "What's wrong now?"

"Must not have secured the gas cans well enough," Trecheon said. "We lost them in transit."

"You guys use miles-per-gallon for fuel expense, right?" Sami asked. "What's the miles-per-gallon on these things? Maybe we could still make it."

"Gallons-per-hour," Trecheon corrected. "At least for watercraft. These run about five and a half GPH. Which leaves us about 15 miles short."

Darvin bubbled along the surface of his body. "This is going *swimmingly.*"

Trecheon rolled his eyes. "Look, I know I screwed up, but you guys have *magic.*" He pointed to Matt. "Surely this windbag can get us the last fifteen miles."

"How?" Matt said. "We have no sails, and even if we did, these things aren't balanced for sailing. One good gust will capsize the whole thing."

"You have *magic,*" Trecheon repeated.

"You think magic is a cure-all that'll fix everyone's problems?" Matt snapped. "Magic still follows a lot of basic physics." He threw up his hands. "I should have figured this out *myself.*"

"Yeah, well maybe you could have if you hadn't been so busy looking for reasons to *hate me,*" Trecheon shouted. "I know my family are scum, and I deserve every scrap of anger you're throwing at me, but it's damn hard to work with someone who'd rather see me *dead.*"

Matt flicked his ears back, furrowing his brow. He frowned. "I don't... I don't wish you dead."

"Bullshit," Trecheon snapped. "Don't deny it. Sometimes I wish I was myself. This life is hell and I'm not worth the dirt I walk on. But Neil needs me, and I'm not going to leave him behind."

Matt opened his mouth like he wanted to speak, but nothing came out. Good. About time he shut the hell up.

Darvin didn't have the same qualms though. He raised himself up in his puddle, dripping ink all around him. "So now what? Your brilliant plan won't work."

Trecheon glared at him. "Oh, *piss off.* I don't see you space aliens offering anything. Just give me a minute. I'll think of something."

Darvin sneered. "Maybe you did this on purpose. Maybe you're trying to delay us so your genocidal brother can--"

"Don't you *dare* insinuate that Ryota and I are working together," Trecheon roared with more poison than he expected. "Ryota betrayed my squad. He betrayed *me* and disappeared after killing dozens of innocent people for his own pointless war. I thought he was dead, and for everything he's done, he damn well should have been. But now I have to clean up his mess. Again. Again!" Trecheon gritted his teeth and held a hand to his forehead, fighting a rage-induced headache. He shook his head, trying to cool down.

Christian's voice immediately shot Trecheon's blood pressure back up. "Your brother is *alive?"*

Trecheon's quills stood on end. He whipped around. "Christian! What--"

"Don't change the subject," Christian said, walking through the sand. He pointed at him. "Is your brother alive? Is this the family emergency?"

Trecheon pasted his ears back. "Christian--"

"Answer me, *Jefe.* "

"He is, yes," Matt said, stepping forward. "And we're going after him."

Christian gave Matt a death glare before turning back to Trecheon. "Are you freakin' serious? You told me just yesterday morning that he was a *murderer* and you're going after him *yourself?* "

Trecheon winced. "It's more complicated than that."

"How?" Christian said, waving a hand. "Don't complicate things. This is a job for the *military,* not *you.* "

Trecheon furrowed his brow. "Christian, it's—"

"No," Christian said. "Screw this. And screw you," he added, pointing to Matt. He turned. "I'm reporting this."

Trecheon's eyes widened. "Wait!"

"Like hell you are." Darvin snarled, and snaked his body around Christian, pressing his three-eyed face near Christian's head. "Listen you--"

Christian screamed, and wiggled in Darvin's grip, pulling his face as far away from the inky abomination as he could, letting out a long string of panicked Spanish. "Let me go, let me go, let me go!"

Trecheon ran to them. "Darvin, if you're hurting him--"

"I'm not hurting him, I'm just holding him in place," Darvin said. He glared at Trecheon. "And it's not like you could do anything to me anyway--"

"Let me *go!* Jesus, Mary, and Joseph! "

"Christian, please," Trecheon said. "Just *listen* for a second--"

"Get off of me, you disgusting thing!"

"I'm not a *thing*, I'm--"

Trecheon bared his teeth. "Darvin, *let him go!*"

"And let him go tell someone?"

"Get the hell off--"

"Enough!" A flurry of sparks flew through the air, biting their noses. Trecheon shook his head and turned to see Sami staring at all of them. "Everyone *calm down*."

Darvin gurgled. "Calm down--"

Sami glared at him. "Darvin, *let him go. "*

"But--"

"Darvin," Matt said, his voice smooth and calm. He spoke with the air of authority that even Trecheon felt compelled to listen to. *"Let him go. "*

Darvin snorted. "Fine. But if he runs off and ruins all of this, don't blame me." He slithered off Christian's body.

Christian took two steps away from Darvin and turned back to Trecheon. "What the hell is that thing? What is going *on,* Boss?"

"Let's find a place to sit," Trecheon said, pasting his ears back. "Because you're getting the long version."

Trecheon took a sip of water from the bottle Matt had handed him, keeping an eye on Christian. He held his Gem in his hand, twisting it in his palm in an absent grip strengthening exercise, as if somehow doing so actually meant something to the biomech.

They sat around the remains of a damaged concrete firepit on the beach on rusting metal benches. The waves lapped calmly at the sand, though for Trecheon, it was just a reminder that Neil and Ryota were a hundred and twenty or more miles away and they were wasting time.

Christian absently sipped water too, staring at the sand, his face blank as he seemed to process all the information Matt had given him. "So. You're from another planet."

Matt nodded.

"And you came here looking for Trecheon because some evil mage king is looking for him. A king that has somehow convinced Trecheon's brother that all humans are evil and is using him to attempt genocide. And you're planning on crossing the channel to find him."

"That's the gist of it, yes," Matt said. The white and blue quilar fidgeted, and he kept tossing glances across the sea at Sol.

Christian eyed Matt. "Let me see it."

Matt frowned. "What?"

"Your magic," Christian said. "I've seen some shit in my time, but I don't accept whatever *babosadas* is thrown at me. Better I see it with my own eyes." He leaned on his hands, glaring. "So let's see it."

Matt raised an eyebrow. "Alright, I can respect that." He held out his hand and the air flashed green, then purple, then invisible. A shield. "Punch me."

Christian smirked. "Gladly." He stood and formed a fist.

Trecheon stood too. "Christian, *wait--*"

Too late. Christian's fist connected with the shield. The whole thing shattered, dropping green and purple shards in the sand before vanishing. Christian yelped and danced around, shaking his hand and swearing in Spanish. *"Dios mio..."*

Matt chuckled. "Sorry. That's usually the most effective way to show off." He turned to Sami. "We have others though. Toss me a fireball?"

Sami grinned. "Sure." She tossed a fireball his way.

Matt caught the fireball in a mini tornado and whipped the flames around in a bright display of power. "I could make this a lot bigger, but I'd rather not attract too much attention."

"Why in God's name didn't you lead with *that, pendejo?*" Christian said. "Didn't need to break my hand for that." Blood dripped down his fingers.

"I did wonder," Matt said, dropping the tornado and extinguishing the flames. "Not every day I meet someone who can shatter my shields with their bare hands." He nodded to Trecheon. "Your boss can handle that one."

Christian eyed Trecheon, eyebrow raised.

Trecheon sighed, then took Christian's hand. Concentrating, he pulled on his Gem's magic and in a burst of light, healed the damage.

Christian let out a low whistle. "Damn, Boss. Forget the shop. Open a healing clinic. You'll be rich in no time."

"Yeah, I don't think I'd last long healing people with magical powers," Trecheon said. "I'd be a government lab experiment in no time."

"Yeah, fair." Christian rubbed his hands together. "Welp. That settles it then." He lowered his gaze, his face growing serious. "I'm coming with you."

Trecheon perked both ears and sat up straight. "What?"

Matt crossed his arms and shook his head. "No. Absolutely not."

Christian glared at Matt. "You can't tell me what I can and can't do, *pelotudo.*"

Matt curled his upper lip, revealing a fang. "You'll be nothing but a burden. You can't fight with no magic."

"I literally crushed your magic shield with one punch, asshole."

Matt snarled. *"And* the Basileus is specifically targeting humans. You can't--"

"I can get you to Sol," Christian said, crossing his arms.

Matt perked an ear. "What?"

"Those skis won't cut it," Christian said. "You don't have enough gas and you're overburdening the weight limit, which will cut into the fuel economy anyway. Magic or not, you can't make it on your own."

Darvin squinted his three blue eyes at him. "How do you even know where we want to go? Trecheon said they were on the Vanishing Island, not Sol."

Christian glanced at Trecheon. "Those fancy new security cameras have damn good mics."

Trecheon's skin burned in embarrassment under his fur.

"So you're an eavesdropper," Darvin said, gurgling.

"Trecheon showed up late to his own business toting some random quilar that he clearly hated with no explanation," Christian said. "I was *worried.* I'm a Marine, damn it. I know what pre-battle jitters looks like. War does things to you."

Matt took a deep breath. "Look, we're wasting time. What do you have to offer?"

Christian narrowed his eyes at Matt, then turned to Trecheon.

Trecheon waved a hand. "Go on. I trust him."

"You don't trust *anyone, Jefe,*" Christian said. "You don't even trust *me.*" He frowned. "Otherwise you wouldn't have kept this from me."

Trecheon winced. He glanced over at Matt who shrugged. He breathed deeply, then turned to Christian. "You're right. I'm not good at trust. But

Neil's at stake here. Hell, a lot of people are. I can't afford to let my trust issues get in the way. So, for *now,* I trust him."

Matt lifted an eyebrow, frowning.

Christian pressed his lips together. "Fine." He stood up.

"Hey, hey, *hey,* " Darvin said, slithering in front of the human. "Where do you think you're going?"

"Darvin," Matt said. "Let him go."

Darvin gurgled angrily. *"Why?"*

Matt glanced Trecheon's way, then met Christian's eyes. "Trust works both ways."

Christian narrowed his eyes, but nodded. "Let me show you then." He waved a hand, and walked toward the parking lot.

Trecheon followed behind, with Matt and Sami in tow, and Darvin slithering slowly beside Christian. Christian had parked his jeep next to Trecheon's truck.

And he had a dinghy attached to it.

"You have a boat!" Sami said.

"Sure do," Christian said. "My nephew and I go fishing in the shallows sometimes." He leaned on the tow hook. "But you're not going without me."

Trecheon frowned. "Christian."

"It's not up for negotiation, *Jefe,*" Christian said. "I won't interfere in whatever magic thing you guys are doing. But if anything, someone has to be outside of this issue to run for help if this gets out of hand."

"As if anyone else on this planet could do anything," Darvin mumbled.

"But it's better than nothing," Matt said. "Trecheon?"

Trecheon shook his head. "This is against my better judgement, but fine. You can come."

Christian grinned at Matt. "Good thing it's windy tonight."

Everyone turned to Matt. He grinned back.

CHAPTER 38

SOL

As much as Matt wanted to get going right away, Christian pointed out the very real problem of the coast guard catching them in the daylight. They had no choice but to wait until the cover of darkness. They took turns sleeping, but Matt was sure he didn't get more than two hours.

Not with Cast haunting his dreams.

The journey took an agonizing three hours and by the time they reached shore, Matt was ready to collapse. But they made it. Everyone piled off and Matt crumpled on the sand. "Good Draso, that was as bad as when I was harvesting elixir with Ouranos. I never want to do that again."

Trecheon helped Sami pull the boat on shore and grinned. "So is this the part where I make a joke about you passing wind?"

Matt glared. "Only if you want a face full of wet sand."

"How about you being full of hot air?"

"I swear to Draso, you're asking for it."

Trecheon chuckled. "Alright windbag, I'll stop."

Matt lobbed a mudball at him, which Trecheon dodged.

Christian wiped his face and mustache clear of sea spray. "So this is Sol."

Matt sat up and looked around. Yes. This was Sol. His home. His literal birthplace.

His parents' final resting place.

He hadn't realized he was shivering until Sami gripped his shoulder. "We're right here, Matt."

He looked up. Sami stood over him, smiling, with Darvin giving his best impression of sympathy through the form of a Cast. Even Melaina curled around him like a protective friend, her eerie eyeballs floating on the surface of her body.

Matt chanced a glimpse of Trecheon and a wave of memories flooded him. Red quilar, everywhere, chasing his family, his friends, his neighbors, chasing the screams, killing, ripping apart, murder--

"Matt." Trecheon bent both ears and frowned, furrowing his brow. "I'm not your enemy."

Matt blinked and looked around. An unnatural wind whipped around them, tossing up sand, mud and pine needles in angry tornadoes all around them. He cursed, then commanded the wind away. The twisters died, raining their contents on the ground. "Sorry."

Christian tossed a worried glance between Trecheon and Matt. "I have a feeling there's more you're not telling me."

"Because it's private," Matt said before anyone could explain. "And you don't need to know." He stood and with a gentle gust, he brushed himself free of sand and water. "Melaina, where is the rip so we can get to Athánatos Island?"

The half-formed Cast bubbled and whistled, then brought the group to a trail that led deeper into the island.

Matt took a deep breath. "Let's go."

They followed Melaina through the woods with Christian's cell phone and Sami's fire as their only light. Trecheon followed behind him, with Sami and Darvin in the middle and Matt taking up the rear.

Even in the dark, Matt felt a vague, uncomfortable familiarity through the trees and moonlight. His mind brought everything back. Glimpses of his nine-year-old sister pulling him and Izzy through the woods at full speed, desperate to escape the Omnirs. The screams of dying neighbors and the cries from their families. The deep stink of blood. The taste of hot magic in the air.

Everything was death.

He tried to summon up some positive memories. His father painting, perhaps. His mother cooking. His aunt Solana and her fiancé playing games in the community room in his home.

But he couldn't even picture their faces, let alone them doing mundane activities in the home he barely remembered. Everything was washed out by red.

"Here," Sami said softly.

Matt looked up and his breath left him.

Dozens of huts dotted the landscape among towering trees and scattered, rotting wood. The air smelled of decay. Decomposing dwellings, wild and tangled forests, the stink of a dead township.

And something else too. Matt lifted his head and wrinkled his nose. It smelled like--

"Smoke," Sami pointed. "Look there!" The forest hid where the smoke came from, but Matt knew where that led. The Sanctum.

Matt clenched his fists without a second thought. Someone was on his island? His home? With *fire?*

Darvin stood a little out of his puddle then turned to Melaina. "Do you know who's here?"

But she didn't answer. Instead, she bounded ahead of the group, slithering up the path faster than Matt had ever seen a Cast move.

"Melaina, wait!" Matt called and ran after her.

Melaina dodged in and out of paths and around huts, leading everyone on a zig-zagging path. Matt kept his eyes trained on her, determined to focus on the here, on the now, and not on his past.

Eventually they hit the town square. A large clearing, paved with aging stones, patterned and once-shining, now overrun by vines, trees, and weeds, just visible in the light of the fire and moon. Dilapidated huts lined the edges of the clearing, and the smell of moldy thatched roofs competed with the bonfire smell. The carvings in the stone-walled Sanctum almost seemed to dance in the flickering light, though it was a dance of fear… of death. In the center, a bonfire roared, casting vibrant orange light on everything around them. The Sanctum's tall entrance refused to invite the light into it and remained stubbornly black.

But surrounding the fire, standing in their anthropomorphic forms, draped in feathers of all colors, stood six Phonar phoenix summons. They turned as one… and stared at Matt.

CHAPTER 39

FIGHT OR FLIGHT

A sharp chest pain awoke Ouranos from his uneasy slumber. His eyes wore a bleary film of tears and his head pounded so hard he could feel his heartbeat in his ears. But the chest pain encompassed everything, making it hard to focus.

His father's biting voice brought him back with immediacy.

They are mine. Face me. Or you shall lose them forever.

"Ouranos?"

He blinked the haziness from his eyes and turned his head toward the sound of the voice. Izzy sat next to him against one of the marble walls of the audience chamber, hugging her legs and resting her head on her knees. Her eyes were puffy and red.

"Isabelle."

She will turn on you. She will hate you.

Ouranos coughed, but no red wet his lips this time. "I appear to have survived."

Izzy nodded beyond them, toward the trees outside the open hall. "I moved the sentries outside. They're lying under the trees. Resting." She shook her head. "I had to use the fabric from their uniforms as bandages though." She breathed deeply. "I tried to heal you, Ouranos, I really did, but it only got worse. I had to do things the old-fashioned way."

They gave their lives for nothing. Sol gave their lives for nothing. The Omnirs gave their lives for nothing.

Ouranos winced, but pressed his father out. "How many?"

Izzy glanced at him. "I didn't count."

"Isabelle."

"You don't need to know," Izzy said. "You'll just use it as a reason to hate yourself."

Ouranos blinked. The words stung, but he knew the truth of them. "Fair enough."

"Why did they fall like that?" Izzy asked, hugging her knees closer. "They didn't even react to the attacks. They just took every wound and fell, like they didn't feel anything."

"They are Drifters," Ouranos said.

They are mine.

"But what does that *mean?*" Izzy asked. "I know that means their souls aren't with their bodies, or whatever. Natassa tried explaining it. But you're a Drifter too, right? You don't act like that. What's different about them?"

Ouranos tried to sit up, but the pain forced him back down. "The state of a Drifter is difficult to explain."

"Please try."

Ouranos sighed. "I shall endeavor to." He closed his eyes, trying to focus on something other than the pain in his chest. "A natural Drifter is an Athánatos whose soul escaped through some poor happenstance. A devastating wound in battle, a catastrophic illness, or in an accident of some sort. Something terribly damaging, but not quite fatal. The soul cannot live in a damaged vessel, so it leaves, to protect itself. In most cases, a natural Drifter's soul can be coaxed back to their body once the wound has healed, if healing is indeed possible."

"Do they lose their Soul Jewels like you did?"

"Rarely," Ouranos said. "And if they do, there is usually no saving them, unless we can preserve the jewels."

Izzy frowned. "Preserve?"

Ouranos nodded, trying to ignore the pain. "If the jewels can be placed in a *féretro* very quickly, the soul will essentially be frozen in time, granting the victim a greater chance for restoration."

"Those little gold boxes we passed by," Izzy said. "Natassa muttered something about them."

Ouranos nodded. "They also house unused jewel sets waiting for their next masters, making it a graveyard of sorts."

"And they can restore a Drifter."

"They are designed to do so, yes," Ouranos said. "Though the Athánatos in recovery is essentially in a coma while they heal, with no waking connection to the real world." He took a deep breath. "Most do not recover from the *féretro*."

"Could we... fix these Drifters with the *féretro*?"

Ouranos chewed his lip. "Unlikely. The Basileus has created decidedly unnatural Drifters. He has forcefully removed the Soul Jewels of the Ei-Ei jewel set from these Athánatos. By doing so, he can keep the soul from returning to the body, essentially creating empty vessels. Because he has a grasp on the soul and the jewels, he can command us like puppets." He lowered his gaze. "Putting their jewels in the *féretro* would put them in comas, making them harmless and unable to be used as puppets, but it would not save them."

"But that's still not your version of a Drifter," Izzy said. "Hell, even when you first met us, you were already fighting against him. You weren't like the mindless zombies these guys are."

"I was lucky," Ouranos said, and he explained about the stranger who bridged his soul. He took a deep breath. "What that stranger started, Matthew finished by fully severing that bond. I am entirely grateful to him."

He will die.

Ouranos sat up, willing the pain and his father's words away. He felt his chest, now covered in scraps from the traditional *osaa*, the diamond shaped fabric hanging from a sentry's belt. He ran his hand over the bandaging, and though it hurt, it did not come back bloody.

"Why are we still here?"

Izzy flicked an ear back. "I can't carry you on my own. It was either wait for you to wake up or leave you here to get help and… I couldn't leave you here."

"I suspect my wound was worse than you were willing to let on, Isabelle."

"It was, honestly," Izzy said. "But you're up now. You're awake and I've stopped the bleeding. It'll hurt like hell for a while, but you should be okay. You shouldn't be moving around too much though. You might open the wound up again."

You will come to me or lose them forever.

"A fine prescription, though I am afraid we may have no choice but to ignore it," Ouranos said, coughing again. "We cannot let the Basileus have Natassa or Neil a moment longer. And where is Roscoe?"

"I sent him to go look for Neil and Natassa," Izzy said. "But he hasn't come back yet."

Ouranos cursed. "Perhaps we will find him when we encounter Natassa and Neil ourselves."

Izzy narrowed her puffy eyes. "I can't let you go after them."

Bring her to ME.

Ouranos frowned. "Surely you are not thinking to go alone. You cannot hope to fight him by yourself."

"No," Izzy said. "We're sticking to the original plan. We're going to find the rip in the Veil. We'll get back to the mainland. I can tuck you away safely in the X-Zero where we can have Trecheon heal you and you can rest. Matt and I will come back and get Neil and Natassa. This is what we're trained for, Ouranos."

Oh, no. He could not let his friends tackle the Basileus and lose yet more people to his father's wrath. He refused it. "And what a fine job you did on Zyearth."

Izzy glared. *"Ouranos--"*

"I am not happy to dredge up old memories, but might I remind you that your entire army struggled to best the Basileus and his relatively small army of Cast," Ouranos said. "And between all the elemental users and trained soldiers we have with us now, we were still driven here by the Basileus' current Cast. And he no doubt has more at his disposal. The entire population of the island is *missing,* and I can only assume they have been turned. Thousands upon thousands. You and Matthew cannot best him alone."

"We don't have to *best* him," Izzy said. "Not right now. We just need to get Natassa and Neil *out."*

Give her to the Cast! You will come ALONE.

"And you think the Basileus will let you walk in and out without opposition?" Ouranos said.

"Of course not, but if we don't get you back to the mainland and some real help, you could die!" Izzy blurted.

Ouranos flattened his ears. His wound throbbed. "You said I would be fine."

"I lied," Izzy said, eyes glistening. "The curse of a healer. Sometimes lying is necessary for peace of mind, but right now, we don't have that luxury. You need help, and I can't provide it, so we need to get you to Trecheon as soon as possible."

It was hard to ignore her near-panicked pleas. And harder still to ignore the stabbing pain in his chest.

But hardest to ignore his father's taunting voice.

They will be lost forever.

"Isabelle," Ouranos said softly, willing her to hear. "They will die."

"Or you will," Izzy said. A tear finally escaped and ran its way down her muzzle. "Either I get you to Trecheon and save at least one of you, or we go after the Basileus and probably lose everyone. I can't do that. Neil and Natassa knew that risk and took it anyway. All we can hope is that Roscoe gets to them. Besides…" She took a deep breath. "I promised Natassa I would take care of you."

"I heard no such promise."

"Ouranos," Izzy said. "It isn't up for debate. I'm not going to let you die, damn it. We're going to Trecheon and that's final. Understand?"

Ouranos watched her for several agonizing seconds. Sighing, he shook his head. "Fine. But let it be known that I do not approve."

"I'm not happy either, but it's the best we've got," Izzy said. She stood and held a hand out to him. "Give me your hand and point me in the right direction."

It was an effort for Ouranos to get into an arrangement that was both relatively comfortable and that also allowed Izzy to support him properly, especially considering their drastic height difference. Once they settled into a decent position, Ouranos pointed the way through the halls toward the Royal Wing and the rip. They walked in relative silence, though Ouranos could not help but scrape his feet as they walked. Every step was agony.

Would he even be able to fight should it come to that? He tried to dredge up a flicker of flame in his free hand, but the pain of the wound was so distracting, he barely managed a spark.

If they met the enemy, they would be helpless.

WAR HERO

Neil ran his sword through another sentry, spilling blood all over his jacket, but wouldn't let himself linger or watch the man fall.

He had people to protect.

Especially since Natassa didn't seem capable of attacking any of them. Or maybe she just wasn't willing. Neil couldn't tell.

Praying a silent thanks to Carter for the skills with the sword and the encouragement to keep training, he stood by Natassa's side and took down sentry after sentry. But he knew it wasn't enough.

"Strike harder!" Neil snarled.

"I… I cannot!" Natassa said, her voice shaking. She pushed back sentries with open hands blasting ice and wind, but nothing more lethal. "They are my brethren!"

"They're trying to *kill* you!" Neil shouted. "You don't have a *choice.*"

Natassa paused, clenching her hands into fists. "I… I must have one."

Neil whipped around and stabbed a sentry running for Natassa. "We can't get through this if you don't fight. I need your help!"

Natassa tossed a weak fireball at another sentry. He took the full brunt of the flames and collapse, though his expression never changed.

Neil bared his teeth and flattened his ears. "Ouranos needs our help. We can't help him if we get killed!"

Natassa perked her ears, then bared her own teeth. She shot a more convincing fireball at another sentry, sending him flying against the wall. He collapsed, unmoving.

"That's the way!" Neil said. Finally some headway.

He refused to die. He refused to leave his brother Philip completely alone. Not after all the hard work it had taken to build up the money to free him. He elbowed a sentry in the face, knocking him to the ground, then stabbed another sentry, spilling hot blood over his bomber jacket.

"Neil! Help!"

Neil smashed one more sentry down and turned. Another Athánatos had Natassa around the neck and was dragging her off down the big hall at the end of the room.

Neil's fur stood on end. "Hang on!" He ran after her, but he didn't get three steps before six sentries dove on top of him and ripped his sword out of his hand. He roared, baring his teeth and claws, and scratched at the eyes of his attackers. He got several deep scratches and one bite in before a sentry smashed a pommel against his head and his vision devolved into stars and blackness.

Everything smelled of smoke and fire and melting rebar. Burned blood and flesh, a coppery, metallic smell. His tongue tasted of it. Singed fur, ash on the wind, caught up his nose and buried the smell in his brain. He stared at his hands and groaned. His head swam. Grime caked his fur and clothes.

Everything smelled *familiar.*

Damn it, not again.

Someone screamed. Neil gazed up at the night sky. He was locked in a nightmare. Again.

A fighter plane flew overhead, visible only because it was bathed in flame. It crashed into a high-rise apartment building, the first of many, drowning the building in fire and smoke.

The screaming stopped.

Panic gripped his chest. His breathing grew shallow, his vision blurred, his ears rang. *Oh God, not again, not now.*

Footsteps thudded next to him. He turned. Trecheon and Carter ran past him. The burning flames around them cast light on the red fur of Trecheon's hands. Still had his natural arms. Neil flattened his ears. Every nightmare he had tried to save his arms. Every nightmare he failed. Each night terror brought fresh guilt.

Carter turned to him. Like usual, he had no face – just filthy white fur with streaks of blue and green plastered in haphazard patterns. He held a hand out to Neil. "Come on, Neil," he said. His voice had three separate octaves and echoed like a ghost. Neil never knew where it came from, as he had no mouth. "We're going after him."

Ackerson. The asshole who had ruined all their lives.

Then Trecheon screamed. Carter turned.

Two sniper rounds. Trecheon thrown to the ground. Carter rushed for him. Both his arms had been blown off. He still couldn't tell how real it was. If he could trust the memory.

But he had failed again. His body buzzed and gripped his head. No, no, no! *"Stop!"*

"Neil?"

Neil flashed his eyes open. He was on the hard floor. Some gentle, pleasant scent he couldn't place warred with a faint, musty smell. A strange light flickered overhead, casting funky shadows on the tan walls. Someone had laid his head on something soft.

He tried to slow his breathing, calm his heartbeat. God, that was a bad one. It had been a while since he had faced an episode that bad. He thought he was done with those. He dragged up old therapy sessions and practiced his grounding exercises. *Five things you can see. Four things you can hear. Three things you can touch. Two things you can smell. One thing you can taste.*

…Shit. Did he taste blood? A second attempt to focus on it said no. Must be imagining things still.

Admittedly it wasn't easy catching all those things lying down with stars in his vision, but it at least gave him something other than the nightmare to focus on. He concentrated on his head cushion, imagining what it looked like based on feel, counting his heart beats. 1… 2… 3… When he got to sixty, he stopped and took a deep breath.

The world he was in wasn't much better than war, but it also wasn't the Battle of DC. He had to remember that. Besides, he'd gotten through DC… he'd get through this, magic or no. He tried to sit up, but the stars flooded his vision again, and he laid back down. "Christ on a bike. Where'd the train that hit me come from?"

"Oh, thank Draso!"

Neil looked up.

Natassa hovered over him, looking at him upside down. She frowned. "Are you okay?"

"Oh." The soft thing with the pleasant smell his head laid on was Natassa's lap. His face flushed, and he hoped his fur didn't let it show through. "Um. Yeah. I'm fine."

"Sisters bless us," Natassa said, releasing a breath. "I was worried they had done permanent damage."

"They may still, if the Basileus chooses him for his experiments, Prinkípissa," an old voice muttered. Neil tilted his head and saw a black quilar with striking green-gold eyes glaring at him. He tried again to lift his head, but the stars in his vision wouldn't let him. The quilar huffed. "Perhaps that would not be so bad, considering."

Natassa glared at him. "Hush, Abrax."

"You have brought outsiders to our island, and then dare hush me?" Abrax snorted. "It was outsiders that brought us to this point in the first place. Outsiders that killed your mother."

"Uninvited outsiders," Natassa shot back. "Enemies. Not friends."

"You think this outsider your *friend?*" Abrax said. "He would sooner use you and leave you."

"Now hold on a minute," Neil said. He pushed his way through the stars and sat up. Shaking his head to clear his vision, he turned and glared. "I resent that. I'd never do that."

"Swine talk," Abrax said. "You mainlanders are all the same. Selfish, hateful, destructive--"

"You don't know *shit* about me, so shut the hell up," Neil said with a feral hiss.

Natassa gripped Neil's shoulder. "My friend, please let it go. He will not be reasoned with." She snorted. "Abrax is one of my father's advisors. He always had outdated views."

"I can see that."

"Those views you call outdated have protected us for centuries," Abrax said. "It was their breaking that opened our world up to hurt."

"Says the man kidnapped by his own king," Neil snapped.

"Listen here, outsider--"

"Shush, Abrax," Natassa said. She turned to Neil, ears pasted back. "Please, leave him be."

Neil glared at Abrax, but let it go as Natassa asked. He glanced around instead. High walls surrounded them, disappearing into darkness that the flickering balls of fire hovering around them couldn't seem to touch. There were no windows or natural light to speak of. The walls faded in the darkness too, to the point where he couldn't even tell how to get out of this place. Everything looked like it was made of… clay, or soft brick or something, even the floor. He also sat on a thin layer of dust. How old was this place?

A handful of other Athánatos quilar lay about the dark room, bathed in the flickering light from the magic fire. Most wore the simple clothing he had seen the sentries wear. Pants, skirts, sleeveless tops, all with that strange diamond shaped bit of cloth at the front. Natassa was the only one of the Athánatos quilar in normal street clothes, which made her stand out. A few stared at her, but most of them huddled together in the corners of the room and several slept. Their faces held the alert, wary, and resigned looks of slaves and captives that Neil wished he didn't have the experience to recognize.

He turned away from his fellow captives and glanced up at the firelight in the room. More magic, likely. In fact, it was amazing he hadn't seen more of that. They had been fighting so many Athánatos at once after all.

"Natassa." He paused, then leaned toward her and whispered. "That is your name, right? I don't think we were really introduced."

Natassa blinked, and smiled shyly. Neil thought he caught a glimpse of a blush under the cream-colored fur on her snout. "Um. Yes, it is. And you are Neil, correct?"

"You claim he is your friend, but you do not even know his *name?"* Abrax exclaimed.

Neil shot him a look, before starting again. "Natassa. How come none of those sentries attacked us with um, magic, like you and Ouranos have?"

"Oh!" Natassa said. "Only the royalty of Athánatos have elemental abilities. The immediate royal family commands all elements, while Archons control one each. Their children and spouses can manipulate the elements, but cannot control them as an Archon can. Regular citizens are only blessed with immortality."

Neil sat down hard. *"Immortality?"* Natassa nodded. "Damn. I guess it's a good thing Trecheon didn't have Athánatos jewels then. He wouldn't take *that* news very well."

"Did I hear correctly then?" Natassa said, frowning. "Izzy helped Ouranos to bind your friend to a Gem?"

"Huh!" Abrax glared. "Just what we need. Some other wild quilar with magic they cannot control, like the red quilar in the Basileus' employ."

Neil perked his ears. "Red quilar?"

"The one with lightning at his command," Abrax said. "If the Basileus does not claim us all in the name of the Cast, that red quilar will certainly dash us to pieces with his wayward powers."

Neil's whiskers shook. "Ryota." That bastard. He started all this. And Neil was going to finish it. He stood, careful of the fire overhead. "Where's the door?"

Abrax lifted an eyebrow. "Why?"

"Because we're getting the hell out of here," Neil said. "Where's the freakin' door?"

Abrax narrowed his eyes, but nodded to the left. "You will never get past the guardian Drifters."

"We'll see about that." He held a hand out to Natassa. "With me?"

Natassa looked up at him, concerned, but also still blushing. She placed her hand in his and he lifted from the ground. She stood nearly half a foot taller than him. Damn, she was tall for a quilar. Not that it mattered. They turned toward the door.

Abrax stood. "You will not take our Prinkípissa from us."

"I'm not taking her from you," Neil said, rolling his eyes. "She made the choice to come." He met Natassa's eyes. "Come on, 'Pringles', let's get going."

Natassa frowned and glanced around at the quilar in the room. A few glanced up at her, but most avoided her gaze. "Neil. These are my people. I cannot leave them."

Neil glanced out too, frowning. She was right. She shouldn't leave them. "Then we'll take them with us."

Every quilar in the room looked at him, though no one spoke.

"You cannot be serious," Abrax said. "What can you possibly do?"

Neil furrowed his brow and bared a tooth. Good god, he was so done with this.

He unsheathed claws on his hands and feet, marched up to the door, and slammed his shoulder into it, knocking it wide open. Both guards reached mindlessly for their swords, but Neil grabbed one by the shoulders and smashed him into the wall. The man slid to the floor and didn't move. The other swung his sword at Neil, but Neil whipped around him and bashed him into the wall too. When he was sure they had both stopped moving, he checked them over. Still breathing. Good. They'd face some consequences for that, but at least they weren't dead. He had killed enough today. He lined them up against the wall, took both swords, and walked back in the room.

"Anyone know how to use this?" He lifted one sword. The group stared at him.

A masculine Athánatos, tall, but young by his looks, stepped forward. His fur was mostly yellow with some thick black streaks across his chest and arms, giving him a tiger-stripe feel. Black splotches covered his eyes almost like a mask. "I have some knowledge of the sword."

"What's your name, kid?" Neil said, trying to ignore the fact that he was probably a thousand years older than Neil.

"Damianos," he said.

"Damianos!" Natassa said. "Your father… The Archon of Electrik… is he…?"

Damianos shook his head. "He vanished not long after Ouranos fell to the Basileus, along with Papa Taras, my lady," he said. "I do not know what has become of them, but since the command of lightning has not fallen to me, I assume he and Papa live. Though where, I do not know."

Natassa flattened her ears. "My condolences."

"It is an old wound," Damianos said.

Neil handed him the sword, hilt first. "Well, Damianos, sounds like you're the man for the job. Want the privilege of helping me protect your Prinkípissa and your people against a bunch of soulless monsters?"

Damianos glanced solemnly at Natassa. She nodded encouragingly. Damianos lifted his chin and puffed his chest. "As heir to the Archon, it would be an honor."

"Good," Neil said.

"One moment," Damianos said. He rushed out of the room for a moment, then returned, holding an oblong, golden-yellow stone.

Natassa perked her ears. "Your amber!"

"It was taken from me when I was placed here," Damianos said. "I am lucky the sentry still had it. Hopefully I will not need it, considering the enemy we face and especially since I did not find my wool, but it is good to have it nonetheless."

Neil nodded to Damianos. He turned to Natassa. "Where can we take them?"

"The rip in the Royal Chambers will take us to Sol," Natassa said. "That is as safe as anything."

"Then let's head out."

Abrax glared, crossing his arms. "I am not leaving."

"Suit yourself," Neil said. "I ain't gonna stop you." He held his sword up. "Anyone who's with us, follow Natassa!"

The quilar slowly got up from the floor and followed, still huddled in small groups. They stayed close together, still carrying that haunted look, but several smiled at Neil as they walked past, relief on their faces. A father herded two children behind him, and two Athánatos helped an elderly quilar walk. One of the mainlanders walked with them to help.

One Athánatos with piercing lime-green eyes and pure black fur approached Natassa. "Do you trust this outsider?" she asked.

Natassa nodded. "With my life, Eris." She smiled at Neil.

Neil flicked an ear back. "Not sure I deserve such a glowing endorsement."

"After what you have done for my people," Natassa said. "I assure you, it is well earned."

Damn. What a thing to live up to.

But he'd gotten involved in this disaster. Time to see it through. He marched the group out of the room, Natassa and Damianos at his side.

ASSASSIN

Neil ran alongside the pack of refugees, following Natassa's lead through the airy corridors and filtered light. Which was fading, Neil noticed. How long had they been at this? Felt like days. Maybe it was. If it was getting dark, that meant they were edging on at least 24 hours of no sleep, aside from a guilt-ridden nightmare. No wonder he was ready to fall over.

Damianos ran next to him, holding the sword, his face a mask of determination. The golden yellow streaks against his black fur caught the light, making him look spotted as well as striped. His eyes were a shimmering magenta, as was the color of his inner ears. And of course, he had those tiny jewels nestled around his eyes like all Athánatos he had encountered. If Neil had to guess his age based on his looks, he'd say the kid was less than twenty, but he was probably way off.

Neil just had to hope he'd be useful if they ran into trouble.

"The Royal Chambers are through this way," Natassa said. They entered a large atrium with thick columns, various small trees, and an open roof.

Sunlight bathed the trees in a haunting light. Walls ran alongside the columns with simple paintings drawn on them. An open door stood on the far end. "Just a moment longer."

"Good," Neil said. "If we can just--"

"Will wonders never cease," a familiar voice said. "The princess of the Athánatos has returned home."

Neil turned, his belly cold.

Ryota walked into the atrium from a side door, arms crossed. Neil's fur stood on end. Damn it all, they should have killed the traitor at the casinos and saved themselves a whole hell of a lot of trouble. Curse Trecheon and his stupid sentiments.

Abrax stood next to him, glaring at Neil. "As I said, my lord," Abrax said. "Attempting escape with an outsider."

Neil clenched his jaw and lifted his sword. *"'My lord?' Are you shitting me? You're seriously helping this asshole after all that trash talk? He's a damn murderer."*

"You play the game you are thrust into," Abrax said, lowering his gaze.

Ryota lifted his chin. "Neil. Long time no see."

Neil bared his teeth. "Go to hell, traitor."

Ryota raised one brow. "Look who's talking."

"Don't," Neil snarled. "Don't compare yourself to me."

"And why not?" Ryota said. "Outlander could have been something big, but you and Trecheon let it fall apart--"

"You think we *let* it fall apart?" Neil snapped. "That shit-eating asshole Ackerson *tore* Outlander apart. He used us. Hell, he used *all* of his teams, then he turned us against each other to cover his own damn tracks. What do you think Angel is? They ain't going to door to door selling holy books."

"You think I give a shit about Ackerson?" Ryota shot back. "Outlander could have been used to help zyfaunos. Take out humans, liberate governments. You could have been *great--* "

"Oh, don't give me that holier-than-thou bullshit," Neil said. "As if somehow being zyfaunos makes you superior to all other races."

"You just don't understand--"

"You know what I understand?" Neil said, tightening his hands around the sword's grip. "June 2nd, 2029. Stratford-Upon-Avon." His ears rang thinking of the memory.

Ryota took a step back. He lowered his gaze and formed fists. "That... that wasn't my fault."

"Do you think it matters whose *fault* it was?" Neil said. His vision blurred. This was it. He didn't give a damn about finishing the job or taking out a murderer. This was *revenge.* "You left us. Clarissa *died* trying to save your ass. Anthony got his foot *blown off* and he bled out. And you *left us.* You ran off like the selfish coward you are!"

"Anyone would have panicked!" Ryota said, snarling. "We could have *died. I didn't want to die.* "

"You're a damn soldier, Ryota," Neil spat. "You don't run, you don't panic, you *fight.* Hell, I couldn't even convince myself to take down half the hits Ackerson assigned us and I still fought for Clarissa and Anthony. And then you ran off with that traitorous team and murdered anyone who got in your way." His voice cracked. "Damn it, Ryota, they were *family. We* were family! How could you abandon all of us like that? "

Ryota flattened his ears and furrowed his brow. "If Trecheon hadn't--"

"No, " Neil said. "Don't put this on him. Trecheon has enough blood on his hands. He doesn't need you dumping more, especially for something that's not even his fault. At least he's trying to make up for it and fight back the corruption."

Ryota pressed his lips together, but then paused. His eyes grew wide. "Holy shit. Trecheon is the White Assassin."

Neil's whole body buzzed and his ears rang. "Wait, what? I-I didn't--"

"All the pieces fit," Ryota said, staring at the floor. "That's the blood on his hands, isn't it? And the White Assassin only takes out corrupt hits." He growled. "It's why he had that high-powered handgun too. Why he could track me down and why he didn't go to the authorities and just went after me himself."

"Oh, Sisters alive," Natassa breathed. Neil flattened his ears and squeezed his eyes shut. Damn it all.

Ryota whipped his head up and stared at Neil. "And you're working with him, aren't you? I heard you were connected with Matron Fawn…. Good god, Matron Fawn's death… It was a sniper rifle. Like that rifle I caught you with. You *killed her.* Both of you are *assassins."*

Neil stepped back. He turned to his allies. Both Natassa and Damianos stared, quills bristled. The Athánatos refugees gaped, confused, but… they knew. Goddammit, they *knew.*

"You damn *hypocrite,"* Ryota said. Neil turned. Ryota gritted his teeth. "Calling me a traitor and murderer while you're going around assassinating people!"

Neil glared, though guilt raged through his belly, making him feel sick. "At least I'm trying to do some good."

"The entire human race has practically enslaved us for centuries," Ryota said. "Killing them off will do far more good than knocking off mob bosses one at a time. Humans *deserve* what's coming to them. Matron Fawn was a person, a zyfaunos, an ally, and you *killed her."* He snorted. "Don't call me coldblooded when you're no better than me."

Neil faltered. Was that true? But Neil killed enemies. People who ruined other people's lives. Ryota just killed whoever got in his way. He created monsters. There was a difference. Right?

But Neil's mind flashed back to the aftermath of the Matron's death, talking with the police officer in charge of the investigation. *She was a living, breathing, sentient creature. Just like your parents,* the policeman had said. The parents who died at the hands of the Matron's assassin sisters.

His message had been clear. By killing her, Neil was no better than she was.

Or Ryota.

Neil's chest tightened and he couldn't control his breathing. The world faded and he fell to one knee. *Fight the panic. Five things you can see, four things you can hear...* But nothing grounded him.

Then a soft, sweet smell wafted by his nose and a gentle hand gripped his shoulder. Natassa. He glanced up, trying to slow his frantic breaths.

Natassa squeezed his shoulder and pressed her forehead to his fur. "Stay with me, Neil. You have put yourself in danger to save my people. He has no power over you."

Neil gripped her hand.

Ryota bared his teeth and shot a bolt of electricity toward them. Neil instinctively held his hand up, Natassa gasped, and several of the refugees screamed.

But the bolt never hit. Damianos stood in front of them, holding the electricity between his hands. His fur and quills sparked with bits of lightning. He glared.

"You will not harm Athánatos any longer," he spat. "Nor will you hurt the puma."

Neil stared.

Ryota glared and armed himself with more electricity. Abrax stepped back, his eyes wide. "I'm Black Bound. You can't kill me."

Damianos narrowed his eyes. "The fact that you believe it is my intent to kill you says more about your fear of death than it does about my actions."

Neil flicked his tail. Damianos had a point. He had thought Ryota just wanted to hurt. Instead, it seemed, Ryota was afraid to die. He stood and put himself between Ryota and Natassa.

He'd give him something to fear.

"Natassa, get the refugees out. We've got this."

Natassa hesitated. "But--"

"Go!" Neil charged Ryota.

CREATION

Ryota snarled and shot a thick bolt of lightning at Neil, but Damianos caught it with one hand and wrapped it around Neil's sword. Neil stared, frozen for half a second, expecting the weapon to shock him. But it didn't. It swirled around in ever-moving bolts, clinging to the edges of the sword, making little crackles and booms as it heated the air around it. *Don't look a gift horse in the mouth.* He swung the sword at his enemies.

Ryota and Abrax leapt out of the way. The lightning dispersed around them harmlessly.

Neil snarled. This wasn't going to be easy. He turned. "Natassa--"

"I know," She herded the refugees into the Royal Wing. She paused. "For what it is worth, Neil... You are forgiven."

Neil took a sharp breath. "What?"

"You are forgiven," she said again. "Hold that in your heart." She pressed her lips together. "I will return with help. Keep yourselves safe."

After that statement, how could he not? "Count on it."

Ryota bared his teeth. "Get back here!" He threw lightning at the entrance to the Hall.

Damianos caught it again and pulled it back. Neil reached up and found the sword attracted the bolts of electricity. Relieved, he turned to swing at Ryota and Abrax, but they had already scattered.

This wasn't getting them anywhere. "Damianos!" The young Athánatos met his eyes. Neil pointed behind Ryota. Damianos nodded and dashed behind their enemy. With effort, Neil swung the sword forward, willing the electricity to Damianos' hand. Damianos pulled it free, lit his own sword with it, and blasted the rest at Ryota and Abrax. Ryota held his hands up and a purple-green shimmer formed in front of him, deflecting the lightning away from him.

Abrax wasn't so lucky. A bolt of the deflected lightning hit him square in the chest, sending him flying against a wall. He yelped and fell to the floor.

Neil flattened his ears. Not a nice way to go.

But Abrax stirred and groaned. He lifted himself on one arm before collapsing again.

Ryota stared at him, jaws slack, eyes wide, as if he couldn't believe what had happened. He flattened his ears and his voice quavered. "H-he should have known better."

Neil's anger burned. Ryota talked a mean game about killing humans, but the moment he actually hurt someone, he couldn't stomach it. No wonder he had run when Clarissa and Anthony got killed.

Now was their chance. Neil rushed Ryota, sword out.

Ryota whipped around Neil and smashed a well-aimed foot in Neil's back, knocking him into the wall. Neil collapsed to the floor, shook himself, then scrambled behind a pillar, hoping to avoid Ryota's magic.

But rather than blast the pair with more lightning, Ryota dashed for Abrax, whipping a small bottle out of his trench coat pocket.

Neil squinted.

"No! Get that bottle!" Damianos shouted. He rushed Ryota.

Ryota threw a bolt of electricity at him. Damianos caught it, but the force of it blasted him back and he slid along the floor, dropping his sword. Satisfied, Ryota turned back toward Abrax.

No. Neil dove for Ryota, sword out, aiming for the bottle. But his aim was off when he hit the floor and he sliced through Ryota's hand.

Ryota yipped and dropped the bottle. It crashed to the stone floor and shattered, throwing the contents in a wide circle around the room. They looked like tiny black pebbles. One landed near Neil, and he reached for it, curious.

"Do not touch it!" Damianos shouted. "It is a Cast charm!"

Neil scrambled to his knees and shrunk away, his skin crawling. "Holy *shit.*"

Ryota snatched one up with his good hand and ran for Abrax again. Neil dropped his sword and threw himself at Ryota, wrapping around his legs and dragging them both to the floor. Ryota hit with a thump, but he landed near Abrax. He wiggled out of Neil's grip, grabbed Abrax by the shoulder, and flipped him on to his back.

Abrax gave a cry of pain and held his hands up, but didn't have the strength to fight back. Ryota lifted the little black pebble.

"Stop him!" Damianos shouted. But Neil wasn't fast enough.

Ryota smashed the pebble in Abrax's eye.

Abrax screamed and his body practically turned inside out as black ink spilled out of his mouth, from between his eyes, and through his nose. Black spurts slashed through his body, spilling ink like blood, until he dissolved into an unrecognizable mess.

"Jesus, Mary, and Joseph!" Neil leapt to his feet and snatched up the sword. It crackled with electricity, but it was faded. "What in God's name?"

Then, three little blue lights blinked into existence on the puddle.

A Cast. He was a *Cast.*

Neil's stomach lurched.

Ryota retched and shook his head, raining red fur on the ground. He glanced once between Neil and the Cast that was once Abrax, scooped up several scattered Cast charms as well as Damianos' sword, then darted toward the Royal Wing.

The newly minted Cast rippled and gurgled as Ryota escaped.

PERSONAL INVASION

Matt's skin grew hot under his fur watching the six Phonar phoenixes stare at him, their faces devoid of emotion. Little representations of their elements swirled around them. Purple and white fire around Excelsis, the raven and Deo, the egret. Electricity around Jústi, the kestrel and soft dirt and sand around Pax, the burrowing owl.

Two others stood around the fire that Matt didn't recognize. A kori bustard with long legs and gray and white peacock-like feathers. They had small, polished stones floating about them. The other was a falcon with blue peacock feathers and tiny rivers of water flowing in circles around their arms, legs, and waist.

Excelsis walked forward and met Matt's gaze with his piercing blue eyes. He waved a winged arm and tiny violet embers floated to the group. Christian and Trecheon leapt back, yelping.

"It's okay," Matt said. "It's not hot. This is how they communicate."

"They throw *fire* at you?" Christian said. *"Dios mio,* did I drop into a fantasy RPG, or what? I'm expecting a raging battle theme to start playing any second now. Gimmie some mana potions and a giant-ass sword."

Trecheon let one of the embers touch his hand. His eyes grew wide.

Matt snatched an ember out of the air and Excelsis voice echoed in his head. *Greetings Guardians.*

Guardians? But Matt was the only Guardian here. "Excelsis--"

Child of Sol. Excelsis caught his eye. Matt winced at the title. *Know that we are outside of time. We see a future that you do not yet know.* His gaze wandered through Matt's group. *And so I call you Guardians.*

Matt glanced behind him. He wasn't sure how to interpret that. The Defender military only had four Guardian positions – the two Master Guardians and the two Golden Guardians. Technically they were all filled. If someone else here was going to be a Guardian, other Guardians would have to die first.

He shook his head. "What are you all doing here?"

We were summoned, and told to wait here for the Guardians, Excelsis said. *It was a summons we could not ignore.*

Matt flicked an ear back. "By who? I thought you only reported to Athánatos royalty."

Excelsis nodded his head. *The Black Cloak.*

Matt's ears burned. That manipulative *bastard.* The strange cryptid who had given him riddled messages, who could practically be responsible for Cix's death after everything he'd done to throw Matt off. *Damn* him. "Of course it was him. Damn it all, we could have really used you all when we were fighting Cast and now I find out that the Black Cloak kept you here? When I see him--"

A blast of purple embers hit his face. *You misunderstand. We were not called by the one who hosts the Cloak, but the Cloak herself.*

Matt paused. *Herself?*

"But why?" Sami asked. "We really could have used your help when we fought the Cast."

The Cast are a symptom, Deo said now, raining white fire on the group. *The Basileus is the disease. We have been summoned to treat it, as we did with the first.*

Matt's jaw dropped. "The first Basileus?"

The Basilea who first created Cast, Deo clarified.

Darvin pulled himself out of his puddle. "Why didn't you do that sooner?" he snapped. "Melaina has been a cast for *decades.* Zyearth has *hundreds* of them with no way to cure them. I mean, from what we got from Natassa and Ouranos, the Basileus has been at this for over a century. And you've just *now* thought maybe it'd be a good idea to try and stop him?"

The Phonar exchanged glances with each other, tiny ticks of emotion flashing across their normally blank faces – worry, concern, shame. Finally Excelsis turned to them.

We are bound to the word of the Cloak, he said. *Her word is what stirs us, and without it, we cannot act on our own against the Basileus. This is the oath we took when we became summons.*

"So the Black Cloak is to blame," Matt said, crossing his arms.

You must understand, Guardian, Deo said. *Our first defeat of the Basilea was won at great cost.* She glanced around at the other phoenixes. *It cost many lives, yes, but also memories, freedoms, and even the sacred peace of death. It was a cost so great, even centuries later we question the worth of that cost. It was, in many ways, no victory at all. Only a tradeoff.*

And that was with us at full strength, with many powerful allies, Excelsis said. *To attempt to fight this Basileus, who is not only stronger than our first enemy, but has stronger Cast, is futile if we are lacking in power. We are weighing the cost of another tradeoff.*

"What do you mean, lacking in power?" Trecheon said. "Look at you! You've got magic floating about you like you're damn *gods*. What power do you still need?"

We are missing members of our Order, Deo said. *Members who, for reasons unknown, have ignored the Cloak's summons to protect those under their care. This can only mean their charges are in grave danger. Without the full Order, we lack strength.*

Damn these things. "Then why are you even here?" Matt asked.

Every phoenix's eyes glowed and their various elements rained down on Matt's group. The Phonar spoke as one, their voices distant, almost omnipresent. *When the Cloak calls, the Order answers.*

Matt flipped his ears back, but didn't say anything.

The falcon with water about them stepped forward and gently splashed Matt. *When we fought the Basilea, we were inexperienced, and despite all our power, we struggled to match her malice. But the Cloak has gathered the Guardians and brought magic to us that we did not have. We may yet stand a chance with you at our side.*

Matt furrowed his brow. That was quite a declaration. No pressure or anything.

Now that the Guardians have joined us, Excelsis said. *We can take you through the rip in the Veil to meet the Basileus when you are ready.*

"We're losing time," Darvin said, slithering out from behind the group. He turned to the Phonar. "Where is the rip?"

All the phoenixes turned as one and pointed to the Sanctum's entrance.

Every fiber of Matt's fur stood on end.

"Where's that lead?" Darvin asked.

"The Sanctum," Matt said. "The rip is in the *Sanctum?*"

The Inner Sanctum holds the gateway, yes, Excelsis said.

"Draso's holy mercy," Matt muttered. The Inner Sanctum. Where his father had been killed. Where he and Izzy had been Black Bound. Where all the nightmares Matt had ever faced started.

His mind flooded with red. The quilar who'd killed his father. The red of blood on the ground. The red in Matt's vision as his Gem bound to himself in his angry energy and fear. His father's scream, the frantic fleeing, the near starvation, the--

"Matt?" Sami frowned.

Matt waved her off. "I'm... I'm…"

"Don't you tell me you're fine, because you're not," Sami said.

"I just… I need to go for a walk," Matt said. "Lay some ghosts to rest. Try and... come to terms with things."

Sami pasted her ears back and furrowed her brow. "If you want company..."

"I don't need it," Matt said. "I'll be fine."

"Matt--"

"I *will* be fine," Matt said, trying to stop the shaking. Just keeping his voice steady was a fight. "Even if I'm not now. I'm going to need a little time before going into the Sanctum. You know why. Can you understand that?"

Sami squeezed his shoulder. "Yeah. I can. Try not to take too long though. We can come back after all the crisis is over, if you need to."

"I won't be gone long," Matt said. "I just need..." He shook his head. "I'll be back."

We will be waiting for your return, Deo said. *Child of Sol.*

Matt stared. Child of Sol. What a title. It carried way too much weight.

In some awful, terrible way, he wanted to hate Trecheon simply for being there. A red quilar… an Omnir… at the place where Omnirs ripped his whole world from him.

But that wasn't fair. Trecheon hadn't done anything. But he couldn't handle being near him. He turned toward the village.

Toward his childhood home.

THERAPY

Trecheon pasted his ears back as he watched Matt walk off.

Matt had his good points. Maybe. He had to tell himself that. But with his xenophobic attitude toward Trecheon, his suspicious tendencies, and his need to control everything, Trecheon had a hard time convincing himself to tolerate him, let alone like him.

Well, to be fair, Trecheon had a lot of those elements too. Maybe Trecheon didn't like Matt because he saw too much of himself in him. Classic psychological analysis, but it seemed to fit.

But seeing Matt broken like that didn't sit well with him. No one should have to feel that. Not even jerks like Matt.

"What on earth is his issue?" Christian asked. "This is just some old ghost town."

"This is Matt's *birthplace,*" Sami said, narrowing her eyes at Christian. "Show some respect."

Christian raised his eyebrow. "He's too young. No one's lived here for almost sixty years."

"Matt is sixty," Trecheon said. He waved a hand at his Gem. "Part of the Gem's powers."

Christian's jaw dropped. "You're kidding."

"I wish," Trecheon said. He turned to Sami. "What's important about the Inner Sanctum?"

"It's where Matt's father died," Sami said. "Specifically, where an Omnir stabbed his Gem and essentially disintegrated him."

Christian winced and glanced back at Trecheon. "So that's why he hates you. I get now why he said that was private."

"And we have to go there, don't we," Trecheon said. "We have to visit the place where he last saw his father."

"Where he saw his father die, yes," Sami said. "And where he bound himself to his own Gem, made himself an enigma, and set himself up for bullying and hate for the rest of his life. Black Bound zyfaunos are feared on Zyearth, and Matt felt the brunt of that fear from the moment he stepped foot on the planet at six years old."

Trecheon shook his head. Too much. It would overwhelm anyone. He met Sami's gaze. "He shouldn't be alone. Not with all this going on at once. Someone should go talk to him."

A purple ember landed on Trecheon's nose. *Child of Sol.*

Child of Sol? Trecheon turned.

Excelsis eyed him. He waved another ember to Trecheon. *You should be with him while he mourns.*

Trecheon's tail fluffed up and he tensed.

Sami flicked her tail. "What did he say?"

"That I should go be with Matt." Trecheon frowned. "You can't mean me."

I do.

"But." The words catching on his tongue. "It was my damn family who did all this to him. Literally my scumbag past that did this to him. I'm the last person he wants to see. Why me?"

Child of Sol, Excelsis said again. *Both of you know loss like few others.*

Trecheon crossed his arms. Why the hell was he calling him a child of Sol? Surely he meant Matt. "You mean misery loves company. Knowing loss doesn't mean I can help."

Experience breeds understanding, Excelsis said. *Understanding breeds empathy. Empathy is a companion to mourning.*

Trecheon flicked an ear.

You underestimate your heart, Outlander, Excelsis said. *Go to him.*

Trecheon stepped back. He'd called him Outlander. He hadn't used that name since the war. If it was up to him, he'd never use it again.

"Trecheon?" Sami asked.

Trecheon shook his head. "Excelsis… he thinks I should be with Matt because I've known loss like him."

"Take this, *Jefe.*" Christian handed Trecheon his phone. "For the light."

Trecheon frowned.

"This… the bird is right," Christian said. "You've known a lot of loss in your life. Your parents, your grandparents, Ayumi, Ryota… Not to mention your war buddies. That's a lot." He took a deep breath. "Clearly Matt has lost a lot too. You might find some common ground." He waved the phone at Trecheon. "Don't let him be alone."

Trecheon sighed. "If he runs me through with his sword for this, I'm blaming you space aliens." Trecheon took Christian's phone and turned in the direction Matt had taken.

The woods were eerily silent. A few critters scurried away as Trecheon walked and there were a few wing flaps in the trees, but almost nothing else.

Homes stood scattered among the trees like ghosts. Small huts at the base of a tree with ladders or steps leading into a treehouse of some kind. Many of the treehouses were burned away, or rotting and falling apart, though the ground huts were mostly intact, albeit damaged. Some of the windows had glass, most broken, but these were obviously made by hand. Secluded. Quiet.

Alone.

He found Matt's ghostly white figure among the huts, running a hand over the door of a home near the edge of the forest by the sea. He looked so broken. Like a smashed shell, with scattered pieces flying off somewhere to the past. Wherever his memories had taken him. Far back, reliving it over and over again, eating away at him.

Trecheon watched him, feeling lost. He couldn't speak into that level of grief. Not when he was one of the reasons for it. He couldn't expect Matt to want comfort from a murderer.

But he had to do something. Bring Matt back to the present. If anything, because they needed his help fighting Theron and getting Neil back.

You underestimate your heart. Time to find out if Excelsis overestimated it.

Trecheon pulled out Christian's phone and activated the flashlight. Matt turned his head and met Trecheon's eyes, his own eyes distant and wild. He shook himself, then turned back to the hut. Trecheon walked up to him, then leaned against a tree.

"I lost my father when I was young too."

Matt looked up.

Trecheon took a deep breath. "I don't remember him. I was… what, two? Maybe three? And I was dumped right into the arms of my granddad and grandma. They had been living with us, so I didn't notice the difference. It wasn't until I was older that I started questioning things. Where was my dad? What happened to him?"

Matt frowned. "And what did?"

"I don't know," Trecheon said. "I asked Granddad, but he never said. He kept telling me 'when you're older' but I guess I was never old enough in his eyes. And then he disappeared."

Matt flattened his ears.

"I always thought that maybe something horrible happened to him," Trecheon continued. "A murder, or maybe he was a thief, or maybe he had been killed in jail or something. I used to make up stories that he was a secret agent on secret missions, or he had died a hero in some forgotten war. I tried looking him up. Never found anything on him or mom. Ever our last name seemed ghost-like. As far as I know, the only people still living that carry the Omnir name are me and Ryota. And my sister, if she's even alive." He shuddered. "I miss that closure. I may not have known Dad, but that doesn't mean I don't feel his absence. And not knowing what happened to him stings." He shrugged. "Maybe not as bad as Carter's mystery, but all the same."

"And you're telling me all this because…?"

Trecheon shrugged. "No one should be alone in their grief."

Matt flattened his ears.

"You have people who are counting on you," Trecheon said. "But I understand the need for closure. Maybe more than some of the others, I don't know. But you shouldn't be alone while seeking it, or it'll consume you."

"And you're the best one to be with."

Trecheon chuckled darkly. "I'm probably the worst one to be with while you go through this. But Excelsis sent me. You shouldn't be alone."

Matt wrinkled his snout. "Excelsis… or the Cloak?"

"Hell if I know."

Matt stared a moment, then shook his head and turned back to the door. "This… this is my house. My home. I didn't think it'd be standing, let alone recognizable."

Trecheon handed him the phone. Matt took it without a word, aimed the light at the door, and put his hand on the door. He stood, frozen.

Trecheon gently gripped Matt's shoulder. Matt breathed deeply, nodded to Trecheon, and pushed. Vines and branches snapped as the door opened.

There wasn't much to it. A spacious living area, complete with a small living room housing basic furniture, a kitchen that had a sink without a faucet, lots of counter space, and a small table with chairs. In one corner stood an easel with a canvas and there was a faint smell of linseed oil. A staircase on their right looked like it led up to the treehouse attachment, though it was hard to determine in the dark. Everything had a thick layer of dust and leaves and it just smelled... old. Like a disused museum.

Matt inched forward, kicking up leaves and dust, until he reached the easel. He held out a hand and blew the dust aside with a gust of wind. The canvas was blank. A set of long-since-ruined oil paints sat on a table next to the easel.

Trecheon leaned down and picked up a dust-covered lump. A toy. A tiny stuffed dragon. It must have been pink at one point, but the grime barely hinted at that. He sighed and placed the dragon on the kitchen table.

Matt leaned against a kitchen counter. "We were about to sit down for dinner when we heard the fighting," he said, staring at the ceiling. "My aunt ran into the room, screaming about some red enemy. Dad put her and mom in charge of us kids and he and Izzy's dad ran into the fray. Mom tried to gather a few supplies and begged my aunt to get us to safety, saying she'd follow. My aunt took us to the beach, hid us, then disappeared." Matt picked up another lump, a once-blue stuffed dragon. "Charlotte wouldn't sit still. She ran back up here and Izzy and I followed. I... I found mom's body in the garden. Twisted. Ruined. I'll never lose that image." He looked at the door opposite the one they entered. "I want to pay her respects, but I don't... I don't know if I can handle seeing her bones out there."

Trecheon frowned. "Want me to check?"

Matt glanced back at him. He pressed his lips together, but said nothing.

Trecheon nodded. "I'll check." He walked out the garden door.

The overgrown garden smelled of overripe pumpkins, tomatoes, and a variety of berries, poorly grown and untended. A pomegranate tree stood in one corner and next to it, a tree with rotting oranges under it. He could faintly make out the patterns and blocks where various garden sections would have been. Some misshapen fruits and vegetables poked out from the decaying dirt. A few scattered signs meant for marking different vegetables still survived, though they were illegible.

But he didn't see bones. He pushed aside dirt and poked at leaf piles, but he couldn't see anything.

As he neared the orange tree, something caught his eye.

A wooden tombstone. Trecheon approached it and leaned down, brushing aside the dust covering it. In crudely carved letters, he read, "Aurora Azure, daughter of Sol, wife, mother, Draso's child. You will be missed."

Trecheon stared. "Matt? You might want to see this."

Matt cautiously poked a head out into the garden. "Did you find her?"

"I found… something else."

GHOST

Matt stared at the tombstone. "What?"

"Your guess is as good as mine," Trecheon said, standing. He took several steps back, giving Matt room.

Matt kneeled by the tombstone. Aurora Azure. His mother's name. Carved into a makeshift marker. The slight mound under the epitaph suggested she had been buried here.

But no one had survived. The entire village had perished. Who could have buried his mom? He wished he could recognize the handwriting, but it was so slovenly written he didn't have a hope to cling to.

Maybe… maybe there had been a survivor.

He shook his head. No. That was dangerous thinking. No one survived. Maybe someone had buried her before they were killed. Or just put a memorial. His aunt perhaps. No one survived.

"I'll let you have some time alone with her," Trecheon said. "But I'll be just inside if you need to talk. Don't be alone too long, okay?"

"Sure." Matt settled into the dirt in front of the tomb. "Thanks."

Trecheon left the garden.

Matt stared at the tombstone. His breath came to him in shudders and his eyes burned.

"Hi, Mom," he said. Draso's horns, that was hard to say. He laid a hand on the tombstone. "I honestly didn't expect to see you here, so I didn't have a big speech planned or anything. Sorry if I ramble.

"I suppose the good news is I survived. Charlotte did too. We've had our ups and downs, but really, it's mostly ups. Jaymes and Amaia took me in. Charlotte chose to live with Uncle Walt. I think it was best for the both of them. They gave each other good company until Walt died last year. She took up painting like Dad and made a living out of it while helping run Walt's business."

He shifted in the dirt, using his magic to brush the tombstone free of dust. Draso's horns, she had missed so much in his life.

"I... I became a Guardian. You probably don't want to hear that considering what happened to Dad, but I'm glad I did. It's hard, but worth it. I hope Dad's proud."

He took a deep breath. "I... I miss you. I don't even know how to put that longing into words. It's not like the way I miss Amaia. Losing Amaia felt like a physical wound to the chest. Losing you... it feels like a ghost. Like it's not real. It's like chasing a memory."

He leaned against the tree. "Maybe that's why this is so hard. It's so distant that I don't know how to react. Everything is just flashes. Brief images. I can't even remember your face. Your laugh. I barely remember the way you held me as a kid. It's like... it's like you weren't real. I don't know how to make sense of it. Except that it hurts. It hurts and I don't know how to make it stop."

Somewhere in the darkness, an owl hooted softly. The wind blew through the trees and a cold breeze brushed through his fur and quills.

"I guess… I need to look forward. I've got so many wonderful people in my life. I wish you could meet them all." He chuckled. "Maybe even Ouranos. Or Trecheon. I think meeting Trecheon would be therapeutic somehow. He's the proof that all Omnirs aren't bad." He paused.

Good Draso. He pinned his ears back. "Trecheon might even be a friend. I've just been too stubborn and too… too hurt to see it." He shook his head. "I can't believe I even let myself think that way, but I did."

He glanced at the tombstone, still silent and unmoving. He sighed. "I need to move on. I thought I had, but I guess I hadn't. It's… been holding me back a long time." He shook his head. "And it almost cost me a friend. I can't let that happen anymore. I don't have to be angry." He stared up through the trees. "I can let Trecheon be my friend."

He turned around and leaned his forehead against the marker. "I love you, Mom. I'll see you again someday. Take care of Dad and Aunt Solana for us." He stood, testing his legs to make sure they still worked. Damn, that was hard.

But it was time to move on. And maybe time to talk to Trecheon. Time to let go of this hate. Trecheon didn't deserve it. He entered the hut.

Trecheon leaned against the wall near the front door. "You okay?"

"Better," Matt said. "Thanks."

"No problem."

Matt leaned against a wall. "…Do you really hate yourself?"

Trecheon perked one ear. "What?"

"You've said it three or four times now," Matt said.

Trecheon splayed both ears and crossed his arms. "Yeah, I do."

Matt frowned. "You shouldn't do that to yourself."

Trecheon chuckled darkly. "You don't know the disgusting shit I've done in my life."

"I know the good things you've done," Matt said. Trecheon turned to him, one eyebrow perked. "You threw yourself in front of a lightning bolt to save my tail. You've put yourself at constant risk to help Neil. You chose to be with me and support me when all I wanted to do was drown in grief. You gave me a lifeline." He tried to smile, but couldn't quite make it work. "I thought I knew who my enemies are. But I was wrong. You're not my enemy, Trecheon."

Trecheon flattened both ears now, but… some hope lingered in his face. He wrinkled his snout and turned away. "Sure. Thanks." He perked one ear and met Matt's gaze. "I mean that."

Matt smiled properly that time. He had so much more he wanted to say, to fix this. But here, in this room, with these memories, he couldn't quite focus them. Mourning first. Apologies after. "I think… I think I want a few more minutes here. If you don't mind. I'll be back out in a bit, I promise."

Trecheon gave him a sad smile. "That's fine. I'll head back. Don't be long."

Matt watched him walk off. Maybe Trecheon had been the right zyfaunos to be there while he went through his grief. Maybe that was the closure he'd needed. Maybe Trecheon actually could be a friend.

But now he had mourning to do and little time to do it. He sat on the chair, closed his eyes, and tried to remember the smell of Dad's paints while he worked.

STATIC SHOCK

Neil stared wide eyed, his whole body buzzing with adrenaline.

A Cast. A damn *Cast.* Memories of a Cast literally trying to crush him to death flooded his brain, threatening to panic him.

Neil shook his head. *Keep a cool head.* They'd have to escape while they could.

Cast-Abrax hardly moved. He just bubbled quietly, sending little ripples over his body. The cluster of glowing blue eyes darted about on the surface, like he was looking for something.

Neil took a step toward the Royal Wing. He nodded to Damianos to follow. If they were careful--

Cast-Abrax shrieked wildly, his screams echoing off the walls. Neil pulled his ears down, squeezing his eyes shut.

"Neil!" Damianos shouted. Neil opened his eyes, just as Abrax leapt for him.

Damianos slammed into Neil, shoving him out of the path of the Cast. Neil rolled along the floor, but he quickly righted himself.

Too late.

Abrax wrapped himself around Damianos and dragged him to the ground. The young Athánatos didn't even have a chance to scream.

Neil's heart dropped. No, no, no! Damianos struggled under the inky body. Sword in hand, Neil rushed for the Cast, not sure what he could do. He had no magic, and using the sword would do nothing to the Cast. It'd probably just kill Damianos.

The sword crackled.

Neil stared. It still held leftover electricity from Ryota's attack.

Just one shot.

With a quick prayer that he wouldn't hit Damianos, he sliced his sword over the Cast, shaving off parts of it.

The electricity expanded tenfold and rippled through Abrax's body. The inky Cast jutted out in weird geometric shapes, like the soft spikes on a dog toy, then leapt off Damianos. Neil moved between them, sword out, staring at the Cast. "You okay, Dami?"

The Athánatos coughed and gagged, then took a deep breath. "I have been better."

"Can you stand?"

He pulled himself to his feet. He staggered slightly, but stayed up.

The electricity on the Cast vanished and it slithered about, disoriented. Little droplets spread out all around him. Neil chewed his lip. "Got a plan?"

Damianos flicked his ear back. "That was the last of the magic electricity."

"Unless you have some yourself," Neil said.

"Your jacket," Damianos said. "It is lined with wool, yes?"

Neil frowned. "I think? Might be fake wool though. I didn't exactly pay much for this."

"Even false wool will do." Damianos pulled out his amber stone. "Give me your jacket. When I give the word, place your sword near the stone and wool."

This was pretty much the wildest thing Neil had ever experienced, but he did as Damianos asked. Damianos rubbed the stone hard on the wool for several seconds.

Abrax started to regain himself, pulling the scattered droplets back into his body. He slowly rose from his puddle.

Neil flicked his tail and flattened his ears. "Any time you wanna get going with this, Dami."

Damianos stepped back. "Now!"

The Cast shrieked. Neil shoved the sword near the stone and wool, just as Abrax leapt into the air after them.

But the Cast didn't get close to them. Instead, he got a face full of electricity, which sent him sliding across the floor.

Neil pumped the air and hollered. "Hell yeah!" He turned back to Damianos for a high five.

The Athánatos stood steady now, his hands alight with electricity, a soft white against his yellow and black fur. Static electricity made his fur stand on end and puffed out his tail as bolts flashed about him, casting stark highlights and shadows over his body.

Neil decided against that high five, but he grinned. "You're a damn genius, Dami."

"There is a reason I keep the amber," Damianos said. "Amber against wool is an effective method to create static, and I can control all forms of electricity, not just magic. It is not as strong as magic, mind you, but it is the best we have."

Abrax pulled himself together much faster this time and attacked again.

Neil turned back to Abrax. "Well, it's cool as hell." He pointed his sword forward. "Do it again."

Damianos lit Neil's sword ablaze with lightning. Neil leapt forward and sliced Cast-Abrax in two. The electricity crackled through his body, breaking him into droplets, but he reformed almost instantly and dove again. Neil managed to avoid him, but barely.

"This isn't working," Neil said. "How the hell do you take down a Cast?"

"You cannot," Damianos said. "Nor will it tire or leave unless its master calls it back."

"Great." Neil flicked his tail. "Your electricity seemed to paralyze him for several minutes."

"That was with magic," Damianos said. "It will not be as effective with natural electricity. It may only hold him for a moment."

"A moment is all we need," Neil said. "Ryota went after Natassa and the others and we need to get there before he causes more damage." He held his sword out. "Give me everything you can!"

Damianos nodded. He squeezed his hands into fists and tensed. The electricity grew in his hands, surrounding him, further puffing out his fur and quills. The air tasted hot and metallic, and the lightning lit the walls up in eerie patterns.

Abrax shrieked and dove.

Neil leapt aside and pierced through Abrax. The sword stuck fast in the ground. It wouldn't hold the Cast normally, but... "Damianos, now!" Neil jumped back.

Damianos threw every bolt at the sword. The weapon acted like a lightning rod and drew all the electricity to the center. Abrax jolted about, shrieking, his Cast body jutting out in spikes again.

"Yes!" Neil punched the air. He waved to Damianos. "The Royal Wing. Hurry!"

The pair ran for the Wing without a look back. *God forgive me for that, but please hold him until we get to Natassa!*

No matter what, he wouldn't let Ryota hurt anyone again.

Mistakes

Ryota dashed through the halls leading to the Royal Chambers, clutching his stolen sword, still fighting the nausea.

I can't die. I CAN'T.

But Neil and Damianos were right behind him. Abrax would only hold them back for so long. Curse Damianos and his lightning manipulation. He'd counter anything Ryota threw at him.

He needed more protection. More Cast. Just a couple of the prisoners. A few for the sake of the many.

He rushed down the hall and entered a large alcove.

Three stragglers hugged the wall, leading an injured Athánatos, trying to keep up with the rest of the group. One of Dustrik's charge stayed behind to help, though they moved at a snail's pace toward the exit.

Ryota paused. Four zyfaunos. Four Cast. His stomach writhed in pain.

He had to hope it'd be enough. He ran for them.

The stragglers turned. One of them screamed. Dustrik's charge scooped up the injured Athánatos and ran.

Oh no you don't! Ryota shot a blast of electricity toward the exit, stopping their escape. The quilar gasped and fell, dragging the injured Athánatos with her.

Ryota moved between them, sword raised. "Don't move." He dove for one of the Athánatos, gripping the Cast charms. They leapt out of the way and Ryota slipped, loosening his fist.

One of the charms fell to the floor and fell between the cracks in the marble.

Damn it! "I said *don't move!*"

The wild rush of fire echoed across the hall.

Ryota created a shield, blocking the flames. He turned.

Natassa. She held her hands out, little embers dancing on her fur. "Stay back." Her voice trembled.

He met her gaze and wrinkled his snout. His heart pounded. *"You."*

Natassa stood there, hands ablaze, shaking. She wore a determined mask, though her fear broke right through it. She glared at him.

"Stand back, or face the flames, Ryota."

Ryota strengthened his shield and glared. He couldn't let her see his fear. *I can't die. Not like this.*

"Do you actually think you can fight me, let alone win?" He shot blasts of lightning into the air, trying to keep his voice steady, his heart under control. "You can't even shield. What do you think you can do to me?"

With a shout, she threw her fire forward, weaving it around the shield, enveloping Ryota.

Ryota held fast against the flames. Good Draso, that was *hot!* Everything smelled like burning. Like melting plastic, hot sulfur… burning flesh. It threatened to drop his mind back into the battle of DC, back into the hell of war.

I can't die! He pushed every ounce of power he could into the shield. Black Bound elixir formed on his fingertips in tiny beads… then started covering his fingers.

He stared. He'd never seen the elixir form that much before. He watched in fascination as the elixir ran up past his knuckles over his palms, toward his wrists. His skin and fur tingled.

But the shield strengthened. Natassa didn't stand a chance.

Then the smell faded. Natassa's fire completely gave out and she fell to one knee, exhausted. Spent.

Ryota smirked. He had survived. Again.

She stared, fear in her eyes.

"Your father always said you were the weak one of the family," Ryota said. It didn't come out quite as strong as he hoped, but he got the intended effect. She glared. Ryota continued. "A shame you don't know how to shield." He charged his magic. She was defenseless.

She was *defenseless.*

His heart raced, his breathing quickened, and his ears flicked back. He held up a shaky hand, trying to calm himself and failing. "I'll… I'll make this quick." He threw his lightning forward.

Natassa covered her head with her hands. Ryota closed his eyes, expecting a scream.

But she remained silent. He opened his eyes.

A Cast had caught her. His mind raced. A *Cast.* Abrax. It had to be. He had taken out Neil and Damianos and now he had Natassa. It had *worked.* He finally had his own Cast!

"Yes!" he shouted. "Finally one of these damn things worked in my favor. Good riddance to that damn puma." Though a twinge of guilt bit at him. He threw it aside. "Abrax, bring the Prinkípissa to me. She'll make a fantastic Cast."

But the puddle didn't move.

"Damn it, obey me!" Ryota shouted. He sent a shock through it, but it didn't seem affected by it.

Slowly the Cast moved toward him. Something glinted on the Cast's surface. Damianos' amber, perhaps. He really had killed them.

His stomach churned again. At least… at least he hadn't had to witness it. Forcing his stomach to calm, he separated one Cast charm from the others. "Open up and hand her to me, Abrax."

Someone roared at him. "You will not take our Prinkípissa from us!"

Ryota turned. Two Athánatos charged him. His fur stood on end and he leapt back, blasting the area with lightning. One Athánatos dove out of the way, but the other got a full chest of lightning, blasting him into the wall.

"Hektor!" the injured Athánatos called.

"I… he…" Ryota stammered. Oh Draso, he was dead. *Dead.* His stomach churned again. "That's… well, he shouldn't have gotten in the way. If he had just… just let me make him a Cast, he'd…" His voice trailed.

"Roscoe, *now!*"

Ryota's heart leapt. *Roscoe?* He turned, but too late. Natassa pounded magic charged hands to the ground and shot a flurry of ice spikes at him.

Ryota held his hands up and shielded, but the spikes tore through the shield and ripped into his flesh. A wound on the arm, one through the shoulder, another on his leg, and two through his left side. Blood splattered from the injuries, staining her ice red. Pain ripped through him, blurring his vision, deadening his hearing. Ryota reached for his voice, for air, but lost it, barely able to squeak above shocked gasps. His sword fell to the ground, but he couldn't even hear the clash.

I don't want to die!

The ice came and vanished in seconds, leaving nothing but ripped clothing, torn flesh, and bloodstains everywhere. His hands flew from wound to wound, almost instinctively, desperate to stop the bleeding. Everything faded.

Then his gaze landed on Roscoe. The Cast's wedding coil floated on top of his body in plain view.

Ryota snarled. He blasted Roscoe with a powerful bolt of lightning without even lifting a hand, and peeled the wedding coil off him.

Roscoe wailed, a shriek riding the line between pain and misery, a sound so loud and so dangerous it threatened to break Ryota completely.

But he didn't care. He shocked Roscoe again and again.

This is your fault. YOUR FAULT. Roscoe squirmed and screamed, his body jolting left and right, out of control, forming spikes and paralyzing him to the spot.

Natassa watched in horror. Ryota snarled. Mustering every ounce of strength he could, he dashed forward and slammed into her with force that surprised even him and pressed her to her back. "You will be my Cast!" He raised a hand, a Cast charm slipping between blood-soiled fingers.

Natassa screamed and covered her eyes.

Someone smashed into Ryota, knocking him off her. Pain shot through his body again and he slid along the marble, leaving big bloody streaks. Through watery eyes, he looked up.

Neil. With Damianos beside him. He stared.

"The Cast, Damianos!" Natassa shouted. "He is an ally. Remove the electricity, hurry!" Damianos pulled the electricity away, holding it in front of him. Roscoe stopped shrieking. He slithered over, snatched up his wedding coil, and moved between Natassa and Ryota, gurgling angrily.

Ryota sat on the floor, still gripping his wounds, helpless.

Neil glared at him, holding Ryota's sword, soiled in blood. "After everything you've done… everything you continue to do… you still find more ways to hurt people."

Ryota flicked his ears back, hunching down. His pounding heart echoed in his wounds. He tried to summon electricity, but only a few weak sparks hovered around him and when he formed a shield, it flickered and died immediately.

Damn it all. He groaned, putting further pressure on the bleeding.

"I should kill you," Neil said. "I should finish what I started in the war."

Ryota shrunk back, trembling and whimpering. *I don't want to die…*

Neil's face hardened. "Look at you. You're such a damn coward. All tough talk and you can't even face your own death with dignity." He shook his head. "Guess it's a good thing I ain't gonna be the one delivering it."

Ryota perked a trembling ear. "What?"

Neil lowered the sword. "I'm sick of being a killer."

Ryota narrowed his eyes. "You're making a mistake."

Immediately Neil brought the sword back up and pressed the tip under Ryota's chin. Ryota stiffened. Neil bared his fangs. "Don't. Test me." Ryota closed his eyes and whimpered. Neil rolled his eyes and moved his sword. "And keep your damn mouth shut. You don't want me rethinking my decision." He turned to Natassa and helped her to her feet. "Are you okay?"

She gripped Neil's hand. "I am fine."

Hektor, the Athánatos Ryota had shocked, groaned and turned over. Ryota felt a strange calm in his chest. He hadn't killed him. He didn't need to see another death.

Neil flicked an ear. "Take him and get your people out," Neil said. "I'll deal with Ryota."

"Deal with me how?" Ryota spat. Neil glared at him and he shrank back, but hardened his gaze. "You already won. You should just leave me. Theron could be here any minute."

"I'm going to bandage you up, get you to the mainland, and let the damn authorities deal with you," Neil said. "Which is what I should have done in the first place. Damianos, keep an eye on him while I work."

Ryota wrinkled his snout, but looked away.

Neil frowned. "Is there any way to keep this asshole from using his magic?"

Natassa flicked an ear. "If there is, I do not know what that might be."

Ryota didn't say anything. Neil narrowed his eyes. "I'll ask Izzy when we see her next. She'll know." He kneeled next to Ryota.

Natassa walked to the puma. "Neil?"

Neil glanced at her, ears perky.

She gave him a soft smile. "Thank you. I mean that."

Neil flicked an ear back and glanced off. Damianos nudged him. Neil shot him a look, then smiled back. "Uh, sure, Pringles. You're welcome, I guess."

Natassa planted a kiss on his forehead. "You are every bit the Defender that my friends are. Never forget that. I will see you soon."

Ryota watched her walk off. He coughed. Blood wet his lips.

Neil stared at him, ears flicked back, tail twitching. "Come on, let's get you patched up."

THE GENOCIDE

Ouranos fought to stay aware as Izzy dragged him through the halls. Everything was agony. The ache in his chest wavered from sharp, nearly unbearable pain to complete numbness, paired with fading consciousness as his body threatened to shut down completely. He was so weak he could not even call on Matt's colors any longer. The absence pained him as much as the wound. He could only hope Matt did not share in it.

Izzy hurried along the halls, as fast as she could with his bulk leaning on her shoulder. The healer's mask had returned, though cracked. She moved too fast, darting her gaze about, her breaths coming in short, ragged gasps.

Guilt rang through him. He should have come alone. He should not have allowed himself to put Izzy in danger.

He had pointed her in the general direction of the Royal Wing, but for the last several minutes, he had been completely silent. The very thought of speaking, or even grunting with the pain, was excruciating.

They were running out of time. Perhaps, after everything he had done, this was suitable punishment. He waited for the Basileus to agree, though he did not speak. Relief warred with fear.

Perhaps his father had given up too.

As they wandered, voices echoed down the hall. Ouranos' heart raced, which probably only aggravated the injury. "Isabelle--"

"I hear them," Izzy whispered. "But we're near the chambers, right? It might be someone we know."

A faint relief filled Ouranos. She made a good point. "Please… be cautious."

Izzy nodded and slowed their pace.

"It is good to see the Prinkípissa in such good spirits," someone said. Ouranos perked an ear. Damianos? "After everything she has faced, she needs that."

"And I'm telling you, she's not gonna want a broken-down HVAC repair man with a smeared record and a kid brother to look after, Dami," another voice said. Ouranos heaved relief, as much as he could in his condition. Neil.

Damianos chuckled. "I like this shortened name you have given me. We do not shorten our names normally, but it suits."

Izzy physically relaxed. "Thank Draso." She hefted Ouranos further up on her shoulder and quickened toward the voices.

They entered the hall. The first voice was indeed Damianos. His yellow, black striped fur was unmistakable, even in Ouranos' blurred vision. The quilar held electricity on his hands. Ouranos chewed his lip. He had known that Electrik and his husband had vanished during the war. That meant Damianos could be the new Archon by default. More lives lost at the Basileus' hands.

Neil was on one knee in front of someone with bright red fur wearing modern clothes, though it was not Trecheon.

Izzy perked her ears. "Ryota!"

Neil looked up. "Izzy! Thank God." He frowned at Ouranos. "Holy shit, what the hell happened to you? Did a sentry get you?"

Ouranos could only nod.

Neil flicked his ears back. He stared at Izzy. "What a time for your healing to stop working."

"Bedside manner," Izzy said, narrowing her eyes. "I need to get him help now." She glanced at Ryota, now covered in makeshift bandages, wearing a scowl. He turned away when she looked at him. "Did you do that?"

"Natassa, actually," Neil said with a grin. He pointed to the entrance to the Royal Chambers. "She left with a bunch of the Basileus' prisoners. The rip in the Veil's in there. Roscoe's with her."

"Then that's where we're headed," Izzy said. She nodded to Ryota. "Might want to get that sword out of his reach."

"Duly noted." Neil picked up the sword and passed it to Damianos. "Light that for me, would you, Dami? You never know when I'll need the extra power." Damianos nodded and lit the sword with electricity, though he turned his gaze to Ouranos.

"Prínkipas Ouranos," Damianos said, shock on his face. "My Lord, I…"

"I… am in good hands… Damianos," Ouranos managed to say. "Fear not."

Damianos' eyes widened. "You can speak! But you do not have your Soul Jewels returned?"

"I… have had my soul bridged," Ouranos said. "Thanks to these… Guardians."

"That is wonderful, but…"

Ouranos waved a hand again. "Trust them." But he could not muster the energy for more.

But Damianos seemed unconvinced. He turned to Izzy. "What happened?"

"No time," Izzy said. "We just--"

"Now this is a sight to behold," a new voice said. "All my enemies in one place."

Ouranos' blood ran cold, and his knees gave out. He lifted his head. Izzy struggled to hold him upright, but she followed his gaze.

The familiar black Athánatos quilar stood before them in a doorway. The tips of his ears were a burnt orange and he had markings above the eyes in the same color. He wore long pants and a diamond shaped piece of cloth in the front, the *kasoa,* light blue with white accents. A gold band laid across the collar bone with small trinkets hanging off it. His Basileus chain. He stared at them all with striking silver eyes.

But most striking of all was what he wore on his arms. Countless braided bands, each with a set of colored, triangle shaped jewels. Nausea waved over Ouranos. Fire and ice, there had to be close to a hundred. They sat in layers on his arms, weighing them down, though he was clearly unhindered by them, physically or mentally. He held a sword in his hand.

Neil twitched his tail. "Who the hell are you?"

"The Basileus." Ouranos choked. "Theron of the Athánatos. My... father."

Ryota laughed darkly. "I did warn you."

"Shut the hell up, Ryota," Neil said. Damianos tossed the lightning-bathed sword to Neil and further emblazoned his electricity. Izzy shifted her hammer up, though Ouranos knew she would be useless against the Basileus while holding him.

The Basileus glanced around the room. He leaned his sword against the wall and crossed his arms, an awkward move considering the bracelets. He flicked his ears forward and turned to Ouranos. "Well then, Prínkipas. Quite the ragtag band of allies you have acquired here." He nodded to them in turn, starting with Damianos. "An orphan who let his fathers die. A healer who cannot heal at all. A pair of white assassins."

Izzy turned to Neil, confusion on her face. He gritted his teeth and stepped back, flattening his ears, but he did not counter the claim. Ouranos frowned. He had known Trecheon was an assassin, but Neil as well? And yet…

Theron lifted a brow. "And you, dear Prínkipas, have convinced them to follow a murderer." He snorted. "Have you told them the truth of the genocide?"

Izzy jolted. She looked him in the eye. "What truth?"

Ouranos' bones buzzed, increasing the pain. Guilt washed over him. "The Omnirs… the genocide…" His voice faded.

"Come now, Prínkipas," Theron said. "Let us hear the truth of the genocide."

Izzy furrowed her brow now. She glanced back and fourth between Theron and Ouranos, unsure, almost afraid.

Ouranos frowned at her, his heart aching. "The Omnirs… were goaded."

Izzy flattened her ears.

Ouranos spat blood on the ground. "They were deceived. Coerced into attacking Sol."

Theron turned up one corner of his mouth. "And who coerced them, Prínkipas?"

Izzy stared.

Ouranos turned his head. This was it. All this time he had thought to hide this fact, but as it grew more and more certain that he would die, he had to cleanse his spirit of guilt. Without looking Izzy in the eye, he spoke. "…I did."

It was a testament to Izzy's shock that she did not even gasp. Her response came as a quiet whisper. "…What?"

"I… coerced them," Ouranos said. "I convinced them to attack. To steal the Gems. Prep them for violent binding. We… we needed the power." Images flashed by. The mad hunt for Gems, power needed for the Cast. The manipulation of the Omnir tribe. The destruction of Sol. The obliteration of the Omnirs. All of it, all at once, bombarding his mind, threatening his sanity, even while pain laced through his chest and he fought for breath.

Izzy stared at the floor, her focus fading as she no doubt replayed the events in her own mind. Neil flattened his ears letting out a quiet whine. Damianos turned his head, rubbing his arm. Even Ryota remained silent, solemn.

But a moment later Izzy's eyes narrowed and she wrinkled her snout. Her ears flipped back and she huffed.

"You said 'we.'"

Ouranos nodded, eyeing her warily.

She tightened her grip on her hammer, making the leather wrap crackle in her hand. "So what he really means…" She turned her dark glare on the Basileus, snarling, raising her hammer toward him. "Is that *you* caused the Sol Genocide."

Ouranos' drew a sharp breath.

Theron frowned, lifting a brow. He stared, gaze darting between Ouranos and Izzy. "Ouranos persuaded them."

"You did," Izzy snapped. "Ouranos was a puppet. Hell, he was *still* a puppet when he was on Zyearth." She let out a feral growl, which made Damianos and Neil step back. "And he was even more so during the genocide. He only regained some part of himself during that War of Eons thing, the one Neil and Trecheon were in. *Years* after the genocide." Her whole body rumbled with growls and she formed a fist with her free hand. *"You* destroyed Sol!"

Theron smiled slightly. "Interesting. I expected you to turn your anger on Ouranos. A pity it seems to be on me instead." He lifted his chin. "Do you wish to take revenge?"

"Neil, get Ouranos to Trecheon," Izzy said.

Neil walked over and with Damianos' help, they took Ouranos from Izzy. Ouranos did all he could to hold in his groans. He wanted to say something, anything to her, but even sucking in breath to speak made him go blind with pain.

Neil frowned as he adjusted Ouranos on his shoulder. "Izzy, about the assassin thing—"

"You and Trecheon," Izzy said, keeping her eyes on Theron. "He means you."

Neil swallowed hard. "Yeah."

"That's what you were doing going after Ryota."

Ryota coughed.

Neil shrugged. "Kinda, yeah. But Izzy, we--"

"What do you mean by 'white assassin?'"

Neil pressed his lips tight. "We only take corrupt hits."

Izzy eyed him a moment. She shook her head. "We'll talk later."

"But--"

"Later," she snarled.

"Yeah… yeah of course," Neil said. "Don't get yourself killed."

"Noted."

Ouranos held fast as best he could. "Isabelle, you cannot--"

"It's Izzy, Ouranos," Izzy said. She turned to him, her expression softened. "You are not allowed to blame yourself for this. Your bastard father is to blame." She wrinkled her snout. "But since I think you need to hear it… I forgive you. Matt and Trecheon will forgive you too. This isn't your fault."

Ouranos flattened an ear. Forgiveness… from a victim of Sol. Decades of guilt screamed in his mind, begging he cling to it, but Izzy's words fought it off. Forgiven. He was *forgiven.* He searched for something, anything to acknowledge her and the weight of her statement, but he could not find the words.

Theron smirked. "And what do you think you can possibly do?"

Ouranos snatched one last look at Izzy before Neil and Damianos dragged him out of the room as quickly as they were able.

Izzy brandished her hammer. Her Gem's whine increased, making Ouranos' ears sting, and that familiar Black Bound elixir formed on her hands. A faint green aura encircled her body, something Ouranos had never seen on any magic user. She faced Theron, body tense, as she answered.

"Avenge the victims of Sol."

AVENGER

Izzy tightened her hands around the hammer, leather pressing through her fur and into her skin to the point of pain. She had never felt anger like this before, but she intended to use every atom of it.

This could not go unanswered.

Theron nodded toward the chambers, oddly calm considering Izzy's rage and unnatural aura. Smug *bastard*.

"Ryota, go after them," Theron said.

Ryota stared at him, incredulous. "You realize I'm literally falling apart here, right?"

"Go after them or I will kill you myself," he snapped.

Ryota sunk down, scrambled to his feet as best he could, and rushed after Ouranos. Izzy just had to hope the others could fight him off.

"And now, Guardian," Theron said. He waved his hands and dozens of Cast appeared in the hall. "You can see I have procured the Black Bound elixir

I need to create Cast. Though I admit, my source is limited and will likely dry up soon. I could use a replacement."

Izzy spat. "Choke on a dead Gem, Theron." Her Gem whined loudly in response.

Theron shook his head. "Such *fury.*" He waved a hand and the Cast rose up out of their puddles, wide, jagged mouths opening up under their trios of blue eyes. "But even rage fire like yours cannot kill a Cast."

Izzy snarled. "I wouldn't take that bet if I were you."

Theron's smug smile dropped. He raised an eyebrow. "Surely you have not cracked the cure."

Izzy snorted, still clinging to anger, though his words confused her. Did that mean he already knew the cure? Maybe she could coax it out of him. "Maybe we have."

Theron looked downright worried now. "You had no idea how to use the acid for…" He shook his head. "You cannot cure them."

Lexi acid. They had been experimenting with that on Zyearth and had had some success with destroying Cast Charms… they just hadn't figured out how to use it to save Cast yet. Aric wasn't even convinced that the acid would work at all. But clearly they were on the right track if even Theron thought so.

She just needed more.

"Certainly there's enough of it to go around on Zyearth," Izzy said. "Just a few drops and…"

Theron narrowed his gaze. "You have given yourself away, Guardian," he said. "You have no cure."

Izzy huffed. It had been worth a shot. "I don't need to cure them." She swallowed all her discomfort and hardened her features. Time to drop the bomb. "I can kill them."

Theron actually laughed. "No one can kill Cast."

"Try me."

Theron lifted his chin. "That bet I will take." He waved a hand. A Cast separated from the group and charged Izzy.

Putting up a mask of determination, Izzy charged her hand full of magic and punched a fist into the flying Cast. Like with all the others, the inky body sunk in on itself, then popped back out revealing a feminine, green tinted Athánatos, before exploding in shrieks, blood, and black rain. Though Izzy drowned in guilt, she kept herself planted, letting the remains coat her, never taking her gaze from Theron's. Just a few for all their sake. To protect herself, she thought. If she could convince Theron that his whole army was at stake, he might stop sending them her way.

Her Gem whined even louder, gleefully, growing her green aura, which waved about her body in ever-moving tendrils.

Theron stared, wide-eyed. Then his expression melted into rage. He gritted his teeth, his quills standing on end.

Izzy narrowed her gaze. "Any more you send my way will meet the same fate." Despite her stoic stance, her voice cracked slightly. Damn it all.

Theron furrowed his brow and wrinkled his snout in a snarl. "You see yourself as an avenger. Are you really willing to be a killer?"

Izzy wrinkled her snout. "Are you really willing to bet your entire army?"

Theron waved his hand. Three more Cast descended on her, but she killed each in quick succession, still never turning her gaze away. Their remains further stained her outfit as their final screams echoed in her head, burning her insides. But she held fast.

She had to avenge Sol.

She glared. "I'm a soldier, Theron. I'm not so weak that I can't stand a little blood."

Theron nodded. "A fair point." He waved his hand and the remaining Cast disappeared into the hallway behind him. "Then we will play on your terms."

He slammed his fist into his hand, shaking the jeweled bracelets on his arms. Fire, ice, electricity, and water all appeared instantly and flew for Izzy.

Not today.

Izzy swung her hammer at the oncoming elements and caught all four on the hammer's head. The magic collapsed in on itself – fire turned ice to water, water turned fire to steam, and electricity ran through the water and grew, expanding all around her. She slammed the hammer into the ground, cracking the marble floor, shaking Theron's sword off its perch on the wall, and shooting the electricity at her enemy in one giant bolt.

Theron crossed his arms in front of his face and a thick slab of stone shot up between them, taking the brunt of the electricity. The stone slab cracked and broke, scattering pebbles everywhere, but Theron was unhurt.

Izzy took a step back, flattening her ears. The plasma and water-based elements she could handle, but earth and stone… that was going to be a challenge.

Theron slammed a fist to the marble, sending a flurry of stone spikes after her.

Shit. She shielded and leapt out of the way, though the line of spikes followed her. Curse this small space! She dashed to her right, nearly running into a pillar.

The pillars… That was her chance. She ran behind one, hoping the spikes would follow. They bit at her heels and wrapped around the column as they chased her. *Hope this works.* She swung her hammer, trying to connect with both a spike and the pillar.

The moment her hammer hit the stone magic, a surge of power rushed up her arms, tingling her shoulders. Rocks stuck fast to her hammer's head, forming sharp barbs, each nearly half a meter long. The sudden added weight pulled her down, but she still hit her target. Her spikey hammer smashed the pillar, shattering it to dust.

Theron smirked. "Clever. I knew your weapons could channel the elements. But to make the stone work for you…" He held his hand out, pulled at the magic, and the hammer jerked from her grip. She fell forward as it left her. "Only you did not think the action through."

Izzy's stomach turned to ice. Lightning and *air*. That was careless.

The ceiling above her creaked ominously and dust fell from the cracks that the broken pillar left behind. The ceiling was ready to fall. She just needed to take one more pillar down.

Theron held her hammer near the ground as a Cast slithered up. The Cast snatched it and disappeared into the hall behind Theron again. Damn it.

"A soldier is only as good as their weapons." Theron sent another blast of stone spikes her way.

Izzy wrapped herself in a shield and dove again. She couldn't take down a pillar on her own. She'd never get Theron to take one down while chasing her. She rolled to escape the stone spikes, trashing her shield in the process. There went that idea. It would never hold well enough against a stone pillar.

Theron huffed. He pushed and the spikes continued after her. She dove, but the stone spike burst through her shield, shattering it. She dove aside, but the spike chasing her burst right through her shield. She dodged the spike and darted behind another pillar.

Damn it all, she needed a *weapon*.

A glint caught her eye and she turned.

Theron's sword. The weapon lay on the ground about four meters away from Theron, near the pillar on the other side of the room.

"Face your *end,* Guardian!" Theron shouted as the stone spikes circled the pillar she hid behind.

One shot.

She dashed from behind the pillar and threw herself forward, tucking into a roll. One stone spike caught her foot, knocking her off balance and cutting right through the bone. Her entire foot seared with pain, making her vision blur. Blood spiraled around her in a grim display. She bit her tongue until it bled, but at least she didn't scream.

But she did snatch the sword.

She raced for the pillar, the stones still right on her tail. Every step was agony, but she willed it away, focusing her thoughts. *Get to the pillar.* She circled around it.

The stones followed.

One shot.

She slammed the sword as hard as she could through a stone spike and into the pillar.

Like with her hammer, the stone magic stuck fast to the sword in thick barbs and smashed through the column in a flurry of dust and pebbles. Immediately the ceiling started to collapse.

Theron looked up. "What? How did--"

She didn't wait. Pushing through the pain in her foot, she dashed for the hall leading to the Royal Chambers, still clinging to the stone-covered sword.

Theron shouted, though the sounds of the collapsing ceiling drowned his voice. Dust and rubble chased Izzy down the hall as she ran. She dove through the entrance to the hall.

Then the stones fell off her sword.

She turned around.

The doorway she had just dashed through was completely blocked by marble, wood, and stone. Dust clouds hovered about it, and the whole thing smelled rotten. Izzy coughed. She'd be tasting dust for days.

She glanced at the sword again. No stones.

She bit her lip. Usually if a magic user dies, their magic dies with it. She glanced at the fallen stones.

The stones cracked, crushed into powder, and flew away in a gust of wind.

Izzy flicked an ear back. She glanced back at the blocked doorway.

She didn't want to believe she had killed him. She didn't know if she even could.

But regardless, if she had killed him, then she'd done what she'd set out to do. Avenge Sol.

And if she hadn't… well, at least she'd bought them some time.

She turned toward the Royal Chambers, her foot aching with every step.

LIFE CHOICES

Trecheon stood outside the hut Matt had once called home and listened. Silence. He wasn't sure if that was good or bad.

At least Matt didn't seem to be living in a different time anymore. He was present. A good start. That was good enough for Trecheon. He headed back toward the town square.

He glanced over the huts, frowning. Granddad might have been here. Chasing around innocent villagers. Killing children. Destroying lives. Matt's included.

Trecheon's legacy. Murder and genocide. No wonder it had been so easy to become an assassin.

Did Ryota like killing?

Did Granddad?

Did he...?

That was a scary thought. He pushed it from his mind, but another thought took its place, making him sick to his stomach.

Had Grandma Solana known about Granddad's past?

The thought sent shivers up his spine. Imagine explaining that to your spouse. This was why you could never think about your actions as an assassin. Rule Number One. The moment you thought about what you were doing was the moment you cared, which became the moment you couldn't finish the job. You realized how despicable killing was. "Damn it all."

Something yellow rushed through the bushes. Trecheon stepped back. He really wished someone had taught him how to make shields. "Someone there?"

Then… a flash of red against the darkness. Trecheon's quills stood on end.

No. Not here.

"Ryota? Is that you?"

Footsteps crashed through the brush. A smell of cigarettes wafted under his nose.

Trecheon stood his ground. "Ryota. Talk to me."

A pathetically weak blast of electricity burst from the darkness, but Trecheon dodged easily. A poor attempt.

"Stay back, Trecheon!" Ryota's voice quavered in the darkness. "I swear to Draso I'll turn you to dust right now!"

Trecheon grimaced. Enough was enough. Matt had lost his family here. He wasn't going to lose his too. "Damnit, Ryota, you're the only family I have left and I don't want to lose you. Just talk to me!"

The area in front of him lit up with an electric blue. Ryota stood there, tiny glowing orbs floating over his head, holding his hands over bandages on his arm and side. A pang of regret stabbed through Trecheon. His big brother. A violent urge to heal him rushed through Trecheon, but he didn't think his brother would let him close enough to do it.

Ryota glared at Trecheon, ears flattened, quills on end. "You get two minutes."

Trecheon clenched his fist. "Why did you leave us?"

Ryota narrowed his eyes. "You get two minutes and this is what you ask?"

"I have to know," Trecheon said. "Please."

"I already told you," Ryota said. "To stop the orchestrators of war. To kill the humans. To--"

"Why did you *really* leave us?" Trecheon asked. "You never used to hate humans. Your best friend was human. Anthony, in our team. You were thick as thieves. Or Clarissa. We all knew you loved her. Carter even caught you guys kissing. So why did you really leave us?"

"I..." He faltered, the electricity cages disappearing. "I... To kill... to stop..."

"Ryota," Trecheon said, trying to soften his voice. "Why did you leave us?"

"Because I didn't want to *die*." Ryota's voice rasped and shook. "Theron offered me an out. Long life, immortality. Damn it, I didn't want to die like... like Anthony. Like Clarissa." He held a hand to his forehead. "Draso's wings, if I hadn't been such a coward maybe Clarissa... maybe she'd still be alive. Anthony, too. I'll never lose that image of his leg being blown off."

Trecheon frowned. He shot a quick glance back toward Matt's hut, then faced Ryota again. "Ryota. Don't do that to yourself. Don't blame--"

"And why not?" Ryota said, glaring at Trecheon. "If I had done something. Pulled her aside, pushed her away, jumped in front of the gun myself, anything, I could have saved her. But I didn't because I was afraid for my own life and she *died*. It's my fault. Anthony died trying to save her and he's a *hero*."

"And how is working with Theron going to fix that?" Trecheon snarled. "He can't bring them back."

"He'll give me immortality," Ryota said. "He *promised* me, Trech."

"He's done nothing but manipulate you!" Trecheon said. "You've been working with him since the war and he hasn't given you immortality yet, has he? What makes you think he'll do it now?"

"This!" Ryota waved his Gem about, though he winced with the action and grabbed his side. "This… it's reassurance. It's long life while he preps me for immortality. It's a promise kept."

"It's a *tool* to *use you,*" Trecheon said. "Because you're Black Bound. Izzy explained it to me. Black Bound Gem users can make Cast."

Ryota flicked his ears back.

Trecheon narrowed his eyes. "I'm right, aren't I? He's using you to make Cast. And as long as you're useful, why bother giving you immortality?"

"You're lying," Ryota said. "I'd be useful being immortal. If I can't die, I can… I can save the world. I can stop the humans. The other humans."

"So you're afraid of death, but you're willing to spend the rest of eternity killing?"

Ryota frowned. "That's... that's not--"

"That's what you're saying isn't it?" Trecheon snapped. "Use your everlasting life to *kill*, Ryota. Kill and be manipulated. Used." He gritted his teeth. "You can't do that. It'll eat you from the inside. And you won't be able to die to escape it."

Ryota narrowed his gaze. "So you know from experience then? Killing, guilt eating from the inside out?"

"Yes!" Trecheon shouted. "Goddamn it, Ryota, I don't want that life for you!"

"That confirms it then," Ryota said. "You are the White Assassin. You and Neil."

Trecheon perked his ears, shock running through his system. "How did--"

"Neil talks too much," Ryota said. "You act so high and mighty. Labeling me a murderer, a traitor." Ryota snorted, shaky. "Yet, you kill humans."

"I kill *corruption,*" Trecheon said, his body buzzing with adrenaline. "Scum. People who deserve it. Humans and zyfaunos alike. And it kills me every single time. I have to fight not to turn myself in. They *deserve* death, Ryota, and I still want to confess. It doesn't matter that they deserve it. I take lives. It kills you." He clenched his fists tighter, his arm hydraulics shaking. His ears trembled and something hot built up behind his eyes.

Damn. Damn it all to hell. Maybe he was no better than Ryota.

I know the good things you've done, Matt had said. *You're not my enemy.*

Draso, he wanted to believe that so bad.

Ryota frowned, his ears drooping. "Trech--"

"Don't call me that," Trecheon said, fighting the heat behind his eyes. "You don't have that privilege. But damn it, Ryota, don't make the same mistakes I did. Don't make killing a profession. Don't do that to yourself."

Ryota wrinkled his snout. "Why do you even care?"

"Because you're my *brother,* damnit," Trecheon said.

"Even after I've done bad things."

"We all have," Trecheon said. "But they can be forgiven." He held out a hand to Ryota, still trembling. "Please, Ryota. Give this up. Come home. I'll find work for you in my shop. We can be *family* again."

Ryota frowned at his hand. He reached out.

Then withdrew. "No. I can't."

Trecheon's stomach dropped. "Ryota--"

"No, Trecheon," Ryota said. He turned. "I can't die. I don't want to die."

Trecheon flattened an ear. He was losing him. He couldn't lose him. "Everyone dies."

"Not me." Ryota ripped lightning through the air.

CHAPTER 51

SPONTANEOUS CONFLAGRATION

Trecheon dove to the left, barely avoiding the lightning bolt. *Shit.*

"Ryota, stop!"

"Stay back!" Ryota snarled, his eyes wide with a fierce panic. His whole body shook, making him stutter. "I don't want to die!" A lightning bolt fell from the sky.

Trecheon dove again, the bolt narrowly missing him. How did Izzy make a shield? She held a hand out, and the air around her went green, then purple, then it disappeared. Maybe if he imagined a shield like he had with healing…

Ryota shot another bolt. No time. Trecheon held his hands up and envisioned a shield.

In a flash, purple and green exploded in front of him. The bolt hit.

The shield shattered instantly. The force sent Trecheon flying backwards, smacking him hard into a tree. He groaned.

"I-I can't let you live," Ryota said. He walked forward, hand outstretched, caged in lightning. The lightning flickered and he wobbled with every step, gripping the bandages on his side.

Trecheon flicked his ears back, fighting to create another shield, but the Gem wouldn't react.

Ryota stared at him with wild eyes. "You know I'm here. If you get back to the others, it'll ruin everything."

Trecheon tried to sit up, but his legs protested. He pushed hard on his magic. *Shield, damnit!* Finally one formed, but it glowed transparent green, like Matt's. Thinner. Weaker. It practically wasn't there at all. He backed up as much as he could. "You won't kill me, Ryota."

"Think so?" Ryota roared, his voice still shaking. "Think I can't kill you? I don't care if you're my brother. I have too much at stake." He built up an arch of electricity over his head. He gritted his teeth, quaking. "I'm sorry. I-I'll make this fast." He shot down the lightning.

Trecheon threw his arms up, panic overtaking him.

Something bright and hot manifested at the edge of his fingers.

Ryota shouted, and leapt back. Fire blossomed in Trecheon's hands and smashed into the lightning, making both disappear in a flash of magic and light. He gasped and jumped, crawling away from it. He glanced around for the source of the flames, but didn't see anyone.

"Where did you get that?" Ryota shouted. "You don't have a Gem!"

"It's not my fire!" Trecheon said, waving his hands. But more fire burst forth, threatening to burn him and Ryota.

Ryota stepped back. "No more of this!" He shot twin bolts at Trecheon.

A blast of wind smashed into them both. Ryota skidded back, his lightning dissipating. Trecheon turned.

Matt stood at Trecheon's side, scowling, his eyes like green flames. He waved a gale around them. "Don't even."

Ryota glared and rebuilt his electric cages. Trecheon pressed himself against a tree, shielding as best he could.

Matt rushed forward and smashed into Ryota, breaking up the cages and knocking them both to the ground. Ryota reached for Matt's shirt, but Matt was faster. He gripped Ryota's jacket, rolled to his back, and kicked Ryota in the stomach, sending Ryota flying into a tree. Matt stood and snarled. "I *said-
-*"

A bolt fell straight for Matt's head. But it smashed a shield and shattered it, scattering the pieces through the forest before they disappeared. Matt rushed for Ryota and wedged his arm under Ryota's neck, pressing him harder into the tree.

"Trecheon may not have the skills with shielding," Matt hissed. "But I do. Don't. Even. Try it."

Ryota bared his fangs. "You should have died with the rest of your family."

"Well, I *didn't.*" Matt pressed harder against Ryota. Ryota gagged, pulling at his arm. "What are you doing on my island?"

"Hunting you," Ryota spat.

A bolt of lightning crashed into the tree Matt had Ryota pressed against. The tree split down the middle and caught fire. Trecheon leapt away in horror, his fragile shield cracking.

Matt leapt back too and waved his hands, while Ryota scrambled away. He whipped up a fierce gale through the forest, aimed at the broken trunk. It swirled around the pieces and held them precariously in place. The fire raged through the trunk.

Ryota growled and formed another lightning cage.

"Don't you dare!" Trecheon threw a hand forward, acting on instinct, and blasted fire at Ryota.

Ryota dodged, glared at Trecheon, then turned and hobbled away into the darkness. Trecheon stood.

"Stand back!" Matt said. "I don't want anything to hit you!" Trecheon stopped and stepped back, frowning. "Did I just see you use fire magic?" Matt asked. Trecheon nodded. "Concentrate on the fire on this tree and imagine sucking it in. We need to get rid of it before it sets the whole island ablaze."

Trecheon held out a hand and concentrated on the fire. Slowly the flames smoldered out. Matt grimaced and guided the broken tree to the ground with the gales, careful to avoid any of the still-standing huts. A thick film of black grew on his hands and flicked away in the breeze, but disappeared the moment the wind died. Matt leaned on his knees, breathing heavily. He turned to Trecheon. "Where the hell did you get fire? I thought you were a healer."

"I haven't a clue," Trecheon said. "But we have to get after Ryota." He turned and dashed after his brother. Matt ran behind him.

Then Matt stopped and gripped his chest, crying out.

Trecheon turned. "Draso's mercy, are you okay?"

Matt fell to one knee, sweat building on his fur and quills. He squeezed his eyes shut. "It's… Ouranos." He coughed, spit running down his lip. "He's on the island… and he's dying."

DESPERATE

Ryota hobbled through the woods, huffing, trying to keep his bearings in the dark. Good god, everything ached.

He should never have let his brother talk him down. Try to convince him that he could be *forgiven*. After what he did to Clarissa? To Anthony? After his cowardice? He was lucky Draso hadn't struck him down yet.

And damn it, he let his emotions get the better of him. His feelings about death, about Trecheon, about… about Clarissa.

Draso's mercy.

He should have dropped this ages ago. He should have taken up Trecheon's suggestion and gone to work for him. Make something of himself. He knew the Basileus was playing him. Trecheon was right. The Basileus just wanted him to make Cast.

Draso's breath, what the hell am I doing?

He slowed to a crawl and leaned against a tree, panting. Damn Natassa and her sudden burst of magic. Damn him for being so slow. Damn his cowardly fear of death.

He was dying. He knew it.

Maybe he should just give up.

No, he thought. If he could just get Neil and Ouranos… if he could actually do what Theron wanted him to, maybe… maybe he'd…

He choked on a sob. Theron wasn't going to give him immortality. Ryota was dying. Fear gripped his chest, churning his stomach, muddying his thoughts.

He bent his ears back. This was out of hand. He needed something to make up for his mistake. Something that would put him back in Theron's good graces, if only to get the jewels. To survive.

"Trecheon!" a masculine voice shouted.

Ryota perked his ears and leapt further behind the tree.

"*Jefe!* Where are you?" the voice continued. "Damnit all, I know I saw that flashy magic this way."

Ryota peeked out from behind the tree.

A human. A human wandering the island of Sol, where no humans were even allowed. No mainlanders at all. And apparently a human that knew Trecheon. His body buzzed with excitement, muffling the pain.

Theron had desperately wanted a human. For what purpose Ryota didn't know, but who cared? A human might make up for his mistake. He limped around the tree.

And immediately stepped on a branch, snapping it.

The human stopped short and turned. "*Dios mio.* You're… you're his brother."

Ryota narrowed his eyes.

The human turned and ran.

Shit! He ran after him, every step sending sharp pains up his legs, and tackled him to the ground. All his wounds screamed at him, but he got his prize.

"Get off me! *Get off!*" The human struggled under him.

Ryota threw five cages of electricity into the air above him. The human stopped immediately.

"Listen here," Ryota said. "You're going to stand up. You're going to come with me. And you're not going to make a *sound* or I swear to Draso I'll fry you so completely you'll be nothing but *dust on the wind*. Do I make myself clear?"

The human leaned back, hands up defensively. He glared, but didn't protest. "…Yes."

Ryota stood up and dragged the human to his feet. He pulled the human's arm around his back and pushed him toward the back entrance to the sanctum. If he could get to the rip and get this human to Theron, he might be okay.

"The hell are you doing to me?"

"Nothing," Ryota said. "That's Theron's job."

"Who?"

"The Basileus," Ryota said. "The Athánatos king."

The human shuddered. "The king that's after Trecheon."

Ryota laughed. "Is that what he told you? Egotistical bastard."

"Oh screw off, you murdering asshole," Christian spat. "Like you can criticize him."

Ryota snarled and yanked on the human's arm. "No, *Trecheon* has no room to criticize. To tell me how to live my life. He's just as bad as I am. Worse, even. *He's* the murdering asshole."

"Trecheon is *not* a murderer."

"Trecheon," Ryota said, his words dripping acid. "is the White Assassin."

The human halted.

Ryota chuckled. "Left that out, did he? Not surprised you know the name, what with his infamous reputation right now."

"You're *lying.*"

"Am I?" Ryota said. "What reason would I have to lie?"

"Defamation," the human said. "Trying to get me to distrust him."

"I have total control over you right now," Ryota said. "What good would defaming him do? You'll never see him again."

The human struggled. "You're lying. Trecheon would never do that. He hates the White Assassin."

"He hates himself, yes," Ryota said. "And who wouldn't? He kills for profit. Innocent lives."

"You are *lying!*" the human shouted. "He wouldn't do that! You're lying, damnit!"

Ryota shrugged. "Believe what you want, but it won't change the facts. He told me himself. Now come along. We have someone to meet."

"I'll prove it," the human said. "Trecheon--!"

Ryota gave him a good shock. The human cried out. "You say one more word and it'll be your last. Understood?"

The human grunted, staggering on his feet.

"Good. Now get walking. Theron will be very excited to meet you."

DYING

Matt ran as fast as he was able for the square. If Ouranos was on the island, he'd like come through the rip in the Sanctum. He had to get to him before--

Sudden pain blinded him, and he fell to his knees with a shout. The colors in his mind blinked rapidly through every emotion he had ever seen from Ouranos, so fast, he couldn't focus on a single one.

Trecheon gripped his shoulders. "Come on, we have to hurry!" He helped Matt up. "Do you know where he is?"

"I think the square… the sanctum…" Matt managed. Damn it all.

Trecheon wrapped one of Matt's arms across his shoulder. "Then let's get to him." They hurried on.

But then suddenly everything… stopped. Matt paused. All the colors, all the pain, every scrap of information from Ouranos, gone. Everything… gone. He poked at Ouranos' mind. *Ouranos, please, speak to me.*

But there was nothing.

Matt slipped out from under Trecheon's arm. *"Run."*

They got to the square and were stunned to find Natassa there with hundreds of Athánatos. A Cast stood stoically by her side, a golden wedding coil bouncing on top of him. Roscoe. The Phonar still stood huddled around the bonfire, seemingly oblivious to the zyfaunos around them. Christian, Sami, Melaina, and Darvin were nowhere to be found though. Matt stepped forward. "Natassa?"

"Matthew, thank *Draso.*" Natassa ran up and hugged him. "You are well? Did you meet the others in the woods? They heard fighting and went looking for you."

"We didn't see them," Trecheon said. He glanced around. "Christian went with them?"

"If you mean the human, then yes."

"Damn it all," Trecheon said. "Sami better bring him back safe."

"Natassa, I sensed Ouranos on the island," Matt said. "Have you--"

"Someone help!"

Matt turned. Neil burst out of the Sanctum holding Ouranos limp at his side. He panted as he spoke. "He's not breathing!"

No.

Matt rushed forward and helped Neil lower Ouranos to the ground. "Draso's *mercy.*"

Neil's voice shook. "Trech--"

"He's dying, we know," Trecheon said. He kneeled beside Ouranos. His Gem glowed brightly and whined as he ripped off the bandages. "Matt, can you guide me here? I have no idea what I'm doing."

"I don't either," Matt said. "But--"

"I'll guide him!" Izzy came hobbling out of the Sanctum, wielding a sword and dragging one foot behind her. Matt's mind flooded with deep jangling sounds, like the tolling of a church bell. Distress. Death. Draso's mercy, it had been too long since he'd had Izzy's emotions clanging around in his head. He wasn't sure if he should be upset or relieved to have it back.

Izzy walked toward them. She was covered in blood and black ink. "I'm here."

Matt felt all the heat leave his face. "Izzy, all that blood…!"

"It's not mine," she said. A short alarm bell ran in Matt's mind. Guilt, uncertainty. Izzy bent an ear back. "Well, most of it isn't." She dropped her sword, kneeled beside Ouranos and pressed a hand to the side of his neck. She faced Trecheon. "He's got a decent pulse. Big wound first. Concentrate on the flesh – you'll get an image of the damage in your mind as its being repaired. Let the Gem guide you. Give it everything you've got!"

Trecheon pressed his hands to Ouranos' wound and pumped healing energy into it. The flesh and skin knitted together while the blood reabsorbed into his body. But it was slow. So slow. And Ouranos still wasn't breathing.

"Trecheon, you've got to move faster!" Matt gripped Ouranos' hand, his eyes glassing over.

"I'm trying!" Trecheon said. "He's not breathing. He--"

"On it." Izzy formed a shield around her mouth and leaned down for mouth-to-mouth. Tiny jingles ran through Matt's ears. She came up after two breaths and checked his pulse. "Dammit!"

Trecheon frowned. "His heart?" The flesh continued knitting, but there was still a gaping hole.

Neil paced back and forth. "Oh god, oh god."

Izzy nodded. "Irregular. Faint." She turned up to Natassa. "I need you to give him a gentle shock."

Natassa stepped back. "I have not the skill--"

"Pass it to me, my Lady!" A yellow Athánatos rushed out from the direction of the huts. "Trust me."

She frowned, but reluctantly tossed a cage of lightning to him. "Damianos, *save him*." Damianos took it.

"Ryota?" Neil asked.

"Sufficiently distracted, according to plan," Damianos said, and gently shocked Ouranos. The prince's body jerked but immediately fell still again. Dozens of the Athánatos watching gasped. Two elderly ones sobbed.

Trecheon pressed harder. "Dammit, move faster!"

Izzy went for more breaths. The jangling bells in Matt's mind sped up, more frantic. "Another shock!" Izzy shouted. One more bolt to the chest. One more jump. Izzy felt for a pulse, but shook her head. "We're losing him." She went for another breath. The bell sounds grew dark. Natassa let out a sob.

"Like hell we are." Matt leaned down and held Ouranos' head in his hands. *Ouranos, reach out to me. Reach me like we did on Zyearth. I know you're there. Come back to us!*

But there was nothing.

Matt squeezed his eyes tight. He pulled at Ouranos with his mind. *You're stronger than this, brother. You've faced worse. You aren't alone. Come back! Come home!*

Then, a tiny flicker of white. A memory of sharing a meal together. Of laughter. Another of Ouranos hanging his head. Fear, shame. But slowly, Ouranos' bright, hopeful blue filled Matt's mind, blowing away all the black. Matt flashed his eyes open.

"He's breathing," Izzy said. Bright bells ran through Matt's mind. Clarity. Relief. Izzy checked his pulse and breathed out, relaxing. "Strong pulse. Oh, dear Draso…"

Trecheon wiped sweat from his brow. "I… I think I've closed it up, but he's lost a lot of blood and the fur won't grow back." He pressed harder, causing his Gem to glow brightly. "Just a little--Gah!" He pulled his hand back. A white, wispy cloud of particles formed around his hands. There was a thick scorch mark on the metal fingers. "What the hell?"

"Lexi acid," Matt said. "I think--"

"Matt, catch that acid right now!" Izzy said. Her panicked voice rang like a gong in his mind. "Don't let it vanish!"

Matt winced, but he gathered it all in a tiny balled-up tornado and hovered it near his hand.

Then Ouranos groaned. And all his colorful emotions flooded back into Matt's mind, drowning Izzy's bell ringing. Ouranos blinked up at Matt. "I appear to have survived." The Athánatos around them collectively relaxed. A blue Athánatos sobbed through a smile and a pack of kits cheer and hollered.

Matt sighed relief, choking back tears. "Thank Draso… I thought we lost you…"

Ouranos sat up slowly and ran his hands over his chest. He closed his eyes a moment, then turned to Trecheon. "Thank you."

"Yeah… no problem," Trecheon said, panting. "Anyone got a napkin or something I can wipe my hand on?"

Neil handed him a handkerchief. "Here, chief."

Trecheon eyed him as he took it. Though Matt caught a flicker of relief on his features. "Don't call me that."

Neil smirked. "Whatever you say, Trech."

"Don't call me that either." Though Matt noticed Trecheon's expression softened.

"Trecheon, Matthew," Ouranos said. "Before anything else happens… I have something I must tell you." He glanced around at the hundreds of Athánatos citizens around him, all of them staring intently at a prince they thought was lost. He sighed. "Privately, please."

Confessions

Matt stared at the campfire in the center of the square, the sphere of acid still trapped in Matt's wind magic hovering near his shoulder. Trecheon sat next to him, staring at the dirt.

Natassa had escorted her people to the nearby creek to clean, drink, and prepare a meal with the food found in the village's gardens. The water Phonar walked with her to test the river. Sémini, she had called the phoenix, nearly in tears. To her, Sémini's presence meant Melaina was still alive, even if she was still a Cast. Matt assured her she was around, probably with Sami looking for Ryota. Natassa couldn't stop smiling. "I look forward to seeing her again… it has been far too many years."

Izzy chose to go with Natassa to wash up. Roscoe moved by her side the moment she had finished with Ouranos.

Matt frowned at her. "Are you sure that's not your blood?"

"For the last time, yes, Matt," Izzy said. A deep long bell sounded in his ears. Confidence. "Do you think I'd be able to walk around like this if it was?"

Matt shrugged. "Ryota did."

"Ryota is also likely to fall flat on his face and pass out at any time looking like that," Izzy said. "I'm a healer. I know better."

Matt lowered his gaze. "Then whose blood is it?"

Izzy flicked her ears back, filling his mind with the toll of funeral bells. "Don't wanna talk about it."

Trecheon tried healing Izzy's foot, but he was so worn out from healing Ouranos that he couldn't get it to work and just created more acid. Izzy assured him it'd come back in time and she'd just treat it the old fashioned way until it did. She walked off after that, favoring her injured foot, with Roscoe sticking to her heels. Matt hadn't even gotten a chance to ask her about her malfunctioning healing powers.

Neil crossed his arms, glaring at Trecheon. "You brought Christian *here?* What the hell were you thinking?"

"He followed me from the garage," Trecheon said. "It was either bring him along or let him go to the authorities and I don't think Earth is ready for this magic shit."

Neil rolled his eyes at him. "Good God." He stretched. "Dami and I will go look for him. We'll keep an eye out for that fox chick too." He pointed at Trecheon. "Stay here. Rest. We're gonna need that healing back, mark my words." Damianos left with him. Both took swords which Damianos had lit up with lightning.

And now it was just Matt, Trecheon, Ouranos, and the remaining Phonar, though the summons paid no attention to them. Ouranos, thankfully, seemed to be close to normal, considering his huge wound. He had thrown off the remains of his shirt and the fur hadn't grown back over the scar, but it was better than the alternative. Having Ouranos, here, safe, occupied everything.

Silence overshadowed them.

Then, slowly, Ouranos detailed his role in the Sol Genocide.

Matt's body buzzed, hanging on every word. Ouranos claimed over and over that it was his fault. But Matt could only focus on one thing.

"I am sorry, Matthew," Ouranos said, after he finished his explanation. He stared at the ground. "If I could have fought my father with greater strength, then perhaps your family could have been saved. There are no words to express my remorse."

"What you're really saying then," Matt said slowly, forcing the words out. "Is that I have even less of a reason to be mad with Trecheon. Because his family was manipulated. Tricked."

Trecheon perked an ear.

Ouranos wrinkled his snout. "Yes. Essentially."

"And I have more of a reason to be angry with the Basileus," Matt said. "Since he orchestrated the whole thing."

Ouranos frowned. "He did so through me."

"Ouranos," Matt said. *"Theron* did this. He used you, he used his people, he uses *everyone*. I refuse to blame you for it. Any more than I blame you for what happened on Zyearth. This is not your fault, understand?"

Ouranos lowered his gaze. "Matthew."

"Don't let the Basileus win," Matt said. "This is on him. Not on you. It was never on you." He gripped Ouranos' hand. "You are not your father, Ouranos."

Ouranos finally smiled. "I… thank you. That means the world to me."

"Of course," Matt said. He eyed him. "What I'm more concerned with is that you took off without me in the first place. Trecheon notwithstanding, you intended to come after the Basileus without my help, and I want to know why."

Ouranos flattened both ears. A heavy black invaded Matt's mind. Ouranos rubbed the fur on his arm. "I… had intended to come here alone seeking the Omnirs. Isabelle… Izzy finding me and insisting on coming along was… unfortunate happpenstance."

Matt frowned. "But why?"

Ouranos lowered his gaze. "You are not responsible for cleaning my messes. And I will not allow you to endanger yourself."

"Ouranos," Matt said. "After everything we've been through." He tightened his grip on Ouranos' hand. "You don't have to fight this alone anymore. You should never have had to in the first place." He pressed all the hope and love he could into Ouranos' mind. "I almost lost you today. I don't want to face that ever again."

Ouranos stared, his eyes glassy. He gripped Matt's hand back, opening his mouth, though he didn't speak.

But Matt felt the words anyway. He smiled. "Let us be your support. That's what we're here for. We protect each other. Okay?"

Ouranos took a deep breath, shuddering. "Word cannot express what that means to be me, brother. Consider the lesson learned. I would not be here if it were not for my friends. And speaking of..." He took a moment to compose himself, then turned to Trecheon. "Trecheon, I must beg your forgiveness as well."

"Why?" Trecheon said. He gripped both knees, baring his teeth. "You didn't do shit. You couldn't help yourself. I wasn't alive during the genocide anyway. And if Granddad was involved with it, he was also manipulated. A victim. Besides, I know what war is like." He sighed. "Heaven knows I'm not innocent either."

"More so than I give you credit for," Matt said.

Trecheon breathed deeply. "I'd argue different, but that's not the point here. Theron's the manipulative bastard in this situation, and I'm sick of him screwing with my family. We need to stop him. Now."

Ouranos sat straight. "Isabelle said you two would forgive me. I did not think it would be so easy."

"Prínkipas Ouranos?" An older looking Athánatos came up to the fire. "Forgive me, my Lord, but if you are finished with your discussion, the Prinkípissa has requested your presence. The people would like to see their Prínkipas whole."

"Hardly whole, Eris," Ouranos said. "Not without the Soul Jewels."

Eris' gaze drifted to Matt. She smiled. "Lady Natassa claims you have found a suitable replacement."

Matt blinked. *"Me?"*

"Indeed." Eris bowed. "Thank you for bringing our Prínkipas back to us. And for freeing him from the Basileus' control. The Lady tells us this was done at great personal risk, when the rest of your people saw him as an enemy. But you did not. You brought him home. You made him whole again. We are eternally grateful."

Matt flicked an ear back. He glanced at Trecheon.

"My Lord?" Eris said. "Are you ready?"

Ouranos stood shakily. "I am."

Trecheon frowned at him. "I'm sorry I couldn't heal you better. I just don't have the skill yet."

"You brought me from the brink of death, my friend," Ouranos said. "I can hardly complain." He glanced at Matt. "I will return with Izzy. Then we will find out why she wanted you to keep that Lexi acid and make a plan from there."

His statements came with a warm, orange-red glow in Matt's mind. Matt smiled at him. It was so nice to have that connection again.

Ouranos smiled back. "It is nice," he said. "I missed your rosy-fingered dawn. And… I shall endeavor to rely on you more. You are right. I should use the support you so willingly give, my friend." He squeezed Matt's shoulder then wandered toward the creek with Eris.

Trecheon glanced between Matt and Ouranos. "I'll never get over that talking through your minds bullshit."

Matt took a deep breath. "…Trecheon, I owe you an apology."

Trecheon flicked an ear back. "You really don't."

"Yes, I do," Matt said. "I have treated you horribly ever since we met simply because of your last name. Hell, even worse, just because of your fur color. I'm no better than Theron if I do that. Than Ryota. I have no excuse for it. You've literally done nothing wrong. You've been actively helping us. And here I am trying to find everything wrong with you when you're innocent."

"Hardly innocent," Trecheon muttered.

"But not a villain," Matt said. "Not my enemy. I should see you for who you are, not for who I expect you to be."

Trecheon took a deep breath. "Thanks. I mean that." He leaned forward, fiddling with his hands. His metal fingers clinked softly. "I'm sorry, too. For what my grandpa's generation did to you. Maybe even my Granddad, I don't know. Manipulated or not, they still hurt you. And I'm sorry that you got stuck with me while trying to process all those memories. I know I'm not making it easy, especially since I'm not telling you everything. You have every right to be suspicious."

Matt flattened his ears. "You don't have to be sorry. None of that was your fault. Hell, I *know* it's not and I still chose to hate on you." He shook his head. "Here I am trying to help Ouranos when he actually *did* hurt me. He really was the enemy, and I turned him into a friend. You've been trying to be my friend all the time and I've turned you into the enemy." He shrugged. "Maybe I don't really know who my enemies are." He met Trecheon's gaze. "You've had every right to dismiss me for all I've put you through and you're sticking with me anyway." He snorted. "I don't understand why."

Trecheon leaned back. "I see a lot of myself in you."

Matt frowned. "What do you mean?"

Trecheon shrugged. "Stubborn, slow to trust, yet trying your best to make the world a better place, however you can. But we all have flaws. I'm full of them. I make mistakes, but I keep trying." He scoffed. "Draso knows why."

"Because you're clearly trying to do what's right," Matt said.

Trecheon's face blanked slightly, like he was thinking. He shook his head. "Maybe. Regardless… Christian says my refusing to give up is one of my better qualities." He perked one ear and glanced over at Matt. "You also keep trying."

Matt smiled. "Yeah, I suppose that's one of my better qualities too. Nice to see we have something good in common."

Trecheon held out a hand and smiled back. "Maybe we should start over. Fewer swords this time."

Matt glanced down at Trecheon's hand. "You sure I'm worth that?"

"Only one way to find out," Trecheon said. "Friends?"

Matt perked his ears forward and took Trecheon's hand. "Friends."

"About time you two made nice," Sami said, coming up behind them. She flicked her white fox tail. "And it only took Ouranos' near death, I hear."

Matt rolled his eyes. "Don't give me that. You were just as bad."

"But quicker to forgive," Sami said with a grin. Neil walked up behind her, and Darvin slithered between them, pulling himself out of his Cast puddle.

Trecheon frowned. "Where's Christian?"

"Can't find him," Neil said, his voice panicky. "Damianos is still looking, but there's just no trace so far. Can you call his cell?"

"Shit," Trecheon said. "I have his phone. We need to go find him *now.*"

"Melaina offered to go looking for him," Darvin said, his voice gurgling. "She knows the island better than anyone."

"Ryota is out there," Trecheon said, standing. "And wild animals and probably Cast and who the hell else knows what."

Matt flicked his ears back. "You make a good point. Everything is on halt. Let's organize search parties." He stood up, wind whipping by his ear.

Neil pointed to Matt's ball of air. "Hold on. Does anyone have any idea as to why Izzy wanted us to save that? It left a huge burn mark on Trecheon's hand, and the last thing I want to do is run around in the dark with that following me. I'd hate to see what it'd do to flesh and fur. No offense, Trech."

"Because that," Izzy said, walking up to the fire with Ouranos, Natassa, and Roscoe. "Is the key to curing the Cast."

PIECING TOGETHER THE PUZZLE

Matt's jaw dropped. "Really? You sure?"

"Not at all," Izzy said. She shifted her bandaged foot, clearly uncomfortable. Distant, asynchronous bells rang through Matt's mind. "But we know several things – The elixir creates Cast. The acid neutralizes the elixir. We've learned all that from experience on Zyearth." She wrinkled her snout. "I think we need to neutralize the Cast charm inside the victims. And Theron mentioned something about it being connected to a cure, so I think it's likely."

"But we've been trying that on Zyearth with no luck," Matt said.

"I realize, but Theron created the damn things," Izzy said. "He had to know more than us just by default."

Ouranos lifted a brow. "You speak of him in the past tense. What happened when you fought him?"

Matt gaped, his heart racing. Alarm bells from Izzy rang through his mind. "You fought the *Basileus?*" he asked. *"Alone?"*

"I had to keep him busy while Neil got Ouranos to Trecheon." Izzy shifted. The bells calmed down, but there was a mild jingling in the distance, like she couldn't let go. "And I'll admit, I let my anger at his hand in the genocide get the best of me."

"Izzy…" Ouranos said.

She rubbed the fur on her arm and recounted her battle. "I'm honestly lucky the stone magic stuck. I don't know what I would have done if it hadn't."

"Don't sell yourself short," Neil said. "None of the rest of us on that island could have done what you did. Hell, the only reason we got away from Ryota is because Dami lured him away while I carried Ouranos."

Natassa hugged herself. "Do you truly believe him dead?"

Izzy shrugged. "I really don't know… The fact that his magic on my sword died the way it did when the ceiling collapsed doesn't look good though. But I wouldn't put it past him to just fabricate the whole thing, if he even can. I don't know enough about how Athánatos magic works to know if he could do that on purpose."

Natassa exchanged a glance with Ouranos. Ouranos lowered his head. "I have not heard his voice in my head since I was healed. So… perhaps he is dead. I am unsure whether to be upset or relieved."

"Someone should go check," Sami said.

"No," Matt said. "Whether he's dead or not, our priority is to find Christian and cure these Cast. If he's dead, fine, but if not, the only real way to fight back at this point is weaken his army."

A flurry of embers rained gently over their heads. *Guardians.* Matt turned. Excelsis, the raven phoenix walked forward, his blue eyes ablaze with understanding and awareness. He stared Matt directly in the eye. *Have you tried freezing the acid?*

"Freezing it?" Matt said. "Why? Is that how they cured Cast in the past?"

Another blast of embers. *The purge of knowledge surrounding the Cast removed all previous understanding of their creation, as well as their cure,* Excelsis said. *The Basilea's Cast were created differently in any case, and any cure would be ineffective against these Cast. However… the Phonar exist out of time. And words from your future follow us, haunting us.*

Acid, Deo said, stepping forward.

Ice, Excelsis provided.

Jústi moved next to Excelsis. *Fire.*

Sémini, the water phoenix, stepped forward now. *Elixir.*

Ouranos gasped and turned to Matt and Izzy.

"But we have already established that elixir turns Cast," Natassa said. "It does not cure them."

"Yeah, but the hair of the dog that bit you," Neil said. "It makes sense."

"In a roundabout way, I suppose." Izzy flicked her ears back. "So what… we freeze the acid… set it on fire… then use elixir? That doesn't make sense."

"What if we freeze the acid, coat it in elixir, then set that on fire?" Matt said.

"Elixir and acid neutralize each other though," Sami said.

"It may not if it's frozen," Matt said. "Or it may at least slow the process. We've never tried that, to my knowledge. Aric and Dad always experimented with it in its natural state."

"Does fire burn the elixir?" Darvin said. "If the fire just unfreezes the acid without burning the elixir away, it'll still neutralize it. And what does fire do to the acid?"

"Fire doesn't burn acid," Sami said. "Aric had me try to burn it off a Cast once when it didn't work to cure it."

"But the elixir?" Darvin asked.

"I don't know," Matt admitted. "But we could try it and see. If we could burn away the elixir and unfreeze the acid…"

"But how does that help the Cast?" Trecheon said. "We have to get it like… inside them somehow. Right? How are Cast created?"

"…Cast Charm in the eye," Neil said. Everyone turned to him. He shifted. "I watched Ryota turn Abrax. It's… it's not pretty."

Darvin gurgled. "I retained myself because I had acid damage in my eye when Ouranos… when Theron turned me. I still think we need to get acid in the eye of the Cast."

"But we've tried that on Zyearth," Sami said. "It just floated on the surface, burning them until they managed to get it off."

"But if the acid was frozen, where the elixir could not neutralize it," Ouranos said. "And if it had the coating of the elixir… the very thing that turned them… perhaps their bodies would be more willing to accept it."

Neil grinned. "Hair of the dog."

"Then we can burn the coating away," Izzy said. "And the acid has a place to work and neutralize the Cast charm."

Everyone grew silent. Izzy's gentle bells mingled with Ouranos' swirling colors, making Matt feel like he was thinking for three people.

Ouranos perked his ears. "It is worth a try," he said. "We can test the effects of fire on our creation first, then see what we can do with a Cast."

"I volunteer," Darvin said.

Sami frowned at him.

Darvin sunk into his puddle. "It's either me, Melaina, or Roscoe. Melaina is looking for Christian, and while Roscoe is more akin to a real Cast than me, he also can't speak. I can talk and give you feedback while we experiment."

Matt frowned. "If you're not screaming in pain."

"Still a better shot."

Sami flattened her ears. "Okay, you make a good point. But I don't like it."

"I don't either," Izzy said. "But I don't see much of a choice."

"Before we get started," Matt said. He turned to Trecheon and Neil. "Trecheon, we got you back to Neil. Christian is missing, and frankly, this isn't your war. You don't have to help us."

Trecheon rolled his eyes. "Look here, space alien. You've already pulled us whisker deep into this shit. I'm not going to stop now. You need all the help you can get."

Neil grinned. "I've always wanted to fight a dragon and save a princess." He winked at Natassa. Her ears darkened in a blush and she smiled.

Matt smiled. "Honestly… Thanks. I mean that."

"That being said," Neil continued. "While you meddle with your alchemy, I'm going to go find Dami and scour the island for Christian. He wouldn't want to miss out on the fun. Anyone you can spare to help would be appreciated."

"I will come," Natassa said, still blushing.

"I'm going too," Trecheon said.

"I think you'd do better work here, Trecheon," Matt said. "You're producing acid, and we're going to need it. Let Neil and Natassa look and we'll join them as soon as we can."

Trecheon flicked an ear back.

"He's got a point, Trecheon," Neil said. "We've got three of us, plus Melaina. We'll find him."

Trecheon sighed. "Okay, fine."

"Then it is settled," Ouranos said. "Let us attempt to make these, ah…"

"We'll call them Lexi Charms," Izzy said. "Let's do this."

CHAPTER 56

CHARMED

It took over an hour of experimenting, especially with everyone exhausted and sleep deprived, but all of them working together made things go smoother than Matt had anticipated. Sami was right – fire didn't burn away the acid. But it did melt frozen acid back to a liquid, making it viable again.

Fire also effectively burned the Black Bound elixir away.

It took longer to figure out how to set up the charms, however. Freezing the acid was easy enough, but getting the elixir coating was far harder. The first charm burned right through it and ruined both the acid and the elixir. For the second, they attempted a layer of pure ice around the acid before applying the elixir. But the elixir wouldn't stick to the ice and just sloughed off.

Matt finally suggested they try freezing the Black Bound elixir too. That worked exactly as they hoped. The elixir stuck. The charm was easy to carry around, and fire effectively burned it away enough to reveal a cloud of Lexi acid.

They just had to test it on Darvin.

Sami shifted from foot to foot, ears flat against her head. "You're sure you're up for this?"

"I have to," Darvin said. "Roscoe and Melaina--"

"I know, I know." Sami twitched her tail nervously. "Still…"

"I'll be fine," Darvin said. "Even if it hurts and even if it doesn't work, I can at least take comfort in the fact that it can't kill me."

Sami didn't look convinced.

"Darvin makes good points, Sami," Matt said, trying to reassure himself as much as Sami. "He knows what he's volunteering for." *As if that fixed it,* Matt thought, but he pushed the feeling aside and glanced around. "Who wants to hit him with fire after I drop this in his eye?"

Sami's whiskers shook. "Don't ask me to do it. I don't want to hurt you."

"I'm still out for the count," Trecheon said.

Izzy raised an eyebrow. "You're a healer."

"I, uh…." Trecheon stuttered. "I can make fire too, I guess."

Izzy's jaw dropped. "You're kidding."

"Nope," Trecheon said. "Though I thought you said Gem's only got one power."

Matt frowned, staring. "Having two specialties isn't unheard of," he said. "But it's really rare to have an element and a support power. Usually it's something like healing and cloaking."

Trecheon frowned and pulled the Gem out of his holster. "What is wrong with this thing?"

"I already told you nothing was wrong with it," Matt said. "It's just unusual. Don't worry about it. But, as a warning, usually if you have two powers, both powers are weaker. Don't expect to get to Sami's level of control or Izzy's strength in healing, okay?"

Izzy shifted uncomfortably and turned away.

"Gotcha," Trecheon said. "But either way, I'm useless right now. I'm still producing Lexi acid. Which will be good if we still need some, but not helpful now."

"Since it was technically my hand that transformed you, Darvin," Ouranos said. "I will volunteer my fire to restore you."

Darvin sunk in on himself. "Ouranos, you know I don't blame you for that."

"Regardless," Ouranos said. "Let me undo the damage my father caused."

Darvin let out a gurgling sigh. "Alright." He lifted his head out of the puddle. "Hit me."

Matt chewed his lip. He breathed deeply, put on a mask of confidence, and pressed the fragment into Darvin's eye.

Darvin screamed.

Ouranos blasted Darvin's face with fire and the puddle collapsed in on itself. The inky liquid exploded off him, dissipating into the air, revealing a black, furry body.

Matt's heart leapt. A *stag*.

Darvin stood and shook himself, the last few remains of Cast ink flying off his black fur like water after a mud bath. The drops hit the ground in hisses and vaporized. He still wore the same Defender uniform he had been wearing when he had been turned on Zyearth, wrinkled, but undamaged.

Sami inched her way toward him, tiptoeing like frightened prey, the tip of her tail twitching. "Darvin?"

He faced her, his eyes soft, intelligent, normal. Well, almost normal. His acid-damaged eye still had the odd bleach spots in the dark green from the splash of Lexi acid he had gotten in it last year.

Sami frowned. "Are you…?"

Darvin blinked at her. He crossed the distance between them in three great strides and drew her close to him in a soft embrace and a kiss.

Matt should have looked away and given them their privacy, but he couldn't help but stare. They needed this. Normalcy. Finally.

The kiss was short and sweet, but when Darvin pulled back, both he and Sami were smiling. The white fox rested her head on Darvin's chest, a glimmer in her eye, and squeezed him tight.

"Welcome back."

He rested his head on hers. "It's good to be back."

Roscoe whipped around Izzy's ankles excitedly.

Matt held up a charm. "Ready for another, Ouranos?"

"Please," Ouranos said. Matt pressed the charm into Roscoe's eye, and before he even got a chance to scream, Ouranos bathed him in flame. The ink exploded off his body, revealing the silver stag. He shook himself, shedding drops everywhere.

"Good Draso, that feels good."

Izzy threw herself in his arms before he even stood up. He held her tight.

Matt picked up Roscoe's wedding coil. "You might want this."

Roscoe smiled and slid the coil on his wrist. "A literal lifesaver."

Sami reached into her side pouch and pulled out two colorless Gems. "Not sure whose is whose, but…"

The brothers each reached for a Gem. The moment their fingers brushed them, color injected into them like pigment into water, restoring them to their previous shine. Roscoe grinned. "Hey, first try." His voice sounded harsh and broken from disuse, but Draso's mercy, did it sound wonderful.

"So," a strangely familiar voice said. "That's how the charms were made."

Everyone turned. Matt activated his Gem. Ouranos, Natassa, and Sami set their hands ablaze. Izzy threw a shield in front of the group.

The Black Cloak emerged out of the trees.

THE BLACK CLOAK

Matt stepped between the Cloak and the rest of his group, snarling. "Stay the hell *back.*"

The Cloak raised an eyebrow, barely visible in the slim eye holes in his mask. "Nice to see you too."

Matt encircled his team with tornadoes, forming a protective barrier. "Don't give me that after all you pulled."

The Cloak crossed his arms. "And what, exactly, did I pull?"

"Manipulating events on Zyearth," Matt snapped. "Throwing vague instructions at Izzy and me. Dropping cryptic messages about how we were supposed to behave. Causing me to practically panic in the battle that cost Cix his life." Matt bared his teeth. "For all I know, Cix's death is *your* fault because of your interference."

The Cloak dropped his arms at his sides. He took a deep breath. "You're right."

Matt frowned.

The Cloak lifted his head. "I manipulated events on Zyearth. I jerked you all around and influenced the outcome." His voice cracked. "I'm not proud of it."

"Then you admit you killed Cix," Matt said through clenched teeth. "You little--"

"Guardian Azure," the Cloak said, his voice shaking. The Cloak met Matt's gaze with shining blue eyes. "We both know that Theron killed Cix, the moment he possessed him. My message to you was a warning of the inevitable, not a forking path to choose. It was inescapable."

"But if you hadn't said anything--"

"You would have helped Ouranos regardless of my message," the Cloak said. "My words focused you, warned you, but it ultimately didn't change your actions. You had too much honor to abandon Ouranos over a prediction from a stranger. You yourself acknowledged that things didn't happen just because strange cryptids said it did."

Matt stared. "How did you…?" Red shot through Matt's mind like a series of arrows, cutting off his thoughts. Ouranos. The prince moved closer to Matt, arms outspread, glaring.

"So that means we should just trust you without question?" Izzy snarled.

"I don't expect you to trust me," the Cloak said. "At least not without endorsement."

Matt narrowed his gaze. "Endorsement."

The Cloak nodded. "Allow me to present my advocate." The Cloak waved a hand and a Cast emerged from the woods. Two eyeballs floated on top of it.

Matt gasped.

"Melaina!" Ouranos exclaimed. The yellow shock in Matt's mind nearly blinded him. Matt winced, but Ouranos calmed the bright yellow with a soft blue as an apology.

Matt eyed the Cloak. But Melaina curled around his ankles affectionately as Roscoe had done so often with Izzy.

Ouranos' emotions ran through Matt's mind – optimistic white, lined with a cautious gray. He turned to Matt now. "My friend… I understand your suspicions, but I trust Melaina… Please."

Matt furrowed his brow, still unsure. He turned to Melaina. "Melaina. We've… we've found a cure for the Cast."

Her body exploded in spikes, and she rippled around, throwing her floating eyeballs into the air.

Matt flicked an ear. "I'm not sure if I should interpret that as fear or elation."

Darvin frowned, looking at her. "Kind of makes me wish I was still a Cast so I could ask her."

The moment the words left his lips, he collapsed back into a puddle.

Matt's stomach dropped, and Trecheon leaped back with a yelp. Sami's hands flew to her face. "Darvin!"

But a moment later, Darvin's proper head popped out of the puddle. He held up his hands, one regular, one inky Cast, staring at them, breathing hard. He opened his mouth to speak, but nothing came out.

Matt leaned down. "Darvin…?"

He shot his gaze up at Matt, eyes wide. He blinked a few times, then shook his head. "I… I think I'm fine." He looked down at his Cast body and, with a motion like walking upstairs, he stepped out of the puddle, forming into his normal body, sucking up the ink as he walked. He ran his hands over his chest.

"What in Draso's name was *that?*" Trecheon said, eyes wide.

Darvin held out a hand and examined it, squinting. He blinked, shook the hand, and it broke apart in an inky form, then solidified again. He tried the same thing with the other hand and it behaved the same way. Then he jumped, and when he landed, he collapsed into an ink puddle. But a second later and he leapt out of the puddle, fully himself.

"Draso's wings," Sami whispered.

"I think," Darvin said slowly. "I can transform back into a Cast."

"Not a perfect fix then," Ouranos said, his sorrowful purple invading Matt's mind. "Roscoe, are you having the same predicament?"

Roscoe stepped away from Izzy and closed his eyes a moment. But he shook his head. "No, I don't think so. I feel completely normal."

Matt rubbed his chin. "Hmm. Darvin had Lexi acid in his eye when he got turned. Maybe that's why he's still partially Cast now." He looked him over. "Do you have a hard time keeping yourself together?"

Darvin shook his head. "No, it seems to happen on my command."

Izzy flicked both ears forward. "That might be a good thing, honestly. I can think of a lot of advantages."

Roscoe flattened his long gray ears. "And a lot of disadvantages too. I know the Athánatos might value their immortality, but they also have an out. Does Darvin?"

Darvin snorted, frowning deeply.

"That's… that's a good question," Matt said. "And I'm not sure how to experiment."

"Later," Darvin said. "That's for down the road and we've got bigger problems now. Last thing I need to do is depress myself over this."

"Alright fair," Matt said. He nodded to Melaina.

Darvin nodded back and sunk down into Cast form, then mumbled something to the Athánatos princess. A moment later he reverted back to normal form.

Ouranos tilted his head. "And?"

"She wants you to try it," Darvin said.

"Despite the consequences?" Ouranos asked.

Darvin glanced down at her, frowning. "She said anything was better than the hell she's living now. Even death."

Matt felt the truth of it like a punch to the gut. He turned to Ouranos and passed him their last Lexi charm.

Ouranos took it, his shoulders drooping. Deep blue worry filled Matt's mind. Matt pushed hope back, trying to drown it with light. Ouranos managed to smile at him, then he turned to his sister.

Melaina bubbled quietly.

Ouranos kneeled beside her. "Melaina… If this does not work…" He choked, unable to finish the sentence. He dropped the charm on Melaina's eyeball.

The screams! A mix of Cast shrieking and sentient cries burst from her body, piercing Matt's ears, making his world go blank. Ouranos' red and orange alarm ripped through his mind. The Athánatos prince tossed the fire on her eye, turning away.

The fire hit her eye – and spread. It engulfed her entire body, so quickly, so completely, that Ouranos was forced to dive out of the way to avoid the flames. Matt watched in horror, and his mind exploded in Ouranos' panicked colors. The shrieking wouldn't stop. The flames wouldn't die down.

Then all at once, the flames blew out like a candle, taking the Phonar's bonfire with it, drowning the whole area in complete darkness. Matt groped around in the dark a moment, then Excelsis and Deo lit the area with white and purple fire. He turned back to Melaina, expecting a burnt puddle of Cast mess.

Instead, he saw a body huddled over itself. Herself. Ouranos took a cautious step forward.

"Melaina?"

The body uncurled, as if uncertain. Matt caught the light of sea-green eyes, staring at him through a film of tears. Cream colored dots lined the arch over one eye, and the ears, bent in the strange way Athánatos ears were bent, were tipped with burnt orange. She wore the same traditional outfit Natassa had worn when she first got to Zyearth, with red and white accents.

Melaina blinked, then a smile, a proper smile, grew on her lips. She uncurled completely and stood, tears leaking from her eyes. "Thank you." Just a whisper. That was all.

Ouranos wrapped his arms around his sister and sobbed. "Melaina. Please, forgive me…"

"There is nothing to forgive, Ouranos," Melaina said, her voice crackling. Ouranos held her tight. Matt sighed, feeling the weight of Ouranos' guilt about Melaina fall off him as well, spiraling rainbows through Matt's mind.

"Now," the Cloak said. "You have an army of Cast and very little time to create enough Lexi Charms. If you'll allow me, I'd like to help you create them."

"Hold on," Trecheon said. "We still haven't found Christian."

Melaina pulled away from Ouranos and stood. Like Natassa, she was quite tall. She furrowed her brow. "I am sorry, Trecheon," she said, her voice broken and raw, likely from so many years as a Cast. "But I could not locate him. He did not appear to be on the island at all."

Trecheon flattened his ears. *"What?"*

Melaina stood tall. "Now that I am myself, allow me to find our allies searching for him and take them through the Sanctum. If he is not here, then he is likely on Athánatos."

Trecheon growled. "Ryota."

"Take Jústi with you, Melaina," the Cloak said. The hawk stepped forward, electricity zapping the air around them. "She'll give you the magic you need and get you out if things go sour. We'll follow after we make these charms."

Trecheon frowned. "But--"

Matt gripped his shoulder. "Trecheon. You're putting yourself in danger if you go after him spent like this. Let the others handle it."

"They've already beat his ass twice today," Roscoe said with a grin. "And with a summon and Melaina, Roscoe won't stand a chance."

Trecheon snorted, furrowing his brow. "Okay, fine. But I don't like it."

"I will return as soon as I am able," Melaina said. She nodded to Jústi and the pair rush into the woods.

Matt turned to the Cloak. "How can you help with Charm creation?"

The Cloak's eyes crinkled like he was smiling. "In a great ironic twist, I'm a cloaker." Roscoe snorted. The Cloak nodded to Darvin. "We all know the tendency for cloakers to overwork their magic."

Their first clue to his identity, Matt thought. A cloaker. That meant he had a Lexi Gem. He shook his head. "Alright, let's get started." He pointed to a corner of the square. "Trecheon, Darvin, Cloak, stand there in a triangle with a good distance between each of you. Roscoe, Sami, Izzy, pick someone and shield them. The last thing we want is Lexi acid damage or poisoning while we harvest this stuff. I'll gather it up as it forms and separate it into charms with my wind magic. Ouranos, you'll freeze them when they're the right size. Once we have enough…" He turned to Izzy. "We're up."

Izzy nodded.

"How many is enough?" Sami asked.

"If the Basileus has enslaved the entirety of Athánatos," Ouranos said. "Over a hundred thousand."

Sami flattened her ears.

Matt took a deep breath. "Then we better get started."

CHAPTER 58

MISTAKES

Ryota pushed the human through the palace on Athánatos, trying not to let him see how weak he was.

Good Draso, everything hurt. So much so that he couldn't even tell where it was all coming from anymore. It had been hard enough trying to sneak into the Sanctum while the others had been occupied with Ouranos. Now keeping the human moving forward in silence took all his concentration, causing him to break out into a terrible sweat.

Draso… maybe it would have been better if he had just been caught.

The human stopped.

Ryota snarled with more ferocity than he actually felt. He poked the human's back. "Get moving."

"Open your damn eyes, asshole," the human spat. "The way's blocked."

Ryota peered around him and frowned.

The path leading to Theron's Lair was plugged up by debris. Marble, stone, clay. Ceiling collapse. That Guardian must have done that.

Did that mean Theron was… dead? Ryota's stomach turned cold and he froze to the spot.

"Hit a snag, huh?" the human said callously. "Maybe you should just let me go."

"Shut up, human," Ryota said. "I'm thinking."

"The name's Christian."

"I didn't ask," Ryota said.

Draso's horns, he couldn't make his brain work.

He just… he just wanted to sleep. Go back before all this shit. Before Theron, before Anthony and Clarissa, before the war, before Granddad left them, back and back and back before all this shit took so much of his life.

"You're in serious trouble," Christian said, his voice softening slightly. Ryota looked up. "Don't think I can't notice it. You're bleeding right through those bandages. I don't know what this king wants with me, but is it really worth your life? Go back up to Trecheon. He won't let you die."

Ryota's body buzzed and he flicked an ear. The human had a point. And yet… "You really want to throw in your lot with an assassin? You can deny it all you want, but he is what he is."

Christian snorted. "My friendship with him is none of your damn business. But even if he is an assassin, he's not going to let you die. Hell, he's been arguing against anyone hurting you during this whole trip. He's not heartless."

Ryota's face burned. But it was too late now. "I'm dying… I know I am. The only way I can be saved is with the Athánatos Ei-Ei jewels… they'll save me. Make me immortal." He tried shaking Christian to make a point, but only managed a weak squeeze of the arm. "The only way he'll give me the jewels is if I give you to him."

If he was even alive. Damn everything…

"Trecheon is a healer," Christian said.

Ryota shot his head up. "What?"

"Trecheon is a healer," Christian repeated. "Mana spell shit right out of a video game."

Ryota flattened both ears. Damn, damn, *damn!* "You know for sure?"

"He's healed himself twice," Christian said.

Draso's mercy… He'd made the wrong decision.

"Ryota," Christian said. "I was a soldier too. Scared shitless on the battlefield. It never leaves. I see you, brother. We've all been there. It's gonna be okay. Let's go back to Trecheon. Start over. It's never too late."

Ryota leaned down. He was tired. So very tired. He should never have gotten involved with Theron. He shouldn't have abandoned his team. He shouldn't be so damn afraid of death.

He took as deep a breath as his wounds would allow. Time to make a change and hope Trecheon's offer still stood. He let Christian go.

"Well then," Theron said from behind him. Ryota winced and slowly turned. "Having second thoughts, are we?"

Christian immediately tried to run, but a Cast wrapped around him and held him in place and gagged him. He struggled in the Cast's grip, but hadn't a hope in hell to escape. Ryota splayed his ears and sunk down. Not fast enough.

Theron glanced at Ryota, eyebrow raised. "Well?"

Ryota wrinkled his snout. "No…. no second thoughts…"

Theron lifted his chin. His fur was ruffled and dusty and his left shoulder had a bloodied bandage, but other than that he looked pretty good for someone who'd probably had a ceiling dropped on them. The jeweled bracelets on his arms practically glowed in the dim light of the moon through the ceiling holes.

He met Ryota's gaze. "You have finally brought me a human."

Ryota's mind blurred. Pain stabbed through his body. He could barely think. He couldn't fight. There was nothing he could do. His gaze settled on the promised Ei-Ei jewels.

Or maybe there was.

He gave Theron a casual shrug, trying to ignore the pain. "I know how long you've wanted one."

"Excellent," Theron said. "We'll bring him to the Lair, as you so aptly call it. I've always wanted to see how the Cast charms affect humans." He turned and led the way out through the audience chamber.

Ryota flicked his ears back and glanced at Christian as the Cast dragged him after Theron. The man was rightfully terrified. Ryota gave him a sympathetic look and mouthed to him. *I'll get you out of here.*

Ryota followed Theron and the Cast holding Christian into the Lair, wishing for the world that he had been just a few minutes faster. Stars invaded his vision, warring with blackness, and the wound in his leg had gone completely numb, running all the way down to his toes. Every step was agony.

Theron directed the Cast to the center of the room. He moved to the far end and casually perused the shelves of Cast charms.

Ryota leaned against the wall on the other side of the shelves. "Theron… I'm dying."

"I have noticed," The king said. "What of it?"

Ryota flattened an ear. Even Christian gave him an "I told you so" look.

"Give me… give me the Ei-Ei jewels," Ryota said. "So I--"

"The jewels would not save you in this state," Theron said, shocking Ryota. "The most they could do is turn you into a Drifter, albeit a far less useful one. Assuming your body survived the binding process in the first place."

Ryota furrowed his brow. "What?"

"You need a magical healer," Theron continued. "Which I cannot provide."

"Then… then why am I even here…?" Ryota said. He slid down the pillar to the floor.

"You are far too gone to fight me," Theron said, picking his way through the Cast charm bottles. "However, once you have died and the Gem is once again without a master, I can force a Black Bind on someone else."

Ryota's gut roiled. "…Why not kill me now?"

Theron hesitated a moment before speaking. "You are so near death. I see no point in wasting energy finishing the job."

Ryota coughed. Blood splattered the floor. "You… you told me that the only reason… you could bind me was because I… was an Omnir."

"I had believed such a thing, yes," Theron said. "You are direct descendants from Zyearthlings. Though apparently all zyfaunos can be bound. It may take some experimenting like it did with the Omnir tribe, but it can be done."

Ryota raised an eyebrow. Breathing was hard now. "What do you mean… with the Omnir tribe?"

"I knew the Omnirs could be bound to Sol's Gems," Theron said. "And what few records I had about Cast creation suggested I needed someone with great power. So I attempted to force a bind on the tribe's leader, Kyo. A shame the experiment just obliterated the whole tribe instead."

Ryota stared at Theron, his body buzzing. "You killed the *whole tribe?*"

"Aside from the one that went missing," Theron said. He picked up one bottle, examined it, then shook his head and put it back. "A pity. It was only by chance I found his offspring later, as my true target managed to escape. He knew I was after him. But a half-blooded Omnir was better than none at all."

Ryota felt a pit grow in his stomach. His grandfather's offspring. His offspring.

Theron's humorless smile dripped poison. "Your father."

Ryota stared at the floor, blood dripping down his chin. His ears buzzed and rang, his vision blackened, every stabbing pain faded to numbness.

Theron killed his father.

"It broke my heart hearing your mother beg for his life," Theron said. "But she hindered me. She had to die. A pity he died as well while attempting the Black Bind. Useless, like the rest of the Omnirs. Your only strength is susceptibility to manipulation."

Ryota slid down the shelves, rattling the bottles, listening to Theron calmly examining Cast charms. He hit hard on the floor.

"Your grandmother hunted me after your father's death, you know," Theron continued. "Took her years, but she finally caught me on the mainland just before the War of Eons started. She had one of Sol's jewels, thinking she could get her revenge with the Gem alone. But without it being bound, it was as useless as a rock. It exploded in our battle, disintegrating her. She achieved nothing, aside from giving me the whereabouts of her family."

Ryota choked on a sob.

"A shame your grandfather caught on," Theron continued. "By the time I discovered where he had hidden you all, he was gone. Mad with grief." He shook his head. "Such a waste. I was forced to turn to you for my needs. Though a quarter Omnir proved more useful in the long run, however temporary." He shook his head with a *tsk tsk.* "Life is so fleeting to mortals."

Ryota's vision and hearing vanished completely now. Everything came apart at the seams. He couldn't even think, couldn't hardly breathe.

Christian managed a muffled sound, catching Ryota's attention. Ryota's vision slowly came back and he stared at him. Christian stared back, a look of horror and sympathy on his face.

That lit a fire in Ryota's gut. Enough was enough. He shouldn't have let his fear of death rule him for so long. His death was upon him. But he didn't plan to go alone.

He forced himself to his feet, pushing through the pain, and snatched a bottle of charms off the shelf.

Theron stopped his casual browsing and immediately held his arms over his face, protecting his eyes. He didn't use magic, Ryota noticed. Maybe he couldn't. Good.

Theron wasn't his target anyway.

He hobbled to the middle of the room and tossed a Charm into the eye of the Cast holding Christian instead. The Cast wriggled in place. Ryota glared at it. "Let him go."

And the Cast obeyed.

Theron brought his arms down. He glared. "Well then. You are a clever one." He called down the hall. "Cast!"

Ryota formed a fist. He threw a handful of charms in the eyes of several more Cast. "Turn Theron." The Cast shrieked and turned to the Athánatos king.

It didn't get far. A dozen more Cast appeared, engulfing Ryota's pack of Cast with wild shrieks. Theron's ripped Ryota's apart, scattering the pieces. Ryota stared, wide eyed, his stomach churning. Could they kill the Cast? He didn't think so, but they were certainly worthless in that state.

Theron turned on Ryota and snarled. Ryota waited for his attack, that final snap of magic that'd finally end him.

But it never came.

Now was their chance.

Christian gripped Ryota's shoulder. "Run!"

Ryota nodded, but then paused. He charged his Gem with all the energy he could muster… and aimed a bolt at the ceiling. The pillars and ceiling crashed down around them, destroying the Cast charm bottles and hiding Theron from view. Ryota glared. Black Bound elixir coated his fingertips. *That's for Mom, Dad and Grandma, you son of a bitch.*

Then he fell into Christian's arms and blacked out.

CHOOSE WHO YOU ARE

Neil picked his way through the trees. Damn branches hid most of the moonlight. Thank God for puma eyesight, but even that only got him so far when it was this dark.

Still no sign of Christian.

Damianos walked up next to him. "Seen anything?"

"Nothing," Neil said. "You'd think there'd be some sign, footprints, something."

"No luck for you either then?" Natassa said, walking up to them. She held a ball of fire above her head for light.

"No," Neil said. "Damn it all."

"Natassa?"

Natassa stiffened, her eyes wide. She turned.

Another black Athánatos that Neil didn't recognize walked through the trees, fire over her head. Natassa drew her hands to her face, tears forming in her eyes. "Sisters alive… Melaina." Melaina smiled. She rushed and Natassa drew her into a hug, sobbing. Melaina sobbed too, hugging Natassa tightly. "Oh, dear sister… I had thought you lost *forever.*"

"My lady!" Damianos said. "Thank the Sisters."

Neil turned and grinned. "So much for your career as a monster movie extra. But I'm glad to see you back to normal."

Melaina looked at him funny, but nodded. "The others are restored as well."

"Thank *god,*" Neil said. "We need every hand we can get looking for Christian. We can't find him anywhere."

"That is actually why I am here," Melaina said. An orb of electricity flew through the trees. Neil and Damianos tensed, but the lightning landed on Melaina's shoulder and transformed into a bird. One of the summons. "Why we are here, honestly. I could not find him either. I believe Ryota may have taken him to Athánatos."

Neil growled. "Shit."

It took an agonizing half hour to get through the Sanctum and around the palace, what with the collapsed ceiling from Izzy's battle with Theron. Neil's nerves were shot. They hadn't seen anyone. No Cast, no sentries, no wandering Athánatos… no Ryota. The longer Ryota had Christian, the less likely Christian would get out alive.

Damianos pointed. "That way will take us back toward the chambers we were being held in."

"Let's hurry," Neil said. Then he paused. "Wait. Did you hear that?"

Damianos nodded. Natassa and Melaina surrounded the group with elements and Neil held out his sword, catching fire, ice, and lightning. Jústi hovered over them, lightning crackling all around.

Then Christian walked into view. He held Ryota over his shoulders in a fireman's carry, blood staining his shirt. He paused when he saw the magic, but relaxed when he saw Neil. *"Gracias a Dios,* Neil, are you a sight for sore eyes."

Neil lowered his sword. "Ryota… is he?"

"He's alive, but barely," Christian said. "He needs Trecheon."

"But is he safe?" Neil asked.

"Considering what he risked to get the two us free, I'd say so," Christian said.

Damianos stepped forward. "Where is the Basileus?"

"Hopefully buried under a shit ton of rock," Christian said. Natassa flicked her ears back, though Melaina seemed indifferent. "Thank Ryota for that. But let's not take chances."

Neil nodded. "Let's hurry." They headed out the way they came.

"Neil." Christian's voice grew dark as they hurried along. "I have a question for you."

Neil's tail twitched. "Uh, sure."

"Is Trecheon the White Assassin?"

Neil flattened his ears. "I-I… I mean…"

"Just give it to me straight, Neil," Christian said. "Please."

Neil's whiskers twitched. "…Yeah, he is."

Christian turned away. *"Maldito sea…"* He glanced up. "And you?"

Neil sighed. "Yeah, me too. We're… we're not proud of it." He twitched his whiskers, "…I honestly hate myself for it."

"Then why are you doing it in the first place?" Christian asked. He honestly sounded sympathetic, which almost made it worse.

Neil flattened both ears. "I thought I was doing *good,* Christian," he said. "Killing is my only good skill. But the military didn't want me anymore after my PTSD issues, so I turned to the… the private sector I guess. I dragged

Trecheon into it too, before you came on. Business was bad and he was one bad month from homelessness. But we only took corrupt hits. Hell, I took out a damn mob boss who's been running this city from the dark for decades."

Christian narrowed his eyes. "Matron Fawn."

Neil took a deep breath. "Yeah."

"She was still a person, Neil."

"Yeah, I know," Neil said. "And I paid the price for it. Triple Fawn had my parents killed after that. Honestly… I want out. I just don't know how to do that yet."

Christian shifted his grip on Ryota, glancing away. He avoided spouting the obvious answer. *Turn yourself in.* But that wasn't an option. Not with Philip.

After a moment, Christian spoke. "Neil… thanks for telling me the truth. I appreciate it." He frowned. "I'm sorry about what happened to your parents."

Neil just shook his head. That unspoken question still hung in the air. *Are you going to turn yourself in?* Neil wished he'd just say it and get it over with.

But he didn't.

"Neil. For what it's worth." Christian took a deep breath. "I forgive you."

Neil stared at him. His mind screamed to dismiss it. After all, what right did Christian have to forgive him for crimes that didn't even affect him? But the comment stuck, stripping a heavy weight off Neil's shoulders. His thoughts darted about, searching for the words to thank him.

Natassa leaned on him. She didn't say anything, but the warmth, her gentle smell, calmed his heart and slowed his thoughts. He gave her hand a squeeze, then turned to Christian. "Thanks."

A chorus of Cast shrieks sounded down one hall. Neil froze, all other thoughts vanishing.

"Draso's breath," Natassa said. "Cast."

"Worse," Melaina said. "If the Cast are still violent, then Father is alive…"

"Shit," Christian said. "Bastard should have died. That asshole boasted about killing Ryota and Trecheon's family. Hell, the entire Omnir tribe."

"Damn it all," Neil snarled. "Battle stations, everyone. Let that magic loose and run!"

Damianos nodded to Jústi. The summon transformed into its anthropomorphic form and built a cage of lightning over the door Christian and Ryota had come through, which Damianos strengthened. Natassa and Melaina weaved fire, ice, and stone around the cage, blocking the way.

"It will not hold them for long," Melaina said.

The lightning in the door flashed. Three words echoed down the hallway.

"You will *die.*"

Neil paled. "Go. Run!" He moved behind Christian in case Ryota fell. Natassa and Melaina ran ahead, and Damianos and Jústi ran beside them, leaving a trail of lightning.

CHAPTER 60

YOU ARE NOT ALONE

Trecheon lay on the soft grass around the square, trying to calm his panting. Draso's wings, that had been a rough hour.

Natassa's refugees had spent the time gathering food and tools to cook, mostly collected from the huts and overgrown gardens in the village. The square filled with fires, massive cooking cauldrons, and the smells of fried fish, roasted nuts, and various stews.

Matt's consistently flat ears and permanently furrowed brow said a lot about how uncomfortable he was about them using the food and utensils from the village. And who could blame him? This was his home. But desperate times, Trecheon thought. At least they had the equipment. Not like there were any burger joints on the island. Trecheon's mouth watered and his stomach grumbled. He hadn't even realized how hungry he was.

Constantly pushing his magic had taken a lot out of him.

But they'd done it. All that magic had created a lot of acid and Matt learned damn quick how to concentrate it and form it into little drops, ready for freezing. And with Izzy's magic going so out of control, they had enough Black Bound elixir in no time.

Her magic still wasn't working right, though. She had tried healing Ouranos further before they got started, but ended up killing a bit of fur instead, adding to the scar.

She sat next to Trecheon, hugging her knees.

Trecheon sat up and frowned. "You okay?" He reached for her.

She recoiled. "Don't… don't touch me. Not yet." She flattened her ears and stared at the ground. "My body is still buzzing with magic. I don't know what'll happen if someone connects with it in my state."

"My hand is metal, remember?"

"I don't know if that'll protect you," Izzy said. "Not when I'm this overloaded."

Trecheon dropped his hand. "Sure."

Izzy hid her face behind her knees. "What if my magic doesn't come back?"

Trecheon wrinkled his snout. "What if it doesn't?"

Izzy stared at him.

Trecheon shrugged. "You're no less of a person just because you don't have your magic. Hell, you're not even less of a healer because of that. You guided me when I healed Ouranos. You started CPR and got Damianos taking care of his heart. You think I'd be able to do that shit on my own? He'd be dead if you weren't here."

Izzy frowned. "I suppose."

"It's dangerous to base your entire identity on one aspect of yourself," Trecheon said. "Things change. You're more than just your magic."

She lowered her gaze. "And you're more than just an assassin."

Trecheon's ears fell flat. Holy *shit*. He turned to find Matt, but he was with Ouranos gathering up finished charms and hadn't heard anything. He turned back to Izzy. "How did you know?"

"Theron said something and Neil confirmed it," Izzy said.

Trecheon leaned back. "Damn it. Look, Izzy--"

"You don't have to explain," Izzy said. "Neil... he said you called yourselves white assassins because you took on corrupt hits. Trying to do good. I don't agree with your methods but..." She sighed. "What's past is past. It's not who you are now, so no use dwelling on it. You've been a huge help to us, Trecheon. I know who you really are. You're not my enemy."

Trecheon stared at the ground. "But Izzy--"

"I'm serious, Trecheon," Izzy said, holding up her hands. "You don't have to explain. We all make mistakes, even... even if some are worse than others." She shook herself. "But it's done. You can let it go now."

Ah. She was deflecting. Trying to tell herself that it was his past so she wouldn't have to deal with it. Or trying to hint to him to get out without getting her involved. He wrinkled his snout.

If only it was that simple.

"Trecheon," Izzy said. "You... you should tell Matt."

Trecheon's gut froze. Shit. *Shit*. After everything he'd done to finally earn Matt's trust? He formed fists. Good Draso... "He'll hate me. Again."

"You don't want him finding out on his own," Izzy said.

Trecheon flicked his ears back. "Okay... Okay, you're right. Damn it all."

"Don't wait too long." Izzy took a deep breath. "Just remember... It's dangerous to base your entire identity around one part of yourself." She stood and walked off.

Trecheon laid back on the grass. Draso's horns. She had to throw that back in his face.

He closed his eyes. What… what if they could get out of the assassin business? Finally be free of this bullshit? It'd be a huge relief. But if they did, how would they get the money for Philip's ransom? He shook his head.

Maybe it was a pipe dream.

Those of them who weren't seriously drained had gathered up the charms and placed them in Sami's field bag. There had to be thousands of them. He didn't know if it was enough, but it was a start.

Matt walked over to Trecheon and flopped on the grass next to him. He wiped sweat from his fur. "Good Draso."

"Tell me about it," Trecheon said.

Matt took a deep breath, one hand on his chest, then glanced at Trecheon. "You okay?"

"I've been worse," he said. "How about you, space alien?"

"Definitely been worse," Matt said.

Trecheon watched Sami gathering up charms. "How many did we get?"

Matt wrinkled his snout. "I lost count around two thousand," he said. "I don't think we have nearly the amount we need to turn the whole island back, but it's a start."

"A good one too," Ouranos said, walking up to them. He handed them each a plate of food. Roasted nuts, bowls of steaming vegetable stew, fried fish with sliced lemons, and a variety of fruit – strawberries, blueberries, and blackberries. The utensils they had found were rusted and ruined so they had to eat with their hands, but Trecheon was so hungry he didn't care. He dug into his meal. Thank Draso for metal hands.

"My compliments to the chefs," Trecheon muttered with his mouth full. A green and black Athánatos looked up and smiled at him. His young daughter danced excitedly and filled another plate. Trecheon nodded to them, then turned to Ouranos. "Do you think we have enough for now?"

Ouranos shrugged. The young Athánatos handed him a plate with a smile and a bow. He thanked her and sat with Trecheon and Matt. "We will need more, but if my father is truly dead, then we have time."

Matt paused mid-bite.

Ouranos shook his head. "I know," he said.

Trecheon shook his head. That damn telepathy again.

They ate in silence until Sami approached. "Here." She held three small pouches. "Lexi charms for everyone. We don't know if Theron is actually dead. Frankly I'd be shocked if he was, the bastard. Best not to take chances. They each have a little more than a hundred charms in them. When we go Cast hunting, make sure everyone is paired up with a fire user. We have enough to go around now."

"Fair point," Matt said, and he took a pouch. He glanced at Ouranos. "Do you think the Phonar's fire would have the same effect?"

Ouranos rubbed his chin. "A good question. I do not know, but before we go hunting, we should check. That could be invaluable."

Sami flicked her ears back. "Will they even work with you? They're under the Cloak's control right now."

"They are indeed," the Cloak said walking up to them. He sat beside Trecheon, clearly exhausted, but he refused food. "I've tried negotiating with the Cloak's entity trying to get her to release her hold on them, but she refuses. For now, the Order follows her will, not mine."

Trecheon wrinkled his snout. "What the hell is it? The Cloak's entity?"

"Stubborn," the Cloak said. But he wouldn't elaborate.

Trecheon finished his food and sighed. Finally his stomach settled. He glanced around. "Neil still isn't back yet, is he?"

Ouranos shook his head. "I have not heard from him, no."

"Darvin saw them all go into the Sanctum, but they haven't come out," the Cloak added.

Trecheon growled. Goddamn it. "We need to go after them." He stood.

"I'm coming with you," Matt said.

Sami frowned. "After all that magic expenditure? I'm surprised you two aren't ready to fall over."

Matt stood. "Yeah, well, I suppose being Black Bound has some advantage. And I'm not letting Trecheon go alone. There's a reason they aren't back yet."

"But Theron…" Sami said.

"I will go with you," Ouranos said. He lay his empty dishes near Matt's and stood. He nodded to Matt. "We support each other."

Sami sighed. "Just be careful, alright?" She rounded up their dishes with the help of a blue and black Athánatos and they headed for the stream.

The Cloak stood. "We should check the island and make sure Theron hasn't created any rips to sneak up on us." He turned to Matt. "Permission to take Darvin and Sami and explore?"

Matt raised an eyebrow. "You're asking *my* permission?"

"You're the Guardian here."

"I'm AWOL."

"Doesn't make you any less of a leader," the Cloak said.

Matt pressed his lips together, but waved a hand. "Sure, if they're willing." The Cloak nodded and walked off after Sami.

Ouranos turned to Matt. "Are you sure you will be okay entering the Sanctum?"

"I don't really have a choice if I'm going to be useful here," Matt said. "I'll get through it. Come on." He led the way.

The three of them got to the entrance. Matt paused as they stood in the doorway, shaking.

Trecheon gripped his shoulder. "You aren't alone."

Ouranos gripped the other. "We are here for you."

Matt closed his eyes a moment, though the shaking stopped. "Okay." They walked inside and turned down a long, wide, high-ceilinged hallway, with stairs leading underground, presumably into the inner sanctum. Where Matt saw his father die.

Matt stopped again. He tensed, ears flat against his skull, his breath shaking.

Trecheon pressed a hand to Matt's back. Matt jumped, but glanced at him. Trecheon smiled. "Today the Omnir's on your side, Matt. I got your back." Matt stared, but then returned the smile.

Ouranos brought them to a small inner room, spotted with moonlight from holes in the ceiling. A pedestal with nine inlays stood on one end of the hall.

Matt kept his gaze forward, studiously ignoring it.

"Here," Ouranos said. He pointed to a thin, almost invisible white line in the wall to their left. "The rip in the veil. This will take us to the throne room."

Matt nodded. He led the way, disappearing through the thin line. Ouranos followed.

Trecheon flicked his ears back, but followed as well. The experience was… strange. One minute he was on Sol, the next in a dark, cool, unfamiliar room. It was less like moving from room to room and more like… like falling asleep on a car ride and waking up at your destination. Disorienting.

Silently, Ouranos jogged out of the throne room toward a massive atrium, waving for them to follow.

But the moment they entered the atrium, they heard shouting. Matt froze and held his hands out in front of Trecheon and Ouranos, shielding all of them.

The atrium lit up with electricity and Jústi flew out of a hall on the far end, shrieking. Neil followed with Christian behind him, carrying Ryota across his shoulders. Natassa, Melaina and Damianos took up the rear, blasting elements all around them.

Neil waved his arm at Trecheon. "Run! Run, Cast everywhere!"

A wave of Cast beat against the marble floor behind them like a flood, shrieking wildly, filling the hall.

Matt grabbed his charm pouch. "Charms up, everyone! Ouranos, stage three firestorm!" The pair of them whipped up powerful fire twisters.

As Trecheon fumbled with his charm bag, several thoughts ripped through his mind.

The Cast were attacking.

Theron was alive.

And Ryota was dying.

CHAPTER 61

HUMAN CAST

"Neil!" Trecheon shouted. "Run, get behind us!" Neil and Christian thumped through the audience chamber with Natassa, Damianos, and Melaina behind them. But Christian stumbled and tipped Ryota forward. Neil caught him and the group stopped along a pillar near the entrance to the throne room, frantically looking over Ryota's limp body.

Draso, let Ryota be okay!

"Trecheon, on your left!" Matt shouted. Trecheon leapt out of the way of a slithering Cast. "Charms!" Matt shouted. He bombarded the monsters with charms. Trecheon did the same, wishing for the dexterity of natural arms. Matt waved. "Fire, now!"

Trecheon held out a hand, but only managed a cloud of acid. Damn it all!

Ouranos moved with Matt instead, creating flame tornadoes and bathing the Cast in fire. The otherworldly wails faded and the fire vanished, revealing dozens of Athánatos and a handful of mainlanders.

Neil punched the air. "Hell yeah!"

Christian lifted his head. "Get the civilians out! Trecheon, Ryota needs help, *now.*"

Damianos waved an arm and broke away from Ryota. "Athánatos, to me! Follow your Prinkípissas! *Viasýni!*"

Natassa stood forward. "Come, to safety, this way!" The Athánatos glanced around a moment, but then followed them. The three Athánatos royals led the cured Cast out of the room, toward the rip in the Veil.

Trecheon ran for Ryota. He kneeled beside him. *"Damn it all."*

"You've got to heal him, *Jefe.*"

"I can't!" Trecheon said. "My magic overloaded saving Ouranos and it hasn't come back yet."

Neil snarled. *"Shit."*

Ryota stirred and opened his eyes. He stared at Trecheon, tears running down his face. "Oh god… help me…"

Trecheon ripped off his jacket and began ripping it up into strips. "Hang on, Ryota." He wrapped the worst of the wounds, praying his magic would return.

"No--!" Ouranos' shout was cut off by a blast of fire and ice magic blasting out of the far hallway. He flew back and slid along the floor. Trecheon turned.

Matt shielded. It held, though spiderweb cracks ripped through it. Matt waved a hand and a vicious gale ripped through the area, wrapping the fire around the ice, turning it all to steam, and hiding Ouranos from view. Matt panted heavily and thick Black Bound elixir soaked his hands.

Theron emerged from the fog, ears back, teeth gritted. *"You."*

Matt's ears flipped back and he waved his hands. Shields appeared in front of everyone. He couldn't see Ouranos in the still fading fog, but something shimmered purple and green in the far corner of the atrium.

Trecheon tried to supplement his with his own shield, but still got only acid.

But Theron ignored everyone around him as he walked. He had his gaze set firmly on Ryota. He held his fingers pinched together, as if holding something.

Neil's pupils shrank. "A Cast charm."

Ryota flattened his ears. "Please… Don't…"

Trecheon and Christian stood, standing between Ryota and Theron.

But Theron wasn't looking at Ryota. Trecheon followed his gaze.

Christian.

Ryota shouted, pulling himself up to a sitting position, soaking his new bandages. He pushed on Christian's leg. *"Run…"*

Christian didn't have to be told twice. He turned and ran toward the throne room.

Theron ran after him.

Matt leapt in front of Theron, whipping up a fierce tornado around them both. But Theron waved a hand and the wind vanished. Matt formed fists and dove for him, but the Basileus whipped around him and kicked him hard in the back, sending Matt careening into the mist toward Ouranos.

Trecheon stood in front of him now, holding his hands up. *Work, damn it! Fire!* But he only got acid. He shook his hands, cursing, then swung a fist instead. Theron thrust a hand up and sharp spikes of stone ripped up from the ground and through Trecheon's arm, pinning him to a pillar. Trecheon screamed, and yanked, freeing himself from the metal arm, then fell to the ground, groaning, the wind knocked out of him.

Christian stopped and turned. "Trecheon!" Trecheon flipped over and waved Christian away, but he couldn't stand.

Neil moved next, but before he could even make a step, Theron blasted ice clumps his way. Matt's shield still held and kept back most of them, but one broke through and slammed hard into Neil's shoulder with a terrifying crack, forcing him to drop his sword and fall. He gripped his shoulder with a roar of pain. Probably broken.

Christian turned and ran again, but a wall of stone raised up between him and the entrance to the throne room. He turned back.

Theron walked up to him, Cast charm in hand, completely unopposed. Christian furrowed his brow and bared his teeth, fists raised.

Theron laughed. "You think you can fight me?" He waved a hand and a pillar of rock shot forward, pressing Christian to the stone wall. Christian gasped and struggled for freedom.

Trecheon sat up, but the phantom pain made it hard to move. *Not Christian!*

A blast of lightning crashed into the stone pinning Christian and shattered it. Trecheon turned. The Basileus stopped.

Ryota hobbled between Theron and Christian, gripping one bloody arm. His powers spun about the room, smashing bolts into the floor, pillars and ceiling, leaving angry scars. Black Bound elixir formed on his fingertips and slithered up past his wrists. He glared at Theron, blood dripping down his snout.

"We… are… *done.*"

Theron scoffed and waved a hand. A rush of fire blew at Ryota.

Ryota held out a hand and blocked it with a thick shield.

Theron perked his ears. "You have some fight in you after all." He held his hands up, calling more elements to his fingers. "But if you push too hard, your magic will kill you."

Ryota snarled, spitting blood, and pushed his lightning even further. The air smelled and tasted of electricity, lighting everything up with a thin blue.

"Maybe there are worse things," Ryota said through clenched teeth. He balled the lightning up into a massive orb.

Theron narrowed his eyes and waved a hand, pulling at Ryota's lightning orb.

But Ryota pulled a hand back, spitting out more lightning. Black Bound elixir ran up to his elbows. He gathered all the electricity into a single, bright bolt and aimed it at Theron. The bolt soared.

But Theron caught it between his hands, balled it back up, and threw all of it at Ryota.

Ryota gasped and shielded, but it did little to soften the blow. It sent him flying back and he crashed into a thick column and collapsed.

Trecheon's heart leapt into his throat. "Ryota!"

Christian moved to his side.

"Once again," Theron said. "You have failed."

Christian turned, snarling.

Theron raised an eyebrow. "This quilar kidnapped you and you mourn his death." Trecheon let out a tiny, choked sound.

"Marines don't die," Christian said. "We go to hell and regroup." He smashed into Theron, knocking him to the ground, forcing him to drop the Cast charm. He scrambled madly off Theron, grabbed the charm, and turned back.

Theron pinned him to the ground with a solid block of ice. Christian fought, but the ice kept him pinned. Theron planted a foot on his chest and leaned down. He pulled Christian's fingers apart and got the charm. "I do admire a fighting spirit."

"See you in hell." Christian spat at him. Theron flinched, growled, then shoved the Cast charm in his eye.

Christian screamed the moment the charm hit his eye. The flesh of his arms and legs cracked and shredded to ribbons, snaking up his body, shooting blood in all directions destroying the ice holding him down. His scream reached impossible high-pitched levels, then a *pop!* drowned out everything and his entire body collapsed in a pile of fine dust, left to soak up the spilled blood.

Numb shock ached through Trecheon's chest. All other pain, all other senses started shutting down.

Theron gave a slight shrug. "Not what I expected. But useful nonetheless."

Neil was the first to find his voice, a violent roar cracking through the atrium and into the woods beyond. "You killed him!" His words clipped with growls and hisses. "You psychotic maniac, *you killed him!*"

That loosened Trecheon's emotions and he gasped for air, fighting a panic attack. Christian, his friend, his teammate, a pile of dust and blood. Neil, a wounded predator, screaming. Ryota dying in the corner. If he wasn't already dead.

And Trecheon, missing an arm, standing in the middle of a battlefield, facing an enemy he couldn't hope to fight. All the memories of the Battle of DC flooded his mind, tearing him from reality, drowning him in hopelessness. His shoulder screamed in pain. He listed to one side, breath and heart heavy.

Someone steadied him, a warm hand on his back, pulling him back to some reality. He looked up.

Carter.

Trecheon stared, trying to process what he was seeing. That… that couldn't be right. Carter was dead. *Dead.* But the face before him, a swirl of blue and green against a background of white, couldn't be anyone but Carter.

"Trecheon, stay with me."

Carter's voice. From beyond the grave, beyond time, beyond his senses. Tears built in Trecheon's eyes and spilled over. *Carter.* He tried to find words, but nothing came.

The swirling face moved closer, and deep green eyes came into focus under a furrowed brow. Carter gripped Trecheon's remaining hand and held it tight. The sweat from his hand soaked through Trecheon's fur and stung the skin.

"Trecheon," Carter said, more firmly this time. *"Stay with me."*

The realization dawned slower than it should have. He wouldn't be able to feel Carter's fur. Or sweat, or stinging, or anything. Not with artificial arms.

That wasn't Carter. Carter was dead. And so were Trecheon's arms. And Clarissa. And Anthony.

And Christian.

Matt's face focused now, drawing Trecheon back to the reality of death, and screaming, and magic, and pain. He gripped Matt's hand. Matt winced, but still held on.

"Don't let go..." Trecheon whispered.

Matt kneeled beside him, pressing his other hand to Trecheon's back. "I won't." He turned to the center of the atrium.

To Ouranos. Standing in the center of it all.

Facing his father down.

No More

Ouranos stood firm on the marble floor, his fists so tight they ached. Magic broiled under his fur, threatening to burst out at any moment.

Ryota lay unmoving in the corner. Unconscious or dead, Ouranos could not tell.

Neil's screams and accusations had devolved into feral roars, then into sobs and gasping breaths. Trecheon's human friend, Christian, lay in bloody ashes. A cold-hearted death he did not deserve. Matt dragged Trecheon toward Ryota, desperately trying to pull him from some memory he appeared locked in.

And the orchestrator of it all, the Basileus of the Athánatos, studying Christian's remains like an artist admiring his work.

Ouranos could stand it no longer.

"Theron!" he bellowed.

Theron looked up. The light of dawn scattered harmlessly around him, catching the myriad of Soul Jewels he still carried on his person. The hundreds of ruined lives in the name of revenge.

Ouranos loosened his magic, letting waves of lightning, ice, fire, and sand ripple through his fur. He gritted his teeth, growling like a feral beast. He spoke, his voice sharp with a barely contained rage. "You have done enough. No more. *Yield.*"

Theron laughed. "Your allies lay broken around you. More Cast approach as we speak. The Phonar have abandoned you. What hope do you have?" Even now, the shrieks of Cast filled the area as they rushed to Theron's aid.

Ouranos glared and pounded his fist into his hand. Massive walls of stone burst up all around the atrium, hiding the forest beyond, blocking all exits, cutting the Cast off from their master, and drowning the room in darkness. Ouranos stomped a foot and swirls of fire lined the walls, giving everything a haunted glow, heating the room.

Theron reached for the fire himself, pulling at the magic, but Ouranos stopped it flat.

Matt's white surprise flooded his mind. "Draso's mercy, Ryota's still alive."

Ouranos looked up. Neil had crouched near Ryota's limp form, angry tears streaming down his face, for Christian's unjust death. Trecheon huddled in place, gripping his ruined shoulder, oil staining his clothes. Matt checked over Ryota, frantic.

Ouranos reached for Matt. *Matthew, get them out of here!*

Matt shot his gaze up, ears flat. *You're not going to fight him* alone, *are you?*

Our allies harbor grave injuries, Ouranos said, straining against Theron's influence. He pulled down the stone wall blocking the entrance to the throne room, and with a gentle breeze, gathered up Christian's remains and piled them safely within the hallway, away from the fire magic. Then he pulled back Theron's stone spike, releasing Trecheon's damaged arm.

The Basileus fought him, but Ouranos pushed back, for now. *He is trying to wrest my magic from me. I cannot protect them. You are the only one who can get them to safety. I know you have offered yourself, but this time I must face him alone lest we lose more.*

Sickly green hesitation flooded Ouranos' mind, but only for a moment. Then Matt's powerful rosy dawn overtook the green, filling Ouranos not only with hope, but with power, allowing him greater control against his father's pulls.

Matt helped Trecheon to his feet, made sure he and Neil could support each other, then picked Ryota up gently. He gave Ouranos one more look of determination.

As long as I live, Matt said. *You're never alone. I'll come back for you.* They escaped down the hall leading to the throne room, careful to avoid Christian's ashes. Ouranos resealed the entrance with more stone magic.

Theron lifted a brow, still tugging on his power. "Do you really think you have saved them by sending them away? You cannot hope to best me. You--"

"No," Ouranos snarled. "For decades your words and puppet strings have dictated my every action. For nearly a *century* I have lived in fear of you. My own *father*. And all of this in the name of revenge against my mother's killers. Do you truly think she would want this? Manipulation of her children? Destruction and death for our people? The eternal imprisonment of the Cast? Planetary *genocide?"* He snorted. "Do you truly think she smiles on you as you destroy everything you touch?"

The Basileus didn't falter. He stood stoically in place, still pulling at Ouranos' magic, silent.

Ouranos stared, wide eyed, his heart aching. "So then. You have confirmed it. This is no longer for Mother's sake, is it? You have become so twisted you have lost sight of your reasons for this."

"Your analysis of my motives only shows your ignorance, Prínkipas," Theron snapped.

"Then enlighten me," Ouranos snapped back.

"I would rather kill you." Theron released his hold on Ouranos' magic.

With Theron's restrictions gone, Ouranos' magic billowed out of control, growing his stone walls ever higher and filling the room with flames. Ouranos sunk in on himself, trying to push the sudden surge of magic back.

Gem users could not be hurt by their own magic. Not so with Ei-Ei jewel users, not without intense concentration and practice. The flames singed his fur and skin, threatening to burn him alive. He shouted.

But it lasted less than a second. A thick shield engulfed him, fighting back the flames, giving Ouranos the time to pull back on his power. His mind cleared.

You're never alone. Matthew's voice, his actual voice, not just a memory, echoed through his mind. Matt's power, literally given to him. Even the power to shield.

But Theron had no such bond with anyone. He would burn.

The flames died. Theron stood, growling, his plan to drown Ouranos in flames ended.

"Remember, Prínkipas," Theron said. "Kill me, and you lose the Phonar permanently."

Phonar or not, Theron had to die. Ouranos' Soul Jewels, bound in a bracelet on Theron's arm, the very thing that forced Ouranos into a Drifter state, a puppet state, glowed bright, reflecting in Theron's own Soul Jewels.

The Soul Jewels. Theron's Soul Jewels.

Sisters alive. Maybe Ouranos had other options after all.

"Well then, Prínkipas," Theron said, elements flying all about him. "Shall we contend?"

CHAPTER 63

Healer

Izzy fidgeted as Roscoe added a layer of bandages over her foot. Blood welled through anyway. Roscoe snorted, filling the air with his thick stag musk, then added more bandages until the blood stopped soaking through. She needed it supported.

Matt and the others had been gone too long.

"Help!" Damianos' voice echoed through the entrance to the Sanctum. "Someone! The Basileus lives!"

Izzy lifted her head.

Roscoe already took off for the Sanctum.

Izzy snarled and ran after him, sword in hand. "Eris, get the Athánatos to the river! Roscoe!" He turned and pulled up a wall of earth, putting a barrier between the Athánatos and whatever enemy came from the Sanctum.

The Phonar remained where they were, stoic and unmoving. Izzy snarled. Curse that damn Cloak.

Damianos rushed through the Sanctum entrance with dozens of Athánatos following him, calling for help. Natassa and Melaina followed behind, elements swirling about them.

Roscoe slowed, nearing Damianos. "Where's the Basileus?"

Damianos leaned on his knees. "The audience chamber… through the rip…"

"There," Izzy pointed down a long, wide, tall stairway, leading to the Inner Sanctum. "Go, run!" Roscoe ran, and she followed. Melaina collapsed to the ground, exhausted, her elements extinguishing.

But Natassa turned and followed. "Izzy!" She threw a fireball her way. Izzy caught it on her sword.

But just as they hit the landing, Matt came out of the Inner Sanctum holding Ryota's limp body. Trecheon and Neil followed, shaking with panicked, raspy breaths.

Matt stepped forward. "Izzy, he's dying. Trecheon's magic is still drained. We need a healer *now.*" Both Trecheon and Neil glanced around like they expected to be attacked at any moment.

Izzy frowned. "But my magic--"

"Izzy," Trecheon's high pitched, panicked cries stopped her short. "Izzy please, he's *dying,* he's my only family left, you have to try, please!" His voice quivered as he spoke. Neil dropped to the ground, hugging himself, favoring his left shoulder, which cracked as he moved.

Izzy flicked her ears back. "Trecheon, with my magic behaving this way, I could just as easily kill him."

Bright bells sounds rang in Izzy's ears. She turned.

"Izzy, you've got this," Matt said. He stared into her eyes with such fierce determination and admiration that she stepped back in surprise. "You're a Guardian. I know you can do this."

Izzy still faltered. "But--"

"You are a Guardian," Matt said again. The jingling bells grew louder, stronger, brighter. "You can do this!"

Izzy chewed her lip. Trecheon's desperate calls made her ears burn. His words from earlier hit her. *So what if you don't get your healing back? You're no less of a healer just because you don't have your magic.*

And he was right. She kneeled down. "Lay him here." Matt obeyed.

Roscoe frowned. "I thought he was on the Basileus' side."

"He nearly killed himself trying to save Christian," Matt said. "Literally stood between them, bleeding out. I don't think he's the enemy anymore."

Damianos jogged up now, still panting. "Where is Christian?"

Matt looked up, ears flat, eyes shining. He shook his head but said nothing more. A deep dark bell sounded in Izzy's ears. She immediately associated it with death.

Both Neil and Trecheon choked on sobs.

Izzy's heart ached. But she had a job to do. She glanced over her patient.

Ryota was in a bad way. Blood all over his bandages, completely unconscious. His pulse was there, but weak. She couldn't tell if he was getting enough breath. But she kneeled beside him and got to work anyway, resting her sword near her feet.

Trecheon shook. "Izzy--"

"My powers still aren't working," Izzy said. "But it doesn't mean I can't save him." She looked up. "I need bandages. Anyone who can spare a piece of clothing, take it and rip it into strips. Use my sword if you have to." Trecheon and Neil ripped off their jackets and Roscoe got to work cutting them into strips. Neil yowled in pain with every movement of that damaged shoulder. Definitely broken. Damianos removed the *osaa* from his belt and began stripping it.

"Roscoe, press your hand here," Izzy said. "Matt, you press here." She met his eyes. "Where's Ouranos?"

"Fighting the Basileus." Matt said.

"Then go to him," Izzy said. "We've got this here." Matt nodded and ran back into the Sanctum. Izzy turned. "Natassa, keep these steady while I wrap the biggest wounds." Natassa sat down next to Ryota. Izzy turned to Neil. "Neil, it looks like you've only got one good arm, but you can still help." She grabbed one strip from the growing pile and wrapped Ryota's shoulder. "Press your hand here. It'll bleed through, but it'll slow it. Trecheon, you're sure your powers aren't working?"

Trecheon pressed his hand near one of Ryota's wounds, but nothing happened. "I can feel the acid building, damn it…"

"Rest," Izzy said. "Take deep breaths. Calm your mind. Your magic will come back in time. We can keep him stable until then." She reached for more strips and covered other wounds. In all honesty, she wasn't sure she could keep him stable. But she had to try.

Neil's eyes held that thousand-yard stare.

Izzy glanced up from her work. "What happened?"

Neil opened his mouth to tell her, but could only manage a whine. He flicked his ears back and concentrated on Ryota's wounds.

"Cast charm," Trecheon said, his voice shaking. He pressed his hands to one of Ryota's wounds. "Don't make me describe it…" He turned, gagging slightly, coughing. He sniffled. "But… he's not a Cast."

Izzy didn't ask further.

Trecheon pressed his ears near Ryota's mouth. "Izzy…"

She checked his breathing. Gone. Damn it! She shielded her mouth, and leaned down for breaths, then checked his pulse. Fading. "Damn it! Natassa, pass electricity to Damianos. Dami, shock him like we did Ouranos."

Trecheon pressed the bandages tighter. "Come on you son of a bitch. You've lived this long. Don't die on me now."

Ryota still showed no sign of waking up. Izzy went for another breath.

"Come *on*, you thorn in my side!" Trecheon shouted. "I thought you were afraid to die! Prove it and live, damn it!" Still nothing. Trecheon's voice shook. "Please..."

Neil flattened his ears, hunching down over himself, glancing around the room like he was seeing ghosts.

Damianos turned to the puma. "Neil, stay with us." Neil turned to him with wide pupils and frantic breaths. Damianos reached out and gripped his hand. "Stay with me, my friend. Your life is here. You are present. You are not alone." Neil gripped his hand back and his breathing slowed, but the panicked look remained.

Trecheon dissolved into panicked pleas.

Izzy watched him, her chest aching. She knew that sorrow. On Sol, during the genocide, watching her father die. She couldn't let this damn island do that to Trecheon too. That was why she became a Guardian. To be the healer.

Her Gem whined in her ear, almost jingling. Inviting.

She pressed her eyes shut. Ryota was dying. If her magic didn't work now, there was no chance in saving him. She pressed her hand to Ryota's wounds and pressed healing magic into him.

Something in him cracked under her hand. *No! This is my magic, my strength, and damn it, I'm not going to hurt anyone anymore! HEAL HIM!*

The cracking stopped.

Ryota's wounds began to heal. Her mind's eye showed the flesh knitting, the body making new blood, the bruises and magic damage healing, and all at once, he gasped for air. His eyes flew open and he sat up, gripping his chest, coughing.

Trecheon whipped around. "Ryota?"

Ryota turned to him, blinking. "I'm... alive?"

Trecheon pressed his lips together, flattening his ears. His voice shuddered. "You... You damn dipshit."

Izzy sighed with relief. Damianos and Roscoe cheered. Even Neil seemed to come back to the present with Ryota's revival. Natassa leaned on Neil, gripping his hand, which brought a smile to his face.

Izzy glanced at her hands. She did it. She got control of her magic. She became the healer again. What she was meant to be. She finally broke this damn island's curse.

Thank Draso. She'd never take her magic for granted again.

"You… you saved me," Ryota said. "Why the hell did you do that? Just so Trecheon could kill me himself?"

Neil smacked him upside the head. "Don't be any more of an ass than you already are and thank the lady."

Ryota yipped and rubbed the back of his head. He frowned. "Still…"

Izzy flexed her hands. "I'm tired of this island stealing everyone's family from them."

Ryota blinked and pinned his ears back. "…Sorry. Thanks." He turned to Trecheon. "Trech--"

"Don't… don't start," Trecheon said, though his voice shook. He took several breaths, clearly trying to calm down. "You survived, but that doesn't mean we're finished here. And don't call me Trech." But he looked relieved nonetheless.

Ryota frowned, but he nodded. "Fair." He stared at the floor. "Trecheon… The Basileus killed everyone. All our family. The Omnir tribe, Mom and Dad, Grandma… maybe even Ayumi and Granddad. I don't know. But he admitted it to me. And… and I should be surprised, but I'm not. He's used me since the beginning. And I'm sick of it." He glanced up. "I'm done with him. And I'm sorry it took so long to get here." He paused. "Thanks for not killing me on the pier."

Trecheon flattened his ears. He pulled his brother into a one-armed hug. "I'm just glad to have you back. It's time we start over. *Really* start over. Once this bullshit is over."

"Yeah," Ryota said. He hugged Trecheon back. "Yeah."

Izzy's chest warmed.

Wait. The Basileus.

Matt.

"Izzy!" Darvin shouted from the top of the stairs. Izzy stood straight, gripping her sword.

Darvin and Sami came rushing down the stairs. Darvin stopped and leaned on his knees, panting. He and Sami both pawed at the fur around their eyes. Darvin shook himself before speaking with ragged breaths.

Izzy furrowed her brow. "What? What's wrong?"

"The Cloak took Sami and I exploring the island looking for Cast," Darvin said. "We got to the edge… and there's an army of Cast headed for the mainland."

THE MAINLAND

Trecheon leapt to his feet, dropping his broken arm to the floor. *"What? You're sure? Are they headed for the casinos?"*

"No, the shipping docks," Sami said.

Neil's tail drooped. "Christ *almighty*. They'll tear those workers *apart.*"

Trecheon felt sick. Oh, good Draso. He stuffed his feelings about Ryota and Christian in the war cupboard in his mind for later processing. Back in war. Again.

"Defenders," Izzy said, standing. "We've got to get to the mainland. They'll need all the help they can get." She turned to Trecheon. "You and Neil have done more than your fair share here. More than you ever should have. But you have your brother back now. Neil is safe. You can go home. We've already asked too much of you all."

"You're kidding, right?" Trecheon said. "You really think you're going to tackle thousands of Cast all by yourselves? Hell no. If you wanted to release me from this whole mess, you should have pushed me harder after I volunteered to help make charms. Way too late for that, space alien.”

“I’m with Trecheon,” Neil said. “I’m seeing this to the end, whatever that end is.”

Izzy flicked her ears back. “Even if that end is death?”

Neil shrugged. “Either I die fighting back, or I face the Cast-pocalypse next week. And I’m not one to sit still.”

“Me neither,” Trecheon said.

Izzy smiled. “Thanks. Both of you.”

“Yeah, well, you guys clearly need all the help you can get,” Neil said grinning.

Trecheon flicked his ears back. “Even…?” He pointed to Ryota.

Ryota pulled himself to his feet. He pounded his fist into his hand, shocking his quills and fur with lightning. “After all the shit Theron pulled, I am not sitting this one out.”

“Good,” Izzy said. She glanced at his hands. Little beads of black formed on his fur. “Ah. So that’s where Theron was getting his Black Bound elixir.”

Ryota paused, and glanced at his hands. He wiped them on his pants. “Sorry.”

“No, no, this is good,” Izzy said. “You’re Black Bound. You won’t tire and lose your magic like most of us. We need that.” She stood tall. “Any ideas on getting to the mainland?”

“Christian’s boat might get some of us,” Trecheon said, his heart aching. “But even with Matt’s magic it was super slow. We need something faster.”

“The Phonar summons,” Natassa said. “They can carry us at much greater speed.”

“If the Cloak will let us,” Roscoe said.

"We'll just have to make him," Izzy said. She turned to Trecheon. "Trecheon. Neil. You chose to help even in the face of all this. That makes you Defenders. You two… and Ryota."

Trecheon perked his ears, surprised. He wasn't sure he was worth that. But what had Matt said? *I've seen the good you've done. You're not my enemy.* He glanced at Neil. Neil smiled and nodded. Trecheon nodded back, then mimicked the sweeping salute he had seen Izzy do, chin held high. Time to… time to finally let go of that self-hate.

Time to be the Defender. "Yes, ma'am."

Neil saluted too, and while Ryota didn't, he still held his ground, lightning flowing through his fur.

Izzy smiled. "Good. Come on." She led the group to the square. Trecheon picked up his broken arm and followed after her.

But as he neared the exit, he heard shouting outside. He exchanged a glance with Izzy, then rushed out into the open.

The Black Cloak paced back and forth in front of the six Phonar summons, growling and spitting, seemingly arguing with himself, his words bouncing between English and some unknown language.

Melaina, and Eris stood near the exit, staring as the Cloak paced. Trecheon walked carefully up to them. "What the hell is he doing?"

Melaina flattened her ears. "I am uncertain."

Izzy wrinkled her snout. "What is he even saying?"

"He is speaking a primitive form of our language," Eris said. "Arguing with the Cloak's entity."

Trecheon lifted a brow. "Well, he did call her stubborn."

Eris twitched her tail and pressed her hand to her chin. "I can make out a few words, but the meaning as a whole is lost to me."

"Arketá!" the Cloak snapped. "If you won't let them go, I'll just *take them."* He held out a hand toward the Phonar.

Excelsis cawed frantically, reformed back to his feral bird form, and dove for the Cloak's hand. He smashed into his palm and exploded into black feathers.

Trecheon gasped, and Melaina shrieked.

The feathers burst into purple flames and swirled around the Cloak in a tornado of down and embers, hiding him from view. But in a surge of fire, the feathers burned up, leaving the Cloak behind. But… changed. Huge black wings weighed down his shoulders. The wing joints folded a whole foot over his head, and the flight feathers brushed the ground. Feathers also formed around his eyes, poking out around the edges of the mask. He let out a long, feral growl.

"I swear to Draso and *tis aderfés sou* that if you don't release the others, I'll take them by force too," he snarled. *"Den boreíte na to alláxete."*

Natassa rested her hand on her cheek. "'You cannot…'" She turned to Eris.

"'You cannot change it'," Eris translated fully.

Trecheon frowned. Change what?

"I don't *care* what it'll do to me," the Cloak continued. "People will *die--*" He paused, then formed a fist, glaring at the ground. He spit off a string of the foreign language.

Eris flattened her ears.

Melaina frowned. "Eris…?"

But before she could answer, the Cloak whipped his head about. His sharp blue eyes glistened as he stared the group down.

Then he locked eyes with Trecheon.

Trecheon stood his ground, furrowing his brow, ready to brandish his broken arm as a weapon if it came to it. Surprisingly, Ryota stood by his side too, lightning flailing about.

The Cloak snorted. "We're out of time." He marched up to Trecheon. "Give me your broken arm."

"Why?"

"We don't have time," the Cloak said. "Give it to me!"

Trecheon furrowed his brow, but tossed the arm to him.

The Cloak stepped back a few paces, then disappeared in a flurry of feathers and flame. A second later he reappeared, holding Trecheon's arm fully repaired. "Here. You really shouldn't fall asleep in your office like that, especially with the door unlocked. It's not safe."

Trecheon sputtered. "Holy shit, that was *you?"*

"Technically it was Theron," the Cloak said. "I'll pay for repairs when this is all over, but you have to survive first, and you won't do that with a broken arm."

"How the hell did you *do* that?" Trecheon said.

"Wait, wait, wait." Neil held up his hands. *"You* were the one who left Trecheon's broken arm on the floor of his office last month?"

"Yes," the Cloak said. "I took his good arm and left the broken one in its place."

"So you're actually a time traveler then," Izzy said.

The Cloak looked away. "Yes."

"Blob monsters, magic healing, bird summons, elemental powers, and now time travel," Trecheon said. "I can't take much more of this BS."

"You had us scared *shitless,"* Neil said. "What the hell gave you the right?"

"We don't have *time,"* the Cloak said.

"What do you mean we don't have time?" Trecheon said. "You're a goddamned *time traveler."*

"But the rest of you aren't," The Cloak spat. "If we don't act now, hundreds are going to *die."* He walked toward Trecheon.

Trecheon took a step back. "Hell no. Pass that to someone else. You're not allowed anywhere near me with your time traveling bullshit."

The Cloak narrowed his eyes. He passed the arm to Sami. Sami frowned at him, but took the arm and pressed it into Trecheon's socket. Trecheon winced at the pain, but everything seemed to work fine.

"Heal up," the Cloak said. "I'm going to talk with the Phonar. We leave in five."

Izzy stepped forward, sword in hand. "Let's get one thing straight here," she said. The Cloak stared, hands limp at his sides. "You've been a tremendous help. But." She lifted her chin. "I'm the Guardian here. *I'm* in charge. My pack is too important, too vital, and too valuable to leave in the hands of someone I don't trust. Is that understood?"

The Cloak paused. He breathed deeply, and nodded. "Yes, ma'am."

"Good," she snapped. "Go do whatever the hell you need to. We'll leave when *I* say we're ready." The Cloak narrowed his eyes, but left.

Izzy turned to Trecheon. "How's your magic?"

Trecheon lifted his newly replaced arm and called fire to it. A fireball blossomed in his hand. He sighed relief. "Good to go."

Izzy nodded. "While the Cloak talks to the Phonar, we'll heal up. Trecheon, you get my foot. Neil, come here and let me see that shoulder. Anyone else needing help, line up behind Neil. We'll take care of this and get out."

"Yes, ma'am!" everyone chorused.

Neil walked up to Izzy. She pressed her lips together a moment, then touched Neil's shoulder. Neil tensed, but not for long. A moment later, he stepped back and rotated the shoulder.

"Good as new," Neil said. Izzy sighed relief.

So did Trecheon. He kneeled down and got to work on Izzy's foot, keeping one eye on the Sanctum.

Natassa flicked her ears back. "There is an additional problem. We cannot cure the Cast on the mainland only to be crushed by more Cast the moment they are cured. Melaina and I must create a rip in the Veil to send them home before we began curing them."

Izzy flicked her ears back. "How long will that take?"

Natassa frowned. "Usually several hours."

Izzy lowered her gaze. "We don't have hours."

"I can help with that," Ryota said. "Theron perfected a method of creating rips that took about half an hour. It's not terribly stable, but it'll last long enough for us to get people to safety."

Natassa looked uncertain, but Melaina smiled at him. "If you got it from our father, I trust you."

Ryota nodded.

Trecheon finished Izzy's foot and stood next to her, healing power still lingering on his fingertips. "Let's hurry and do this."

CHAPTER 65

A FAILED ARMY

Matt dashed through the Inner Sanctum, trying not to look at the Gem Pedestal in the corner. The spot where his father died. Where he was murdered. By an Omnir.

But not Trecheon. Or Ryota, for that matter. Finally Matt could truly see them as allies. He could almost hear his father's spirit shout at him as he ran by the pedestal. *Forgive them.* Or perhaps Dad just rolled his eyes and muttered *about time.* Matt smirked slightly at the thought.

Regardless, he knew who his enemies were. Ryota was an ally. Trecheon, a friend.

And Theron was the enemy.

He burst through the rip in the Veil.

And stopped.

Dozens of Cast lined the floor, wobbling about, like newborn fawns on unsteady legs, gurgling and whistling like Melaina had when she first met them. Eyeballs floated on the tops of each puddle, rolling about. He stared as one-by-one, the creatures rushed the stone wall blocking the way to the audience chamber, as if trying to break it. But they didn't have the strength of a full Cast and hardly even made a noise, let alone a crack.

Matt flicked his ears back. "Draso's *mercy.*"

As one, the Cast shifted and turned their floating eyeballs on him.

Matt stepped back, wind ripping at his heels… but he stopped. Melaina had still had her will, her mind. Did these Cast? "Can you… Are you trying to get to Ouranos?"

One Cast separated from the group. Their shimmering red-gold eyes glanced up at Matt, almost with sympathy.

Matt crouched near them. If only he had fire.

Two more Cast, one with pink eyes, and another with pine-green, slithered up to Matt holding a decorative urn. They passed it to him. He took it, confused, and almost opened it, but then something clicked. This was a funeral urn. He glanced at the Cast. "This is Christian."

The Cast gurgled excitedly.

Matt held the urn to his chest. Trecheon should have this. He closed his eyes a moment. "Thank you." He turned and gently placed it on the throne, quietly speaking last rites over it.

He stared at the stone wall. There was no way he could take it down with his magic in time. He turned to the Cast. "Does anyone here have magic that can take down the stone wall?"

Six more Cast moved forward. The other Cast slithered back respectfully. Matt took that as a yes. He kneeled beside them. "I can cure you all."

Rippling sounds mixed with quiet, broken sound, as the Cast moved as one. Matt chewed his lip.

"But I need fire," Matt said. "Is there a torch or a hearth nearby? Some place I can make fire?"

The Cast turned, and flooded down a side hall, leading away from the audience chamber. Matt took a deep breath and followed. *I'll come back for you, Ouranos.*

Ouranos leapt to the left, narrowly avoiding a blast of rocks that hurtled his way.

In the time it had taken his friends to leave, he had managed to stabilize the stone walls blocking the exits, though the fire was no longer necessary, as the light of dawn poured in through the ceiling holes.

But Theron still kept him at bay.

Ouranos snarled. The Basileus was playing with him. Like a lion playing with its food. Toying, trying to wear him down, showing little interest in finishing the job.

This was not working.

I see into your mind, Prínkipas, Theron said. *You cannot best me.* Ouranos winced at the pain.

He needed Matthew.

Then his mind filled to the brim with the warm, rosy colors of Matt's dawn, renewing his resolve and strength. *I'll come back for you, Ouranos.*

Ouranos stalled. *Matthew?*

Theron bombarded him with fire and ice. Ouranos shielded and returned fire with a bolt of lightning.

Oh, thank Draso, Matt said. *You can hear me again.*

Ouranos thought fast. *Ryota?*

Alive and well, Matt said. *He's headed to the mainland with the rest of the pack. The Basileus sent the whole Cast army to the docks.*

Ouranos stumbled in shock. *Sisters have mercy. You should be with them. They will need you!*

You *need me.*

Theron pounded his fist to the ground, shooting spikes up in all directions. Ouranos dodged most, but one sliced through his shoulder, spilling hot blood. He bit his tongue against a scream.

You need me. Matt repeated. *I'm coming after you. Can you drop the stone blocking the way in?*

If I do, my father will notice and bombard the area with magic and kill anyone there, Ouranos said. Theron smirked at Ouranos' words, confirming his fears. *He… he hears me again, Matthew.*

A pause. Matt's voice growled through Ouranos' mind, not aimed at him, Ouranos sensed, but at the Basileus. *I have allies, you murderous bastard. We're going to take you down. Mark my words.*

Matt's voice faded, but he left a bright white light swirling through the ever-present rosy dawn. Matt's magic swelled through Ouranos' body, forming a shimmering shield in front of him.

Ouranos drew on every ounce of its strength. *Hurry.*

Matt ran after the Cast as they slithered along. Not much time. His own shoulder ached, echoing Ouranos' pain.

The Cast exited the palace into the open air. Dappled light from the sunrise filtered through the trees, caressing dozens of statues, topiaries, and columns. The Cast slipped between them and finally stopped in a wide garden surrounded by dragon statues.

Matt glanced around, walking slowly after them. Not just any dragons. Draso's ArchDragons. Michalus, Gavriíli, Rafaili, and others.

And in the center, a low bonfire.

Two Cast slithered off into the woods and came back out with sticks and fallen branches, which they tossed onto the fire. Sparks lit the area, forcing everyone back.

A third Cast approached Matt with an unlit torch.

He took it. He stuck the torch into the bonfire and lit it. "Who's first?"

The Cast parted and the six volunteer Cast slicked forward. Matt nodded to them. "Fair warning… this may be painful. And it will be messy."

The Cast gurgled in response, focusing their floating eyes.

Matt took a deep breath and dropped charms in each of their eyes.

The Cast wailed.

Matt whipped wind around his torch, bathed the charms in fire, and leapt back as the flames engulfed their bodies. The Cast around them shrieked and bubbled.

Then the fire blew out.

Six Athánatos of various genders stepped out of the steam. Unlike Ouranos and Natassa, who were mostly black, these were had different base colors in their fur – blue, brown, silver, green, brown and… yellow.

Matt's jaw dropped. "Fire and ice. You're Electrik."

The yellow Athánatos' perked his ears. "You know my name?"

"Yes." Matt nodded. "From your son."

Electrik's eyes widened. "Damianos! He lives?"

"He does," Matt said. "He's been a great help to us."

The Athánatos heaved relief, his face relaxing. "Sisters be praised."

The silver Athánatos walked forward. His fur and ears frosted over, and ice chunks flew about his person. Matt thought strongly of Lance. The Athánatos glared. "Reunions later. We need to get through that wall."

"First," Matt said. He turned to the Cast. "I need a handful of Cast volunteers to remain as you are, for the moment. Someone willing to tackle the Basileus full force. I have a plan."

"Hold on," a green Athánatos said. She narrowed her eyes. "How do you know the Prínkipas?"

Matt stood tall, holding his ground. "In every sense besides blood, he is my brother."

"And you are?" the blue Athánatos asked.

"Matthew Azure, Golden Guardian of Zyearth," Matt said. "I helped bridge the gap to Ouranos' soul. He's still a Drifter, but he has full control over himself now. We share a social bond between our focus jewels, which allows us to share power. He's using mine to fight off the Basileus as we speak."

The silver Athánatos eyed him. "And all of this is thanks to you."

Matt nodded. "Correct."

The quilar exchanged glances.

The silver one turned to the Cast. "Eva. Isaák. Kyros." Three Cast slid forward – the one with the fire-gold eyes, and the two that brought Christian's funeral urn to Matt. The silver Athánatos furrowed his brow. "My children, I know it has been far too long. But may I ask you to remain as Cast for a bit longer? For the sake of the Prínkipas?"

The three Cast gurgled politely.

"Your volunteers, then," the silver Athánatos said.

Matt nodded. "Thank you, um…"

"Frostrik."

"Mmm," Matt said. "I'm sensing a pattern here. I don't suppose there's a… ah, 'Firik' or something among you? It'd make curing the rest much faster."

"Embrik has been missing from our number for quite some time," the green Athánatos said.

"Damn." Matt pulled more charms out of his bag. "Then we'll have to do this the slow way. But it'll go faster if you help. Drop a charm in the eye. I'll catch them on fire. And if any of you have wind magic…"

The green Athánatos stepped forward. "I do. I am Windrik. Please do not make light about the name. I have heard it all my life."

Matt smirked, in spite of everything. "I have too. You're in good company." Matt whipped up a few short tornadoes. "Let's do this."

The Athánatos nodded, took the charms, and began.

CHAPTER 66

THE DOCKS

Trecheon clutched to the leg of a kestrel that should absolutely not have the strength to lift both him and Neil. And yet, here they were. Sailing over the water at what felt like a hundred miles an hour, wind and water spray whipping through his fur and quills. He tried not to look down.

The Black Cloak led the charge on his own wings (well, technically the raven's wings) with four others following, each one carrying a pair of their pack. Roscoe and Izzy took the burrowing owl, an even smaller bird carrying even bigger zyfaunos, much to Trecheon's surprise. Damianos paired with Ryota on a kori bustard, and Natassa and Melaina flew with a falcon. Sami and Darvin took the water route – Darvin had reverted back to a Cast and now glided along the water with Sami on his "back." She'd be soaked, but it was better than overtaxing one of the phoenixes.

After all, the Black Cloak had insisted they leave the final bird, the white egret, back on the island. For Matt and Ouranos.

A distant scream echoed over the water. Trecheon glanced at the docks.

The Cast had already entered the harbor. They worked as one being, lifting giant black tentacles out of the water, dotted with glowing blue eyes, like some eldritch horror emerging from the depths. A kraken no one could hope to fight. They wrapped their bodies around small boats and squeezed, cracking them in half and dragging them under, along with whatever crew was on board. They left nothing but bubbles.

Trecheon winced. Earth really wasn't ready for this magic shit.

The Cast moved quickly, ripping up boat after boat, before gliding up the docks themselves and going after the workers. Everyone scattered, but many of them disappeared under the waves of Cast.

"Defenders!" Izzy shouted over the wind. "As we planned! Keep the Cast busy while we get the rip in the Veil open. The moment it's open, herd and cure!"

The Phonar flew low over one of the docks. Trecheon dropped, tucking into a roll, his heart pounding. Neil landed beside him. Just like back in the war. Except this was a war with magic and monsters.

He lit a hand on fire. Good thing he was one of those with magic.

The Cloak flew ahead of them, set himself ablaze with purple fire, then crashed into the mess of Cast, scattering them. Several Phonar followed him, lighting their feathers with their elements.

Natassa, Melaina, and Izzy landed nearby, with Ryota, Damianos, and Roscoe next to them.

Ryota pointed to a spot near a shipping container. "Start a rip," he directed. He turned. "Damianos."

Damianos lifted his head, raising one brow.

Ryota tossed several orbs of lightning at him. "You'll need this."

Damianos caught the lightning orbs. "Thank you." He nodded to Neil and they rushed off after the Cast and the Cloak.

Natassa and Melaina poked at the air, their fingertips glowing bright white. Long threads of red light snaked into the air like seaweed in water. Natassa ran a hand down to the ground, leading the threads until they formed a thick line of red in the air. She began prodding at the threads.

Melaina turned to Ryota. "Whatever help you can supply, now is the time to offer it."

Ryota pointed to a thin thread floating to Melaina's left. "Pull on that."

She raised an eyebrow. "We would normally pull on the thick strands."

"For a stable rip, yes," Ryota said. "Not for a quick escape chute." She eyed him, but did so, and a small ray of white light poured through the red strings. Her eyes widened.

"Sisters alive," Natassa said.

"There's a pattern to it," Ryota said. "I'll guide you." He turned to Trecheon. "I'll be here a while. Don't get yourself killed in the meantime."

"Same to you," Trecheon said. He nodded to Izzy and they ran toward the docks. The rest followed.

"Cloak, Darvin, cover those workers!" Izzy shouted. "Everyone else, containment!" She turned to Trecheon. "Have you seen Matt and Ouranos use stage magic?"

Trecheon flicked his ears back. "Maybe once."

"We'll just have to wing it then," Izzy said. "Follow my lead. When I call a stage, send fire my way!" She rushed the Cast.

Trecheon followed, calling fire to his hands, fighting the adrenaline rush. Good Draso, there had to be *thousands* of the damn things. Far more than they could handle on their own for long, even with the Phonar.

Half a dozen workers, both human and zyfaunos, rushed past them, with a mess of Cast at their heels. A wolf zyfaunos whined in fear, and two human workers carried an injured fox with them, panic in their eyes. Trecheon snarled and snaked a wall of fire between the workers and the Cast. The Cast shrieked and turned on him and Izzy.

"Trecheon, stage two!" Izzy called. "Fire on my sword!"

Trecheon weaved fire around her sword, trying to remember how to make a shield. He pushed hard at the air. It shimmered green, then purple, then invisible, just as the Cast crashed on him like waves on the sand. He slid back, but the shield held. Trecheon smirked. He was finally getting the hang of this. Izzy sliced the sword through the Cast, breaking them apart and scattering them. The workers escaped to the relative safety of the shipping containers.

Izzy frowned, ears flat. "I thought Theron only wanted humans. But the Cast are going after zyfaunos too."

Trecheon wrinkled his snout. "I noticed." They dove back into the fray.

With the Cloak and Darvin hiding the fleeing workers from view, the Cast turned their attention on their group in large droves, allowing them to herd them more effectively. Trecheon worked well with Izzy keeping the Cast herded on their side, and Sami kept fire trained on them on the other side.

Roscoe, the silver stag, was something else entirely though. He was an earth user, a magic Trecheon hadn't seen a lot of, and his power was surreal. Controlling earthquakes and ripping sand from nearby sandbags to tear through the Cast, breaking them into droplets. They never stayed that way for long, but it was enough to slow them significantly. At one point a mess of Cast gobbled up two workers, but Roscoe ripped them apart in seconds with sand, clearly reveling in having his magic back.

But as much as the Cast clearly feared fire, it was Damianos' lightning that stopped them in their tracks, paralyzing them for several seconds as they tried to flee or attack. Neil took great pleasure in this, snatching up Damianos' lightning and driving it through the Cast with his sword, whooping and hollering. Trecheon swore he caught them counting points for ripping up Cast. At least Neil's PTSD seemed under control.

He wished he could say the same for himself.

Trecheon counted at least a dozen crushed bodies, humans and zyfaunos, and likely there were dozens more buried under the Cast, not to mention the lost sailors. But he refused to look long. The last thing he needed was to add to his already terrible nightmares.

Focus on the survivors. Fight off the Cast.

They just needed to hold out until Ryota and the others got the rip open and--

"Trecheon, look out!" Izzy shrieked.

Trecheon turned just as a wave of Cast washed over him from the ocean. He gasped and exploded flames all around him, but the Cast engulfed him immediately.

And the flames burned through his oxygen.

He scratched and pulled at the Cast bodies, exploding fire where he could, pushing, pushing, pushing, trying to get to the surface, trying to get to *air*. He wrapped himself in a shield and blasted fire up, breaking through the Cast.

But he was lost in a sea of black. The wave dove on him again.

He took as deep a breath as he could and pushed his shield wide, giving him a bubble.

Then the black submerged him again, bathing him in darkness, trying to smash his shield.

His heart raced and he fought to control his panicked breathing. *Can't use up the air, breathe slow, calm, quiet--* But it did little good. He was dead. He knew it. After everything he'd been through, he didn't want to die.

He didn't want to die.

Somewhere behind the muffling of Cast, shields, and fire, he heard people calling his name. Defenders. His allies. His *friends*. And one voice stood out among the rest.

Ryota.

CHAPTER 67

SOUL JEWELS

Sweat soaked Ouranos' fur and his muscles ached as he pulled hard against his father's hold on his magic.

And yet, his stone walls cracked and crumbled. Any second they would fall.

Theron's magic was simply too strong. There was no hope. He would win. After everything Ouranos had done to stop him, the Basileus would *win*.

Once again, you prove yourself too weak, Theron said, penetrating Ouranos' mind. *Give up, before you die of exhaustion.*

You will not hold my mind any longer! Ouranos said. *I am not your PUPPET!*

You are, and will forever be, something to be used, Theron said.

NO. Ouranos pushed harder, forcing his father from his mind. *I am not your TOOL. YOU HAVE NO POWER OVER ME!*

You are a murderer, Theron snapped.

"I am *forgiven!*" Ouranos shouted. He drew on both his strength and Matt's, pulling hard. "And we are finished!" He ripped Theron's grip on his magic away.

Theron flew back against a wall, grunting, gripping at his injured shoulder. He snarled.

Ouranos held his magic tight. His own shoulder ached. The reprieve would not last long.

Sure enough, Theron stood and Ouranos once again felt the pull on his power.

But just a small pull. And only on the entrance to the throne room. Ouranos narrowed his eyes, concentrating on the magic.

That… was not Theron's magic.

It was Archon Bouldrik's.

Ouranos' chest swelled with relief and he let go of the stone Bouldrik pulled on.

Theron noticed it as soon as Ouranos did, and tried to block the Archon, but Ouranos pushed his father's power aside.

Matt rushed and the Archons funneled into the room through the break in the stone wall, all their magic at full strength, shouting at the Basileus.

The Basileus bared his teeth and held his hands out. Ice-crusted rock, fire tornadoes, and lightning orbs whipped around him. He threw his hands forward, bombarding the group with his magic, but Matt held a shield out and deflected it all.

Theron stood still a moment, clearly conflicted, gaze darting between Ouranos and his new allies.

Then he turned to a stone wall, pulling at it, trying to run.

"You will not escape again!" Bouldrik shouted. She pulled walls of stone around Theron. The other Archons let loose their magic, lining the stone wall with sharp ice spikes and the spikes with lightning. Earth and water swirled under Theron's feet, trapping him with a thick mud. Wind whipped up, catching loose sand and blinding Theron.

Ouranos pressed his magic into the Archon's manifestations, hoping to strengthen it. He turned. Three Cast slithered under Matt's feet. Ouranos got their meaning immediately.

Brilliant.

"Matt, quick! The Ca--"

Theron roared, breaking all the magic in an instant, including the stone walls blocking the exits, waving the stone and earth away in a hurricane wind, dispersing the plasmas to the skies. Ouranos, Matt, and the Archons flew back with the exploding elements.

Theron glared, teeth bared, breathing heavy. *"You think you can hold me?"* he snarled. "Let me remind you who won the war!" He lifted his hands, magic building at his fingertips.

Matt shielded everyone. "Ouranos!"

No. He could not be allowed to do more harm. Ouranos reached for his own magic… but stopped.

Ouranos pushed instead, drawing on Matt's magic and strength, seeking his father's mind.

Theron gasped, and the magic faded.

And Ouranos drowned in his father's thoughts. The anguish of losing his wife. The fear of the humans who killed her. The desperate, chaotic need to get revenge, fading, fading, fading, until only anger remained and all true motivations vanished, leaving only unbridled, unrelenting, unfounded hate, a shell of who he once was. The Theron Ouranos had known as a child drowned and dead, his remains in a corner, rotting.

Lost.

Ouranos' heart ached to the point of pain.

But despite his father's loss, despite his pain, despite everything… he had done too much to be allowed freedom.

Cast shrieks filled the room. The three Cast slithered out from behind Matt and snaked up Theron's body, holding him in place. Theron tried to fight them off, but the Archons surrounded him, holding their elements around them, daring him to move.

"Hold your magic, Archons!" Ouranos called. They stepped back to give him room. Ouranos walked up to his father, breathless. He called magic to his hands. "I will deal with him."

Theron struggled and glared. "Kill me and lose the Phonar."

Ouranos furrowed his brow. "I never, ever, wished to kill you," he said. "Even after everything you did to us. To Melaina, to Alexina, to Natassa…. to me. I watched you fall into despair, but I still clung to a hope that you would one day realize your mistakes and come back to us. I missed the father I had as a child. I still miss him."

Theron spat. "He is dead."

Ouranos closed his eyes a moment. "I know that now. And yet… I still do not wish to kill you. And now that I have seen your mind, felt your pain, I know I never could." He lit his hands with magic and brought them up to Theron's head. "But I can no longer allow you to hurt as you have." He reached for the Soul Jewels.

Theron's eyes grew wide and he wiggled, trying to escape Ouranos. "Turn me into a Drifter and you are no better than I am!"

"It is far too late to discuss morality, Father," Ouranos said. "I am sorry it has come to this." He pressed his hands to Theron's Soul Jewels.

The Basileus' body went rigid and the Soul Jewels fell into Ouranos' hands.

Theron's expression blanked, his jaw slack. A Drifter. Soulless. Mindless. Ouranos shook his head. "Lower him gently." The Cast did so. Theron sat on the floor, breathing shallowly, eyes unfocused, no different than any other Drifter. Harmless.

Matt gripped Ouranos shoulder. Ouranos patted Matt's hand, though he could not tear his gaze away from his father. He sighed. "We are finished."

But are you?

All the heat left Ouranos' face. That was Theron's voice. "Sister's alive."

You want to know one of the benefits of creating a Drifter? Theron said. *They also allow me to anchor my soul. Which means I still hold control over the Drifters I created. And the Cast.*

Footsteps echoed through the halls and dozens of Drifter sentries entered the room from all sides, lining the pillars, blocking the exits.

The Archons moved immediately, but Ouranos stopped them. "No! They are Drifters, still controlled by the Basileus!"

The inside of Matt's ears paled. "Wait, what? But he's a Drifter now!"

"Apparently creating Drifters anchors his soul," Ouranos said. "His body may be a Drifter, but his mind and soul are still connected."

Matt paled. "Meaning…"

"Meaning he still has control over the Cast."

Matt's eyes widened. "The mainlanders."

Ouranos clenched his jaw against a scream. *Even when he loses, he still wins!*

The Drifters ran for the group. The Archons responded in turn, knocking them down. While their magic was weak, not intending to kill, several Drifters fell anyway. Bouldrik cursed, mumbling about how the decades without practicing her magic had ruined her.

Ouranos' chest ached. Oh, if only he could cure them… stop them…

Wait. The *féretro* - the coffin boxes for Ei-Ei jewels. Putting a Drifter's Soul Jewels in one would put the user in a coma.

In theory it would work the same for Theron.

"Matt!" Ouranos said. He gripped Matt's shoulders. "Get to the mainland. Help the rest of our pack. They will need it. I need to get these jewels to a *féretro.*"

Windrik blasted back a handful of Drifters. "Oh, that is brilliant, my Lord!"

Frostrik threw up a wall of ice, blocking the Drifters coming forward. They clawed at the wall like manic wolves. "We need to hurry then! This will not hold them long!"

"Go, Matt!" Ouranos said. "I have the Archons. We will join you as soon as we can."

Matt flicked his ears back. "Ouranos--"

"Go, *please,*" Ouranos said.

Matt frowned, but gripped Ouranos' hand. "Take care of yourself."

"And you, brother," Ouranos said.

"Please," Electrik said. "Let me come with you."

Matt nodded. "Of course. I could use the help." The two of them left.

Ouranos faced the waves of Drifters coming after them. He clenched his fists over the Soul Jewels. "We finish this now."

CHAPTER 68

CRACKED

"Trecheon, look out!"

Ryota whipped his head around at Izzy's screech. *Trecheon?*

He could hardly make out anything in the disaster. The battlefield – because that's what it was at this stage – was a mess. Shipping containers had been smashed open, dropping their contents all over the deck. Workers ran as the Defenders fought the Cast back, trying to save as many as they could. At least one crane had fallen, laying bent and broken over several containers. Bodies of workers had been strewn about, Cast covered the entire deck in black, elemental magic flew every which-way. The Phonar took turns dive bombing the monsters to break them up, but there were so many of them it didn't last long.

That ever moving ocean of Cast…

Where was Trecheon?

"Trecheon, no!" Izzy again, pointing, trying to fight the Cast back. She nipped at them with some kind of magic, breaking off bits of them – her broken healing magic, perhaps? – but she couldn't even begin to separate them.

Ryota followed her gaze. He caught a flash of red among a sea of black. Then Trecheon burst through the monsters in a fountain of flame, took a deep breath, and collapsed back under the waves of Cast.

Ryota's jaw dropped and his body buzzed with fear. "No!"

"Go!" Natassa said, shoving him. "Help him, please!"

"Keep pulling at the small strings!" Ryota shouted and rushed after the Cast, lighting his hands with electricity. "Trecheon!"

No answer. No flames. Nothing to indicate where Trecheon had vanished beneath the monsters. He couldn't lose his brother. Not now. Not *again*. "Trecheon, I'm coming, hold on!"

A weak blast of fire through the black mass was all the answer he got. But it was something to cling to. *Don't take my brother from me!* He rolled waves of electricity over the Cast.

The monsters on the surface froze up and sloughed off, but they inadvertently protected the ones underneath. His magic didn't even make a dent.

He snarled. What had Izzy said? *You're Black Bound. You won't tire and lose your magic like most of us.*

But Theron's voice ran through his mind. *You are too weak.*

I'll show you weak. If he really wouldn't tire, then by God, now was the time to push it. He dragged on the Gem and blasted a massive bolt through the Cast.

The bolt successfully parted them, but only a sliver.

Ryota roared and blasted another bolt, shoving the monsters away in great, black, wailing waves. Black bound elixir formed on the tips of his fingers and ran up to his palms.

Theron's words bounced around again. *You are too weak.* He shoved them aside.

Trecheon's shield bubble poked out of the mass of Cast. Ryota blasted more monsters away, fully exposing Trecheon's shield, and ran for him.

Trecheon's bubble popped and he collapsed.

"No!" Ryota ran and stood over Trecheon, blasting back wave after wave of Cast. The elixir ran up past his wrists, making his arms tingle. "Trecheon, get up, *get up.*"

Trecheon stirred, and stood, shaking himself. "Ryota?"

"Stay close," Ryota said. He encircled the pair of them with massive bolts of electricity, drowning out the Cast's wails. The elixir ran up past his elbows. His fingers no longer just tingled… they burned.

You are too weak.

But the Cast formed high walls around Ryota's electricity, cutting off their help, threatening to collapse like tsunamis and drown them. He couldn't be too weak. He couldn't give up now or they'd both be dead. He spread his lightning across the walls, pushing them back.

Trecheon tried to help by shooting fireballs at any Cast that managed to work their way over Ryota's electric walls, but even those got overwhelming. Trecheon pressed his back to Ryota. "We're dead…"

"No we're not," Ryota said. "I am sick and tired of Theron taking everything. He can't have you, he can't have the Cast, and he can't have me, damnit!" He pressed his power further, harder, stronger than he could ever remember doing.

The elixir ran up to his shoulders. His fingers and palms burned like they were positively on fire.

You are too weak.

But the wall of electricity expanded, growing higher and wider, pushing the Cast further. His face tingled now, his chest ached, his fingers felt ready to fall off. He wasn't too weak. He was Black Bound. He was *strong*.

And yet, they kept coming.

Trecheon called out, pointing above. The final summon, the white egret Deo, flew a good half-mile offshore, carrying Matt and some Athánatos, maybe Ouranos.

But not quick enough.

The Cast were closing in fast, pushing back in massive numbers against Ryota's electricity, shrinking their little circle. Ryota's energy waned, and he didn't know why. Black Bound users weren't supposed to get exhausted.

But then why did this hurt so much?

You are too weak.

The Black Bound elixir coated his neck now, running up his face, snaking around his snout in little tendrils. Everything it touched burned like fire. His fingers ached in ways he didn't think possible.

Why wasn't this limitless like he was told?

Why wasn't this *working?*

You are too weak.

NO. Get the hell out of my head!

Trecheon roared now, enhancing the electric walls with his fire. But it still wasn't enough. The Cast wails drowned out their magic.

The Gem whined loudly, stinging Ryota's ears. He glanced down at his Gem holster. It glowed so bright it hurt his eyes.

But something in the light… cracked. He blinked at it. His Gem…

His Gem was breaking.

For a moment, his world stopped. Cracking… breaking… Broken Gems killed their users.

Panic ripped through him, racing his heart, his breath, his very soul, he couldn't die, *he couldn't die.*

But if he let go, he wouldn't be the only one to die. Trecheon would die too.

Unacceptable.

He shut his eyes tight. There was no choice. He had failed Clarissa. He had failed Anthony.

He had failed Christian.

He wouldn't fail Trecheon.

Theron's voice ran through his mind. *You are dying.*

Ryota took a deep breath, trying to calm himself. *Maybe there are worse things.*

"Trecheon, shield yourself."

Trecheon blinked and faced Ryota. He stared, gasping. "Ryota, your snout--"

"Shield yourself."

Trecheon frowned, but did so.

Ryota scrambled for every scrap of power left and pushed with everything he had.

Lightning exploded outward, blasting the Cast in all directions, widening their safety circle.

The Gem cracked in two.

A surge of power rushed through Ryota's body before all the pain vanished in an instant, and everything went completely black.

CHAPTER 69

DON'T WASTE THAT SACRIFICE

Trecheon covered his face with his arms, trying to keep himself from blowing away. Something near him crashed like glass breaking. Lightning blasted the Cast a good twenty feet or more away from them, giving them a wide berth. Enough breathing room. They seemed frozen in place, too, like the electricity had temporarily paralyzed them. Good. Maybe they could call the Phonar, or Matt could come in and help them keep the damn monsters away long enough for Natassa and Melaina to open the rip. He dropped his arms. "Ryota--"

But Ryota wasn't there.

Trecheon's body buzzed with shock. He glanced around, frantic. The Cast had been blasted back. None of them could have gotten him.

So where was he?

Deo hovered overhead and Matt landed with a thump near Trecheon, blowing wind all around them. A scrap of cloth smacked Trecheon's face.

It smelled strongly of cigarettes.

He pulled it off his snout and glanced at it. Black, thick cloth. Like from a jacket. Or a trench coat. He stared.

This was Ryota's trench coat. Just… just a scrap.

He looked around again, frenzied, desperate. Ryota was here, right here, just a moment ago, fighting the Cast, saving Trecheon's life. He was just *here,* he couldn't be far, he *couldn't.*

But the only other person in the safety circle was Matt. He walked up to Trecheon, still blowing wind around them, keeping the Cast back.

Trecheon glanced at the scrap of cloth. Ryota's last words ran through his mind. *Trecheon, shield yourself.*

Trecheon's last image of Ryota flashed in his mind. That Black Bound elixir covering his fur and face. The bright light from his Gem. That devastating sound of cracked glass.

The Gem had shattered.

Matt had warned him. Shatter the Gem and you die. It was how his father died.

He stared at the cloth again.

Trecheon went numb with shock. He finally had his brother back. He finally had his *family* back.

And now… he was gone.

Cast shrieked all around him, but he didn't have the energy, the heart, to fight back. Let them come. Let them end this.

But Matt was at his side, shielding them both, though the Cast seemed unable to move much, still held in place by Ryota's lingering magic. Matt gripped Trecheon's shoulder. "Trecheon--"

"He's gone," Trecheon said. "He's… he's…"

"I know," Matt said. "I saw it from the air." His brow furrowed. "I'm sorry, Trecheon."

Trecheon clung to the scrap of trench coat. He stared blankly at the dock. "I'm done. I don't care anymore. I'm sick of losing everything."

"Trecheon," Matt said firmly. Trecheon whipped his head up. Matt scrunched his snout. "Ryota gave his life for you. Do you understand that? He gave his life for *you*. He used every atom of power he had to save your life." He closed his eyes a moment. "Just like my dad did for me. Like Izzy's dad, for her. He finally let go of that fear of death… for *you*. Because you're *worth it.*" He met Trecheon's eyes. "Don't waste that sacrifice."

Trecheon stared at him, trying to process Matt's words. *Don't waste that sacrifice.*

Don't waste that sacrifice.

"Defenders!" Natassa shouted. "The rip has been opened!"

"Rise up, Defenders!" Izzy shouted. "Herd and heal! Get those Athánatos home!" She started throwing charm after charm into the eyes of the Cast. Sami, Natassa, and Melaina cured them with fire, and Damianos and Neil began guiding the freshly freed and bewildered Athánatos through the rip.

A new Athánatos joined them, one that was almost pure yellow. Damianos stopped short when he saw him, and they shared a deep embrace before resuming their work.

Trecheon blinked. "That's…"

"Archon Electrik," Matt said. "One of Damianos' fathers."

Trecheon stared for what felt like ages. Damianos and his father worked hand in hand to herd and cure Cast before sending them home. Family restored.

While his family had been obliterated.

Wind blasted all around them, making Trecheon turn. The Cast had finally escaped Ryota's final blast of electricity, but Matt kept them back. "Trecheon. You're not alone. Ryota might be gone but," he looked Trecheon deep in the eye. "You still have us. For whatever that's worth."

Trecheon stared back, unable to respond.

"Matt, Trecheon, heads up!" Roscoe called. He ran up and pounded a fist to the ground, shaking the Cast about, stopping their advance. He tossed charms into their eyes.

Matt pulled out his charms. "Ouranos has made his father a Drifter."

Trecheon's eyes widened. "What?"

"He's basically made him soulless like he is," Matt said. "But the Basileus has anchors here, allowing him to still command the Cast. However, Ouranos thinks he can break those anchors. We only need to hold them off a bit longer." He nodded to Trecheon and held out a hand. "With me?"

Trecheon watched him a moment, then took his hand. Matt nodded in solidarity, then turned to the Cast. Trecheon pulled out his charms. This is what Ryota would want. This was what he had died for. *Don't waste that sacrifice.* He lit his hands ablaze, letting the fire build in his chest as well, trying to steady his voice.

"Let's do this."

BROTHERHOOD

Ouranos dashed through the palace, headed for the *féretro* garden, nursing his damaged shoulder. He had to move fast. The Archons ran alongside him, their magic lit up, ready to push back. Frostrik assured Ouranos that the other cured Athánatos had gone through the rip in the throne room and were safe.

The three Cast that had held Theron down still remained as Cast, following alongside them, struggling to keep up the pace.

But they might need their strength.

Do you truly think you can win, Prínkipas? Theron said. *The sentries will kill you all.*

Sure enough, dozens upon dozens of Theron's Drifter sentries appeared from all over, rushing at Ouranos and the Archons.

Ouranos snarled. "Do not kill them!" He pulled on his own magic and stopped several sentries – one caught in mud from dirt and water, another blocked by slabs of rock, yet another slowed with a bump to the head from a blast of wind.

The Archons followed suit, pinning sentry after sentry down, with the Cast helping as they could.

But several sentries escaped and bore down on them anyway. One knocked Frostrik to the ground and held his sword up for the kill. Frostrik shielded himself with a block of ice.

Ouranos knew too well how ineffective that could be. He whipped about and crashed into the sentry, pushing him off Frostrik. He held the sentry in place with stones, then pulled Frostrik to his feet. Ouranos' shoulder burned with pain, but he could not stop.

They ran.

You will not win, Theron said.

But Ouranos ignored him. This time, he would.

They entered the botanical wing and Ouranos ran for the *féretro* garden. He only needed one open box.

They rounded the hall leading to the garden… and all stopped.

Each open box was guarded by three sentries, swords out, faces blank.

The heat left Ouranos' face.

But Windrik stepped forward. "This is over!" They pulled on their powers and blew a hurricane wind through the garden, knocking the sentries back. The sentries stumbled and flew, their blank faces unchanged.

But they left the *féretro* unguarded.

"My prince, now!" Bouldrik called.

Ouranos rushed forward and pressed the Soul Jewels into a box.

No! Theron shouted. *You cannot--*

Ouranos slammed the box shut, sealed it, and spoke the rites of *féretro.*

His father's voice subsided.

The Drifters all around them jolted left and right, gripping their heads, their faces losing those blank, empty stares. They blinked and looked around, confused. But alive. They may not have their souls, but they had the connection to them again, as Ouranos did. Saved, as much as they could be. Perhaps they could find a way to return their souls to them, once this was done.

Ouranos heaved relief. Finally the nightmare was over. It worked. Theron was sealed away. His influence gone.

He could only hope he had been fast enough to save his friends and the residents on the mainland.

Matt pressed Cast back with his wind, letting only one or two escape long enough to drop a charm in the eye and cure them with Trecheon's fire. A terribly slow process, but at least he had the charms. He reached into his bag for more… and came up short. Only three left in his hand. He used them up in seconds.

Yet there were thousands more Cast.

"I'm out of charms," Trecheon said, his voice nearing panic.

"I am too," Matt said. He glanced around. Nearly everyone around him had stopped throwing charms. Probably all of them were out. Lightning and air, they needed more time!

They had barely made a dent in the Cast mess. And they hadn't stopped attacking. Maybe Ouranos had failed. Maybe they were just… stuck.

Damn it all!

A wave of Cast crashed down after Matt and Trecheon.

Oh, hell no. Matt called on his power and whipped the Cast back with hurricane winds.

Yet, they still kept coming.

Matt pushed harder. Black Bound liquid formed on his hands now, running up his fingers, coating his palms. The tips of his fingers tingled.

And they still kept coming.

Matt roared and blasted them harder. The elixir continued to grow, expanding past his wrists now. The tips of his fingers burned slightly. But he couldn't let up. He couldn't--

"Matt."

Trecheon's panicked voice startled Matt. He turned. Trecheon stared at him, pleading. "Slow down."

Matt stared back. "But--"

"Please," Trecheon said. "I can't lose someone else."

Matt wrinkled his snout. "I… I didn't…" he shook his head.

"Let me help," Trecheon said. "We're a team. Defenders."

Matt perked his ears. Defenders.

Guardians.

"Okay… okay, you're right." He faced the Cast. Trecheon did the same, pressing his back to Matt's. "Give me all the fire you can. Stage firestorm!"

Trecheon surrounded the pair of them with flames. Matt snatched up the flames and whipped them into fire twisters, blasting them at the Cast. The monsters wailed and fell back, keeping their distance.

"Another!" Matt called.

The two of them worked together, fighting the Cast back. Matt struggled to keep his powers under control, never letting the elixir extend past his palms.

But this was a losing battle.

The Cast swelled up like great ocean waves, crashing through their magic, rolling toward them like death incarnate.

Matt threw up a shield around them. Trecheon doubled up, forming a protective bubble. The Cast crashed against it, cracking Trecheon's shield.

Matt squeezed his eyes shut. His heart pounded, his body buzzed with adrenaline, his magic rippled through his fur. This was it.

This was *it*.

Trecheon reached over and grabbed Matt's hand. Even though Trecheon couldn't feel it, Matt gripped it right back.

"I'll see you on the other side, brother," Trecheon said. Matt didn't know if he meant him or Ryota.

Then the sweeping wall of black melted away.

Matt stared.

The Cast calmed. Almost as one being, they ebbed away and flattened, like the sudden calming of the sea after a storm. Their glowing blue eyes floated about like debris from a hurricane, blinking in and out of existence.

Matt leaned on his knees, finally feeling like he could breathe again. Ouranos had done it. Thank Draso.

Trecheon leaned down too, panting. Then his panting morphed into slow sobs.

Matt flicked his ears down. He rubbed Trecheon's back. "It's okay. Let it all out."

Izzy jogged up to them. Jangly, uncoordinated bells rang through Matt's mind. Uncertainty. "Matt…"

Matt nodded to her. He leaned closer to Trecheon, gently gripping his arm. "Ouranos did it. He stopped Theron." Izzy sighed. The bell sounds lined up in a gentle wave, then faded away.

Natassa walked up behind them. "Did… did he… Is my father dead…?"

"No, at least I don't think so," Matt said. "Ouranos turned him into a Drifter, the way Theron had done to him. Then he did something to the Soul Jewels."

"He intended to place them in a *féretro,* my lady," Electrik said, walking up behind them, with Damianos and Neil in tow. "I can only assume he succeeded."

Melaina held her hands to her face. "Oh, Electrik… you are safe. Praise the Sisters. Are the other Archons…?"

"Alive and well, my lady," Electrik said.

Melaina flattened her ears. "Even… Embrik?"

Electrik flicked his tail and closed his eyes. "Embrik escaped to the mainland during the war. We have not heard from him since. Though perhaps now that we are restored, we can start looking for him."

"We need to take care of this mess first," Matt said. The rest of his team moved closer, including the Black Cloak. Matt started issuing orders. "Fire users, herd the rest of the Cast into the rip and get them off the mainland. Izzy, have Darvin cloak you and heal all you can. Everyone else, let's see if we can clear some of this mess and find survivors. Cloak, hide everyone. Move fast. I don't want anyone really seeing us if we can avoid it. Especially Trecheon, Neil, and the Athánatos, since they're locals."

Neil flicked his ears back. "We won't really be able to hide, you know. There's bound to be some idiot who caught something on their phone."

"Don't worry about that," the Cloak said. Neil gave him a skeptical look, but the Cloak lowered his gaze. "Time traveler, remember?"

Neil just rolled his eyes. "Of course. Thanks, I guess." He turned to Trecheon. "Hey, uh…"

Trecheon just shook his head, ash raining off his red quills. Matt rubbed Trecheon's back. "We'll join you in a minute."

Izzy frowned, chewing her lip. "Ryota…"

Matt furrowed his brow. "Gem overload. He's… he's gone."

Izzy watched Trecheon a moment. She kneeled by him. "Trecheon. Just remember. You're not alone. All of us are here for you. Okay?"

Trecheon stared at her with glassy eyes, but said nothing.

Izzy smiled sadly and squeezed his hand. She turned to the others and started directing everyone.

Trecheon sat hard on the ground. He stared forward, saying nothing.

Matt sat with him. "I won't ask if you're okay, because I know the answer."

"I know," Trecheon said. "I just feel numb."

"That's understandable."

He took a long, deep breath. "But… Ryota gave himself up for me. He chose that. I… I want to make sure it's worth it. That I'm worth that."

"Trecheon." Trecheon turned. Matt stared him deep in the eye. "You've always been worth that."

Trecheon stared back. "Yeah. Yeah, you're right." He stood. "Get the Cloak. I'll have him cloak me while I heal people. We've had enough death today."

Matt stood too. "I'm here if you need me."

Trecheon nodded. "I get that. Thanks." He shook himself. "For now… let's just get to work."

It took another half hour, but the pack managed to clean up the mess as best they could. Roscoe healed cracks in the deck and fixed sandbags. Matt worked with Natassa and Melaina to set up fallen shipping containers and get the broken crane in a position where their own crews would have a chance to move it. And between Trecheon and Izzy, they were able to save a lot of lives, more so than Matt had expected. Darvin and the Cloak's magic had kept many of the dock workers from harm as they ran.

Trecheon worked especially hard, pushing his magic to the brim, stopping only when he said he could feel the acid buildup. But he saved a lot of lives. "To make Ryota's sacrifice worth it," he said.

Izzy also worked with renewed vigor. Her very aura spoke of pride and relief at having her magic back. Not a single incident where it went wrong.

"What do you suppose happened?" Matt asked her.

She shrugged. "I don't know, honestly. But right before this trip, I had been wishing again for offensive powers. Maybe the Gem reacted based on that."

Matt flicked an ear back. "That's not how Gems work."

"That's not how *normal* Gems work," Izzy said. "And we have a lot to learn about Black Binding. But for now, I'm just grateful I can be useful again." She jogged off to help a bleeding zyfaunos before Matt could say anymore.

Not that they were without casualties. Matt spoke last rites over the bodies he found. Too many.

The rip stayed open long enough to get the remaining cured Athánatos and Cast through, something Melaina said would not have been possible if Ryota hadn't helped. She and Natassa shut it down once they herded the last of the Cast. Sirens wailed in the distance as Matt stepped through the rip. Good. More help on the way.

They landed on Athánatos island, somewhere in one of the massive gardens Matt had only seen glimpses of in his mad dash to save the half-Cast. The remaining Cast had been quarantined to one side of the gardens, all sitting in a big pile, quiet and calm. Rather than the angry gurgles Matt was used to, a few Cast cooed and purred, like kits. Several poked at the garden's flowers and one had curled up under a dragon statue, rippling softly, almost like it was sleeping.

Then he caught some movement coming from the palace. The five remaining Archons walked out, along with three other silver-accented Athánatos that Matt took to be the three who had volunteered to remain as Cast. Cured, finally, thank Draso.

Melaina ran up to one of them and took her hands. "Oh, Eva, thank the Sisters. You have been restored. I am so sorry I was unable to prevent you from falling to my father…"

Eva squeezed Melaina's hands and bowed. "Do not fret, my lady. In the end, all is well. My family is safe now, and the Basileus' rule ended."

Ouranos emerged, looking tired and harried, favoring his bloody shoulder, but also relieved. A soothing, calming blue fluttered through Matt's mind.

Matt crossed the distance between them and drew him into a bear hug. "Thank Draso." Ouranos hugged him back, amplifying the colors further.

Melaina turned to him. "Ouranos! Father… is he…?"

"Alive, but declawed," Ouranos said, breaking his hug with Matt. "He can no longer hurt us."

Melaina perked one ear and flattened the other, as if she wasn't sure how to react.

Ouranos turned to Matt. "My friend. My brother." Matt nodded and Ouranos smiled. "The Basileus is finished. But there is still much to do."

"Then let's get started," Matt said.

RESTORATION

Restoration began for both the physical and the mental.

But first they had to deal with the Basileus.

Matt followed Ouranos to the depths of the Athánatos Palace, with Izzy at his side. The Athánatos Prince placed Theron's body, in its coma-like state, deep in their catacombs, his *féretro* locked away.

"No one can restore him with these separated," Ouranos said. "Even if they managed to free his Soul Jewels from the *féretro*, he would still be unable to reach his magic, and soon he will no longer have Cast to command. He is harmless."

Izzy frowned, staring at the Basileus' body. "But won't he starve to death?"

"The Ei-Ei jewels will preserve his body from starvation," Ouranos said.

"And the Drifters he created?" Matt asked.

Ouranos shook his head. "We will work to restore them, though I am unsure how. We cannot use the traditional method. I will not trade lives for trapped souls."

Matt shuddered at the thought. "What will you do with him long term?" he asked. "He can't stay like that forever."

"As long as he is a danger to himself and others," Ouranos said, his voice firm, cold. "He will."

That evening after they finished their first truly calm meal since the mess had begun, Matt passed Christian's funeral urn to Trecheon.

He had held the urn in his hands, staring, as if searching for words. Eventually he sought out the three Athánatos who saved Christian's ashes, Isaák, Kyros, and Eva, Frostrik's children, and thanked each one of them. They accepted his thanks gracefully.

Then he passed the urn to Neil. "Find a safe place for him."

"Of course," Neil said.

With Ouranos' permission, Neil and Matt placed the urn in the *féretro* garden, a place of honor. Neil stared at the urn, tail twitching. "I'm not sure what we're going to tell his family."

Matt stood by him, arms crossed. "Can't exactly give them the truth."

"He was at the docks," the Cloak said, walking up to the group. Matt turned. The Cloak looked at them both with sad eyes. "They found the remains of his fishing boat washed up on the water break."

Neil eyed him. "And I suppose you set that up already."

"Hours before the attack, yeah."

"Damn time traveler," Neil muttered.

Matt flicked his ears back. "Good excuse as any I suppose."

Neil sighed. "A place of honor for the Marine. See you in hell someday, buddy."

Trecheon didn't speak again for the rest of the day.

Restoring the thousands of remaining Cast was quite a task. They set a procedure – spend a few hours creating Lexi charms, rest, then spend a few more hours restoring Cast. The Black Cloak helped a lot, though he only showed up when they needed him and vanished soon after, like a ghost.

Or a time traveler. That still sent shocks up Matt's spine.

But he lingered on the third day of restoration. He passed an envelope with a wad of cash to Trecheon for his broken arm.

"This should cover it," the Cloak said. "There's extra too, to cover your new security system, since that's technically my fault. It also covers what your business lost while fighting the Cast."

Trecheon eyed him. "Why is my lost business your responsibility to pay?"

The Cloak lowered his gaze. "Because it was my dummy job that made sure Neil saw Ryota on the casino cameras." He walked off after that, leaving Trecheon stunned.

Because the Cast restoration took so long, Natassa and Melaina eventually created a rip in the Veil that appeared in the old casino strip. Trecheon wanted to deposit his money and both he and Neil were eager to rest in their own beds again.

Matt offered to go along on their first trip home.

Trecheon stared at him, his expression dull. "Maybe another time. I need… I need isolation for a bit."

Matt frowned. "Are you sure? You don't have to do this alone, Trech."

Trecheon blinked at him after he used the nickname.

Matt flicked his ears back. "Sorry, should I not have called you that?"

"*I* can't even call him Trech," Neil said smirking. "And I survived a bloody war with him. Two now, technically."

Trecheon tilted his ears back. "That's… that's unfair of me. Sorry, Neil. You can call me Trech."

Neil's eyes widened, and he perked his ears. Then he grinned and patted Trecheon's shoulder. "About time, *Trech.*"

Matt expected a sarcastic remark, an eyeroll, something, but Trecheon didn't react. He just turned and left through the rip. Neil frowned, flicking his tail. He turned to Matt.

"Don't worry. I won't leave him alone." He followed after Trecheon.

The cured Athánatos went between Sol and Athánatos and gathered food, equipment, and whatever else was necessary to get their island running again. This time, Matt allowed them to take whatever they needed from Sol. He couldn't imagine a better memorial. His dad had died a Defender. He'd understand, and so would Sol. But Matt could already see that what they had wouldn't be enough for long. They needed help. Help that the Defenders could provide.

Matt contacted Lance the next day. Probably overdue considering the Master Guardian had dropped over a hundred messages during the last week.

"Thank *Draso,*" Lance said after Matt explained the whole situation. "I'll start prepping restoration teams here, so we can get back out there soon after you come home. See if you can bring some charms home with you, but not at the expense of your health. We've got Lexi acid here we can use if need be."

"Thank you, sir," Matt said.

Lance lowered his gaze. "And you're sure Trecheon is okay?"

Matt crossed his arms. "Not yet, but I think he will be, in time. He risked far more than he ever should have, considering he's brand new to Gem magic, he's untrained, and he's not even a Defender."

"Agreed." Lance eyed Matt. "And we will still be talking about your reckless actions when you come back. Regardless of the results, what you did deserves discipline. Is that understood, Guardian?"

Matt took a deep breath and saluted. He held in a smile. Guardian. That meant Lance didn't intend to court martial or dismiss him. He'd happily take whatever discipline Lance had for him, for all the good they had done down here. "Yes, sir."

"Good." Lance rubbed his chin. "So you're aware, I've sent some authorization codes to Caesum for Defender pendants."

Matt tilted his head. "For who?"

"Your allies," Lance said. "Trecheon, Neil, Damianos, and the Athánatos royalty, all three of them. Caesum's already working on fabrication." He smiled. "I wouldn't call them Defenders, but allies, yes. They deserve it. We should be able to contact them when we visit." He eyed Matt. "And stay within silent planet rules this time."

Matt smirked slightly. "Yes, sir."

"Regardless," Lance said. "This is the start of a long-term relationship with allies on Terra again. We should start off on the right foot."

Matt nodded. "I wholeheartedly agree, sir."

"Just… be careful of Trecheon, despite how you feel about him," Lance said.

Matt frowned. "Why?"

"There was a reason we were looking into him," Lance said. "Connected to the White Assassin."

Matt wrinkled his snout. Trecheon had had a newspaper on his desk about the White Assassin. Hell, several newspapers over the course of weeks. And Christian had said Trecheon had been going off for several days at a time. "Are you implying…?"

"I think maybe you should ask him yourself," Lance said. "Keep me posted on when you intend to come home. Master Guardian out." He ended the call.

Matt sunk down.

Time to find Trecheon.

"Are you sure you've got that?" Neil asked Trecheon as they got off his bike.

Trecheon hoisted his backpack higher up on his shoulders. It weighed heavy on him, but it was a burden he had to carry. "I've got it, Neil."

"Trech, you really shouldn't do this all on your own," Neil said.

Trecheon glared at him. He was going to regret letting him use that nickname. "I've got it, okay? Just trust me."

Neil frowned. "Yeah, sure."

They left the bike and wandered toward the rip in the Veil. Trecheon dragged his feet.

"Hey. Trecheon."

Trecheon stopped and turned.

Neil rubbed the back of his head. "I've… I've been meaning to talk to you about something."

Trecheon flattened his ears now. "This better not be bad news. I've had enough of that shit lately."

"It's not… bad," Neil said. "But it is going to make life difficult for us for a bit."

Trecheon sighed. "What?"

"I want out of the assassin business."

Trecheon perked his ears. "Really? But Philip…"

"We'll have to get Philip through legit means," Neil said. "I can't do this anymore. I don't want to pay for Philip with any more blood money. I hope you can understand that."

Trecheon blinked at him. What a relief, honestly. "I absolutely understand," he said. "I'm sick of the bloodshed too. I don't want to think about all this every time I look at Philip." He furrowed his brow. "The question is though, will the Fawns let us?"

Neil opened his mouth to reply when something crackled in Trecheon's ear.

"You can leave," a cool, feminine voice said. Trecheon froze and pawed at his ear. Holy *shit.* He still had his earpiece in!

Neil reached for his ear too, shock on his face.

"You can leave," the voice said again, gentler this time, almost somber. *"We have enough. And you've done more than could be asked of you."* A pause. *"Your allies' secrets are safe with us. We'll be in touch soon. Thank you for your service... Outlanders."* The radio clicked off.

Neil flicked his tail. "Christ. That was one of the Fawns. *Directly."*

Trecheon's body buzzed. Good. Draso. On the one hand, they didn't seem upset. But they also said they'd contact them soon. Draso's hot blood, he didn't need any new worries. He took the earpiece out and made sure it was really off.

Neil twitched his whiskers, clearly wanting to say something about the Fawn, but nothing came out. He pulled his earpiece out too, then looked away. They were silent for several minutes.

"Christian knew, by the way. About us." He looked into Trecheon's eyes, his glassy.

Trecheon wrinkled his snout. "And...?"

"He forgave us," Neil said. "For what it's worth."

Trecheon slumped his shoulders. The heartache warred with relief. "Honestly... it's worth a lot."

"Yeah," Neil said. "To me too." He rubbed his arm. "Most of the team knows too, but they're... accepting. And I think it'll help if we drop it."

Trecheon flicked his ears back. "Even Natassa?"

"Even Natassa."

"And she's really not bothered by it?"

Neil lifted his tail, smiling slightly. "She's more understanding than I'd expect, honestly."

Trecheon snorted. He supposed that was good, especially considering she showed some interest in Neil. He sighed. "Matt doesn't know. At least, I don't think he does."

"Then you should tell him," Neil said. "Before someone else does."

Trecheon stared at the ground. He lifted his pack higher. "…You're right. I'll tell him when we get back." They headed through the rip in the Veil.

But Athánatos wasn't Trecheon's ultimate destination. Omnir Island was.

Slipping through the rip on Sol with Excelsis in tow, Trecheon managed to get to Omnir island with little difficulty, clinging to the bird's legs as it crossed the channel from Sol to Omnir.

The moment he stepped on the ground, the ghosts of his ancestors seemed to be all around him. But… welcoming. Comforting. Even though he had never been there, the connection was instant.

Like with Sol, the island had tiny, decaying huts hidden between trees. Rotting food and untilled, overgrown crops littered the ground. Tiny stone paths weaved their way around the homes.

Unlike Sol, however, there were black, quilar-shaped shadows all over the walls, floor, and trees. Like the shadows from the atom bombs of World War II. Yet… no other destruction. Terrifying.

He hated the Basileus even more now.

But he wandered about until he found what he assumed was the Omnir graveyard. A small patch of land with little stones and wooden monuments, etched in some unknown language.

He found a patch of soft earth, then reached into his pack and pulled out a shovel.

"Want help with that?"

Trecheon turned. Matt stood there, his face sympathetic.

Part of Trecheon wanted to scream at him. How dare he show up here? He needed to be *alone* for this.

But then again, Trecheon had been there with Matt for his mourning. *Experience breeds understanding,* Excelsis had said. *Understanding breeds empathy. Empathy is a companion to mourning.*

And of all people, Matt would understand empathy here.

"Sure," Trecheon said.

Between Trecheon's shovel and Matt's wind magic, they were able to dig a shallow grave quickly. Trecheon reached into his pack again and pulled out a box. He lifted the lid.

Ryota's trench coat scrap sat on a satin pillow inside. Stuffy and pretentious, the exact thing Ryota would loudly complain about, but also secretly love. Trecheon managed a smile thinking about it.

He wiped tears from his eyes, then shut the box again. Carefully, he placed the box in the dirt, and he and Matt covered it.

One more thing.

Trecheon pulled out the last thing from his pack – a headstone. Unofficial, flat, hastily made. Real headstones were too expensive anyway. With Matt's help, they pressed the stone into the ground on top of the box.

Then they sat back in silence. The wind blew casually through their quills.

"Why did his Gem crack?" Trecheon asked, his voice breaking. "I thought you said it was hard to break a Gem."

Matt shook his head. "I think it was a Black Bound thing, but we know very little about Black Bound individuals. I can only theorize."

"Theorize, please."

Matt crossed his arms, staring at the grave. "Well. Based on my own experiences and what we know of other Gems, I think his Gem overloaded. You've seen how Lexi acid forms when you push your magic. It's a failsafe to protect against overload. But Black Bound elixir prevents the acid from forming. It prevents that failsafe." He closed his eyes. "The Gem overloaded and broke because it had nothing to limit it."

Trecheon sighed deeply. "That makes sense, I guess." He shut his eyes and moved closer to Matt. "…Don't let that happen to you, okay? You or Izzy."

"We won't," Matt said.

Silence fell again.

Now, of all times, would be the right time to talk to Matt about being an assassin. When they were alone, and he could deal with all the repercussions coming his way. "Look… Matt… I have something I need to tell you."

"Is this about the White Assassin?" Matt asked.

Trecheon's body buzzed. "You know?"

"I kind of put two and two together," Matt said. "Wasn't exactly hard. All those papers about the White Assassin on your desk. Christian talking about you going off for days at a time. It's pretty obvious."

Trecheon shut his eyes. *Damn it all.* "Matt, I--"

"You've been hunting the White Assassin down, haven't you?"

Trecheon blinked. "What?"

"You don't have to explain," Matt said. "I'd probably do it too if I were you. We're both the type. That's obvious after you ran wholeheartedly into the Cast battle on the docks. You didn't have to do that, yet you did. You felt the need to help." He turned to Trecheon. "But you should let it go. Even with your magic, hunting down a vigilante is dangerous. Let the authorities take him down. I'd rather not lose a new friend." He smiled. "Okay?"

Trecheon blinked at him. Wow, he couldn't have gotten that more wrong. He started to correct him… but stopped.

Matt had originally hated Trecheon because he thought he was a murderer. His mind changed when he separated Trecheon from the Omnir of his past.

So if Matt knew he actually was a murderer… What would that do to their friendship? After all they had been through together, Matt had become a dear friend. One he could rely on. Really and truly rely on. Like the teammates he had in war.

He had already lost Christian. Ryota. So many friends and family.

He couldn't lose anyone else. The very thought of it sent his heart racing.

He couldn't lose Matt over the mistakes of his past.

"Trecheon?"

"You're right," Trecheon said. "I'll let it go. I'm done with it." Nice, vague confirmation. Not exactly lying. Not exactly the truth. Safe. Matt would never have to know. He was quitting the assassin business anyway. All in the past.

Trecheon wouldn't have to lose him.

Matt smiled and gripped his shoulder. "Let's head back. I've got something for all of you."

Matt sat in the throne room with his entire pack scattered around the room, including the Athánatos royalty, Trecheon, Neil, and Damianos. Both Damianos and Natassa sat close to Neil, which didn't escape Matt's notice. He stood in the middle of the room.

"Defenders," he said. "Today we finished curing the rest of the Cast. We've finally erased the last of Theron's damage, as much as we could." The group applauded, and Neil whooped, pumping the air. "However, Athánatos is a long way from being fully restored. I've already talked with Lance about it. The Defenders are prepping a team as we speak. We plan to head home, then come back with them and help with restoration."

"We are grateful for all you have done for us," Ouranos said, swirling pink gratitude with a mix of black shame through Matt's mind. "I only regret that there is nothing we can offer you in return."

"As if we're doing this for a reward," Izzy said with a chuckle. "Hardly. We're family now. This is what family does." Natassa smiled and gave Izzy a gentle squeeze, which she returned.

Ouranos smiled. Matt's mind filled with his white hope, chasing away the shame. "Still, we are grateful."

"That being said," Matt continued. "We'll need a way to communicate when we come back." He reached into his bag and pulled out the Defender pendants Caesum had fabricated. "And I think all of you here have earned this honorary rank."

Trecheon perked his ears. "Those are the pendants you guys wear."

"Defender pendants," Matt said. "Used for identification and communication, newly authorized by the Master Guardian himself. For all of you who helped us during this. Izzy and I can help set them up for each of you. But you all get one. Part of our thanks for helping." He turned to Trecheon. "I'll start with you if you don't mind."

Trecheon perked both ears. "Uh… Sure." He stood.

"Normally we'd pair it to a thumb print," Matt said. "But this'll have to be different for you, obviously. We'll do a facial scan."

Trecheon flicked his ears back. "What if someone finds it?"

Matt laughed. "No one native to this planet has the technology to hack into a Defender pendant. You're safe."

Trecheon shrugged. "If you say so."

After a bit of finagling, Matt was able to capture the scan and set the pendant with Trecheon's information. It set him as Defender-Z, the base

Defender rank. It fit… but Trecheon was more than that. Guardian material, if Matt had anything to say about it.

Maybe that's what the Phonar had meant when they'd called them Guardians. Who knew.

He slipped the pendant over Trecheon's head. "Welcome to the Defenders."

For the first time since the battle of the docks had ended, Trecheon smiled. A real, proper smile. Matt smiled back. Finally they could start healing.

"We'll be back in a couple of months," Matt said as they boarded their X-Zeroes.

Trecheon crossed his arms and smiled, watching the Defenders pile on to their respective planes, carrying canned goods and other supplies for the trip back. The last few days had been spent healing and creating more Cast charms to take home to Zyearth. Trecheon was grateful. It gave him time to really come to terms with Ryota's death. Surrounded by allies. Friends.

He wasn't alone. And he'd never have to be alone again.

Izzy had her hammer back on her hip, and it made a soft thumping sound as she walked about, catching bits of light from the streetlamps. It was dark, just like when they had first landed here. Trecheon didn't know how much that kept them hidden, but it was better than nothing.

Matt continued. "Keep in touch with Ouranos in the meantime, yeah? You'll all need to support each other while we're recovering from this."

Trecheon bounced a two-fingered salute off his forehead. "Aye-aye, Captain."

Matt rolled his eyes. "At least call me Guardian."

"I'll probably just call you asshole," Trecheon said with a grin. "It's how I talk to all my friends."

Matt smirked. "You're just a bundle of joy, aren't you?"

"He gets it from me," Neil said, leaning on Trecheon's shoulder. He winked at Matt. On his side was one of the Athánatos swords – a gift from Damianos. It had a piece of wool around the hilt, with a bit of amber tied onto it. Trecheon hadn't asked what that was yet, but it had made Neil giddy. Trecheon turned back to Matt.

"Hurry back," Trecheon said. "And bring a boat this time."

"Space-faring plane!" Darvin called over his shoulder, but he grinned.

Izzy waved to him. "Don't do anything I wouldn't do," she said.

"Doesn't narrow that down much, but sure," Trecheon said. Izzy grinned at him. Roscoe snuck up behind her and pulled her into his arms. He kissed her, then carried her inside with her giggling.

"I'm gonna go warm up the bike," Neil said. "See you space aliens in a couple of months." He walked off. Matt waved to him.

"Matt," Trecheon said. Matt turned. Trecheon rubbed his quills. "Thanks. For everything. Whether you were here or not, we were going to get involved with Ryota and Theron eventually, and you saved our asses."

"We saved each other," Matt said. "I wouldn't have gotten through this without you either."

"I doubt that, but I appreciate it," Trecheon said. "That was hard. But in the long run... I think I needed it. It lit a fire under my ass. Kind of makes me rethink like... everything."

"Hopefully in good ways."

"For the most part," Trecheon said. He held out a hand. "So, thanks. I'm glad we met."

Matt grinned, shook his hand, then wrapped his arm around Trecheon's shoulder. "I am too. You helped me work through a past I didn't know needed working through, and fought the xenophobia out of me. I needed that." He gave Trecheon a quick hug.

Trecheon froze a moment but hugged him back. Relief flooded him.

He wasn't going to lose Matt.

Maybe now he could work on reminding himself that he was worthy of that relationship.

Matt gripped Trecheon's shoulder. "See you in a few months." He boarded the plane.

Trecheon stepped back several yards and watched as the two planes hovered into the air, slipped out over the water, and vanished from sight. The last indication of their presence was a powerful sonic boom as they left atmosphere.

Trecheon smiled. "Later, space alien."

The End

About the Author

R. A. Meenan was born in London during the golden age of science fiction, but somehow time traveled to the Modern Era (some say a mad man with a blue box was involved). She was dropped on the doorstep of a house owned by anthropomorphic cats and though they were disappointed she didn't have furry ears and a tail, they took her in to teach her the ways of elemental magic. After setting fire to her furry cat friends' tails one too many times (final score – fire: 2612, cat's tails: 0) they called an exterminator and sent her out on her way.

Others would call this "going to college" and "getting a job" but she disagrees.

Now an adult (physically, not mentally), she ride-hops intergalactic military spacecraft, combing the outer reaches of space and time, writing science fiction and urban fantasy stories based on her experiences. She's also hoping to find the perfect cup of coffee and a better way to grow dinosaurs. Humans kind of look at her funny, but she's managed to make herself an honorary ambassador for furry and anthropomorphic aliens and space dragons.

She carefully feeds and brushes her wonderful husband Joe and the pair have four furry children (which are really cats, but don't tell them that) and a human child named after a video game character. She also spends her spare time teaching essay-writing haters, molding them into people resembling Actual Students and Lovers of English.

She may not win the hearts of stiff military men or students who want good grades for no effort, but she certainly captures the spirit and imagination of time travelers, magic users, nerds, Students-In-Training, and fantasy lovers. Welcome to her nonsensical world. We hope you like it here.

You can email R. A. Meenan at r.a.meenan@zyearth.com. Check out more of her works at www.zyearth.com. You can also follow her on BlueSky at @zyearth.com.

If you enjoyed this book, consider reviewing it at the retailer where you purchased it!

Enter the World of Zyearth

Liked this book? You can get FREE Zyearth short stories when you sign up for the newsletter at Zyearth.com! Here's some sneak peeks:

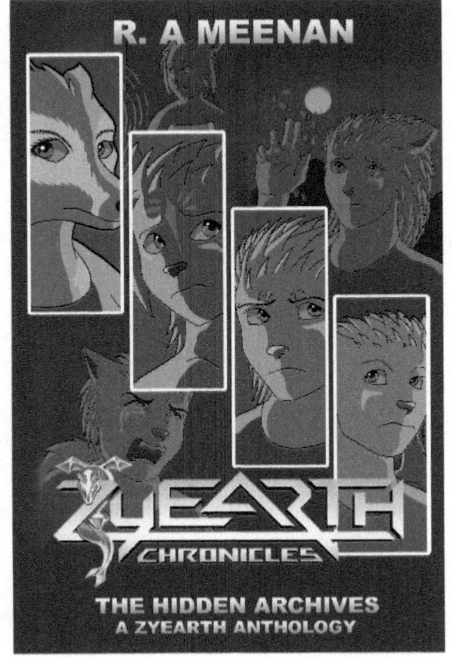

Five stories from the world of Zyearth...

Two rivals falling in love. An artist discovering a horrific secret. A Guardian saving a prince. A genocide survivor discovering his lost wife. A soldier just trying to survive.

Greetings, Traveler. Your curiosity has led you to the Hidden Archives, where I document stories important to the history of the Defenders of Zyearth.

These stories are short, often tragic, sometimes humorous, but they may reveal connections, hidden knowledge, or special insights to the greater Zyearth world, and therefore must be protected.

Read on, Traveler, if you dare, and if this does not satisfy your curiosity, know that I add to the Archives frequently. There may be many more stories for you to discover.

Go forth and may Draso shine upon you.

Get more information by signing up for the newsletter at Zyearth.com!

464

Glossary

Learn more about the World of Zyearth at Zyearth.com!

Zyfaunos: Zyfaunos are anthropomorphic animal-like bipeds. All zyfaunos have similar characteristics -- plantigrade or near plantigrade legs, human stance structure in the spine, humanlike eyes and sometimes lips, generally short snouts, and have humanlike, five fingered hands, usually with tiny, somewhat sharp retractable claws instead of fingernails. Zyfaunos tend to have the same height range as humans, with a few extreme examples of very short or very tall species. All zyfaunos can interbreed regardless of the individual's species. Unlike most faunos, zyfaunos are not always "traditionally" colored, and often have unnatural colors in their fur, such as red, blue, green, purple, and others. Though relationships are rare, humans and zyfaunos can produce children. Zyfaunos are named as such because the DNA strain originated from the planet Zyearth and Zyearth has the purest forms of this species.

Quilar: Quilar are perhaps the most unusual of all zyfaunos, as it is unclear what animal they evolved from. They have several key characteristics

-- catlike ears and snout, slightly humanlike lips, though usually black or dark pink, humanlike feet and hands, tails, and quills of various lengths on their head in place of hair. Quilar quills are hard, though not usually sharp like a porcupine or hedgehog. Instead of fingernails, quilar have tiny retractable claws on each hand. These claws are not very sharp and are mainly used for scratching. Quilar can be divided by color and physical characteristics into three different categories.

Zyearth Quilar: Zyearth quilar have very short, very soft fur and generally longer, thicker quills on their heads. Their snouts are short and flat and many even have human-like lips. They tend to  have catlike ears and human-like eyes. Quilar are the most human-like of all faunos. Human-faunos relationships usually involve a quilar. Zyearth quilar tend to have browns, whites, blacks, and grays for their colors. Jason, pictured on the previous page, is wearing the Defender Elemental uniform colors, indicating his status as an elemental user.

Jason is modeling a Zyearth quilar. Jason's fur is soft golden brown.

Earth Quilar: Earth quilar are physically very similar to Zyearth quilar, though their colors tend to be more vibrant. They also generally have streaks of color in their fur and quills while Zyearth quilars tend to be one solid color.

Trecheon is, reluctantly, modeling an Earth quilar.

Athánatos Quilar: Athánatos quilar are typically taller than their Zyearth and Earth kin. They have ears that bend backwards and more animal-like tails and feet. Their snouts are short and flat and like other quilar, they can have human-like lips.

Ouranos is modeling an Athánatos quilar here.

Focus Jewels: Focus jewels are found on many different planets throughout the universe. The term refers to any jewel that can be bound to a user's skin, soul, or lifeforce that grants supernatural powers. Sometimes focus jewel power only grants simple powers, such as long life, but others exhibit more extravagant powers.

Lexi Gems: Lexi Gems are focus jewels bound to the user's soul and grants users several powers. Average Gem users are granted long life, up to four hundred Zyearth years, and slow aging. Advanced users develop "Gem

Specialties" through the Gem "breaking" usually after a stressful, dramatic, or difficult event in the user's life. Military personnel are the most likely to have broken Gems and most Gems break in training.

There are a variety of specialties that users can develop. The most common specialty is healing, followed by elemental fabricators and manipulators, and a select few specialize in cloaking and shielding. Users are usually granted only one specialty, though a rare few have two. In the case of a duel specialist, both specialties are significantly weaker than those in a single specialist.

Lexi Gems are usually about the size of a user's fist. Gems often take on the colors of their users in one of several forms, but they lose their color if the user doesn't touch their Gem for extended periods of time or if the user dies, which also results in the Gem's bond breaking with their user. Gems can be used again by another user after a previous user has died.

Ei-Ei Jewels: Ei-Ei Jewels, like Lexi Gems, are focus jewels and are the source of magic and power for a member of the Athánatos tribe. Ei-Ei jewels are small and they are fused to the skin of the user just around the edge of their eyes. Ei-Ei jewels also come in pairs. Each eye has one set of the pairs. There are three jewels, but all of them work together to properly function.

The first jewel, the Mind Jewel, is yellow, representing the sophia flower, a symbol of wisdom. This jewel set keeps the user's mind fresh and free of deterioration. They even protect against mind aging issues like Alzheimer's and dementia.

The second set, the Body Jewel, is red, representing the purity of blood and flesh. This jewel set keeps the body from deterioration. Athánatos tribe members are immortal because of this jewel, but they are not invincible.

The final set, the Soul Jewel, is the color of the users eyes, representing the user's soul. This jewel set keeps the soul pinned to the body. Together the three sets make the user immortal.

Wishing Dust: Wishing Dust is created from ground up focus jewels and is used by applying the dust to the eye while making a "wish." Wishes are very specific, detailed spells that do one thing really well, but with a cost. Wishing Dust users are called Wish Dusters.

Wishing Dust is very volatile and a majority of attempted users wish too large for the wish to compensate. If the wish cannot properly compensate, the user will go insane and physically rip themselves apart trying to remove the dust. If a wish goes wrong, the user will always die. There is no saving them. Because the dust is so powerful and so deadly, most major civilizations in the universe have banned it. As a result, Wishing Dust is mostly found in black markets and smuggler's groups.

Wishing Dust comes in a variety of colors and will add a light, very subtle dusting of that color to the user's eye. It's difficult to identify a Wish Duster until they've used their magic. Common wishes include magic tracking, object manifestation or enhancement, body morphing, and various magical defenses.

Continuum Stones: Continuum Stones are a pair of magical stones that manipulate time and space. They're almost exclusively used by the zyfaunos bat species of Vanguard from the Tribus continent. Users wear the stones attached to the skin in the inner parts of their ears.

Most Continuum Stone users live beyond their biological lifespans, but how long that is depends on their time powers. Powers are granted randomly as the user grows.

Time powers include healing, which reverses time on the user's body, scrying, and very temporary time freezes, with limited range. Each one has their own down sides. Too much healing can put a user outside of time, which takes time and effort to fix. Scrying is very imprecise as a whole. Time freezing robs the user of time off their lifespan – one hour for every second of frozen time.

Space powers include telekinesis, or the ability to lift things with the mind. Telekinesis users can only lift objects that they would otherwise be able to lift with their own strength. Teleportation, or space jumping, which allows users to jump 50 or 60 feet from where they stand. This is very energy intensive and needs a long recovery time between jumps. Finally, gravity manipulation, which allows a user to increase or decrease gravity on an object or in a small radius for a very short period of time. This is also energy intensive and cannot completely negate natural gravity, which means a user cannot eliminate gravity completely and send someone into space.

Jewel Shards: Jewel Shards are a relatively new focus jewel discovered on the Paleofaunos-inhabited planet Erdoglyan. Jewel Shards are pointed cone-shaped jewels and bound physical to a user, usually grafted onto bone or teeth and held in place with ornate metal holders. As they are a permanent fixture, they're often on the face or snout and positioned to face forward like a unicorn horn.

Jewel Shards manifest a single elemental magic, one of the main seven elements. The inhabitants who own jewels call themselves the Forged and name themselves off the element they have. For example,

"Fireforged" or "Lightningforged." The element it manifests will also determine its user's remaining lifespan. Some shorten the lifespan, such as lightning, which only grants 30 to 50 years of life after binding. Others lengthen it, such as stone, which can grant up to 350 years of additional life after binding. Some claim the element manifested is a reflection of the user's personality, though this has yet to be proven.

Jewel Shards are powered by UV rays. If they are left uncharged for too long, it causes psychosis in the user.

Blood Crystals: Unlike other jewels, Blood Crystals are shaped to look like things, typically something that their users find solace in. Blood Crystals are unique in the sense that they need two or more users to work properly. When bound, users will borrow magic or energy from their partner (called the Bleeder) and use it to create massive, destructive spells. Blood Partners can kill each other if they're not careful with how they pull magic.

Blood Crystals are highly regulated by Galactic InterPol because they were once used to bring people back to life, though very temporarily. The process is all but forgotten now, except for the knowledge that in order to use a Blood Crystal to revive someone, someone else had to be sacrificed.

Defender: The Defenders are a military group run by a small country called Zedric on the continent of Yelar on the plant Zyearth.

Guardian: Guardians are an essential part of the Defender military. Guardians are high ranking, highly trained individuals that perform tasks that average Defenders aren't trained for. There are two important types of Guardians.

Master Guardian: The role of Master Guardian is usually held by two people at the same time, often a former Golden Guardian pair. Master Guardians have a duel task – they are both the head of the Defender army and the leaders of the country of Zedric. Master Guardians must be smart, strong, courageous, and influential. Master Guardians are usually in office for life, though there are checks and balances that can remove a Master Guardian if the governing Assembly or the people of Zedric feels like they are not properly performing duties, and some Master Guardians choose to retire. Master Guardians are generally considered by most Defenders to be the most powerful zyfaunos of their time.

Golden Guardian: Golden Guardians are a team of two Defenders specially trained to handle delicate situations and complete covert and difficult missions that need small strike teams. Golden Guardians are selected by the Master Guardian of their era, and are given an extra five years of special training beyond typical Defender training. Usually the team has one healer and one elemental user.

Defender Pendant: Defender pendants are worn by all Defenders, regardless of their position in the army or Academy. They carry holographic identification cards and are the most common means of communication among Defenders. The pendant also carries several symbols. On Zyearth, a legless dragon is a sign of peace, so the Defenders made the legless dragon the center of their pendant. The dragon's  neck is tucked under, a classic move that prevents strangulation in battle. This represents defense. The outstretched wings are a sign of openness and welcome. Finally, the Gem at the dragon's side represents the world of Zyearth, since nearly all native Zyearthlings are bound to Gems.

Discover other titles by R. A. Meenan

Black Bound

Golden Guardian

Shadow Cast

White Assassin

Brothers at Arms

Umber Sky

Gray Matter

Mage

Angel

Crimson Footprints

Viridian Jewels

Judgement

Greetings from Earth: Zyearth Tales Vol 1

The Hidden Archives Vol 1

Facets of Color: Vol 1